# The Whole Wide World

To Miss Laurie Thank you so much for everything & Peace & God Bless always —

By
Yvonne Castañeda

PUBLISH AMERICA

PublishAmerica
Baltimore

First printing

ISBN: 1-4137-3692-0
PUBLISHED BY PUBLISHAMERICA, LLLP
www.publishamerica.com
Baltimore

Printed in the United States of America

*This book is a work of fiction;*
*however, some aspects are based on my*
*whacky life.*

*For my mom, dad, and very cool brother.*
*I couldn't have asked for a better familia.*

## Additional acknowledgments:

This book never would have been sent to a publisher had it not been for three wonderful people: Tiffany Maxwell, Allyson Keller and Judy Macias. Thank you for reading it when it was just a sparkle in my eye, for egging me on and giving me the confidence I needed to send it off. I owe you so big time. Thanks to my husband, Ben Brain (yeah, that's really his last name), for your endless patience, your ability to handle my mood swings, your support, your very existence.

Thanks to the following people for their kindness and generosity: to George Papadopoulos and the crew, Ray Faez, Bobby Cross, George "Turkey" Tsouroullis (for making me laugh so damn hard); Roxanna Noonan and James Keller, for letting me make my own schedule at work. Who knows when I would've finished this book had you not let me take this or that day off; to my entire family outside of my parents and brother. I'd name you all but there's too damn many of you. Thank you for helping me become the person I am.

Words cannot express how thankful I am to Lisa and David Brown and their entire family (that includes you too, Roadie). Thank you for being my "white" second family, for making me tell you stories about my mom over and over again. Without you, I probably would've forgotten them! Thanks for all the love you've given me over the years. You took me in as one of your own and treated me like family. You never made me feel out of place, and for that I will be eternally grateful.

Thank you Jenny Brain, Pollyana Brain, Oxo and the Osbourne clan. You made this crazy American/Hispanic girl from across the pond feel welcomed and loved on that first trip to England. Thank you for accepting me and my wild family.

Thank you, Chris aka Liquidmuse aka Minedmuse aka The Coolest Friend Ever; for being my personal editor and for *being* there; for making me take a good look at myself when I least wanted to. You *rock*.

Thank you thank you thank you Todd Nordstrom aka Sister aka Beverly

*THE WHOLE WIDE WORLD*

aka Mary, for always being optimistic and funny and so, so wonderfully *bitter*. If you ever turn straight, I'm leaving Ben.

Thank you Stephen Clark, for filling me with a sense of wonder and amazement at the world. You are an eternal bubble of love and light, and I am lucky to have met you. Thanks to all the people I worked with at Bristol Hotels and Resorts for letting me be a clown. Your laughter kept me alive. Thanks to every student I ever had. Without you, this book never would have been written. You taught me something about the world and I will always remember you, yo!

Thank you Publish America, for taking my silly little dream and making it a reality.

Thank you, Dr. Willoughby, God rest your soul. I know you are looking down on me and smiling.

Lastly, I'd like to thank all the people who have made a difference to me, large or small. You know who you are. Thank you for making me feel special and different and capable of anything. Thank you for telling me to get off my ass and write a book. I hope it makes you proud.

7

# Chapter 1

Imagine this: a young woman in her early twenties with perfect brown curly hair all the way down to her waist standing in front of a classroom, a classroom full of perfect teenage kids sitting quietly as she calls roll. Her name is written on the chalkboard, a brand new computer is on her desk and the soft hum of a new air conditioner is in the background. It is the only sound you hear. You see a young woman fully in control of her class, strict but nice, the captain of the ship. The kids say "Present" as she calls their names, and one by one she checks them off in her brand new roll call book in a brand new everything kind of classroom. She asks them to take out their homework and the kids with perfect white teeth and brand new clothes oblige her willingly. She smiles at them and they smile back. A perfect day in a perfect school begins.

Congratulations. You just imagined my polar opposite.

My hair was long but far from perfect. It was out of control, a wild animal permanently glued to my scalp. It was neither curly nor straight. It had a mind of its own and tended to get into fights with the hairbrush. My classroom had an air conditioner, but it was an old wall unit that only came to life when beaten with a stapler or during a full moon. *A moody bitch*, my brother would say. I was the only teacher who had to shower more than three times a day and show up for work with towels and extra deodorant. I had no computer, not in a million years. What I did have was an old attendance book that looked as though it had been passed down from one century to another.

The only time there was silence and order in my classroom was a) during a national holiday or teacher workday, b) during after school hours, or c) whenever I gave up and stuffed my ears with cotton. I didn't have a perfect name kids could pronounce easily, like Mrs. Smith or Mrs. Jones. My full name is Bibiana Maria Castellanos. My students called me Miss C simply because they gave up on trying to pronounce the whole enchilada. When I was born, my older brother Erasmo nicknamed me Bibi and it just stuck.

Later on his nicknames for me would be *moron* and *dumb ass*, but to my eighth grade class of maniacs, I was Miss C.

My students were rarely obedient, never dressed properly and always said "yo" instead of "present" or "here." I was the captain of a ship that looked like it was about to sink. For over one year of my almost-adult life, during which I contemplated everything from admitting myself to a mental institution to feeling like I was born to inspire, I was in charge of kids from the hood. Hard to believe Orlando, Florida has a less than perfectly manicured neighborhood, but it does. The Mouse can only control so much. Orlando has more than a few neighborhoods that look like an after school special gone wrong.

The job: First year teacher.

The school: Howard Middle.

The mission: Stay sane.

The school was located on the "right" side of the I-4. It was considered an "inner city" school and I had no idea why. The neighborhood, Thornton Park, was nothing short of beautiful. It was full of tree lined streets with old storybook houses, houses inhabited by families with the right equation: 2.5 kids, two new cars and one perfect looking dog with no fleas. To me, it looked exactly like those neighborhoods you see in movies. The ones where rich kids turn into drug addicts and daughters commit suicide. Thornton Park was all about nice cars, new clothes, clean streets and a thousand illegal Mexicans mowing lawns. To the rest of the world, it looked like an ideal neighborhood where nothing ever went wrong. I knew better because I grew up with cable. I watched too many movies about wealthy tormented teenagers.

Another world existed on the other side of the I-4. My students called it The Wrong Side, and they would say this with pride, as though not having adequate plumbing or living in fear of dope pushers and drive by's was completely acceptable. Six lanes of highway separated those who have and those who wish they had. The streets in the hood were cracked and full of potholes, homes were kept together strictly by cheap, inventive ways and the only dogs you ever saw were usually starving strays running out into the street out of sheer desperation, as though the only way out of the hood was suicide.

Even though it was in a dreamlike neighborhood, Howard Middle School was home to kids from both sides of the I-4. Thrown into the mix were a small population of Hispanics, Asians and, of course, Goths.

I kind of fell into teaching. *Collapsed* would be a better word for it.

Teaching wasn't something I'd wanted to do more than anything. I hadn't been dreaming about it since I was a kid. No, teaching was simply the thing I most wanted to do rather than bartend for the Hard Rock Café, which was where I found myself three years after graduating from college. By that point, I was desperate to do anything other than pouring draft beer after draft beer and mixing Long Island Ice Teas for people who thought leaving a tip was a rumor. Most customers were Germans, Brits, Aussies, Kiwis, and yes, more Germans. Added to that were bitter salesmen on business trips, families from a small town in Ohio or Wisconsin and local people who didn't mind loud music, people I was always happy to see because they knew how to tip. Their generosity kept me sane and my bank account intact.

Working at the Hard Rock Café wasn't a terrible job to have. Bartending was fun most nights. I thought it was a cool job at first. I met people from all over the world, all walks of life, people who were always more than ready to tell me all about their vacations while I stood behind the bar and asked them questions like, "So, what's Germany like?" "Where do you live in Switzerland?" "Do the French really hate Americans that much?" And these nice people, even though they couldn't tip to save their lives, would answer my questions with smiles on their faces, as though they came all the way from across the Atlantic to be on my personal talk show.

If I wasn't in a horrible mood, I would stand there and give them my undivided attention, only because it's always a good thing to learn a thing or two that you'll never learn in a textbook. But catch me on a day when I hadn't had enough sleep and, well, let's just say I'd give the French more than enough reason to hate Americans.

The money was more than good, I'll admit. I will never make that much money again, bad tippers and all. For every person who left me a twenty-five cent tip on a thirty-dollar tab, a nice divorced man from Nebraska or Oklahoma on vacation with his kids would give me ten bucks on a twenty-dollar tab. My mom taught me to balance the bad with the good, and every time someone would hand me a tip in coins, I'd smile and remember her wise advice even though every bone in my body would want to smash their empty beer bottles over their sunburned heads.

Okay, so I have a temper.

I got bored with bartending quickly. Too quickly. Day in and day out, I found myself asking the same questions over and over again. "Where are you from?" "Oh, you're driving across the country?" "You're going to Key West after this?" I felt like a robot programmed to keep people on vacation in good spirits, whereas my own were vanishing into thin air with every hurricane I poured into a souvenir glass. *There has to be something better out there.*

The life of a bartender after working hours can be detrimental to anyone's health. It was the only time I ever did anything considered social. I never went home and went to sleep. Who could sleep after five espressos and three YMCA routines? I never thought to myself, "I can't wait to get home to read my book," as I put up the last barstool. Usually, my only thought was, "I need a drink. And fast. A cold beer and some chicken wings." Some could argue I was headed straight towards Friends of Bill W. meetings, but I beg to differ. Most of my uncles are professional drunks, drunks who wake up in the morning with a shot of tequila. I was far from that. I only drank tequila after six pm.

When I wasn't out after work trying to drink myself into oblivion with other employees, I'd get home around three in the morning and have a glass of wine or two or three while I watched the Home Shopping Network and reruns of "The Brady Bunch." You see, the life of a bartender is not what it's knocked up to be. You've got to trust me on that one.

One movie came along and changed the face of bartending forever. *Cocktail.* It glorified the world of bartending. Tom Cruise made it look like the job of a lifetime, a dream come true for young single men who wanted to get laid non-stop and make tons of money overnight, but it failed to show the side of bartending that can only be seen through the eyes of people who work until four in the morning mixing drinks for idiots who think a one dollar tip is enough for putting up with them for three hours. Thank you, Hollywood. The bottle flipping, admirable and entertaining, never happens in real bars. One time I watched one of the bartenders flip a bottle for about a minute just to pour a vodka tonic. The customer, who looked as though he needed a drink yesterday, slammed his hand on the bar and screamed, "For Christ's sake, pour me the *&%$# drink and get it over with! You're not Tom Cruise and we're not in a movie, so cut the crap." The bartender nodded and poured his drink and never flipped another bottle. Of course, I bought the guy a drink when the bartender wasn't looking.

Anyone who's ever been a bartender knows working the night shift is the only way to make any real money. The day shift at the Hard Rock was boring. Tourists usually came in for one thing: a free pin, air conditioning and a chance to do the YMCA. They would come in dripping in sweat, order a hurricane, and watch and clap as the staff mimicked the Village People. Souvenirs in hand, they would walk out the huge doors of the Rock without so much as a backwards glance at the bar. Yeah, the day shift sucked.

I was lucky enough to get put on the night shift schedule. I would go into work at four in the afternoon and slave away till about two in the morning. On nights when I couldn't conceive watching yet another episode of *My Favorite Martian*, I'd give in to temptation and head for a local bar with other waiters and bartenders. Conversations rarely ever involved the latest natural disaster or the future economy of the former Soviet Union. Conversations usually started with, "You won't believe what happened to me tonight!" or "God, I was sooo weeded." Or it would revolve around who was sleeping with who, who was getting fired, who was starting their own band. I always felt oddly out of place in these situations.

Even though I'd wish somebody would talk about something else other than work, I'd sit there and laugh with everyone anyway. Pretend I wasn't grossly self-conscious. And it was nice to sit on the other side of a bar. After multiple beers and too many garlic Buffalo Wings, I would fall into bed smelling like a giant draft beer and a pack of cigarettes, too tired to think about anything except that I needed to change my life and fast. I'd slip into a beer-induced coma and promise myself I'd do something different the next day. It's easy to make promises to yourself when you're lying in a comfortable bed, knowing full well you don't have to set the alarm.

I'd wake up every morning, sorry, *afternoon,* take one look at myself in the mirror and cringe. *Today is the day,* I would think. *From now on, I'm going to come home straight after work, take a long bath and settle into my book.* Then I'd force myself to go for a run in order to sweat out all the beer, if only to make myself feel like I wasn't a complete alcoholic with no life and no real friends. I'd go to work and remind myself of my promise, but as soon as the last barstool was up and the last drunk escorted to a taxi, my promise would fade into nothingness as I drove to the local dive.

*Tomorrow,* I'd think, as I bonded with my best friends Jose Cuervo and Corona.

Being a bartender was like being a comedian, an actress and a therapist all rolled into one person, on top of being a mom or a potential lover. It never ceased to amaze me how alcohol could completely change a person. An average Joe would walk in, order a drink and a burger and I'd think, *Wow, he seems nice.* After a few drinks, Average Joe would turn into a cross between Psycho and Jack Nicholson in *One Flew Over the Cuckoo's Nest.* Suddenly, I would become their sounding board, their overnight therapist with all the solutions. I'd want to kick myself for asking that fatal question: "So, where are you from?" Average Joe would start telling me about the wife he no longer understands, the kids he can no longer relate to, the boss he wants to murder, the neighbor who won't let him sunbathe in the nude. I would listen patiently, hoping he wouldn't get too drunk and forget to tip me the 20% he owed me for listening to his very average problems. Occasionally, Average Joe would start crying, which was always a clear sign that he'd had too much to drink and perhaps needed a cab.

There was probably nothing that annoyed me more than having to deal with annoying women in positions of authority somewhere in the corporate world. Female executives on a mission to prove something to the world. They would stroll into the bar with their expensive suits and very expensive taste and always start off with a high class drink like a martini, drinks they would order as they looked down their noses at me and the wild animal on my head. I had been a bartender long enough to know I had to ignore these looks otherwise I would end up in jail or on welfare. Besides, they were too predictable.

After one or two martinis, these women who thought they walked on water would start talking to Average Joe and switch to shots. Just one B-52 or Lemon Drop shooter would immediately replace their arrogant airs with a twisted set of booze goggles. I would go from being some loser bartender to their best friend in less than one hour. *Hey, bar girl!* would be replaced by *Hey, sweetie, can you get me another drink?* Sooner or later, they'd start telling me their problems, and how could they not? Once the booze kicked in, their mouths would start going a mile a minute while I stood there trying to look understanding and compassionate. *Men suck, honey, the world sucks, my job sucks, my dad was an asshole, my uncle abused me, my first boyfriend cheated on me, men suck, men suck, men suck.* Average Joe would always be too wasted to argue, so he'd raise his beer and toast to the fact that *Men Suck!*

It was always one thing or another, one more thing to make me pray I'd win the lottery. Sometimes I'd go to bed wondering why Oprah didn't serve alcohol to her guests. It certainly made people open up. But who was I to judge? I would just as easily get off work, guzzle a few beers and tell my coworkers things about myself that would make me cringe in the morning.

But there I was, living in Orlando three hundred miles away from my mom and dad in Miami, in my very own apartment, doing my own laundry, my own shopping, getting the oil changed in my car all by myself. I was proud to be making it on my own without having to call my dad for money, but inevitably, I got tired of my wake-up-at-noon-work-out-get-ready-for-the-Germans routine. When I woke up one day and couldn't remember anything about the night before, not even where I'd parked my car, I realized it was definitely time for a change. One look in the mirror at the bags under my eyes and the pasty quality of my skin told me the time was now. Not tomorrow, not the next day, but now.

I wanted to do something fun, something easy, but there was no circus I could join on a part time basis. I contemplated getting a part time job at Dunkin' Donuts, if anything for the free coffee, but having to go to work at six in the morning just to pour coffee and put donuts into a bag was simply unreasonable. I thought about getting a job at Borders Books and Music but knew I'd probably get fired for spending more time reading than helping customers. For weeks, I went through a list of possible jobs and discarded them one by one: bus driver (I didn't know Orlando too well), toll booth collector (I would've wanted to talk to every car), or taxi driver (I would've had to leave bartending and buy a gun). The fact that I couldn't find something else to do started to depress me. I started ignoring all the average Joe's and stopped listening to bitter women who just needed to get laid.

Just when I thought I was going to spend the rest of my life playing an actress/therapist/comedian/lover/friend/mom, a solution fell into my lap.

I was talking to Tommy, one of the other bartenders at the Rock. It was early in the evening and we were standing around waiting for the night rush.

"So, Bibiana, I heard you moved up here from Miami." Tommy was very cute in a cuddly way but I never entertained the thought of dating him. It was a rule among bartenders; never eat where you shit. Crude, but true.

"Yeah, about three months ago."

"Cool. Why'd you move?"

"I needed to get away from Miami for a while. I just wanted to live on my own and do something different. Hand me a garbage bag, will ya?"

"Why didn't you just move out and get a place in Miami?" He handed me a bag and I tied it around the smelly trash bin.

"Are you crazy? News flash: my parents are Hispanic, which means you basically don't move out *ever* unless you're moving somewhere far away or you're getting married."

"Right. Gotcha. So how you liking O'town?"

"Huh?"

"O'town. Orlando. Mickey Mouse central. Tourist hell."

"Oh. It's okay, I guess. I like being on my own, but to tell you the truth, I don't know how long I can do this. You know, *bartending*." I picked up a bottle and started wiping it down.

"Hear you on that one. Money's good, though."

"Yeah, it is." I sighed and shrugged my shoulders.

"What?"

"What do you mean?"

"What's up with the sigh and shrug?"

I put the bottle back in the rack and started wiping down the bar.

"Well, I went to college, you know? I actually graduated and everything. I just feel like I should be doing something else with my life. Something other than the YMCA. I don't know, I just get the feeling there's something better out there for me."

"I hear you on that one. Well, what do you do during your free time? Days off? Do you have any hobbies?"

I stopped wiping the bar and thought about it.

"Well, let's see. I wake up at noon, go for a run, take a shower, read a little bit and then get ready for work. On my days off, I go for drives. Sometimes I go to Cocoa Beach if the weather is good. That's about it."

"Oh."

*God, my life is so boring*, I thought.

"What about hobbies?"

"Hobbies? Reading, reading, reading…oh, I like to write once in a while."

"What do you write about?"

"Crap. Nonsense. I've started writing a book about a million times but I never seem to get past the first chapter." I was growing uncomfortable so I decided to change the course of the conversation. The night shift was only beginning and the last thing I needed was something to remind me I was going nowhere at a hundred miles an hour.

"What do you do?"

"Me? Don't laugh, but I'm actually a substitute teacher."

"No shit? Cool, Tommy. Do you like it?"

"Yeah, it's a lot of fun and pretty rewarding. Kids have a way of reminding you it's still okay to have a Slurpee and a donut for breakfast. The money's decent, too."

"Really? What do I have to do to become a substitute teacher?"

"You serious?" He seemed surprised.

"Yeah, I'm serious, I'd love to do something like that. I like kids, and if it will get me out of bed before noon, even better. I'm starting to feel like I'm going to spend the rest of my life restocking beer and changing kegs. I didn't work my ass off to pay for college so I could end up getting people drunk. It sucks, you know?"

"Trust me, I know. All right, if you're serious, I'll give you the information about who you need to call. Just remember, though, you can't turn up for an assignment reeking of alcohol." He smiled at me and winked. *Great*, I thought, *he thinks I'm nothing but a boozer.*

"Gotcha. Hey, here comes our first customer and he looks German. You deal with him and I'll start getting the cases of *Budveiser* ready."

"You got it."

Before I even had time to think about whether or not I'd really like being tortured by teenagers, I called the number Tommy gave me. I thought it would be a few months before anyone decided I was mentally stable enough to look after kids, but the process of becoming a sub was painless and quick. It took approximately one day of my time filling out paperwork and checking off the appropriate boxes and less than one week of waiting for my first "assignment." I was convinced the school system would lose my paperwork or decide I wasn't competent, but oh boy was I wrong. My first assignment was only a week after I'd applied, definitely not enough time for me to reconsider my options.

When my phone rang at five in the morning, only a few hours after I'd crawled into bed, I looked at it as though seeing a telephone for the first time. *Why is it ringing?* I asked myself. *Funny, I didn't know it could do that.* I almost didn't answer it, but panic set in when I realized it might be my mom or dad with terrible news. *Who else would dare call me at such a ridiculous hour?* All I heard when I picked up the phone was an automated operator asking me to accept a job at Ocoee Middle School. Not for the next week, not for the next day. That day. My bed was warm and soft and begging me not to leave, but I reminded myself I'd wanted a change. I reluctantly accepted the job and shot out of bed before I had any time to think. I'd only had three hours sleep.

Ocoee Middle School was my baptism by fire. I walked into the main office wondering if they would send me home for looking like a monster, but the secretary gave me some forms to sign and directions to the classroom without even hesitating. There was no time to be nervous, no time to grab my keys and drive back home. I walked out of the office and made my way towards the classroom while kids ran past me, all of them yelling and laughing and playing tag in the hallways. I bartended at a place where the music was loud and the people louder, but nothing could have prepared me for the attack on my eardrums that morning. *Jesus,* I thought, *were we that loud when I was in school or am I just getting old?*

All it took was one day of looking after caffeine-addicted kids to realize how much substitute teachers suffered. Every class was an exercise in my patience. They misbehaved, they talked out of turn, they made fun of each other and took turns laughing at my name. Somehow, I managed to look on the bright side. I was getting paid to basically baby sit a group of kids for one day. All I had to do was keep them from killing each other or killing me. No tests to grade, no parent/teacher conferences and no drunks to worry about. Piece of cake. I embraced substitute teaching because it was a lot like being a circus performer. All I had to do was entertain them, make them laugh and stop them from abusing me and the animal on my head.

I never got a chance to work in another school. Ocoee was so desperate for subs they simply told me to show up every day. I went from one classroom to the next, each one a new performance. Having to get up early was great for my health, too. I couldn't get off work anymore and drink six pints of beer and wake up at six o'clock in the morning and expect my body to function properly. Neither could I show up smelling like the Marlboro Man. I was proud at how disciplined I was, and even though I was bone tired from working two jobs, I was having more fun than I'd expected.

There's a lot to say about directing an innocent game of charades.

I quickly earned the reputation of being the "cool" substitute. My antics spread quickly among the student body with lightning speed. The kids would take one look at my name on the chalkboard and say, "Awesome! We got the cool substitute." One kid stopped me in the hallway one day and asked me if I could take the place of his teacher for good. I got more attention and love from a bunch of teenagers than most boyfriends I'd ever had. Even though I made sure they did their assignment, I wasn't a bitch about it. They would do their work quietly and quickly, after which I'd let them ask me questions about my life, entertain them with silly facts about the Hard Rock and join in when the kids played "Simon Says." As irresponsible as my behavior was, the administration of Ocoee Middle School liked me and made the sad mistake of thinking I was a nice, responsible young lady. Each morning when I walked into the main office, the receptionist would give me a sincere smile and hand me my assignment for the day. I would smile back and feel horribly guilty. I'd feel like I should fess up and tell her I had no idea what I was doing.

One day into my third week, the vice principal, Mr. Sean Kline, asked me to take a walk with him. *Uh-oh,* I thought, *here it comes. Somebody must have complained about the noise level in my last class.* Charades got out of hand when I imitated an Oompa Loompa from Willy Wonka's Chocolate Factory.

"Miss Casta…Miss Quesa…Miss…"

"Castellanos. Just call me Bibiana."

We were walking the halls of the school, which were thankfully quiet. I liked Mr. Kline. He was a very handsome young black man. Handsome, charming, dedicated and obviously crazy enough to let me be a substitute teacher.

"Miss Bibiana, I was looking at your résumé today. I had the county fax it over to me. I hope you don't mind."

"No, not at all." *Shit, shit, shit,* I thought. *He's going to realize I can't really do anything except pour a mean draft beer.* "What's up? Did I do something wrong?"

"Oh, God, no. You have been wonderful. The kids love you. Teachers are asking me to request you for their absent days. I don't know what you're doing, but whatever it is, they love you." He gave me a smile and I wondered where on earth he was going with this conversation.

"Okay, so what's up? Why the walk?"

"Well, I wanted to look at your résumé because I was curious. You're funny and you obviously love kids. Most substitute teachers walk around with scowls on their faces muttering to themselves, but you're always smiling when you show up for work."

"It's the Dunkin Donuts coffee, I swear it. I'm convinced they put happy pills in it."

"I'll have to give that a try, Bibiana. Anyway, the reason I wanted to talk to you is because I was wondering why you didn't apply to be a full-time teacher."

"Really?" I was shocked. Being a full-time teacher hadn't crossed my mind, and I didn't think I could be one anyway. "To be honest, Mr. Kline, I didn't think I could be a full-time teacher."

He looked confused. "Why not?"

"Well, I didn't study education. My degree's in International Relations. What on earth could I teach with that?"

"Yes, I know, but you also have a minor in Political Science, which means you can get a two year temporary certificate. I've done the research for you."

"Oh. But what would I teach?"

"There are a few things, but before we even discuss that, I'd like to ask you a question, and you must be honest with me. I rarely ever do this for anyone, but I'm doing it for you because I knew you were different the first day you showed up here."

"Different how?"

"I don't know. Different. Funny. Smart. Or as the kids say, cool."

"Oh, okay. I like the 'cool' part. Anyway, what's your question? I promise to tell you the truth, the whole truth, and nothing but the truth so help my crazy mom Isabela."

"Crazy mom Isabela?"

"Yep, she's nuts."

He laughed and shook his head and then stopped walking. He turned and looked me in the eye.

"Do you really want to teach? Do you think you would enjoy it?"

I stopped walking and scratched my head.

"Yeah, Sean, I think I would. I mean, I've had a lot of fun so far. It can't be that hard, can it?"

"Well, just remember something. Being a substitute teacher is very different to having your own class. As a sub, you get to go home when the bell rings without having to grade papers or call someone's mom. Being a full-time teacher is a major amount of responsibility and a lot of hard work and dedication. Are you up to that? I mean, are you ready to give up your fabulous lifestyle of bartending?"

"You mean leave the Hard Rock Café with music loud enough to blow one of my eardrums?"

"Uh-huh."

I thought about the night before. An intoxicated customer had leaned over the bar and had tried to grab the animal on my head. Tommy had grabbed his arm and yelled at him before having security kick him out. Yeah, I was up to it all right.

"I'm more than ready to leave bartending, Sean. I've always wondered what it would be like to have a real job."

He chuckled and shook his head. "Okay, I'll contact the right people down at the county and make sure they take care of you right away."

"Wow, thanks a lot, Sean. I really appreciate it."

I wasn't 100% sure I wanted to be a teacher. I wasn't sure I wanted to be anything. Having to choose a profession for the rest of your whole life can be pretty intimidating. I'd held on to the silly idea that I wanted my life to resemble a salad bar. A little bit of this, a little bit of that, not too much of this and not too much of that. And everything had to taste great. I figured I would never get bored.

When I was in college, confused over what to do post the most-irresponsible-time-you're-ever-going-to-have phase, everyone from family to friends to complete strangers felt the need to tell me what I should do with the rest of my life, as though I had a sign on my forehead that said, "I Accept Unsolicited Opinions."

"You should go into sales.

"You should go into public relations."

"You should be a stripper."

"Have you ever thought about law school?"

"Why don't you go into communications?"

Rarely did anyone ever ask me what I enjoyed doing. To most people, what you enjoy bares absolutely no relation to how much money you should be making at the age of twenty-five. If you're in medical school and up to your ears in debt, it's okay, because after all, you're going to be a doctor. If you're a bartender who's making three hundred dollars a night, it's not okay, because after all, you're just a bartender. It's not a "real" job.

Only a few people had ever told me I should go into teaching, but I'd always met this advice with disbelief and confusion. Me, a teacher? Me, in charge of America's future? Don't think so. But Mr. Kline's words got to me that day. I knew I was capable of more than changing kegs and throwing out garbage at three o'clock in the morning. The thought that I could actually do something with my life, something that might benefit the future, only reinforced it. And besides, I was bored with bartending. It was no longer spectacular and fun.

I went to work that day after my talk with Mr. Kline and had a terrible night. *It's a sign*, my mom would've said.

My mom is a big believer in signs. She's Mexican and it kind of goes with the territory. She's always taught me to listen really hard to what God is trying to tell me. To her, everything that happens can be interpreted as a sign. My mom can be silly sometimes when it comes to her superstitions, but she is usually right. When my first boyfriend showed up at my house with a bouquet of roses, my mom told me it would never last if they died within the first day. They died in about two hours. Six months later, he cheated on me. My mom said the roses were a sign. I said she was crazy. When the next boyfriend showed up with a box of chocolates, she said the relationship would be painful if the chocolates made me sick. They did. Three months later, boyfriend number two punched me in the arm because I beat him at Trivial

Pursuit. She said it was another sign. *Another sign you're crazy*, I thought.

But for once, I took my mom's advice and took Mr. Kline's offer as a good sign.

True to his word, Sean gave me the information I needed. I had no idea what I was in for. Everything I knew about teaching stemmed from movies, books, and my own experiences with inspiring teachers. I didn't let this hold me back. The more I thought about it, the more teaching seemed like a good idea. *You said you wanted to make a difference when you were in college, right? Here's your chance.*

Because I'm Hispanic, Sean put me in contact with the minority recruiter for the school system. I had pretty much grown up in Miami, so it was a shock to think of myself as a minority. I grew up in a city where most street signs were in Spanish and Cuban flags hung everywhere, but if it meant an easier way into the public school system, so be it. The minority recruiter determined I would be an asset to an inner city school. *Inner city?* I had thought. I had put down on my application that I thrived under stress and enjoyed challenges, but it had never occurred to me that I might be sent to a school in a less-than-safe neighborhood. I thought I'd end up teaching in a school with beautiful landscaping, perfectly behaved kids and wonderful cafeteria food. I didn't think I'd end up in the hood.

I was excited at the prospect of doing something else with my life and decided not to ask questions. I didn't want to blow it. I prepared myself for my first and what would be my only interview at Howard Middle School in downtown Orlando.

# Chapter 2

Howard Middle School was a red brick schoolhouse, two floors high and supported by massive columns in the front. *How can this be considered inner city?* I had thought. I was sure the minority recruiter had made a mistake. The words "inner city" made me think of metal detectors, graffiti, guns, drugs. There wasn't a sign of that to be found anywhere.

I loved it the minute I laid eyes on it because I've always been a sucker for old buildings. It had that special smell, too, one that instantly propelled me back to my kindergarten classroom. A wonderful combination of paste, lead, paper, old books and cafeteria food. For some reason, I loved these smells. They reminded me of a time when the world was much easier to live in and things were never so complicated that they couldn't be solved with a bowl of ice cream. A time when I never wondered what would become of my life.

I made my way to the front office and prayed I'd get the job. I had always been funny like that. If I liked the way a building looked or made me feel, my first thought would be that I wanted to work there. *So what if it's a mental hospital or funeral home*, I would think.

I interviewed with the principal, Dr. Lawrence. *Holy shit, what a huge man,* I thought as he stood up to meet me. He was absolutely massive and towered over me like the Jolly Green Giant. He had big hands, a big smile, big shoulders, and big expectations. His size intimidated me but he still made me feel comfortable. Dr. Lawrence was an easy person to talk to, so we dove right into conversation. He asked me all the right questions and I charmed him (or so I thought) with all the right answers.

That's not to say I lied in any way. By then, I was truly convinced I was born to teach, to change lives, to inspire, to have summers off and great benefits. The beauty of the school was a clear sign. I wasn't too sure what I wanted to teach, but I told him I was up to any challenge, any subject except Math or Science, any type of student. He smiled and nodded as I explained what I studied in college. He said very little as I went on and on. I wondered what was going through his mind. The way I saw it, what could I possibly teach? I couldn't imagine the school had a course in Soviet Foreign Policy in the 1950's or Middle East Relations. It didn't really matter, though, because I was ready to teach anything to get me in the door of that old school. Inner city or not.

I laid on the charm and did my best to impress him just in case he was going to interview anyone else. Little did I know there was a shortage of teachers all over the city, the state, the entire country. An endless need for people ready, willing and brave enough to educate raging adolescents. After about an hour of questions about who I was and why I wanted to teach (to make a difference, of course), Dr. Lawrence offered me a position with little hesitation and told me I would be perfect for the At-Risk program.

"Just perfect," he said as he smiled at me.

I was flattered he had decided so quickly, but my initial happiness diminished as the words "At Risk" bounced around in my head. *Shoot*, I thought, *maybe this really* is *an inner city school.* I was desperate to leave bartending, but not so desperate that I wasn't willing to ask him a few questions. I didn't know what "At Risk" meant, but the words "belligerent" and "insubordinate" came to mind.

"At Risk? At risk of what?" I smiled and pretended I wasn't wondering if I'd need to buy a bulletproof vest. He smiled.

"Miss Castellanos, most of these kids are from broken homes and a poor neighborhood. They are at risk of dropping out. Most of them live with their aunties and grandmas, and a few of them have already had brushes with the law. Nothing too serious, I can assure you." Yeah, like *that* made me feel better. "All of them have the potential to graduate someday, however their poor behavior in mainstream classes has held them back. These kids have all been taken out of regular classes and put into one classroom to better target their specific needs."

*Okay*, I thought, *forty badly behaved kids in one classroom, with me as their guide. Hmm, this could be interesting if not an introduction to Prozac.*

"Oh, I see. Like a *Dangerous Minds* kind of thing, right?"

"Yeah, I guess you can say that. Only you're not Michelle Pfeiffer and this is not a movie. This is real, Miss Castellanos, and I feel obligated to tell you that these kids have managed to go through three other teachers."

*Were they killed? Tortured? Stabbed with razor sharp pencils?* I managed to find my voice again.

"Oh, what happened to them?"

"Well, let's just say they couldn't handle it." He gave me a long look while I mulled over his last words.

*Couldn't handle it*, I thought. At least they were still alive, a very good sign. Maybe they had decided teaching wasn't their calling after all. *C'mon, you're no chicken*, I said to myself. *When you were a little girl, you chased lizards, rode your bike barefoot and let your brother paint your face with permanent marker. You are fearless.*

"I said I was ready for a challenge so I'm not going to back out now. I really want to teach and that's why I'm here. I accept the position, Dr. Lawrence."

He smiled and got up from his desk, his large body towering over mine as I stood up to shake his hand. He came around his desk and put both his hands around my trembling one.

"I can tell you're going to be different, so don't worry. I think you're going to do a great job. Gut feeling. But I'm here if you need my help with anything. I know most of their mommas and aunties and grandmommas, so I can call them if things get out of hand."

I gave him my best I-won't-let-them-get-to-me smile. "I hope it doesn't come to that, but I'll keep that in mind."

When I got home after my interview, I checked my messages. Tommy was begging me to work for him (no way, I needed to celebrate), my friend Linda in Miami had called just to say hi, and my mom had left a message asking me to call her back immediately because it was "bery important." The last message was from my brother. "Hey, shithead, call me back. I need some advice." I put off the messages and decided to go for a run. Running always made me think better. I put my Walkman on, threw in my favorite tape and started running. As soon as I hit a steady pace and felt my legs warm up, I thought back to my interview. I couldn't believe I'd gotten the job so easily. For a split second I felt guilty that I hadn't called my mom back. I quickly shrugged it off because her version of "bery important" usually involved asking me to send her money for bingo. I started thinking about my future class.

I was going to teach Language Arts and Social Studies to a group of eighth grade kids who were falling behind, kids who basically couldn't sit still and listen to the teacher. *Brushes with the law*, I thought. *What kind of brushes? Assault and battery, theft, jaywalking?* I wondered if Dr. Lawrence hadn't really told me the truth. And suddenly, the job didn't seem so interesting anymore. Suddenly, making a difference didn't sound so exciting. *Oh, well,*

I thought. *Too late now.*

I would have the kids for three hours every morning for English and Social Studies. I had an hour break to plan lessons and yet another hour for lunch. After lunch, the students would come back to me for study hall. During my break, the kids would go to Mr. Connelly, the other fortunate At Risk teacher. Mr. Connelly would teach them Math and Science while I planned my lessons and gathered my wits. I wondered why they didn't have music or art or Phys Ed, but I figured it was part of the program. Dr. Lawrence told me Mr. Connelly was a former New York City schoolteacher who had moved down to Florida to get away from the cold. He said the kids lived in fear of him.

*Good,* I thought. *I have backup.*

I figured it couldn't be that bad. My mom managed to raise my brother and me without being committed to a mental institution and God knows we weren't the quiet type. She didn't speak English very well but she had no problem getting through to us. She usually got her point across with her sandal. When she spoke in her funny accent, we listened. When she raised her voice, we cowered, but when she took off her sandal, *we ran.* We really respected my mom. I couldn't imagine the kids would be that bad. If my mom could handle us, I was arrogantly sure I could handle them, even without a sandal.

There was one thing bothering me, though. One little aspect of my fabulous new job that scared the hell out of me. The thing is, I'd never dealt with those kinds of kids. You know, black kids. In fact, all the kids I'd ever known had been disguised as obnoxious adults. Thus far in my life I had been a college student, a waitress, a bartender and a cruise ship purser. The only people I'd ever dealt with were annoying tourists and miserable drunks. *Black teenage kids?* I thought. *Piece of cake.*

I ran for about thirty minutes. By the time I got back to my apartment, I was drenched in sweat, no surprise for someone running in Florida. It is so damn humid. I took a cold shower and poured myself a glass of red wine. It was not uncommon for me to have a glass of wine by myself. It didn't depress me in the least because I was used to it. I liked the people I worked with at the Hard Rock, but not enough to hang out with them on a regular basis. I would've ended up losing my liver.

I turned on the television and flipped through the channels. There was nothing exciting on except a sitcom called "Friends." I had always worked nights so I'd missed out on the Seinfeld-Friends mania. But at least I could say I'd seen every single Brady Bunch episode and purchased a sock dryer from the Home Shopping Network. There didn't seem to be anything on, so I turned off the television and crawled into bed, feeling guilty that I hadn't called my mom back. *Oh, well*, I thought, *one night without bingo won't kill her.*

The next day, I headed over to the school and picked up old files about the program from Dr. Lawrence's secretary, Mrs. Green. As she handed me the files, she gave me a half smile and said something that sounded like, "Good luck." In retrospect, what she probably said was "You're nuts." I smiled back and thanked her as I put the files under my arm. I made my way to the classroom on the second floor. The emptiness of the school spooked me. The hallways were clean, the floors were shiny and there was no graffiti anywhere. I took it as a positive sign. I found my classroom and peered in. I wanted to go inside and have a look around, but I thought it would be a better idea to go back to my apartment and read the files. If they were too depressing, a glass of red wine was only a few steps away.

Instead of going straight home, I stopped at the Rock. In my excitement to finally have a real job, I'd completely overlooked the fact that I had to formally quit the Hard Rock. I had mixed feelings about quitting. The Rock had treated me more than good. When I decided to transfer from Miami, they welcomed me with open arms and gave me a dream schedule. Plus, it was a fun place to work. I was probably the only employee without any weird piercings or tattoos. Loud music blared throughout the restaurant as employees tried to outdo each other with stunts and pranks. There was a swooping staircase that connected both floors of the Hard Rock. To most employees, the staircase was a slide. Sydman had the most guts. Everyone called him Sydman because every other word out of his mouth was "man."

For example: "Hey, man, so, uh, uh, yeah, man, cool, man. That sounds great, man. All right, man. I'll catch you later, man."

Or: "Hey, Bibiana, man, can you, uh, man, I forgot what I was gonna say. Oh, yeah, man, I remember. Can you hook me up with some oj, man?"

Sydman's favorite trick was sliding down the banister of the staircase with an empty plate on his head. Until he fell off the banister halfway down and landed right on a plate of half eaten nachos. The nice family from Iowa innocently thought it was part of the Hard Rock experience and laughed it off, but Sydman got into major trouble and never slid down the banister again.

Sydman is just one example of the kind of people I worked with. Everyone at the Rock had their own personality, their own quirk, their own way of delivering chicken wings. As I walked through the huge doors, it was like closing a chapter of my life, a chapter I had once thought would always keep me entertained and amused.

I walked in right before the day shift started. Tommy was setting up the downstairs bar. He smiled when he saw me and I wondered if it would be okay to date him now that I was quitting. Instead of going straight to the bar manager and giving him my notice, I sat at the bar as Tommy set up.

"Hey, you. I called you yesterday."

"I know, Tommy, but I wouldn't have been able to work for you anyway. Sorry."

"Don't worry about it. I found someone else. What are you doing here? Aren't you off today? Something wrong?"

"Yes and no."

"Yes and no? That's like saying you're somewhat pregnant." I gave him a funny look. "Oh, shit, don't tell me you're…"

"No, don't be ridiculous. Getting pregnant involves having sex. I have more chances of getting struck by lightning."

"Cute, Bibiana, cute. I happen to think you're hot so cut the I'm-a-loser attitude. What's up?"

My face was beet red. I wasn't good at taking compliments. I debated asking Tommy out on a date right then and there but quickly changed my mind. If teaching didn't work for me, the Hard Rock would be my fall back plan. Fooling around with Tommy would've made it awkward to work with him again. Especially if the sex turned out to be horrible.

"Tommy, I'm here to resign. I'm quitting."

He stared at me and smiled.

"You're full of shit. Come on, what are you really doing here?"

"No, I swear. I got another job."

"Doing what? Don't tell me you got a job at Planet Tragicwood. I'll have to kill you."

"No, I got a real job."

"A real job?"

"Yeah. You hooked me up with substitute teaching, remember?"

"Yeah, so?"

"Well, that sort of turned into a job as a full-time teacher. I have to start planning tomorrow and classes begin next week."

"Holy shit! You, a teacher?" He sounded surprised.

"Hey, don't be so shocked. I'm not as much of a loser as you think I am."

"I never said you were a loser."

28

"No, but you probably thought it."

"Did not."

"Did too."

"Bibiana, stop being a moron, okay? Why would I even think that anyway? If anything, you've always confused me. I happen to think you're way too smart to be stuck behind a bar."

"You have?"

"Yeah. I kind of hated you when you first started here, and do you know why? Because no matter what country a person came from, you always knew something about it. The capital, the president, the civil unrest, everything. You're like a walking encyclopedia. I couldn't understand why you were here with us, restocking beer and doing the YMCA." He started picking up bottles and wiping them down. "I never asked because I didn't want to pry, but you're way too smart to be a bartender. Not that all bartenders are stupid. I just think you should be doing something else. Something better." He stopped and smiled at me. "I'm so glad I told you about substitute teaching."

"I'm really not that smart, Tommy. I just have a good memory." The nerd in me screamed and yelled but I shut her up quick. "To be honest, Tommy, I'm actually scared."

"Scared? Why?"

"I don't know. I'm going to have to be responsible. I'm going to have to be in charge of kids. I'm going to have to do something I know nothing about. I'm going to have to grow up and I'm not so sure I'm ready. "

Tommy stopped setting up and leaned over the bar. He got really close to my face and I suddenly wondered if I'd brushed my teeth.

"Bibiana, can you be honest with me?"

"Uh-huh."

"Can you see yourself bartending for the rest of your life?"

"Hell, no."

"Could you see yourself being a teacher for the rest of your life?"

"I don't know. Maybe."

"Why don't you know?"

"Because I've never done it before. And because I've never been able to stick to anything. I'm scared I'm going to get bored like I do with everything else."

"Why not take a chance, though? Would you rather stay here and wonder? Would you rather go to sleep every night until you're too old to lift a bottle of rum and wonder what would've happened if you had done something else?"

"No, of course not."

"So why are you hesitating?"

"I'm scared. I just told you that."

"Scared of what?"

"I'm scared it won't be fun. I'm scared I won't be able to handle it. I'm scared I'll fail."

"But you won't fail."

"How can you be so sure?"

"I'm not, but there's one thing I've noticed about you. You don't like to be less than perfect. It's kind of annoying, to be honest. But, oh well, some of us were born to be slackers. Don't worry, Bibiana. You're going to be a great teacher."

"If you say so."

"I know so. Now, get your ass into the office and turn in your notice. Otherwise you'll leave me no choice but to pick you up and drag you there myself."

"Down, boy." I was laughing. "You've convinced me."

"Thank God. Don't be a stranger, okay? Keep in touch and let me know how the real world is treating you."

I turned in my resignation that day and walked out of the Rock for good.

When I got home, I changed into sweats and put the files in front of me on the coffee table. I poured myself a glass of water and dove into a sandwich, already wondering if it would be wrong to open a bottle of wine at one in the afternoon. I was nervous, I'll admit that. I was scared of what I would find. I sat on the couch and ate my sandwich, silently willing myself to open the files and get it over with. *It can't be that bad*, I told myself. I picked up the files.

Notes from the last three teachers (all in one school year) had been left for me, most of them scribbles that made me think they were truly insane by the end of their teaching career. *Not able to teach lesson due to argument between two students which resulted in fist fight. Need a drink.* Hmm. *Various disciplinary problems today: Taquila wearing too-short skirt but refused to listen; Tevaris and Jean-Pierre got into fight over Haitian and African American heritage; unable to quiet students and therefore gave out ten detentions; only one student showed up. Need to see doctor about prescription for Valium.* Finally, I came across a positive note. *Good class today, was able to give lesson on letter writing; however, one-third of class missing due to suspension for fighting and failure to show up for detention.*

Once again, I started doubting my abilities to control a group of teenagers.

Controlling a group of drunks was easy because one phone call to security and they were out. I couldn't do that with students. The idea that I might not be able to hold their attention terrified me. But it was too late to turn back, too late for me to head back to the salad bar for a second helping of bartending.

I spent the whole day looking through their notes. The desperation of their scribbles made me want to laugh and puke at the same time. I managed to make it through the day without downing the bottle of wine, though, and after a long hot bath, I went to bed ready to face the next day. No matter the obstacles, I was going to tackle my first real job with a vengeance.

The next morning I woke up too early, which annoyed me. It was only four thirty in the morning and I had set my alarm for six. *Damn it*, I thought. *I should've had a glass of wine.* I lay in bed with my eyes open, praying for sleep. I eventually fell asleep again, but only minutes before my alarm went off. I rubbed my eyes. I looked outside from my air-conditioned apartment and knew it was going to be a scorching day. It was August in Orlando, enough to put anyone in a foul mood. I spent an hour working on my hair and picking out the right clothes, but I was drenched in sweat by the time I got into my car, which was parked not ten feet from my apartment. I vowed to cut off the animal on my head as I turned on my car.

Despite the heat, I stopped at Dunkin' Donuts for my routine medium coffee, cream and sugar. Mac, the old man who owned the store, smiled as I walked in. I grabbed a napkin and wiped the sweat off my forehead.

"Well, well. Look at you! What are you doing up at this hour? Not working nights anymore?"

"No, Mac. No more night shifts." As nervous as I was about being a teacher, the fact that I'd never again have to come home at four in the morning instantly filled me with happiness. I smiled at the realization.

"Oh, is that right? What happened? Let me guess, you finally found a nice rich man to take care of you?" Mac was sweet. He constantly tried to set me up with his nephew. I must have looked really lonely because his nephew was forty-seven years old and unemployed.

"No, Mac. No rich man. I got a job as a teacher."

"A teacher? You're shittin' me!"

"Nope. I'm going to be a teacher."

"Wow, Bibiana, that's great. What school? What grade? What subject?" Mac was clearly impressed and more than happy to see me doing something other than entertaining tourists.

"Uh, well, I'm teaching the At-Risk program. You know, it's a program for kids with special needs."

"Oh." He gave me a funny look. "What school is that, dear?"

"Uh, Howard Middle School. It's downtown, right by Lake Eola."

"Uh-huh." He was starting to look pained. "You sure you wanna do this?"

"Yeah, Mac, why not?"

"Well…" He looked ready to say something but changed his mind. He grinned as he handed over my coffee. "Honey, you'll do a great job. Keep me posted, okay? And this one's on me. God bless you, dear."

"Okay, Mac. Thanks for the coffee."

*Is there something no one's telling me? Something Dr. Lawrence failed to inform me of? Do I look like someone who would never survive teaching?* These questions ran through my mind as I drove to the school. I threw in a Van Morrison CD and calmed down. Van has that effect on me. Van has every effect on me, if I think about it. I listen to him when I'm sad, when I'm angry, when I'm lonely, when I'm happy, when I'm drunk. He's my music-for-every-mood guy.

I found Mrs. Green at her desk. She jumped up when she saw me, as though she was truly surprised I came back after looking through the files. She gave me a permanent set of keys to my classroom and a key to the storage room, a place where I could find everything from posters to books to slide projectors. I spent the morning tacking up old maps and battered posters. The wooden desks weren't too bad and the chalkboard was in decent shape. My desk, however, was ancient. And heavy. I tried to move it but gave up after the third try. I sat down in the wooden chair.

I loved the feel of it, loved the way I felt at the front of the classroom. In charge. Empowered. Passionate. I let my imagination run wild. I pictured myself sitting at my desk with inquisitive young scholars hanging on my every word. They were asking me to read Whitman, begging me to indulge them in Keats or Tennyson. "Just for a few minutes, Miss Castellanos."

I was about to stand up and give them a passionate speech on the importance of the English language when Dr. Lawrence's voice boomed into my classroom. "All returning teachers and staff, please report to the school library." I was excited to meet my peers. Scared, but still looking forward to it.

I walked down to the library and took my place with the rest of the Language Arts and Social Studies teachers. I noticed there was only one black teacher, Mrs. Styles, and I also noticed she was the only one who smiled at me sincerely. The rest of the group glanced at me briefly and went back to staring really hard at the table. The minute I sat down, Mrs. Coleman, the Gifted English teacher, turned to me and gave me a smug grin. She asked me what I planned to assign as required reading for the first term.

"Uh, well, since I'm new to this, I was hoping for some suggestions." I looked around the group and gave everyone a *please let me into your cult* smile.

Mrs. Davis spoke first. She looked like she'd been a teacher since the last century.

"Humph, a new kid. What are you teaching?"

Whenever I'm uneasy, I have a terrible habit of associating people with animals. One look at Mrs. Davis and I saw a turtle. Something about her face reminded me of slow movements.

"I'm teaching the At-Risk students."

She snickered and gave me a sarcastic smile.

"Well honey, I hate to tell you, but you're the one at risk!"

*Wow*, I thought, *she went from turtle to snake in 1.2 seconds.*

The rest of the teachers snickered and laughed while I thought about which one I would poison first. Everyone thought her joke was cute and funny, everyone except Mrs. Styles. She cleared her throat and spoke on my behalf. I made a mental note to put her on my Christmas list.

"Hi. My name is Namisha, and your name is Miss Casta...Miss Castenda...uh..."

"Castellanos. Just call me Bibiana, please." I thanked her with my smile.

"Bibiana, don't be nervous. It's always rough your first year. Is there any book you think the students would like?" She glared at Mrs. Coleman as she said this. Mrs. Coleman looked away and rolled her eyes.

"Well, like I said, I'm new and I'm not sure what the students are like, but based on what Dr. Lawrence told me, I think I'll start them out with a book they might be able to relate to. Like *The Outsiders* by S.E. Hinton." Little did they know I pulled the idea straight out of my ass. I hadn't given required reading any thought at all. I had been too preoccupied with my sanity.

"*The Outsiders*?" Mrs. Coleman replied. Too bad for Mrs. Coleman. She reminded me of a cat, a shame because I don't like cats. She was extremely petite and had an oval shaped face, a tiny mouth filled with equally tiny teeth. She spoke to everyone in an I'm-way-too-intellectual-for-you-losers manner. Give me a nice dog and I'll play with it for hours. Give me a cat and I'll simply want to run it over.

"Yeah. What's wrong with *The Outsiders*? I read it when I was in the eighth grade and I loved it."

"Bibiana, please don't take this the wrong way, but these kids live in a totally different world than that of Ponyboy and Sodapop. How are they going to relate to a story about poor white kids in the Midwest? And as you probably know by now, they don't exactly have the best reading skills."

Her tone of voice made me feel like I, myself, was back in the eighth grade. I shrugged and gave her a challenging look.

"If I remember correctly, *The Outsiders* is a book about kids who feel left out, kids who come from broken families and a bad neighborhood. Everyone can relate to that, black or white. And maybe this book will get them more interested in reading, because I don't think Shakespeare will be able to do that."

Silence.

The Cat coughed and looked at the rest of the group, but the group had gone back to staring at the table. Mrs. Styles was the only one looking at me and she was smiling. I knew I'd found a friend. The Cat cleared her throat again.

"Well, it's your class after all. Dr. Lawrence asked me to help you, so I'll be here if you need anything." *Sure*, I thought, *I'll be running to you in a hurry.*

"Great, thanks." She gave me what could have been an innocent smile, but it was too late. *She's a snotty cat*, I thought.

The rest of the meeting was a blur. I started to panic because I felt like there was no way I was going to make it through the school year without wanting to trip Mrs. Coleman in the hallway or put speed in Mrs. Davis's coffee when she wasn't looking. I said very little during the meeting and pretended to take notes. I knew I was being unfair to judge them so soon, but I hate it when people make me feel uncomfortable and out of place. It makes me think of childhood.

During the meeting, while Mrs. Coleman droned on and on, I dreamed up ways of torturing her but eventually forced myself to stop. I'm Catholic. We're not supposed to imagine stapling someone's lips together.

After the meeting, I stood in a corner of the library feeling slightly nauseous. I felt like an outsider, a poser, someone merely acting as a teacher. *I've been cast in the wrong role*, I thought to myself. *I don't belong on this movie set.*

I turned when I felt a warm hand on my shoulder. A tall guy with jet-black hair and sparkling blue eyes introduced himself as Mr. Connelly. I took in his enormous presence and sighed in relief. Here was someone who would keep me safe, someone who would watch my back. He must have been about six foot four because I had to strain my neck to look up at him.

Mr. Connelly took my breath away.

His eyes looked as though they'd once been sparkling blue diamonds in another lifetime. His eyelashes were longer than mine and they made the diamonds stand out even more. He wasn't *oh my God* beautiful, the kind of guy who looked like he walked straight out of *GQ Magazine* and into Howard Middle School to save me, but he had that something I loved: a New York accent and good body odor. A deadly combination for me. He also looked in shape, not at all like the bartenders I used to work with whose idea of exercise was running to the liquor store and back. His teeth were slightly crooked and he had tiny wrinkles around his eyes, wrinkles I hoped were from staying up watching television and not, I prayed, from changing diapers or arguing with a wife.

I'd never been a believer in love at first sight. I'd had terrible luck with relationships and the idea that I had a "soul mate" would always strike me as hilarious. *How ridiculous*, I would say. *Someone made just for me? Nah.* That pretty much changed two seconds after I met Matt.

Something about him set my insides on fire. It wasn't the accent or the body odor or the fact that he made me feel like I'd just been given a lifelong bodyguard. It wasn't anything that had to do with raw sexual desire. It was something I couldn't put my finger on. Time stood still as I introduced myself. I tried desperately to enunciate every single word without spitting all over him. We made small talk…*I'm from Miami, I'm from New York, never done this before, don't worry you'll be fine*…and as I watched his mouth open and shut as though in slow motion, my heart beat uncontrollably and my palms started to sweat. *How on earth can I work with this man? How am I going to concentrate with all these new sounds in my head and feelings in my body?*

It was love at first sight. It had to be. Nobody else had ever made me feel that way so quickly. Usually it would have taken at least a few beers. Standing not two feet from him, I felt the hairs on the back of my neck stand and felt a strong desire to fall into his arms. I knew right then and there, standing in the middle of the library, that Matt was my soul mate. No doubt about it. Just like that, I sealed our fate.

I've always been a determined young lady.

While I contemplated what our wedding would be like, Mr. Matt Connelly told me all about himself; his large Irish family, his education, his passion for kids. I tried to focus on his words, but all I could think about was whether or not we would honeymoon in Ireland or Mexico and what our kids would look like. I checked his hands and noticed he wasn't wearing a wedding ring. *Whew.* I pictured us living together, talking about our students over a bottle of wine, soft music in the background as we discussed how to change the world...

"...and that's why I really wanted to teach, you know?"

"Yeah, I know what you mean. I know exactly where you're coming from."

"Hm hmm. So, listen, since our classrooms are right next to each other and we're sharing the same students, we should sit down and go over a few things."

*Of course. The ring, the church, bathroom rules.*

"Definitely." I kept smiling at him like a crazy person. Somehow, I managed to compose myself. "We'll do that."

"Cool. I'll see you around, Bibiana."

"Okay, Mr. Connelly."

"For Christ's sake, call me Matt, okay? Mr. Connelly's my dad."

"Oh, okay. Sorry." I half smiled in an attempt to look sexy. I turned and walked away, hoping I wouldn't do something stupid like trip over myself. Too late. I ran into a chair and caught myself before I became one with the floor. I looked at him and shrugged.

"It's my first time walking."

Matt laughed out loud. "See you soon, kid."

*You bet you will,* I thought.

I wanted to take the job seriously and put all else aside, but all I could think about was Matt. I went over our brief conversation a thousand times, wondering if I should've said this, or I should've said that. I loved the fact that I had something to look forward to every day, but I couldn't let him stand in the way of my mission, my first real job. I managed to push him all the way to the back of my already too-crowded mind and concentrated on getting organized.

I got my hands on twenty copies of *The Outsiders*, which was no good because I had over thirty-five students. I considered buying the rest of the copies myself, but when I did the math, I decided sharing would have to do. I planned my lessons for the first three weeks; lessons revolving around Geography, American History, Grammar, Reading. I'd always been an organization freak, so making files for every student was a momentous occasion. I actually derived pleasure from such a menial task. Big Nerd. I made neat little files with everyone's name on them, names that were going to take some getting used to. Chancy, Tevaris, Jazelin, Taquila, Marcdala, etc. I practiced saying their names because I wanted to get them right. Chaancee, Teevahriss, Jayzulin, Taqueela, Marcdaala...I'd never before seen such names. I was used to names like Josefin or Israel or Juan Manuel or Luisito or Ana Maria.

My first real task was deciding whether or not to have assigned seating. One memory of childhood popped into my head and I decided against it. The first day of third grade, my teacher assigned me to a desk at the back of the classroom next to Rudy, a little boy who loved to torture lizards in the playground and pull my hair. I cried and begged and pleaded with her to move my seat to the front, but she ignored me. She told me we all had to get used to uncomfortable situations in life and I should just *deal with it*. When you're eight years old, an uncomfortable situation means having to wait for the bathroom after you've had three gallons of fruit punch. I tried making peace with Rudy, a little blond kid who could've been cute had he combed his hair once in a while or brushed his teeth. My peace offering (a Snickers) was met with pinching and more pulling of the hair. I told my parents and they came to the school armed with their strong Hispanic accents, ready to do battle with the *teecher*.

You have to imagine my parents at this point. My mom is under five feet tall, my dad is nearly six foot. She is small and a little on the chubby side and always wearing funky colored lipstick like bright orange. My dad has a full head of silver hair and a belly that makes him look like a proud soon-to-be mother of triplets. They both have kind, understanding eyes and a timid demeanor. More than anything, they are polite and respectful, but when it comes to their children, nothing else is more important than their happiness.

To them, having to sit next to a mean little boy was a serious threat to my safety and education. They missed half a day's work to come to the school and resolve the matter. It took all of fifteen minutes. My mom stood in front of the teacher, large rollers in her hair and orange lipstick on her lips, and tried to get her point across in very broken English. My dad calmly asked if he could speak to Mrs. Bonney outside where he could smoke a cigarette. After ten minutes, Mrs. Bonney walked back in with a smile on her face and moved me to the front of the class.

To this day I have no idea what my dad said to Mrs. Bonney, but it worked. For a long time, I was convinced my parents had mysterious powers. And these powers could only be evoked with a lit cigarette. I mean, how else could my parents figure out that my brother hadn't done his homework or that I hadn't brushed my teeth? Powers or not, I knew one thing. When it came to my happiness, my parents would always be there for me, cigarette in hand and rollers in place.

The night before my first day as an official teacher, I lay awake for hours, tossing and turning and worried that maybe I had made a mistake, chosen the wrong profession. *What if they think I'm just another stupid white woman? What if they don't listen to me? How will I get them to like me and trust me on the first day? Oh, no, what if I don't like it?* All night long, questions and doubts tortured me, but eventually fatigue kicked in and I slept for a few hours before the alarm went off. Fifteen minutes later, I was off and running towards my new career as a school teacher.

With my Dunkin Donuts coffee in hand, I walked into my classroom an hour before the bell and went through my plans for the day. Anxiety hit me fifteen minutes before the bell rang, so I did what I always do when I'm troubled or scared. I called my mom in Miami.

"*¿Aló?*"

"Hi, Mami."

"Oh, my choogar. How are joo?"

"I'm okay, Mami, a little nervous."

"Oh jess? Why? Oh, wait, I know! Today es your first day, no? As a school teecher?"

"Yes, Mami, but maybe I can't do this. I'm really nervous. I'm afraid they won't like me."

"Don't be craysee, baby. Joo are bery funny and smart. Joo will be okey, okey?"

"Okay, Mami."

"Joo call me when today es over. Joo call me and tell me everysing, okey?"

"Okay, Mami. I will. Bye."

"Okay, *que Dios te bendiga, mi'ja.*"

"Okay. God bless you too."

I hung up the phone and enjoyed my last few minutes as a sane person.

# Chapter 3

I was born in East Los Angeles and spent the first seven years of my life surrounded by alcoholic uncles, their crazy, obsessive wives, and what seemed to me like three thousand cousins and just as many animals. Tia Esmeralda had six kids, Tio Sammy had three, Tio Cesar had two, Tio Jose had four (that we knew of), Tio Antonio had five. No such thing as birth control. Everyone in our neighborhood owned at least one dog, a few chickens, a rooster, cats, rabbits, you name it. We had our very own petting zoo and didn't even realize it. Our neighborhood was predominantly Mexican, but we did have a token white family and a crazy Italian family. And it worked for us.

There weren't any signs of gangs or drugs or crime back then. It was a relatively peaceful neighborhood in spite of the reputation Cheech and Chong were giving it. My brother and I went to St. Anthony's Catholic school just a few blocks from our house. During the day, while my brother wreaked havoc on the nuns and I charmed them, my dad worked as a construction worker and my mom…well, we were never sure what the hell she did during the day, but she was always there when we left and always there when we came back. Instead of chocolate chip cookies and milk after school, my mom would feed us Hawaiian Punch ice cubes. Her rationale was that it was "froot" punch and therefore good for us.

We would sit at the kitchen table like good little soldiers and do our homework. She couldn't help us because she couldn't speak English. Added to that was the fact that she only had six years of formal schooling in Mexico.

She'd pretend really well, though. She'd look over my shoulder as I worked on my alphabet lessons and say, "Oh jes, bery good. Bery bery good. Joo are bery smart." My brother never got so lucky. He had the attention span of a corpse and hated everything related to the prison he attended Monday thru Friday. Whenever he'd try to sneak out, my mom would grab him by the ear and bring him right back to the table. One look at the smug grin on my face and he would kick me under the table.

To put it bluntly, we never saw black people in our neighborhood. Not that we were constantly on the lookout, but it's just one of those things you notice when you look back on your childhood. Their homes and their lives were in South Central LA, which could have been another planet for all we knew. My parents didn't talk about black people. It was never a topic of discussion at the dinner table. In our house, it was the Cuban vs. the Mexican factor. My parents constantly argued over who was the superior race or who had the better country.

"Cuba has de most beautiful beechess on de whole world," my dad would say.

"*¿Qué? Estás loco.* Joo has neber been to de Mexican beeches," my mom would argue back.

"No, no, I know what I'm telling joo. No place like Varadero."

"Hmph, es because joo neber been to Acapulco."

Or.

"All de best baseball players, they come from Cuba."

"*¿Qué? ¿No me digas?* What about Fernando Valenzuela, eh?"

My brother and I would sit there like two kids at a tennis match. A point for her, a strong serve for him, a great come back for her. Back and forth. Erasmo and I would look at each other and shrug, because it was pointless to take sides. We were neither completely Cuban nor completely Mexican. We were stuck in the middle.

My only recollection of "black" was my brother's version of the "boogie man." Lying in bed at night, he would try to scare me by saying that the boogie man, an evil ghost dressed in black, would crawl through the window and take me to hell if I didn't let my brother play with my toys. When you're a little kid, anything is possible, and the *dressed in black* boogie man scared the hell out of me. I wet my bed, I had nightmares, I insisted on sleeping with my parents. Instead of telling them the truth, though, I let Erasmo terrify me for months.

Until something terrible happened and Erasmo got a major ass whoopin'.

I was three years old. We were at the local supermarket a few blocks from our house, a typical supermarket in East LA. The shelves carried traditional cereals and canned foods along with products for every single Mexican dish you can imagine. Mole, red chilies, nopales, etc. Piñatas hung from the ceiling and behind the counter you could always find a Loteria or a Mexican version of Chutes and Ladders.

I sat quietly in the shopping cart as my mom pushed it up one lane and down the next. She questioned my dad on every item he put in the cart. "No, no, that one es no good," or "No, no, *ay Dios mio,* joo know nothing!" One big power struggle. When it came to groceries, though, my mom always won. Without her, my dad would've starved. He couldn't boil a pot of water to save his life. So the grocery store was her domain.

I was a mild-mannered little girl, so my mom says. These trips to the store were a treat because I'd always be rewarded for my wonderful behavior. I'd get a piece of candy, a cheap plastic toy, or any other object I found extremely amusing. These objects included, but were not limited to, dental floss (I loved yanking all the string out), empty egg cartons (boats for my Fisher Price Little People), or rubber snakes (they terrified the Little People in the bathtub). I realized quickly that being the good kid would always get me things easily. Not Erasmo. Erasmo was like a trouble magnet, so he'd always stay behind at a friend's house and drive that mother crazy.

We made it to the checkout line, my dad utterly defeated, my mom triumphant and happy. I may have been the good kid, but that didn't stop me from being restless. I tried to get myself out of the cart while my dad laid the items on the counter and my mom made small talk with the cashier, who happened to be from the same city in Mexico. No surprise in East LA. Unfortunately, my chubby legs were holding me prisoner. I struggled and twisted and turned and tried to get out of the cart. My dad grabbed me and hefted me out in one motion and placed me in his arms, my head landing on his shoulder and my eyes staring right into the face of a black woman behind us. Time stood still as she caught my eye and smiled at me.

Instead of smiling back, I *screamed.* Yes, I *screamed.* My mom and dad froze and the cashier looked around in bewilderment. Unphased, the black lady continued to smile at me. To make matters worse, I screamed again.

"What? *¿Qué pasa? Eh?*" My dad asked me.

"A monster! A monster!" I yelled as I pointed at the lady. "Boogie man!"

My mom started to panic. "*Ay Dios mio,* how embarrassing. I'm so sorry, lady, I..."

People in the other check out lines started getting interested in the commotion. Everyone always loves a good drama in the supermarket.

"Bibi, ees okay, ees no monster. Please no cry." My mom was mortified.

"A monster, Papi. A monster!"

I desperately tried to get out of my dad's arms. The black lady looked at my dad with raised eyebrows, as if to say, *Is this what you're teaching your*

41

*child?* My dad, so peaceful, so soft-spoken, shrugged and apologized. "I so sorry, lady," he said, as he explained in broken English that I had never in my life seen a black person. "I sink so maybe she scared for that." Maybe it was the way my dad spoke to her or the fact that his eyes conveyed nothing but sincerity. Perhaps she thought his accent was funny and too hard to understand anyway. The lady started laughing, a loud laugh that caught everyone by surprise, even me. I stopped struggling momentarily and looked at my dad for an explanation.

He smiled at the lady and shook her hand. She kept laughing and said she couldn't believe I'd never seen a black person. My dad raised his hands in the air as though to say, "I don't know," and my mom wrung her hands and said, "I'm so bery sorry, lady. Bery bery sorry, *Dios mio.*"

On the way home, my parents took turns explaining that black people were just like everyone else and not monsters. After very little prompting, my parents got it out of me that Erasmo had been tormenting me about the *dressed in black* Boogie Man. Boy did he pay for it. I've never seen my mom handle her sandal the way she did that day. Utter perfection. He never again mentioned the Boogie Man and I stopped being afraid to sleep with the window open.

I don't remember seeing another black person in the flesh for a few years, thankfully enough time for me to realize the world was full of colors and shapes. Thank you, Sesame Street.

The year I turned seven, my dad decided our neighborhood full of nice, hard working Mexican families was going down the drain. He saw graffiti everywhere and young Mexican *cholos* wearing bandanas and sporting knives in their pockets. And then the crimes started. The supermarket was held up, a fight broke out in the parking lot of Winchell's donuts and someone got stabbed, two gang members were found dead in a dumpster, etc.

At a gas station two blocks from our house, my mom was mugged by a group of young *cholos. My own people*, she said sadly. They only took her purse, but she was a nervous wreck for weeks. She even stopped freezing Hawaiian Punch. We stopped walking to school and my mom became our chauffeur. We started keeping the door locked at all times. We stopped leaving our bicycles on the front lawn overnight. The crime was definitely a valid reason to leave, but there were other things my dad had a problem with.

Like my mom's brothers, for instance.

My mom got a job during the day (once again, we were never quite sure what she did), and it became my uncles' responsibility to watch us after school until she got home. I don't think my dad approved of their tendency to drink beer for breakfast and their inability to hold down a job, but Erasmo and I loved the arrangement. Besides, my dad really had no choice. It was either my uncles or a stranger, and to Hispanic families, leaving your child in the care of someone you don't know from Adam is a disgrace and downright shameful.

So this is what it was like: Erasmo would come home and tell my uncles he had no homework to do. I would come home and tell them I couldn't do my homework unless I had a bowl of ice cream with chocolate sauce. It's not that they were lenient or too lazy to argue with us. We just had an agreement, you see, a simple pact between two smart-ass kids and a few morally flexible men. My uncles were all married to extremely jealous and hot-tempered women. The idea that their wives could fly off the handle for cheating on them didn't seem to hold them back. If anything, it gave them motivation. One of my uncles would walk in the house, put the beer in the fridge and head to the bathroom to freshen up. The doorbell would ring within seconds and we'd open it to find yet another stranger.

The first time it happened, we wouldn't let the lady in a tiny red dress and high-heeled shoes come inside. Tio Antonio came to the rescue. He told us to go into the kitchen and wait for him there. After a few minutes, he strolled in. He looked incredibly uneasy and nervous.

"Okay, guys. She's just a frien', okay? Uh...um...we working together."

I piped up. "Tio, you don't have a job."

"No, well, sometimes I work at dees place, and she...she come working sometime too. *Pero* she's just a frien'." He was starting to sweat and kept looking into the living room to make sure she was still there.

"Does my tia know her?"

"Bibi, would you stop asking stupid questions?" my brother said.

"I just want to know. So, does she know my tia?"

"Ehm, no, *mi'ja*. And your mami no know her *tampoco*." He bent down, looked me in the eye, and whispered, "Please no tell your mami or your aunt, okay?"

I whispered back, "Only if I can have a bowl of ice cream before I do my homework."

"*Sí, sí,* es fine. Have what joo want, *pero* clean up your mess before your mami gets home."

Feeling somewhat slighted, my brother spoke up. "Hey Tio, I promise not to tell if you let me go outside when I get home from school and play with my friends."

"Okay, as long as joo no has no homework."

And that was the arrangement. My brother's grades hit the bottom and my Catholic school uniform shrunk overnight. My brother made me swear not to say anything or else. I only swore not to tell because Erasmo was my idol. I would do anything to get me on his list of cool kids. Oddly enough, the ladies who came to see my uncles were really nice. They never snuck into any of the bedrooms, and from what I saw, the only thing they ever did was talk and hold hands, maybe sneak in a kiss here and there. Yuck. I enjoyed doing homework so I didn't really pay attention to them, interrupting them only to ask my uncle to buy more ice cream before my mom got home, which he always did.

Even though my uncles weren't setting the best example for us, we were still safe inside our homes. We knew better than to talk to strangers, we looked both ways before crossing the street and we had nice if not eccentric neighbors. The Italian man who lived across the street from us would sing at the top of his lungs in the shower. The old American lady who lived next door to us would often come over and help my dad with his vegetable patch or the petting zoo.

When we first moved into the house, all the neighbors came over with funky little housewarming gifts and genuine smiles. I never felt afraid to walk outside or ride my bike in the street. My Tia Esmeralda's six kids were like our best friends. Every weekend seemed to hold surprises and adventure. We weren't the kind of family who traveled to Europe over the summer or spent weekends at beach resorts. Instead, we'd all pile into my Tio Santiago's totally rigged up van and drive to Ensenada or Rosarito Beach for the weekend. We'd go to Yosemite or Big Bear. We'd have birthday parties at Rosemead Park or picnics at Legg Lake Park.

There always seemed to be a get together somewhere in East LA that usually went smoothly until one of my uncles would get rip roaring drunk and decide to fight anyone who gave him enough reason.

It was, in a sense, an idyllic childhood. We were surrounded by family and friends. We didn't have a whole lot of money, but it never seemed to matter. There was always money for the circus, for Magic Mountain, for the local swimming pool. Idyllic or not, nothing could stop my dad from wanting to get the hell out of Hell-Ay and fast. He used the assault on my mom as the perfect excuse to put the house on Vandorf Street up for sale. My aunts and uncles were shocked.

"Federico, Miami is no good. I'm telling joo. No work." My uncle Sammy would plead with him.

"No, no, no, Sammy. These *cholos* are going to ruin my children. Es time for a change. Miami es growing. Many construction for me, joo know?"

"Joo are craysee, Fico. My seester, she has no family in Miami. She es gonna be bery lonely, joo know."

"*Sí, sí,* I know, *pero* es better. We are moving."

Even though both my uncle and my dad had no need to speak English, my dad refused to slip into his native tongue. He spoke English as much as he could because it was the only way to get ahead. When it came to Erasmo and me, however, we were forced to speak Spanish in the house at all times. No if's, and's or but's about that. My parents would speak to us in English and we had to answer them in Spanish. Of course, being the smart asses that we were, we gave them our opinion on the matter.

"We're American, Dad, so we don't have to speak Spanish," my brother said.

"Jess, joo are American, *pero* let me tell you somesing, es important no forget Spanish."

I tugged on my dad's pants. "But why, Papi? We live in the *United States.*" Like he didn't know.

He put his hand on my head and stroked my hair. "Es better to speak two ways, that way joo no forget who joo are, okay? Spanish only. Joo learn English en school, joo learn Spanish en la casa. *Punto.*"

We knew better than to argue with him. He never hit us or raised his voice, but we knew he could snap at any moment. And it terrified us. So we grew up speaking Spanish while my parents learned to speak English in a country so different to theirs, a country they were still trying to understand.

My mom never really said much about moving to Miami. She spent most of the time wringing her hands and muttering *Ay Dios mio* under her breath, as though the end of the world was near. In retrospect, her own little world was coming to an end. My brother was older and therefore better able to handle the news, but because I was desperately in love with my second grade teacher, Sister Mary, and permanently attached to Donna, the little girl next door, they told me we were merely going on vacation. I was amazingly gullible and unable to imagine anyone lying to me, so the news of our upcoming vacation thrilled me.

It's amazing the kind of crap you fall for when you're seven. Like the time my brother told me my parents found me in a dumpster behind the supermarket, or the time he convinced me Mr. Rogers was talking to him and him alone (boy did I cry over that one). I believed we were going on vacation in Florida because the information came straight from Mom and Dad and not from Erasmo.

We helped my mom pack up our belongings. We cleaned, we scrubbed, we argued incessantly and nearly destroyed every nerve in my mom's body. The packed boxes, the "SOLD" sign on the front lawn and my sad relatives failed to enlighten me. Everyone came over the day we were leaving and helped lift the remaining furniture into the moving truck. And still I had no clue. *Doesn't everyone take their bed on vacation?* My friend Donna couldn't contain herself and held on to me for dear life. It was so flattering. "Don't cry, Donna. We'll be back soon, and I promise to bring you something from Florida, like maybe a toy or something."

She cried and cried along with everyone else. With the kind of production they put on, you would've thought we were moving to Mars. Nothing phased me, though, because a great vacation was ahead of us and already I was praying my dad would stop at motels with swimming pools.

On a cool, sunny day in November of 1978, we drove out of East LA. Little did I know we would never actually drive back.

The vacation was pretty boring at first, and I couldn't make out why we had to get up so early every morning. *Why aren't we stopping at any theme parks? Why is Papi driving for hours and hours without stopping? And why is Mami in tears every five seconds?* The vacation was not what I'd expected, but I still believed things would get better once we reached Miami, once we found a hotel with a slide and a diving board. In the meantime, Erasmo and I entertained ourselves by working on paint by number sets (no small feat in a moving vehicle), playing Tic-Tac (the object of which is to spot a VW Beetle before anyone else), and listening to an eight track my Uncle Sammy gave us as a going away present. We sang along to The Bee-Gees, The Doobie Brothers, Donna Summer, and Chicago as we cruised through the Southwestern United States.

During the trip, singing was the only thing that made my mom happy. We'd sing right along with her, too. Sometimes Erasmo and I would collapse into fits of laughter whenever my mom got lyrics all mixed up. She would end up singing something that made no sense.
*Ooh, Night feeber,*
*Night feeber,*
*Joo no has to do it.*
*Night feeber*

*Night feeber*
*Show me we can sew it.*

Just one wrong word or funny pronunciation and we'd giggle for hours, my mom either completely unaware we were laughing at her or just flat out ignoring us. She liked to sing even if she got the words wrong. She had a nice voice, thankfully. Her one saving grace. My dad didn't say much as we made our way to Miami. Occasionally, when my mom's threats to pull our ears off or make us walk to the next town didn't stop our fighting in the back seat, my dad would stop the car, slowly and calmly get out and light up a cigarette. My mom would not so calmly get out of the car, take off her shoe and point it at us and then join my dad for a cigarette.

My mom's threats kind of scared us, but nothing scared us more than my dad's silence. It was like the calm before the storm and it scared us to death because it meant one thing; sooner or later Mt. Federico would erupt and all the cool things he'd bought us along the way would come to an end. So we'd lean out the window and apologize and promise not to fight anymore, *cross our hearts and hope to die.* My mom would give us a frustrated look. My dad would look at us out of the corner of his eye as he put out his cigarette and say, "Okay. We see." Erasmo and I would get along fine for a few miles, but inevitably, he would find a way to make me scream at the top of my lungs.

Lord knows we certainly didn't help their smoking habit.

Miraculously, we made it to Miami, Florida on Thanksgiving Day, 1978. Bruised, tired and fed up with the Bee-Gees, we got out of the car and walked into Sergio's Café on Bird Road. It was a rinky dink kind of place with checkered tablecloths and colorful paper menus. A waitress came over as soon as we sat down and took our order. In Spanish. That was lesson number one. For a split second I wondered if we had taken a wrong turn and ended up in another country. Years later I would come to the realization that Miami was, in fact, like another country. We ordered fried eggs, buttered Cuban bread and café con leche. A heart attack waiting to happen. While the waitress took our order, I had one of the stupidest grins on my face. I couldn't help it. I couldn't stop smiling at the fact that I had, I thought, outsmarted Erasmo. After the waitress left, my dad asked me why I was smiling.

"Oh, Papi, you are going to be so proud of me."

My brother turned to look at me and raised his eyebrows. "Why, smartie pants? What did you do this time?"

"Shut up, Erasmo. You're gonna be so jealous when you see—"

"Ah, ah, plees stop right now, okay? *Ahora,* tell me what joo do."

47

I took my time to draw as much attention to myself as possible. That should have been clue number one for my parents. *Bibiana will always want to be the center of attention.* They sat there waiting patiently for an explanation as to why I was grinning like a mental patient.

My dad bought me a wonderful little purse on our last trip to Tijuana. It was a small, brown leather pocketbook with painted flowers and a braided strap. As I pulled it onto the table, my grin got bigger and bigger until it seemed my whole face was nothing but teeth and two stretched lips. One by one, I pulled them out and laid them side by side.

Every motel we had stayed in had given us a set of keys. Not the new, high-tech swipe keys, but the kind you actually have to pay for if you lose. Instead of leaving the keys in the room like we were told to do, I had snatched every single one of them along the way and hidden them in my bag. There they lay before me, six hotel keys, the shiny copper lighting up my eyes and making me feel like the smartest person in the whole wide world.

Silence. Complete and utter silence. I looked at my dad. He wasn't laughing nor smiling. He wasn't frowning either, but instead he looked pained, almost constipated. My mom simply said, "*Ay Dios mio,*" and my brother...well, Erasmo smacked the table and nearly fell out of his chair. I couldn't understand why he was laughing when it was clear to me and (I hoped) everyone else that I had done a very clever thing. My dad, after a few seconds during which he contemplated everything from a lashing to tying me to a tree, cleared his throat.

"Bibi, why joo take the keys, eh? Why joo do this?"

He was calm, he wasn't yelling, so in a confident voice, I proceeded to explain. Clue number two: *Bibiana is a know it all.*

"Well, I kept them 'cause you said we were going on vacation and I thought we could save time on the way back by keeping the keys. This way we won't have to stop by the office or anything; we can go straight to the same room." I looked at my brother. "You see? Humph, and you thought I was stupid."

Once again, my brother started laughing and this time, much to my horror, my parents looked at each other and broke down. Everyone except me had tears streaming down their faces. I sat there trying to figure out what I'd done wrong and why I felt like such an idiot. Gratefully, our food arrived and everyone calmed down, but still nobody congratulated me. I sat there and sulked over my greasy fried eggs, which looked like two eyes. I grabbed a piece of bacon and turned it into a mouth and used half a sausage link as a nose. But even the face on my plate wouldn't thank me for being so smart. I stabbed an eye with a fork. My dad eventually took the keys from me and trying not to laugh again, muttered, "Sank you bery much, Bibi. I keep them safe."

We never again went on a long road trip as a whole family, and as weeks turned into months and months into years, one day I woke up and finally realized we were never going back to California.

# Chapter 4

The bell rang and my nerves rattled one more time before settling down. *Okay, no backing out now.* One by one, the kids made their way into the classroom and took their seats. I expected pandemonium, chaos, even a fight within the first five minutes. But they surprised me. As they walked in, each one looked at me and gave me a shy smile and one or two were actually brave enough to say hello. I smiled back and took mental notes of each student as they took their seats. *Wow, his pants are going to fall down... she looks sweet...Lord have mercy, that skirt is way too short....* But not one looked like a hardened criminal with a record; in fact, most of them looked like regular middle school kids on the first day at any school.

When I was pretty sure everyone had arrived, I turned around and wrote my name, Miss Castellanos, on the chalkboard. I took a deep breath as I set the chalk down and turned around to face my future. Panic hit me. I felt like I'd just sat on the toilet only to realize there was no toilet paper.

"Hello, class, uh, my name is Miss Castellanos and I will be your teacher this year."

One of the girls raised her hand.

"Yes? What is your name?"

"My name's Ebony."

"Yes, Ebony. Do you have a question?"

"Yes, Miss Ca, Miss Caste, Miss…"

"Miss Castellanos."

"Yeah. You really gonna be here a whole year?"

"Yes, of course I am."

One student snickered. "Miss, you crazy or somethin'." He was sitting towards the back of the class.

"Oh, why is that? And what is your name?"

"My name's Jazelin. Shoot, miss, you ain't gonna last. We ain't a good class, ain't they told you that?

I smiled and lied, of course. "I've heard nothing but great things about you guys, really."

More giggles and another snicker. I waited for them to settle down.

"Okay, well, if you'll just be patient I'm going to call roll. If I can't pronounce your name, just let me know, and if you have a nickname, let me know that as well."

I turned around and picked up my roll call book as tiny beads of sweat broke out on my forehead. *So far so good,* I thought. *They're not as bad as I thought.*

When I turned back around, one of the students was walking towards me. A description is in order here. His pants were closer to his ankles than to his waist. He was wearing a comb not in his pocket, but in his hair, as if he'd been picking at his fro that morning and had simply forgotten to take it out. His high top sneakers looked three sizes too big and the laces were untied. *He's going to trip before he gets here,* I thought. Just what I needed. A boy rushed to the hospital on the first day. Miraculously, he sauntered up to the front without falling. Before he could get any closer, I asked him his name.

"My name? Chancy."

"Chancy?"

"Yeah.

"Okay, uh, Chancy, you got our of your chair without raising your hand, but I'll let it slide this time since we haven't gone over the rules yet. What is it?"

"Right. Yo, Miss Ca, Miss Caste, Miss Questa…shoot, how you say your name?"

"Just call me Miss C."

"Yo, Miss C, I can go to the bathroom?"

"Chancy, 'May I go to the bathroom?'"

"What, Miss C? You gotta go too?"

*Oh, dear.*

When it came to controlling a group of unruly adolescents, everyone told me I had to be as serious as possible on the first day. In other words, just short of a bitch. If I didn't lay down the law, they would think I was too nice and too lenient and too lazy and therefore a target for abuse. *But I don't like to be serious,* I remember thinking. *And I like kids.*

When Chancy came back with such an innocent question, I couldn't help but giggle. Okay, I'm lying. I roared. I have the kind of laugh that can scare people because it's explosive. I sat at the edge of my old desk and laughed my head off, and then something bizarre happened, something I didn't expect on the first day. The class calmed down and waited for my next move. It was a weird feeling. It was like being a strange animal at a zoo that everyone's watching. I gathered my composure and reminded myself I wasn't in a comedy club. Not yet, anyway.

I gave Chancy a pass to the bathroom and told him I'd wait for him to come back before starting my fabulous first day of school speech. He came back in less than two minutes. *He really didn't need to go*, I thought. *He was testing me and I failed. Shit.*

One by one, I outlined the class rules and discussed the importance of obeying them. *Please raise your hand before speaking. No fighting, no name-calling, no stealing, and absolutely no swearing. Participate, cooperate, take responsibility for your own actions.* The list went on and on and still nobody said a word. I was starting to bore myself. I ended my first day speech by telling the students they had to have fun in my class. "And that's an order," I added.

"What do you mean we have to have fun? I *hate* school." Marcdala said. Marcdala was a very pretty girl and darker than most of the students. She also spoke with a slight accent, and when I looked at her last name, Baptiste, I figured out she was Haitian. I don't know how I knew that, but I chalked it up to the fact that college had taught me at least a thing or two.

"Marcdala, didn't I just ask you to raise your hand before speaking?"

"Oh, sorry, Miss C." She stopped scowling and gave me such a remarkable smile it took my breath away. *Jesus, her teeth are so white and perfect.*

"I know most of you hate school and homework and waking up at six in the morning, but if we don't have fun, it's going to be worse. Don't you guys want to have fun?"

"I don't understand, Miss C. How we gonna have fun? You gonna tell jokes or somethin'?"

"No, but I promise to teach you everything you need to know and make you laugh along the way, how's that?"

"Yeah, whatever," Jazelin said.

"Shut up, boy, Miss C's tryin' to be nice," Marcdala retorted.

"Why don't you shut up, stupid girl? I ain't talking to you. Why you always gotta open your..."

"Don't you call me stupid, boy. Your momma..."

"Ah, excuse me?" I interrupted. "Marcdala and Jazelin, this is unnecessary and rude. You are not showing each other respect and..."

"Miss C, he started it."

"No, I didn't."

"Yes, you did."

*Prozac, here I come.* By now the rest of the class had started to put in their two cents.

*Breathe, Bibiana, breathe.*

"Enough!"

I didn't want to yell on the first day. I didn't want to get hysterical and start throwing things. I most certainly did not want to lose my cool. I thought back to elementary school and remembered a trick my teachers used to use.

"If you can hear me, clap your hands once."

A few stopped and clapped.

"If you can hear me, clap your hands twice.

More hands.

"If you can hear me, clap your hands three times."

Everyone clapped three times and nobody said another word.

"Listen, we have a lot of work to do and we can't waste any more time talking about each other's mammas and aunties and whether or not you're stupid. Enough. I'm not going to tolerate this behavior."

For the second time that day, they surprised me. Nobody said a word when I asked them to take out a sheet of paper. While they rustled through their folders and backpacks, I wrote four questions on the chalkboard. I wanted to know if they were as illiterate and "At Risk" as I'd been led to believe. *I'll show you, Mrs. Coleman.*

"Okay, I want you to answer these four questions as best as you can. The first one is, 'What do you like about school?'" I heard a few snickers but continued talking. "The second one is, 'What don't you like about school?'" Like a disease, the snickering spread. "Quiet down. The third question is, 'What do you want to learn?'" Silence. "And the fourth one is, 'What kind of person do you want to be when you grow up?'"

Chancy raised his hand. *Good, they're catching on.*

"Like, you mean do we wanna be a basketball player or a doctor?"

"No, no, no. That last question is very important. I want you to tell me what *type* of person you want to be. You know, honest, respectable, cooperative, friendly, helpful, etc."

"I wanna be cool," Chancy stated as he looked around the class. Jazelin laughed and shook his head.

I scratched my head. "Cool? No, you're not getting the point. What's so great about being cool?" I asked him.

"Well, 'cause, it's like, if I's cool, then when other people be my friend, it's like they gonna be cool too."

*Okay, Bibiana, that's really funny but now is not the time to laugh. Not when they've calmed down.*

"Okay, you can tell me you want to be cool. But I want you to add to that, and don't tell me you want to be cool and rich. It has to be something intangible."

"Intangible? What that is?"

I knew I should've been correcting their grammar but I was too excited that they were listening to me.

"Well, uh, let me see if I can explain this. If you can physically touch something with your hands, it's tangible." I wrote the word on the board. "If you can't touch it, if it's something you can't get your hands on, then it's intangible." I wrote the word intangible underneath it and underlined it for emphasis, as though underlining it would make him understand.

"My daddy, he never around and I ain't get to touch him or see him. That make him in-tan-gible?"

*Uh-oh.*

"Uh, not exactly, because he really exists, and, uh, uh, if he walked in right now, you would be able to touch him."

"Shoot, my daddy ain't gonna walk in the door. He gone, Miss C."

*Oh, super shit.* I could handle reading problems, I could handle grammatical disasters, I could handle bad behavior. I wasn't so sure I could handle the fact that most of the students came from broken homes and problems I knew nothing about.

Chancy stared at me and waited for me to say something, but the girl who could usually spend an hour talking to the wall couldn't find the right words. I shrugged and gave him a smile. *Way to go, you dumb white girl. First day of class and already you've reminded a kid that his dad's gone.* He didn't say anything else, just sat there and stared at me before he picked up his pencil and started to write down his answers. The rest of the class joined him.

It took them most of the morning to finish the assignment. While they sat there writing down their answers, I sat at my desk waiting for the first sign of chaos. I pretended to be hard at work with lesson plans when in reality I was sitting there doodling on a sheet of paper, wondering how to fill up the rest of the morning. It was taking them a long time to answer four questions, but I couldn't stand there and yell at them to hurry up.

Finally, after what seemed like an eternity, I gathered up all the papers and put them in a neat stack on my desk. My goal for that year was to get them interested in reading and writing, so I asked them what books they'd recently read. I was greeted with an awkward silence. Nobody raised their hand or said a word. I cleared my throat.

"Okay, well, um, why don't I tell you about the book you're going to read this term?" I got a collective groan. "No, no, come on, you'll like it. I read it when I was your age and I loved it. They even made a movie about it. When we finish the book, I'll bring in the movie."

"Miss C, where are you from?" Marcdala asked. *So much for discussing books.*

"I'm from California, Marcdala."

Ebony raised her hand and I nodded. "Miss C, you have babies?"

"Babies? Oh, you mean kids? No, no, I don't have any kids."

"Miss C," DiAngelo said, "you like football?"

"Yeah, I like football."

"What team you like?"

"Oh, uh, the Cowboys."

Everyone started booing and talking. Chancy silently stared at me until I smiled at him. He shrugged his shoulders and raised his hand.

"Yeah, Chancy."

"Miss C, what that book is? The one you gonna read to us?"

"Well, I'm not going to read it to you. We're going to read it together. It's called *The Outsiders*."

"*The Outsiders*? Man, I ain't never heard of that book."

"You haven't? It's pretty awesome." *Great, Bibiana, now you sound like a surfer chic.* "I mean, it's a very good book. It's about some kids who come from the wrong side of the tracks. It was written by S.E Hinton, and guess how old she was when she wrote the book?" As if they would really care.

"Miss C, how old you is?" Jazelin asked. Before I could say anything, the whole class decided to answer for me.

"Twenty-five."

"No, no, she thirty."

"She look twenty."

"I say twenty-nine."

"Uh-uh, you crazy, she forty."

Chancy came to the rescue.

"Yo, man, be quiet. Y'all crazy." He looked around the class and everyone

quieted down. *Great, now I have both Mr. Connelly and Chancy as backup.*
"So, Miss C, how old she was?"

"Who?"

"The lady who had wrote that book. What you say her name was?"

"Oh, S.E. Hinton, and she was only sixteen years old."

"So what?" Marcdala replied. "Big deal."

Jazelin turned to look at her and practically barked.

"Why you so mean, stupid girl? You ain't never gonna do nothing like that. Stupid ass Haitian."

His last words took my breath away. I'd forgotten how cruel kids could be. Before Marcdala had a chance to say anything, though, Chancy jumped out of his chair and walked right over to Jazelin. *Oh, shit, here it comes, the first sign of chaos.* I looked around the room for a phone just in case I needed to call 911. Jazelin slumped down in his chair as Chancy stood in front of him. The whole class sat quietly in anticipation, and what did I do? I stood there rooted to my spot at the front of the classroom and let the drama unfold.

"Yo, Jaz, we cool?"

"Yeah, Chancy, we cool."

"Why you gotta say shit like that, yo? That ain't cool." A cuss word and a potential fight on the first day. *Wonderful.*

"Come on, Chancy, I was only playin', yo."

"Don't mess with Marcdala, Jaz, you know what I'm sayin'? You feel me?"

"Yeah, yeah, I feel you, man." Jazelin was so slumped down in his chair I thought he was going to slip out of it.

"A'ight. Be cool, man, be cool."

"A'ight. I'm cool." Jazelin nodded his head and straightened out as Chancy walked back to his desk.

I was shocked by the way Chancy had taken control of the situation without my help. Actually, it kind of annoyed me. *I'm the teacher here,* I thought. *I'm the one who's supposed to put out fires.* I said it to myself a few times before launching into a description of the book. I was a huge fan of *The Outsiders* and overly enthusiastic about the story, so they listened and didn't give me any problems. We spent the rest of the morning talking about Ponyboy, Sodapop and Johnny. They slipped in a few questions about my personal life, but it didn't bother me. The lives of my own teachers had always fascinated me as a kid. It was like I couldn't imagine they went grocery shopping or to the movies. I thought they lived at school.

During my lunch break, I headed to the cafeteria. I bought a sandwich made with processed ham and cheese and a carton of skim milk. I didn't want to eat in my classroom so I went to the teacher's lounge. Matt had my students so there was no chance of seeing him. When I walked in, Mrs. Coleman, Mrs. Davis and Namisha were seated at a table and invited me to sit with them. I hesitated, but because Namisha had stood up for me at the meeting, I decided to give the Cat and the Turtle another chance, which was, of course, a mistake.

"Hey there. How's it going?"

Namisha was eating something she'd brought from home. It looked and smelled so good I wanted to snatch it and wolf it down.

"It's going okay."

I sat down and picked up my government ham and cheese sandwich. The Turtle looked at me as I was taking my first bite,.

"So, how do you like your students? How many detentions did you give out today?" *God forgive me, but I can't stand her.*

"None, Mrs. Davis. They're okay, actually."

"Uh-huh. They're always okay on the first day, but you wait. Your kids are enough to make anyone want to pull their hair out."

"Really? I didn't get that from them." I was trying so hard to be nice it was making my face hurt.

Mrs. Coleman was eating a no-calorie-no-fat-no-fun salad. *Of course.* She put down her Diet Coke and gave me a shallow smile.

"I'm glad they finally hired someone who can understand those kids."

"Really? What do you mean?"

"Oh, you know. The best thing they could've done is hire a minority teacher because you'll be able to relate to them."

"What?"

"Oh, come on, Miss Casta...Miss Cesta..."

"Bibiana. The name is Bibiana. Not your typical minority name like Maria or Yolanda or Taquisha, but I'm sure you'll remember it, being that you're the *gifted* teacher."

"Don't be so dramatic. I was just trying to say—"

"Say what?"

"Well, you probably come from the same background, you know, a bad neighborhood and whatnot. But I have to tell you, I'm very impressed that you rose above your situation and became a teacher." She smiled at me. She actually thought she was paying me a compliment. I had visions of putting thumbtacks on her chair.

"I come from the same background? Mrs. Coleman, did you actually go to college? I mean, did you get a degree?" All the color drained from her face and I loved it. Nothing like the shock factor.

"What are you saying?"

"Well, for someone who's in charge of 'gifted' kids, you're pretty damn ignorant."

"Ignorant?" She went from being shocked to angry but I didn't care. I'm Hispanic, which means I can go from zero to Satan in less than a second.

"Yes, *ignorant*. What makes you think I come from the same background? You think I know what they're going through just because I have a Hispanic name?"

"No, but, let's face it, you *are* Hispanic."

"Of course, you're so right," I said sarcastically. "We're all in the same boat, aren't we? We're all dealing with typical stereotypes created by people like you. You can't regard us as equals but damn, you sure love having that Mexican food, don't you?"

There was nothing but silence for a few seconds.

Mrs. Coleman looked at me coldly, probably confused at the fact that a Hispanic had managed to string a whole sentence together, verbs and all. She threw out the rest of her two-calorie salad and picked up her things. As she walked out, the Turtle suddenly became engrossed in her lunch and I looked at Namisha. I thought she was going to berate me, but the corners of her lips started tugging upwards and that was all I needed. We burst into laughter.

I can be a mean bitch when I want to.

After lunch I went back to my classroom and just sat there. *How could she think I can relate to my students just because I happen to be a minority? Ignorant moron.* I knew nothing of their lives, but I was pretty sure it was miles apart from what I'd grown up with.

Instead of sitting there fuming, I decided to make my planning session productive. I started looking through their answers to my four questions. *Whoa,* I thought as I looked the first one over. I read through their answers and shook my head, trying hard not to laugh.

Jazelin wrote: *I don't like nothing bout scool sorry Miss C but I like scool cuz I can see my boys. I wanna learn how to rap Puff Daddy is cool and I wanna be like him. I wanna be strong cuz my momma had told me you gotta be strong to make it in this wurld and my momma she strong, she tuff she don't take nothing from nobudy.*

Ebony wrote: *I like school sumtimes but my teachers are boring sumtimes. I wanna learn how to sing good like Whitney Houston. I wanna be smart cuz my bruther always telling me I'm stupid but he ain't got no job cuz he stupid I wanna be better than him sumday.*

DiAngelo wrote: *I hate school sory Miss C I don't like home work. I wanna be rich someday becuz my auntie always working and she don't got no time for nuthin not even for me sometimes I wanna buy a nice crib for her so she can say I did good the end.*

Marcdala wrote: *I hate school. All the other kids make fun of me and I was happier in Haiti. I don't like anything about school, so, I'm sorry, Miss C. What do I want to be? I want to be successful. My dad was a doctor in Haiti and he's the smartest person I know. I don't care what people say about my accent because I know I'm better and smarter than them. Someday I'm going to prove to the world that I can be somebody.*

I looked out the window and sighed. Marcdala was way too smart to be in my class. I made a note to look through her file. I wanted to know how she'd ended up becoming an At Risk student.

Chancy wrote: *School is okay, but sum teachers are so boring and mean. They all think I'm dumb cuz I'm black and I ain't got no parents but my grandmamma luvs me and so does Uncle Morris. I wanna learn how to be a riter becuz it's fun becuz I can make up storys about other peoples and I can make myself laugh. Maybe I can be a riter sumday and get paid to write storys. I don't care about my daddy becuz he's dumb but sumday I wanna make my grandmomma and Uncle Morris proud of me.*

Aside from Marcdala, their grammar was atrocious but it didn't phase me. A misspelled word or verb in the wrong place doesn't mean kids don't have their own thoughts and dreams. Everyone, no matter where you come from or what color you are, has a dream. Chancy wanted to be a "riter," Marcdala wanted to be somebody and Ebony wanted to sing at the top of her lungs. There they were, all but thirteen years old and convinced they knew what they wanted. And there I was, completely unsure if teaching was my calling, a confused girl in her mid twenties wondering how to make the students listen to her.

# Chapter 5

For the first couple of weeks after we arrived in Miami, we stayed in motels while my dad tried to find an apartment in a safe neighborhood. He was waiting for the closing on our new house, a house we'd only seen in pictures. It wasn't hard to find a safe neighborhood, really. In 1978, Miami was a relatively safe place. A few years later, the Mariel Boat Lift would turn the whole city upside down, but back then it was quiet. The fact that we were going to *move into a house* could not stop me from believing we were on vacation.

Every morning, my dad would take my brother and me to get breakfast: *café con leche* and *tostada*. We'd walk into one of the many cafeterias on Calle Ocho, a long road known as the heart and soul of Little Havana. It should've been called *Northern* Havana because it was nothing but Cubans and more Cubans standing around talking, playing dominoes, drinking *cafecito*. We enjoyed going with him because everything was so different compared to East LA, and we knew that for at least a few hours, we'd be safe from my mom's sandal.

Little Havana was like no place I'd ever been before. For one, there seemed to be a lot of yelling going on. It wasn't hostile or anything, it was just the way people spoke to each other. I wondered if maybe all Cubans had a hearing problem and whether or not I would succumb to such an affliction. To my horror, my dad yelled just as loud as everyone else. The veins on his forehead always looked ready to explode. And the hands. Oh Lord, the hands. I'd never seen him use body parts with such abandon just to get a point across. This other side of my dad kind of freaked me out because I didn't know what else was in store. But I took it as a sign that he was enjoying the vacation.

Some people say Cubans are only six degrees apart and I'm almost convinced it's a known fact. After those first few days, I started to believe Cuba was so small that you could yell and someone on the other side of the island would a) know you, b) answer back and c) invite you over for coffee.

My dad seemed to know everyone, and everyone seemed to know him. I was proud to have a dad that was so popular.

As we walked the streets of Little Havana, my brother and I would have a contest. We were so competitive we'd bet on the weather. We'd try to figure out how much time it would take for my dad to recognize someone from Cuba. My dad would spot a long lost friend within seconds, no lie, and we would stand there staring at him as he hugged yet another man tightly as though they were long lost brothers. I suppose in a way they were.

Brothers lost *en el exilio.*

We'd sit in a little café on bar stools and wolf down our breakfast while my dad and his friend shouted at the top of their lungs, shouted even though they stood right next to each other. It's such a vivid memory. Everyone standing within inches of each other trying to out-shout each other. Nobody ever seemed to mind the noise level. They were together, talking about Cuba, and that's all that mattered.

I could never make out too much of what my dad said, but I remember hearing the word "Fidel" about a million times and always with a heated tone of voice. I didn't know who Fidel was, but judging by the way my dad spoke about him, I knew he'd probably done something terribly serious to get my dad so worked up. He was the one person I hoped we wouldn't run into in Little Havana.

And then there was my dad's version of Spanish.

You see, Erasmo and I learned Spanish way before we learned English, but it was Mexican Spanish, and let me tell you, there's a huge difference. We learned to say things like *orale* and *¿qué onda?* My dad and his friend would sound like they were speaking in a foreign language. And not Spanish. They'd speak rapidly and cut words in half. They would casually drop letters from words as though they couldn't be bothered with that s or that r. They said things like *vaya* and *chico* and boy was I confused. I secretly wondered how on earth we'd managed to communicate the first seven years of my life. My dad and his friend would spend a few hours talking about how much better things were in Cuba (it's a Cuban pastime, I've learned). Erasmo and I would get so bored that we'd actually get along. He always made me ask our dad to take us home, so I'd tug on my dad's pants and look up at him sadly. He would pat me on the head. "*Sí, mi'ja, ya voy.*" With our bellies full of Cuban bread and café con leche, we would go back to our grimy hotel room and find ways to amuse ourselves without causing my mom to take off her sandal.

I thought the vacation was going well. I still thought we were on an adventure, but I wondered why my mom insisted we go to school. My dad kept telling her to wait, because after all, he hadn't found an apartment yet. In the darkness of the hotel room, I would hear their whispered conversations about whether or not they'd done the right thing, whether or not my dad would find work in Miami, whether or not I was getting too fat. I ignored them and hoped he'd find somewhere with a swimming pool. Nobody had a real swimming pool where we lived in Los Angeles. Every year my dad would buy us a plastic one that we could barely move in, but we never complained. We were happy enough to play with the water hose or the sprinkler once in a while. My friend Donna had a Slip 'N Slide, which was always more amusing when you applied dish soap, but I was fascinated with real pools, the kind that had slides and diving boards.

My dad found an apartment on Bird Road a week after we arrived in Miami. It had a pool just like I'd wanted but it looked like it hadn't been cleaned in years and more like a home for every dead bug in Florida. The day after we moved into a tiny apartment already inhabited by a battalion of mammoth-sized cockroaches (that could fly), my parents woke us up and got us ready for school. I knew the vacation was taking a different turn, but I figured it was my parents' way of making sure we didn't miss any school, God bless them. We didn't say a word as we drove through a quiet neighborhood on our way to Tropical Elementary. Only in Florida could a school have a name like that.

I looked out the window and saw palm trees everywhere, houses painted a soft pink or coral. Not a sign of graffiti to be found. I thought Miami was the most beautiful place in the world, far more beautiful than Tijuana or the east side of LA, but I kept looking into the distance hoping to see mountains. Nothing. *What a flat place,* I remember thinking. *Where are the mountains? The snowcaps? Why is every other tree a palm tree with coconuts? Why is Erasmo pinching me so hard?*

I knew he was trying to make me angry but I ignored him. Sometimes it was the only solution. I was terrified at the prospect of making new friends, but more than anything, I was confused about the fact that I wasn't wearing my Catholic school uniform. *What kind of school is it?* I remember wondering. *Will there be nuns? Will we go to church every morning? Will I still get nap time after graham crackers and milk?*

We walked into the school and thankfully, the receptionist spoke Spanish. My parents went through the normal routine of filling out forms and handing over our birth certificates. According to my parents' records, my brother was supposed to be in the fifth grade and I was supposed to be in second. The principal, Mrs. Garcia, looked over our records and calmly explained to my parents that we had to be tested, because after all, they didn't know what the school system was like in East Los Angeles, let alone the *Catholic* school system. My parents were shocked. They insisted we were at the same level as all the other kids our age. There was no way we were going to get put back just because we'd spent about three hours in mass every day. My dad lost the fight and testing was scheduled for the next day.

To be honest (you'll realize how much of a nerd I really was), I wasn't bothered about being tested or annoyed at the fact that we had to go to school. I was one of those irritating kids who despised summer break and looked forward to school shopping days. I loved the smell of fresh paper, new notebooks, metal lunch boxes (thermos included), pencil boxes, rulers, markers, etc. I loved sitting at an old desk on an old wooden chair. I loved the idea that I had a teacher, that there were rules I had to obey. But most of all, I loved learning and boy did I love homework. Erasmo was the complete opposite. He loathed anything related to homework, tests, and rules.

On the way home, he complained nonstop about having to go to school until my dad stopped the car and lit up a cigarette. I looked at him and gloated while he silently vowed to beat the shit out of me later.

I don't know what it was about a schoolroom that filled me with happiness. I don't know why I always felt safe around a teacher; on the right path. Whatever the reason, my test results the following day confounded both the principal and my parents. According to my test results, I had an extremely high IQ and an ability to read on a fourth grade level (who knew!). My parents, very proud of their chubby-but-starting-to-get-too-fat daughter, refused to let them put me in a grade above. They were worried the older kids would pick on me. They shouldn't have bothered. Kids my own age took care of that. Erasmo, to no surprise, was right where he was supposed to be. Metal lunch boxes in hand, we walked with the principal and my parents to our classrooms. Erasmo looked like a man walking to his own hanging, whereas I practically skipped the whole way. *So what if the vacation is over?* I thought. I really missed school and graham crackers in the afternoon. I even missed praying.

After my brother was safely escorted to his classroom (I think my parents were worried he might try to make a run for it), we arrived at the door of my future second grade friends. I walked in with my parents and greeted my classmates with a huge smile. I waved at everyone but nobody waved back.

My parents saw my teacher first and started to panic. You see, my teacher, Ms. Connor, was black. My parents looked at each other and braced themselves for another "monster" episode. They were convinced I would freak out and run out of the room.

When Ms. Connor walked over to me, her bright red blouse and large bosom looming closer and closer, I looked at her and nearly fainted. She was walking over to me with the largest bowl of peanut M&M's I had ever seen. My dream come true; a teacher with candy.

She smiled at me, showing her perfectly straight teeth, and scooped up a handful of candy. She handed it to me while I continued to stare at her, unable to look away from her incredibly long fingernails.

"Hello, there. Welcome to my class. What is your name, pretty lady?"

I couldn't say anything. I was taken aback. I couldn't even find my voice because in that instant, I fell in love with her skin. It was a rich brown color, like the color of milk chocolate. Instinctively, I reached out and placed my hand on her arm, half expecting the color to rub off on my hand.

"Well, young lady, what is your name?" she asked me, still smiling.

"Uhm, my name is Bibiana Castellanos, but everyone calls me Bibi. Are you a nun? Why aren't you wearing a robe?"

The other kids in the class started giggling and the principal looked at my parents.

My mom put her hand on my shoulder. "Bibi, plees, this no more Catolic escool." My mom nervously looked at the teacher. "I'm sorry, lady, she still think we take her to Catolic escool, okay?"

"It's okay, Mrs. Castellanos, I'm sure she'll be happy here. I'll make sure she gets the best education."

"Educachun? Jes, es bery important, no?"

"Of course. I understand your daughter is very smart."

"Oh jes, bery much. She like de homework, and she like many things about escool, okay, lady?"

The teacher grabbed her hand and squeezed it.

"Don't you worry, okay?"

"Okay, lady. She give joo any *problema*, and joo just call me, okay? We bery good family, joo know? Ehm…"

Before my mom could develop diarrhea of the mouth, my dad told her it was time to leave. He was relieved I hadn't flipped out and called Ms. Connor a monster. They shook hands with my new idol and left with Mrs. Garcia.

Miss Connor dropped more M&M's in my hand and led me to my new desk. It was in the front row, which made me want to jump up and down. All the other kids stared at me in horror as I sat there shoving the candy into my mouth, my fat legs swinging back and forth. Swoosh, swoosh. *Fat kid*, they must have thought. *Great, we got a whale as a new student.* You see, those bowls of ice cream weren't the best thing for me. And I wasn't what you'd call the active type. I loved to read. I enjoyed sitting in my bedroom for hours playing the tiny toy piano my dad bought me on my fourth birthday. I was never allowed to play outside with Erasmo and his friends, so cardiovascular exercise was never part of my daily activities. I lived in my own world filled with Fisher Price Little People and crayons. My own world full of ice cream, Oreo cookies, and Chunky's. But damn, watching Sesame Street had paid off, because I was apparently very smart.

Fat and smart will get you nowhere in elementary school.

The other kids in my class were terrified of Ms. Connor, but my obsession with the color of her skin drove my love for school to a new level. I refused to be absent, panicked on Fridays when I knew we'd be away for the weekend and tried my best to be her favorite student ever. It wasn't really hard. It's like I was born to be the teacher's pet and I loved it. No matter what the question, my hand would be up first, and you better believe I always had the right answer. I would stay after school for a few minutes and clean her chalkboards, put away books, anything to be around her and her chocolate skin. I didn't have a crush on her. I was simply fascinated with her silky skin. I loved the way her skin smelled and looked. It was soothing.

Ms. Connor gave me way too much attention. She treated me like her own daughter. Whenever the kids teased me in the playground about my funny clothes, my weight, or the fact that I was the teacher's pet, she'd come to the rescue. I didn't care at first. I was too engrossed in being super student to make friendships a priority.

I started making up excuses just to get close to her. I would walk to her desk with an assignment, give her an innocent smile and tell her I didn't understand. She would pat me on the back and take the paper from me, taking her time to explain what I had to do. She must have known I was full of crap but she never said anything. She would patiently explain the assignment. I would place my chubby hand on her arm and rub my fingers up and down, amazed at the absence of hair, in awe of the smooth texture and rich color. Finally, she turned to me one day and looked at me tenderly.

"Miss Bibi, why are you always touching my skin, baby? Does it bother you?"

I was shocked and embarrassed that she'd totally busted me.

"Uhm, I just like it."

"You like it?"

"Oh yes, very much."

"Really? Why is that?"

"I love the color because it's like chocolate and I *love* chocolate. I wish my skin was the same color. Do you think if I pray hard enough, I'll wake up one day with the same color skin?"

Ms. Connor caught her breath and tears welled up in her eyes. She gave me a long, sad look.

"Oh, my sweet Bibi, I wish everyone saw the world through your eyes."

Years later I would look back on that day and fully understand why Miss Connor was so moved. And I would think to myself, *Yes, it would be nice if everyone looked at the world through the eyes of an innocent, chubby second grader.*

But nobody saw the world the way I did back then, not even my parents. If I was ever too sick to go to school, I would cry because I couldn't bear the thought that I was missing out on something. My mom would shake her head and wonder if it was normal for me to like school so much. I would do my homework the minute I got home, relishing every task that challenged my little brain in my larger than average body. On Saturdays, she would take me to the local library as opposed to the park, and I would check out about thirty books and read them within two weeks. Life to me was all about books and school, and it was easy.

I failed to make friends, even with Maggie, the little girl who lived across the street. I spent one day playing with Maggie, enough to convince me there was something not right about her. She tried to make me smoke a cigarette, and when I refused, she hit me in the arm. I didn't hit her back because after all, I'm Catholic. She tortured her dog and looked through her mom's purse. When I told her I wanted to go home, she threatened to tie me up to her bunk bed. Instead of being afraid, I told her it would be fun if I tied her up and painted her face with her mom's make up. "I'll make you look really pretty, Maggie," I said. Like an idiot, she agreed. I tied her up with shoe laces and pretended to be into the game, but as soon as she was tightly bound, I picked up my Barbies and left. She never asked me to play with her again and told everyone at school I was weird.

The bitch.

All through elementary school, I was picked on, pushed, teased, made fun of. Somehow I managed to coast through it. I realized crying would only make it worse, so I kept my mouth shut and ignored everyone. Lucky for me, I was teacher's pet every single year. At least one person liked me.

My world was books and jelly donuts. My teachers loved me and it was all that mattered, but once in a while, whenever I'd find myself sitting alone on the bus on the way to a field trip or hiding in a shaded corner during recess, I'd get sad and wish for a friend. Occasionally, someone would take pity on me and be nice, but it would never last. They'd soon realize I was the odd ball out and stay away from me.

My mom would often ask me why I didn't have friends over.

"I don't know, Mami. Nobody likes me."

"*¿Qué?* Why?"

"I'm fat and ugly and smart."

My mom's eyes would get sad.

"Oh, *mi'ja*, joo are not ugly. Joo are bery pretty, *mi'ja*, just a little *gordita*."

"It's okay, Mom. It doesn't matter."

It did matter. It mattered because I grew up thinking I could shut out the world forever, that if I tried hard enough, I could dive into one of my books and live there for the rest of my life. I could make up my own story, my own friends, pretend I lived in a beautiful two story house with a cute dog and parents who never worried about money. I thought it was normal that I went to the movies with my mom, to the mall with my mom, to the fair with my mom, everywhere with my mom. Wherever we would go, I would see girls huddled together, giggling and talking about this or that boy they had a crush on or showing off their new cherry flavored lip gloss. I would watch them from a distance, envy the way they moved their hands or flicked their perfectly straight hair. I'd try to imagine what it would be like to be one of them. One of those girls everyone liked. But I never could. I'd always see myself as some fat kid.

At least we lived in a good neighborhood. One less reason to pick on me. My dad bought a four bedroom home for practically nothing when we moved from California and it was the biggest house we'd ever lived in. The idea that we had a "Florida Room" confused us. We'd never had a "California Room," so for the first few months we all sat in the living room trying to decide where, exactly, we should adjourn as a family. Finally, my dad moved the television into the room with wood floors and high ceilings. From then on, we only sat in the living room when we had guests over, which was practically never. My mom's entire family lived in either Mexico or East LA. My dad's family lived in Cuba. It was quiet, peaceful. For me, lonely.

Whereas I made no friends, Erasmo managed to draft an entire army of buddies within the first week we moved into our new house. We were the first Hispanic family to move into the neighborhood, but the fact that we were "different" didn't stop all the other American kids from thinking my brother was the coolest ever.

We lived across from Westwood Lake. Erasmo loved to go fishing and knew more about it than the rest of the boys, so within minutes Erasmo was King. One of his friends was always at our house eating dinner or joining in when my brother teased me about my nerdiness and weight problem. They loved having dinner at our house because my mom cooked everything except traditional American food. Enchiladas replaced fried chicken. Tortillas and refried beans replaced vegetables. She made Cuban food for my dad, and I swear my brothers' friends would fight over who could stay for dinner whenever my mom made black beans and rice, steak and sweet plantains. We had the "come get your free serving of incredibly fattening and starchy food" kind of dinner.

Our living room had a bay window with a bench. I would sit there during my reading marathons, a day to day occurrence. I loved nothing more than to read and dream. Judy Blume and Beverly Cleary were my heroes. I would sit on the bench engrossed in my novel about true love or getting my period, but sometimes I would look out the window and watch Erasmo and his friends playing tag football, in awe of my brother's charm and athletic ability, silently wishing he would come inside and ask me to play with them. I loved my books, but I was always ready to drop *Super Fudge* just to hang out with Erasmo and his friends. After my tragic experience with Maggie, boys seemed safer than girls.

I was sitting on the front porch when my brother ran outside and nearly fell over me.

"Hey, dumb ass. Be careful."

"What did I do?"

"I nearly tripped, you idiot."

"So? That's your fault. You should've looked."

"No, you shouldn't be sitting here. What's the matter, dork? Did you run out of books to read?"

"No."

"Then what are you doing here?"

"I wanna play football with you and your friends."

He snickered and laughed. "Forget it. Get back inside."

"No. I live here too, you know. I can sit wherever I want."

"Why do you always have to be such a pain? God, you're so annoying."

He walked down the front sidewalk and like a magnet, his little army of men gravitated towards him out of nowhere. They huddled by the lamppost as though trying to figure out how to build a pipe bomb when one of them turned and pointed at me as though he'd found a way to annihilate Planet Earth. I could tell something was up because Erasmo kept looking over at me and shaking his head. Finally, after they'd stood there arguing for what seemed like hours, Erasmo walked over to me with the football in his hand.

"All right, dork, looks like you're going to get your way." Tiny beads of sweat formed across his upper lip and he wiped them off with his Dallas Cowboys t-shirt. "Just don't screw up."

"What do you mean?" I looked up at him and squinted my eyes from the sun. From my position on the floor, Erasmo looked like Roger Staubach himself.

"I mean, we're going to let you play, but only *this* time. Billy has the chicken pox and we need an extra man, so you're it. Do you remember how I taught you to catch the football?"

Did I ever. It had been one of the few times in our hostile relationship that he'd actually been nice to me. He'd taught me how to catch, throw, dive, turn, run, run, run. He'd also made me memorize the names of every single football team. All this when I was four.

He would stand at his display of miniature helmets and quiz me for hours.

"Who's this?" He would ask as he pointed to a helmet.

"Miami Dolphins."

"This one?"

"Minnesota Vikings."

"And this?"

"Uhm, Dallas Cowboys."

"And what did I tell you about the Dallas Cowboys, Bibi?"

"They're the greatest team in the whole wide world."

"Good girl."

God forbid I ever got one wrong because he'd punch me in the arm and make me start all over again. To me, those moments with my deranged older brother were heaven. Getting a chance to play football with him was the next best thing. As I got up from the porch, I went over all the things he'd taught me. Touchdowns, safeties, first yard downs, rushing. I took my place along with the rest of the guys in the middle of the street and prayed I'd make my brother proud. My chubby self intercepted a pass and I ran ten yards before Greg tagged me. I tackled a very surprised Jimmy when he tried to get by me (lots of bloody elbows), and I scored the winning touchdown when, to my surprise, my brother threw me the ball instead of throwing it to Andrew.

Billy got over the chicken pox by the following week and I never got to play with the boys again, but I don't recall feeling sad. All I remember when I look back on that hot Saturday afternoon was the way my brother looked at me and what he said.

"You know what? You're pretty damn good for a lard ass. You made me proud, sis."

I didn't hear the "lard ass" part. All I heard was the fact that I'd made him proud, and it was enough to keep me from annoying him for the next few days. Too soon I realized it was my God given right to drive him crazy. Isn't that what little sisters are for?

My brother went back to being a jerk and I went back to my Judy Blume novels and fantasy world. Elementary school flew by like a bad nightmare I wanted to end. Before I knew it, I was in junior high school, shaving my legs, learning how to attach a gigantic kotex to my underwear and walk straight even though cramps threatened to cripple me for life.

I would love to say I managed to make friends in a new school, but my weirdness followed me like a relentless ghost. The cliques formed in elementary school strengthened and only reinforced the fact that I did not belong. So I spent my days trying to keep my grade point average at 4.0 and avoided dressing out in Phys Ed. Having to undress in front of mean-spirited skinny chicks was worse than anything I'd ever been through. I would purposely take my time opening my gym locker so I'd be the last one to expose flesh. I got an A in every class except gym because I was always late for roll call. My B in PE was hurting my grade point average, but I dealt with it. No way was I going to let anybody see my size fourteen waistline.

My mom was my only true friend. When I told her I couldn't wear the super sized Kotex she was buying me, she bought me something that didn't look like a pamper. When I told her I wanted to join a bowling league (a true fat kid sport), she drove me to the bowling alley and signed me up right away. Anything to make me happy. I could've walked to school, but she insisted on dropping me off and picking me up every day. Sometimes, when she wasn't too tired, she'd take me to McDonald's and buy me a Happy Meal even though I was way past the age of toys.

The things my mom did for me. She was quick to calm me down whenever I'd had a nightmare that I'd lost my homework. "Es okay, *mi'ja*, es only dream." Whenever I had a bad fever, she would sleep with me the whole night. One time I asked her why she insisted on sleeping with a sweaty fat girl.

"If I esleep with joo, the fever pass to me and joo get better, and then joo can go back to escool, *mi'ja*."

"But Mami, if I give the fever to you, then you'll be really sick."

"Es okay, *mi'ja*, es no problem. I drink somesing and I be okay. Go to esleep now."

I didn't wake up one day and realize how much my mom loves me. I didn't go through that horrible teenage phase when I thought I knew more than she did or criticized her for being old fashioned. I carried her love with me like an invisible security blanket I could always wrap around me no matter how far away I was. She would always hold me whenever I complained about being different. She would always say the same thing.

"Joo are especial, *mi'ja*, I know joo are. Someday joo will do somesing good and be bery happy, and if joo ever feel sad, don't joo worry. Mami will always be here for joo."

And she meant it.

# Chapter 6

My first semester as a teacher was full of surprises and well, more surprises. Like my first paycheck.

I was making a whopping $22,000 a year to educate the future, whereas I'd been making double that to inebriate the present. When I first found out about the salary, I accepted the fact that my bank account was going to suffer. It didn't bother me at first because after all, I had a "real" job. Nevertheless, my first paycheck horrified me. I stared at it and prayed for someone to tell me it was a joke. I did the math and figured out I was making in two weeks as a teacher what I would've made in two nights as a bartender, and it hit me hard, hard enough to make me contemplate bartending part time. *How do teachers survive?* I thought. No wonder most of my teachers had driven ancient cars and eaten bologna sandwiches for lunch. The bar manager at the Hard Rock had offered to keep me on for just two nights a week, but no, I couldn't do that. I wanted to give teaching my all. Having to think about whether or not I'd restocked the beer cooler at the end of a shift would've been too much for me. That and the fact that with very little sleep, I could be classified as mentally unstable.

Challenge number one was getting used to the pay cut. Challenge number two was getting used to my students.

As the kids got more comfortable with me, their real personalities starting to shine through and my insanity became a very possible reality. They were good on the first day but the honeymoon came to a screeching halt. Out went their politeness. Goodbye, manners! See you later, respect! Au revoir, shyness! The little angels I met on the first day quickly turned into little monsters I had no control over.

There's a lot to say about comfort. For example, when you first start dating someone, you show them that side you think they'll fall in love with. The side that's always happy, kind, caring, compassionate, simply wonderful. You never burp, you don't swear, and God forbid you fart in front of each other during those first three months. Once the sex is out of the way and you've set up a mini-camp in each other's apartments, it's fair game. You both ease into that comfort zone you both wanted, and all of a sudden you're having farting contests.

God I love it when that happens.

Same goes for any kind of relationship in which you spend a significant amount of time together. As the kids got to know me, they tried me. That's what they called it: "trying." Chancy would always stroll into the classroom *after* the bell. Marcdala would deliberately act like she wasn't smart, Jazelin would say it was too hot and then complain that he was too cold when I'd smack the air conditioner with a stapler to bring it to life. I'd ask them to take out a sheet of paper and more than one would tell me they forgot their backpacks at home. They would raise their hands in the middle of lesson and ask me questions that, of course, had nothing to do with what I was teaching.

"Yo, Miss C, what car you drive?"

"Miss C, where you stay at?"

"You got a man, Miss C?"

"Miss C, you in love with Mr. Connelly?"

"Damn, Miss C, how long it take you to grow your hair? I can touch it?"

Getting through one lesson was like trying to get through an obstacle course with my arms and legs tied together. Impossible.

But I carried on like a soldier in a war he's not sure he believes in. I'd say "Please be quiet" more than a hundred times in one hour. I'd say "Raise your hand first" more than double that. I tried being cool, I tried being patient and I even made the sad mistake of bribing them with candy. Big mistake. Giving kids sugar was the worst way to get them to calm down.

I'm smart, but I'm no Einstein.

I was sitting in the teachers' lounge one day into my third week. I was trying to find the last string of patience in my soul when Namisha walked in. We had lunch together just about every day but I hadn't had the energy to open up to her. No, it wasn't that. I was too afraid to admit I wasn't good at something.

"Hey, girl. How you doin'? Those kids getting to you?" She bought a Coke from the vending machine and sat next to me on the couch.

"Nah. I'm just tired. Long day." I was staring at the ceiling counting all the little black dots in the tiles, something I found oddly soothing.

"Come on, now, you need to talk it out. I've seen that look before."

I turned to look at her. "What do you mean?"

74

"Oh, you know, that Oh-my-God-I'm-going-to-kill-one-of-those-kids look. We've all had it at one point or another."

I sighed loudly. "I'm so frustrated, Namisha. I can't figure out what I'm doing wrong."

I realized trying to hide anything from Namisha was pointless. She had a caring face, the kind of face that could look you in the eye and make you confess every bad thing you'd ever done in your life and make you feel okay about it. She reminded me of a black lab.

"What happened?"

"What happened? Jesus, what didn't happen?"

"Don't use the Lord's name, girl."

"Sorry. Okay, why don't you ask me what didn't happen? Let's evaluate my situation, shall we? It's week three. So far, I've managed to stop two fights, give out a million detentions, and dear God, oops, I just can't get them to stop arguing with each other long enough to let me teach a lesson. And then when I start teaching the lesson and think I've got them, something happens. Chancy gets up without raising his hand. Marcdala and Jazelin start picking on him because I reprimand him and the next thing I know, the whole class is telling the whole class to *shut up and let Miss C teach.* Voila."

She took a sip of her Coke. "Hm, sounds normal."

"What?" I couldn't believe it happened in other classes.

"Yeah, girl. It always happens with a new teacher. They're just trying you."

"Trying me?"

"Yep. That's all it is. They're trying you. They wanna see how far they can go until you snap. Until you walk out. Until you give up on them like every other teacher has."

"Damn. They're getting to me."

"I knew it. Girl, you can't lie to me." She was shaking her head and smiling whereas I felt like crying my eyes out.

"You know what, Namisha? I'm starting to think I'm not the right one for these kinds of kids. Dr. Lawrence should've hired someone with experience."

"Someone with experience probably would've turned down the job, honey. You don't think you're cut out for it? What? You think someone else could do it better? Let me tell you something, Miss C. It ain't about what color you are or where you come from. It's about how much you want to teach. That's it."

"How'd you know I was worried about the color of my skin?"

"It's the same with every white teacher trying to teach black kids. Not that you're a typical white woman. But just remember one thing: that's your issue, not theirs. If you make a big deal out of it in your mind, chances are they're going to see that and try to eat you alive even more. They'll know you're some white teacher trying to do good for the poor black kids."

"But that's not why I wanted to teach. My desire to teach has nothing to do with skin color."

"It doesn't? Tell me something, Bibi, why did you go into teaching?"

"You really want to know?"

"Yeah, of course."

I sighed and looked at the little black dots again, wondering if I'd find the real answer.

"To be honest, I'm not too sure. I think I felt like I was wasting my life as a bartender. I felt like I had to make my parents proud of me. I went to college, you know. I got a degree. I, I, I—" I was too embarrassed to put it into words.

"You what?"

"I had a dream."

"A dream? You mean a dream dream? Like something you have at night?"

"No, the kind of dream you have when you're in college and think you can single-handedly change the world. That kind of dream."

"Uh-huh. Explain."

"When I was in college, I wasn't exactly sure what I wanted to do with my life, but I wanted to make a difference. I know that sounds super cheesy and clichéd, but it's true. I wanted to make the world a better place somehow. After college, I put that desire on the shelf and embraced the *I want a spectacular life* dream. Well, now I've decided to pull my original intention off the shelf and do something about it. You know, inspire someone." I cringed. "Ugh, that sounds so stupid."

"What's so stupid about wanting to make the world a better place?"

"It's not stupid, but I'm wondering if I really meant it. I mean, I have a golden opportunity to make an impact on these kids, but the only thing I can think about is the fact that the money sucks. Or that it's not really exciting. Or that I might get bored. I have to keep reminding myself that teaching's not something you do for the money, but I'm starting to feel like I'm not making a difference at all. I'm only making myself crazy and poor."

"Bibiana, do you really care about what happens to your students? Really?"

I thought about Marcdala's ambition, Chancy's desire to be a writer,

Ebony's passion for music.

"Of course I care. I can't help but care. They're just kids, and part of me is hoping they're gonna start listening to me sooner or later. I'm hoping they're gonna wake up one day and see me as a role model. I'm hoping they're gonna realize I care about them, that I want their dreams to come true. I don't want them to give up so easily when they're so young and have so much ahead of them."

Namisha nodded and smiled at me reassuringly.

"Remind yourself of that every morning when you wake up. Besides, what kind of example would you be setting if you just gave up?"

"Hm, I know. A really bad one."

"Hm hmmm, and just remember this: kids will only rise to your level of expectation. If you think they can't learn, chances are they won't. If you forget about the fact that you're white and different and just teach, they'll rise to the occasion. But don't give up and make it even harder for the next teacher."

"Yeah." Once again, I started counting the little black dots.

She sighed and got up from the couch. "Look, I have to get going. Papers to grade, lessons to write, and a crazy ass husband to cook dinner for. But call me later if you want to. I'm here for you, okay?"

"Okay, thanks, Namisha."

"Anytime."

She walked out of the lounge and left me alone on the couch with nothing but my misery and fatigue. I was so tired my eyelids were staring to droop. *I can't give up.* A part of me wanted to, but giving up meant I'd have to think about what I was going to do. Again.

I'd moved to Orlando because I was convinced the only way I could grow up was by leaving the comforts of living at home. My mom did my laundry and my dad changed the oil in my car. She cooked, she cleaned, she did everything for me. My parents doted on me like some freak gifted child they'd accidentally picked up from another planet. They thought I was special. Talented.

But I had to get away from them. I had all these expectations to live up to, this feeling that I couldn't end up doing what they were doing, no matter how humble their jobs. My dad was a construction worker and my mom worked in a cafeteria at an elementary school. Just the fact that I'd graduated from college was enough to make them think I'd go where no other relative had gone.

To a job with benefits and a 401K plan.

When I was in college, I used to stay up most nights studying or writing a paper. My mom would come into my room every hour just to make sure I was still alive and not setting fire to my books. She'd always walk in with something to drink or eat and ask me questions about what I was studying.

"Oh, Bibi, joo are estudying bery hard. What are joo estudying, *mi'ja*?"

"Uh, I'm reading about the Intifada, Mom."

"*¿Cómo?* What is Entefada?"

"It's about the conflict between Jews and Palestinians. They're always fighting." I knew she would never understand but it was hard to ignore my mom, especially when she'd just brought me a cup of hot chocolate and a donut.

"Why they fight? They no like each other?"

"No, Mami, they don't."

"*¿Porqué?* Es problem with families? Like de way your Tio Jimmy and Tio Cesar always fighting?"

Usually my uncles would fight over whose turn it was to get more beer, but I didn't wanted to spoil my mom's attempt to learn something about the world.

"Uhm, sort of."

She'd nod her head as though she understood Intifada better than anyone and set the treats down on my desk

"Okay, *mi'ja*, joo keep estudying. I go to sleep now. I'm bery tired."

"Okay, Mami, thanks for the hot chocolate."

My parents never worried about what I was doing. As long as I was happy, they were satisfied. But I always wanted to do more for them. They'd worked hard their whole lives to give us the opportunities and choices they'd never had. Even though they never put any pressure on me, I knew my being a school teacher would make them proud. Not because I was going to contribute to society or do anything marvelously noble, but because it meant good benefits, a steady paycheck and a solid retirement plan. Hate to say it, but it's the mind of a blue collar worker. Not having to wear a uniform or punch into a time clock was a surefire sign I was going somewhere.

When I put in for a transfer to Orlando with the Hard Rock, I told my parents the news and waited for them to take out chains and lock me in my bedroom with flowered curtains and ten-year-old waterbed. Instead, my dad looked at me out of the corner of his eye, a cigarette hanging out of his mouth. He looked like a Cuban version of the Godfather.

"Why? Why joo want to leave so bad? Joo no happy here?"

"Oh, no, Papi! Not at all. I love living here with you and Mami, but I need a change. I'm not happy. I feel like I'm going nowhere."

"Why? Why joo feel like that?"

"I don't know. I just think I need to get out there and experience another life. Do something on my own. Buy my own groceries, do my own laundry, make friends for once. If I stay here, I'm going to end up killing the next person who cuts me off on the Palmetto Expressway."

I blamed Miami for everything. Funny how you can blame a whole city for your anger, your lack of direction, your depression, your rage. I felt like Miami was holding me back from another life, a more exciting life. The Hard Rock in Orlando accepted my transfer request and nothing could stop me. Not even my dad and the cigarette in his mouth.

"Okay. Joo go. *Pero*, let me tell you somesing, *mi'ja*. No matter where joo go, there joo are, okay?"

"*Sí, Papi*, of course. I know what you mean."

But I ignored him anyway. I hated running into people from high school and telling them that in spite of my good grades and college degree, I was nothing but a bartender still living at home. I loathed the fact that I could go to any bar in Miami and strike up a conversation with the bartender, only to find that we knew all the same people. People like us who went from one bar to another looking for a better gig; more money, more money, more money. I hated everything, but I convinced myself that transferring as a *bartender* to the Hard Rock in Orlando would enlighten me and open other doors. I felt like moving to Orlando was going to be like being on "The Price Is Right"; I would be offered three doors to choose from and behind one of them I would find not a new car, but a new me with an exciting life.

I was about to fall asleep on the couch in the teacher's lounge. As soon as my eyes closed, I imagined Mrs. Coleman walking in and suffocating me with one of the throw pillows. I quickly got up and straightened out my shirt. I bumped into Matt Connelly as I was walking out the door.

"Hey, you."

I suddenly forgot how to breathe.

"Hey, Mr., I mean, Matt." *Please, God, tell me my zipper is not undone and that I don't have a huge piece of black pepper stuck between my front teeth.*

"What's going on? I haven't seen much of you."

"Yeah, our schedules are different. Besides, I've just been trying to get used to things."

"I got you. Hey, sorry we never got together before the first day, but I had to fly up to New York, you know, family emergency."

"Oh, really? Is everyone okay?"

"Yeah, it was nothing major. My dad got into a car accident, and of course, my mom flipped out and exaggerated the whole thing. I flew up there expecting to see my old man on his death bed, but he was sitting in his recliner with a cold beer in his hand when I walked in the door." He chuckled. "My old man."

"Oh. Well, thank God it was nothing, right?"

"Yeah, but I tell ya, I was pretty upset that I'd flown up for nothing. I kind of wanted to pick him up out of that chair and slam him a few times. You know, put him in the hospital for real, make my trip worthwhile."

I started laughing and prayed it was a joke. I couldn't marry a potential wife beater.

"Hey, I'm only kidding. I love my folks, but my mom has a habit of exaggerating everything, you know?" *More than you can imagine.* "Hey, you going somewhere? Am I holding you up?"

I wanted to tell him that I could very well stand there all day and into the night and probably for the rest of my life talking to him, but I decided to play it cool.

"Yeah, I mean, it was a rough day so I'm just gonna go home and contemplate suicide."

"Come on, now. It can't be that bad. Don't forget, I have the same students."

"Yeah, but you're six foot four and have that tough guy accent going for you. I'm half your size and the only thing that could possibly work in my favor is this wild animal on my head." I pointed at my head.

"What are you talking about? Your hair's beautiful. It's so long."

He grabbed a piece of it and held it in his hand. He let it drop too quickly. I stared at him for a few seconds because I was reeling from the fact that he'd touched my hair. I felt like a seventh grader.

"Oh my God, where are my manners? Uh, thanks, but I still think my hair is a pain in the ass." *Pain in the ass, Bibi? For God's sake, be a lady.* "Sorry, did I say that out loud?"

He laughed and looked me in the eyes. "Hey, you wanna talk about it?"

"What, my hair?"

"No, funny girl, the students."

"Well—"

Truth is, I was desperate to talk to someone. I couldn't talk to my parents because I would've had to pronounce Marcdala and Chancy for them a million times. I was sure Namisha had heard enough. I decided to let him be the sounding board.

"Look, I really don't mean to bitch or complain because I'm really not like that, but you have a kind face and you asked so I'm gonna tell you these kids are driving me *crazy* and you see I don't make nearly enough money to justify the fact that I'm actually contemplating getting a prescription for Prozac, not when I was making double the money as a bartender as a waitress too and I just wish they would listen to me once in a while and give me a chance to actually teach something because if they don't I'm going to lose it completely and tie all of them to their chairs and put tape on their mouths."

"Oh." Matt put his hand over his mouth and tried not to laugh. I had been hoping for a little more sympathy, but at least I'd made him giggle.

"Are you headed home now?" I asked.

"Me? Well, I was gonna go to the gym and then grab something to eat. You can join me, but I'm warning you, I'm not gonna try to talk you out of jumping off a building."

"Haha, cute, Matt. I would never jump off a building. I'm afraid of heights, anyway."

"Good to know. I'll give you a call in a little while, okay? Is it okay if I get your number off the contact list?"

"Sure. If I don't answer, don't panic. I'll probably be in the shower. You know, it's Wednesday."

"No kidding? Is Wednesday your day too?"

"Yep. On Saturdays I wash my hair."

He laughed again and held the door for me as I walked out of the teachers' lounge. I managed to make it down the hall without tripping myself or knocking someone over. I was smiling from ear to ear when I got into my beat up Honda Civic with the broken air conditioner, smiling even though I was already sweating from head to toe.

*Matt is smart. Matt is nice. Matt has a solid brain, solid muscles and a sense of humor. But Matt has no clue what he's about to get into.*

We decided to meet at the Ale House on Kirkman Road. It was a halfway point for the both of us. I was kind of nervous because it was a Hard Rock employee hangout. I didn't want to run into three million curious waiters and waitresses and bartenders. I didn't want to answer questions about how I liked teaching and whether or not I had adjusted to being poor. Matt offered to pick me up, but because I wasn't exactly sure if it was a real date (he only said I could join him, as though it was an afterthought), I decided to play it safe and drive myself. I figured I could always drive myself home if he pissed me off within the first five minutes. Something told me it was the last thing he was going to do.

I spotted him as soon as I walked in the door because, let's face it, the guy was my soul mate. They tend to stand out in bars. He was wearing jeans and a t-shirt, nothing too spectacular, but he still made my heart stop. He was confident but not arrogant, sweet but not too nice, smart but not nerdy. Handsome in a rogue kind of way. Not the kind of handsome that makes you think of Barbie and Ken. He was handsome in an Old Spice commercial way, and that was a good sign because my dad wears Old Spice. Still, I couldn't help but wonder why he was still single. *There must be something wrong with him,* I thought. I decided then and there, standing in the doorway of a very crowded Ale House, that Matt was either bi-polar or in the closet. If he was mentally unstable, there was a chance I was going to hit him up for prescription drugs. If he was gay, he was going to be my new best friend. If he was neither of those, I would still be in the running to be Mrs. Connelly.

He had his back to the door so I just stood there and watched him. You know, typical stalker-like behavior. All the women sitting at the bar kept looking at him and smiling. When I saw a blonde with breasts bigger than six of mine put together idle up next to him, my deranged, insecure self kicked in. I walked over and sat next to him as the Implant Queen tried to make conversation with him.

He jumped when he turned and saw me. *Not a good sign,* my mom would've said. *Your face scares him.* "Damn, you scared me, sneaking up on me like that."

At least he didn't say, *Damn, that wild animal on your head scared the shit out of me.*

"Sorry. You were talking to someone and I didn't want to interrupt."

I looked at the blonde bimbo sitting next to him. She stared at me and tried to figure out if I was his girlfriend. Good thing I'd made more than an effort to look decent. A fashion expert I was not. I'd spent so much time wearing a uniform that I was truly happy to hang out in jeans and boots. But Matt was a different kind of guy, the kind I wanted to impress and convince that once in a while I could pull off lipstick and nail polish. I was wearing a black skirt (not the come-get-me kind but it was still cute), a dark red casual top and black sandals. For once, my hair was tame and I had even sprayed on my favorite perfume, Paloma Picasso. I thought I looked okay even if I didn't have huge breasts and fake blonde hair. I smiled at the Implant Queen as she looked me up and down and then up and down again and decided not to choke the poor thing. I figured sooner or later one of her implants would explode and that alone was enough to make me feel better.

Matt asked me what I wanted to drink. I asked for a beer because wine makes me talk too much. The last thing I wanted to do was throw Matt the details of my entire life on the first date. Besides, that's what second dates are for.

Matt paid for our beers and looked around for an empty table. The Implant Queen shrugged her shoulders and turned to another guy at the bar. Matt didn't seem to notice or care. We found an empty table in the back by the dartboard and pool tables. I loved the way everyone was staring at us as we sat down, loved the way women were looking at me with envy. *How do you like me now?* I wanted to scream.

"You're not from Orlando, right?" He sipped his beer.

"No. I moved here about eight months ago from Miami. I was a bartender for the Hard Rock in Miami and I transferred up here."

"You left bartending to be a teacher?"

"Hard to believe, but going home every night at four in the morning smelling like vodka and ashtrays got kind of old, so I decided to teach."

"Is that why you decided to teach? You got sick of bartending?"

"Kind of, I don't know." I hadn't expected such direct questions.

"What do you mean you don't know? Teaching's not something you do just for the hell of it."

"No, it's not, but I wasn't really trying to be a teacher. I started out subbing and one thing led to another, so here I am. And you know what? I have no idea what I'm doing." I took a long sip of my beer. *Slow down. He's going to think you're a drunk.*

"Don't be so hard on yourself. The kids really like you, you know."

"They do? Really?"

"Yeah. They talk about you in my class a lot."

"They do?!" I was truly shocked.

"Why are you so surprised?"

"Matt, wake up. You were born to teach. You have some mechanism I don't have. So, what do they say?" I pretended to be casual about it, but I was dying to know. Being liked by the students was really important to me.

"They just say that you're funny."

"Funny? That's it?"

"Yep, pretty much."

"Shit."

"Shit? Why do you say that?"

"Well, I was hoping they said they loved school because of me, that they want to go to college, move out of the hood, get a good job, stuff like that."

"Bibiana, kids only say that kind of crap in movies, okay? I'm not saying you're not doing a good job, but you have to remember these kids are facing all sorts of challenges you probably never had to deal with. College is a million miles away for them, let alone graduating from high school. Be happy they at least like you. Trust me, once you've got them to like you, they'll do anything to make you happy."

"But they don't."

"Don't what?"

"Do anything to make me happy. They spend most of the time ragging on each other. It's hard for me to teach them anything when Jazelin calls Marcdala a cat killer, Ebony gets up and smacks DiAngelo for taking her pencil, Princess calls Taquila a who'e and—"

He laughed and took another sip of his beer. "Calm down. You just need to find your thing, that thing that will make them listen. Don't bother bringing them candy or any other kind of crap because it doesn't work. It's gotta be something original."

The beer hit my central nervous system and I relaxed. "So what's your thing? Why do they listen to you?"

"Me? I don't know. I don't treat them like idiots and I don't address them as the At-Risk students. I treat them like regular kids."

"That's it?"

"No, of course not. When they get out of hand I threaten to make them lick the chalkboard until it's clean."

"No you don't!" I laughed.

"Oh, believe me, I do. It works."

The waitress came over and took our order. I ordered wings because some habits never die. I ordered them garlic free because I was praying our "date" would turn into just that and Matt would be possessed with an insane desire to ravish me in the parking lot. After she left, Matt went back to interview mode.

"What do you like about teaching?"

"Uhm, do you really want to talk about work? I was only kidding about the suicide thing, you know."

"I know you were kidding. We can talk about something else if you want, but I'm just curious, you know, just trying to get to know Miss C." Blue eyes twinkled at me from across the table, eyes that were looking straight through me and directly into my whirlwind of a mind. I was ready to give him the interview ready answer, but he was looking at me so intently that lying would have been pointless. *Matt should have been a cop*, I thought. I shrugged and smiled shyly.

"To be honest, I love kids, always have. I love their energy and the funny things they say. I don't know, I just feel comfortable around them."

"Uh-huh, so?"

"I don't know how I like teaching because, to be honest, I can't say that I'm actually teaching them anything except how to raise their hands or how to stop picking on each other." He said nothing and kept staring at me, waiting for more. "I don't know why I decided to do this. I guess I was sick of bartending. And I knew it would please my parents, not that they've ever put any kind of pressure on me." I shrugged again and took another sip of my beer. "Someone very close to me once told me I'd be a good teacher someday, and that someone made a difference to me. I don't know, I guess I'd like to die knowing I made a difference in someone's life." *God, that is so cheesy.* "That and having summers and holidays off is way cool. You know what I mean?"

Matt took a sip of his beer and looked around the restaurant. His eyes stopped roaming and settled on me as I gulped half of my beer. I saw our wedding plans running out the door.

"You're making a difference already, Bibiana."

"You can call me Bibi. It's my nickname."

"Bibi? How'd you get that?"

"My brother couldn't pronounce my name when I was born, so he came up with Bibi."

"Bibi? I like that. Anyway, as I was saying, you're already making a difference."

"Yeah, right. I don't see it."

"I do. The fact that you haven't given up says a lot. By now, any other teacher would've run out the door and left the kids to torture someone else. I've seen it happen a million times."

"Yeah, I know. I guess I stay because I don't like to quit. And well, Chancy has great momma jokes."

"You see? That's what it is. That's it right there."

"What?" I was totally confused. I didn't think letting my kids tell momma jokes was appropriate, even though I'd call Erasmo and repeat them.

"Give me a good momma joke," he said. "I love momma jokes."

I didn't hesitate for a second.

"Okay, here goes, 'Miss C, your momma's so fat she slid down a rainbow and Skittles popped out!' How can you not laugh at that?"

He tilted his head back and clapped his hands. "You see? That's what I mean. That's hilarious. You let them be who they are, and that's good. But don't try to be something you're not, trust me. If they like you because you're funny and you can relate to their sense of humor, use it to your advantage. Make them laugh right back. I don't think momma jokes are the PC way, but once you find your groove, they'll listen to you. Promise. Just do me a favor, okay?"

"Okay." *Please ask me to marry you, please, please, please.*

"Don't quit. You're the only cute teacher around and I happen to think you're hilarious. If you keep me laughing, I'll keep you sane. Deal?" He raised his beer to toast me.

I picked up my beer and toasted him back. "Deal. Do you wanna do a shot?"

"Let's do it."

We did a shot of tequila and let ourselves get lost in conversation. We talked about our families, our friends (he had more than I did), college, cures for hangovers, etc. We covered everything from movies like *Better Off Dead* to Vivaldi, everything, of course, except past relationships. I didn't want to admit I'd never had a real one. But we covered just about everything else. I felt like I was in heaven.

We stayed at the Ale House until last call. As we walked out, I made a quick run for the bathroom, desperately wishing I could brush my teeth. I rinsed my mouth out with cold water and fixed my still-tame hair.

He was waiting for me outside the bathroom and grabbed my hand when I walked out. His fingers squeezed mine and he looked at me as though we were sharing a secret. The butterflies in my stomach went into a frenzy. The minute we got to my car, Matt let go of my hand. I almost wanted to cry. I didn't want the night to end so I made a huge production of looking for my keys. He stood there and watched me as I pretended to fumble. When I looked up, he was laughing at me.

"What the hell is so funny?"

"Bibi, I have your keys."

"You do? Why didn't you say so?"

"Because you looked so adorable trying to find them. Were you trying to prolong the night?"

"No way!"

"Yes you were!"

I raised my hands. "Okay, you got me. Sorry, Matt, but I had a great time tonight. I don't think I've ever felt so comfortable talking to someone of the opposite sex. Anyway, you and I have to wake up early and face the same monsters, so I guess I'll go now. Give me my keys."

"One condition."

"Condition? Matt, they're my keys, dork. Oops, sorry. I didn't mean that. Come on, the sooner you give me the keys, the sooner you'll be driving away from a raging lunatic."

"A cute lunatic."

"Haha." I wasn't sure what to do next.

"Close your eyes."

"No."

"Come on, don't you trust me?"

"Sort of."

"Just close them and hold out your hand."

I sighed and closed my eyes and held out my right hand. He grabbed my left hand, gently dropped the keys into them, and then pulled me close. I laid my head on his strong chest. He smelled so good. Clean. Manly. He held me away from him and I didn't open my eyes until he cleared his throat.

"Bibi?"

"Yeah?"

"I really want to kiss you."

"Me too."

"You want to kiss yourself?"

"You know what I mean!"

"But we work together."

"So?"

"Are you going to get weird on me if I kiss you?"

"Newsflash: I'm already weird."

"You're right about that, but are you sure you want to do this?"

I had never been more sure about anything else in my life. "Am I sure I want to kiss you?"

"Yeah."

"What do you think?"

He hesitated for a moment. "I think I'd love to brush my teeth."

"Me, too."

We started laughing. He leaned over and my knees trembled at the thought that he was actually going to kiss me, the weird, neurotic, former fat girl. I felt his lips on mine and tasted beer and tequila, my favorite combo. It wasn't a short kiss. Actually, we made out like two teenagers who've just figured out what their tongues are for. We managed to pull away from each other before clothes started coming off and said good-bye. I got into my car and he leaned over for a last kiss, a kiss that lasted another five minutes.

He finally pulled away and straightened his shirt out. "Whew. I better go."

"Me, too."

"Okay, Miss C, I'll see you tomorrow."

"Okay. Drive safe."

"You too. Bye."

"Bye. Drive safe."

"You said that."

"Just in case you forgot."

"One more kiss, Miss C."

One more quick kiss and I turned my car on before I changed my mind and followed him home.

I got home, slipped a Chopin CD into the stereo my parents bought me as a going away present and lay down on the floor. My apartment, though small and full of neglected plants, was still nice. It had vaulted ceilings I loved to stare at from my position on the floor. My favorite nocturne filled the emptiness of the apartment and I slipped into a cloud. I thought back on the night and thanked God I hadn't done anything stupid like knocked over my beer or tripped the waitress by mistake. I fell off the cloud the minute I thought of my students.

Matt said I had to find my *groove*, the thing that would make them listen. *But what? What can I do?* I couldn't think of anything. I gave up on trying to find a way to preserve my sanity and let my mind drift back to the teachers who'd inspired me. The teachers who championed my love for books, the ones who protected me when I was a fat kid everyone picked on, the ones who encouraged me to go to college, and of course, the man who once told me I'd be a great teacher someday.

The coolest teacher ever. Doc Keigwin.

# Chapter 7

The summer before my sophomore year, I finally decided to stop stuffing my face with donuts and ice cream and switched to salads and water. The weight dropped off me at an alarming rate. Even my parents started to worry. I listened to no one about my strict diet and rigorous exercising. Instead of staying in my room reading book after book, I borrowed my brother's old ten speed and spent hours riding around our neighborhood. I stopped eating chocolate cake for breakfast, turned down that second slice of pizza and developed a love affair with sunflower seeds. Truth is, I was tired of being picked on, tired of sitting by myself in the cafeteria, and really tired of being the last person picked for any athletic event. Cheerleading tryouts were two weeks before school started and I was determined to be on the squad. Fat girls never made the squad. No way. Fat girls stood around during pep rallies hating cheerleaders, wanting to be one at the same time.

If you'd asked me back then why I wanted to be a cheerleader, I would've tried to justify it by saying I thought it looked fun, but damn, that would've been a load of shit. I wanted one thing: to be accepted, to be popular, to be one of those girls everyone liked. I also wanted straight hair and teeth that didn't make me look like a rabbit, but some things you just can't change. My weight was something I could control. I rode the bike, ran around the local park, went to bed hungry and looked at myself in the mirror every ten seconds to see if those last ten pounds had magically disappeared. By the time tryouts started, I'd gone from 165 pounds to 125 pounds, and boy did that make a difference. The cheekbones that had always been hidden under layers of fat made a long awaited appearance. They drew attention away from my teeth, which was a blessing. My hair grew out and no longer looked like an old mop. I was elated to look in the mirror and not see rolls of fat threatening to take over my whole bedroom.

Erasmo's friends showed up at the house and spent more than ten seconds talking to me, each one unable to look me in the eye, each one casting glances at my body in ways I'd always wished for. Most of my brother's friends were serious rednecks who thought chewing tobacco was a sport, boys I would never in a million years consider kissing, but that didn't matter. They thought I was cute and it was enough for me. I was no longer Erasmo's fat sister.

Tryout day was sunny and typically humid. My mom fussed and fretted around me that morning as I did my best to make my hair listen to the comb. I tried on at least six different outfits and finally decided on a new pair of white Nike shorts and a pink t-shirt I'd begged my mom to buy me. My boobs were finally more than two pairs of blob and my legs actually looked a little muscular. My mom, unwilling to accept my refusal to eat breakfast, toasted some bread and handed me a cup of black coffee as I turned in front of the mirror.

"*Mi'ja*, please, joo must eat something. Joo are too skinny, *mi'ja. Ay Dios mio*, joo look so different."

"I know, Mami. But I'm happy."

"Jes? Joo feel good now?"

"Yeah, Mami, and I want to be a cheerleader."

"A sheerleader? What is a sheerleader?"

I sat down on my bed, a piece of toast hanging out of my mouth and put my tennis shoes on.

"A cheerleader cheers for the football team, Mami. They're the coolest girls in school."

"Oh jes? Why? What is so cool about sheerleaders?"

I sighed and looked at her. "Oh, Mami, you wouldn't understand. They just are."

She nodded and shrugged her shoulders. "*Andale, mi'ja*, joo go and become sheerleader. Joo ready?"

I checked myself in the mirror one last time to make sure any cellulite hadn't mysteriously reappeared. I smiled at the taut skin on my thighs. "Yeah, Mami, let's go."

No matter how much I wanted to show up for tryouts by myself in a convertible red sports car, I had to settle for a ride in my mom's 1974 Caprice Classic. It was red, it was old, and oh my God it was huge. Erasmo and I called it The Plane. The Plane had brought us safely across the United States from California to Miami, and even though my parents probably could've afforded a new car, my mom hung on to it for dear life, as if leaving it or selling it would somehow erase every memory of Los Angeles. Besides, it had an eight-track player. How can you get rid of something like that? We rode the short distance to the school in silence, me envisioning myself on the sidelines of football games and my mom still confused about the role of a "sheerleader."

My mom wanted to stay for the tryouts, so I had to beg her to leave.

"Why I no can stay?"

"Mami, please. Don't embarrass me. You'd be the only mom here."

"Es okay, no? *Porqué* the other mamas no come to the tryout? They no care?" She was looking at me sadly and it made making her leave even harder.

"Mami, I can't explain, but please, come back in two hours. I'll tell you everything when you pick me up, okay? I promise."

"Okay, *mi'ja, andale.* I know joo will be great. Joo go become sheerleader. *Dios te bendiga.*"

I smiled at her. "Okay, Mami, see you in two hours."

I walked towards the group of girls standing around the bleachers on the football field. Behind them, gorgeous guys were stretching out, the marching band was warming up their instruments, athletic trainers were running back and forth with towels and water bottles and coaches were yelling incessantly for no apparent reason. The whole scene was so intimidating I considered running back to my mom and the Plane. I had no time to change my mind, though, because as I got closer, one by one the beautiful popular girls turned to look at me. They all looked at me like they were trying to figure out where they knew me from. Cheryl Parker, senior and captain of the cheerleading squad, spoke to me first.

"Hi."

"Hi."

"Can I help you?"

"Yeah, uhm, I'm here for the tryouts." I held my breath as I waited for her to tell me fat girls weren't allowed to try out.

"Oh, okay. Are you a sophomore?"

"Yeah."

"What's your name?"

"Bibiana Castellanos."

"Castellanos?"

"Yeah. Why?"

"Do you have an older brother?"

"Yeah. His name is Erasmo."

"Of course! Your brother is so cute! He was so popular."

"Oh, yeah? I didn't know that."

That was a load of bullshit. Erasmo had been a star baseball player and part of the in crowd. I used to hate him for it, but at that moment, with so many eyes on me, I was grateful to him for opening a door to the Land of Coolness.

"All right, Bibiana. Tryouts will start in about five minutes. Have you ever been a cheerleader?"

*Oh, crap.* I'd completely overlooked that.

"No, but I learn quickly, really. All my teachers say I'm a fast learner."

*Way to go, nerd. Why don't you just pull out your report cards?*

Cheryl smiled. I smiled back because she wasn't being mean or nasty. She gave me an approving look.

"Don't worry about it. I'm sure you'll do fine."

She turned back to the other girls and began giving out instructions. I tried to become invisible but the other girls started asking me questions I was totally unprepared for.

"Weren't you fat?"

"Did you lose a lot of weight?"

"What did you do to your hair?"

"I love your shorts."

"You look so thin."

"Weren't we friends in elementary school?"

I was bombarded for a full five minutes. I loved the attention but something about it still bothered me. I wanted to yell at them and hug them at the same time. Most of the girls had been part of my nightmares. Nearly all of them had picked on me and called me names when I was fat, and all of them, with the exception of Cheryl, had snubbed me for being "different." Yet there I was, surrounded by a bunch of super popular rich girls, reveling in the attention and admiration. I warmed up my legs with the other girls and tried to feel comfortable, but I couldn't. The whole situation was *wrong wrong wrong*, but when you're fifteen with a desire to be cool, everything is justifiable.

I made the squad, plain and simple. During tryouts, I jumped higher than everyone else, yelled louder than the football coaches and ran faster than the athletic trainers. I learned each routine and perfected it. I was on a mission to prove myself and I did. When my name was called my heart stopped. I stood up from the bleachers before Cheryl changed her mind and took my place next to the other fortunate girls. Did I look at the other girls who didn't make it and feel sorry for them? No way. Did I smile when the "cool" girls congratulated me? Hell, yes. Nothing else mattered to me at that moment, not even the fact that my mom had snuck her way back and was sitting in the bleachers a few rows above us. That is until she stood up and started clapping and yelling.

"Oh, Bibi, joo was so bery good! Oh, jes! Joo bery good sheerleader!"

*Oh dear God. I've made it this far and now my mom's going to ruin it for me.* I looked at the other girls as they laughed at my mom. Anger welled up inside me. *How dare they laugh at her?* Before I could grab the nearest girl and body slam her (I was a nerd with a temper), Cheryl came over to me and put her hand on my shoulder.

"Hey, Bibiana. You did a great job. Is that your mom? Is Bibi your nickname?"

"Yeah, that's my mom and yeah, you can call me Bibi," I answered coldly as I stared at the other girls.

"That's really sweet of her to come. I wish my mom was here."

I turned to her. "You do?"

"Yeah, but my mom's always busy working. She never shows up for anything."

*Wow,* I thought. *She thinks it's cool that my mom is here.* "Yeah, well, I was hoping she'd come." I was a nerd with a temper and obviously a good liar.

"Hey, don't worry about some of the other girls. Most of them I can't stand, and to be honest, I don't really like to hang out with them. But they're good cheerleaders. Just be careful who you pick as friends."

"Really?"

"Yeah. Cheerleading's not all it's knocked up to be, okay? Don't take it too seriously. There's more to life than jerkys and pyramids."

"Okay, Cheryl. Thanks a lot."

"Anything for Erasmo's adorable little sister. Congratulations, by the way!" She hugged me sincerely and I nearly broke down in tears.

She said I was adorable. She actually liked me! As I walked back to The Plane with my mom, her talking a mile a minute about my sheerleading skills and how "bery" good I was, I was thinking to myself, *Bibiana, welcome to the land of keg parties, designer clothes you'll never afford, nice cars you'll never have, lunchtime with the popular crowd, and oh yeah, football hunks with an IQ smaller than your shoe size.*

It never occurred to me that I wouldn't like it. The realization that my homework and grades would suffer dramatically failed to hit me, and I was totally unprepared for the physical attack on my newly formed, newly thin body. We had practice after school every day for two hours. After that, we'd have boring meetings during which we'd discuss how to raise money for better uniforms, how to be cuter than all the rival schools, who the hottest football player was and where to get the best, absolutely best manicure and pedicure. I went from being surrounded by total geeks in Honors and AP classes to having discussions about who was having the latest sale at the mall. The first few weeks were somewhat bearable only because it was something new and different but...wow, it was so *boring*. Meaningless. Being a cheerleader and part of the "in" crowd doesn't necessarily mean you really enjoy parties and pep rallies and football players puking all over you.

It was too late for me, I discovered. I'd spent too many years as an outsider, and no matter how hard I tried, I couldn't get into discussions about which cosmetic line was better. I could care less about the latest sale at the mall. I was, at heart, a nerd. I missed reading. I missed having time to do homework. I missed watching the news, annoying Erasmo and helping my dad mow the lawn. I was going to parties I never felt comfortable at. I hated making polite conversation with football players who had two things on their mind: cold beer and sex, in that order.

Halfway through the football season, Cheryl came up to me in the locker room after practice. I was sitting on a bench in front of my locker getting my stuff, trying my hardest not to worry about my Geometry midterm. She tapped me on the shoulder. I looked up expecting to see her smile, but she looked concerned.

"Hey, Bibi."

"Hi, Cheryl."

"How you doing?"

"Me? I'm okay. Why?" *Here it comes*, I thought. *I suck after all.*

"No reason. It's been kind of crazy, and I haven't really gotten a chance to talk to you about everything. How are the other girls treating you?"

"Uh, okay, I guess. I mean, I don't really know them too well." I decided not to tell her most of them teased me about my good grades and the way I practically ran away from any football player with beer on his breath.

"Well, are you happy? I mean, do you like being a cheerleader?"

"Yeah, it's okay. I mean, it's not what I thought it would be, if that's what you mean."

"How so? Is it too physically exhausting? I'm only asking because you've lost so much weight."

"I have?"

I thought about what I'd been eating. Salads, cold sandwiches without anything fun like mayo or cheese, sunflower seeds, water and more water. I'd been so busy running from one end of the football field to another that I'd totally stopped thinking about my weight.

"Yeah. Don't get me wrong, you look great, but just be careful. I don't want you to get too skinny and then have your sweet mom yelling at me."

"Oh, don't worry about that because even if she did yell at you, she'd be hurling a stream of insults in Spanish you wouldn't understand. Really, I'm okay."

She looked me in the eyes and I started to panic. She knew I didn't like it, and what's more, she knew exactly why.

"Bibi, why did you try out for the cheerleading squad? You can tell me the truth, I promise."

I looked at her for five seconds before I unloaded everything on my mind. I told her about my life as a fat kid, a nerd, a teacher's pet, a dork, a freak, a weirdo. I told her about the girls who'd called me names in junior high, the girls who so desperately wanted to be my friend now that I was a cheerleader. I told her my grades were suffering, that I loved reading, that I longed for real conversation, and that my desire to belong was playing a mean trick on me. I told her I'd done everything for the wrong reasons. After forty-five minutes of semi-neurotic rambling, Cheryl with the beautiful blonde hair and compassionate blue eyes took me in her arms and told me I should quit.

"Quit?"

"Yeah. Fuck it, who cares? *Just quit.* I mean, don't get me wrong, you're a really good cheerleader and you always have so much energy, but if it makes you feel that way, you should quit. You don't belong with this crowd, Bibi."

Her last words hit me like a bucket of cold water.

"I don't belong?"

"No, but believe me, that's a good thing. You're smarter and more mature than the whole squad put together. Hell, you remind me of me when I was a sophomore, but I didn't have a choice."

"What do you mean?"

"Well, imagine this. My mom was captain of the cheerleading squad, all my sisters were cheerleaders, all my brothers played football. Everyone I've grown up with does the same thing. You cheer, you date the cutest guys, you're always popular and God forbid you decide to do something else."

Cheryl looked sad, tired and bitter and I felt sorry for her. Normally, I wouldn't feel bad for someone who looks like the Barbie doll was modeled after her, but she was different. She was being honest with me.

"You know, I never thought it would be like this."

"Like what?"

"Like I just told you. I've spent my whole life trying to belong, trying to feel accepted, trying to have real friends. And now that I've got the chance, I hate it. It's just not me, you know?"

"Bibi, more than you know."

"You're right, I'm not cut out for this, and besides, my grades are dropping. I want to go to college, you know? Nobody in my family's ever been to college. Hell, my brother was like the first person to graduate from high school."

"I know. Look, don't worry about it. Leaving the cheerleading squad is definitely not the end of the world. I'd like to think it's the beginning of something better. Why don't you drop one of your electives and take chorus?"

"Chorus?" *Where on earth did that come from?* "Why chorus?"

"I've heard you singing to yourself. You have a nice voice. I took chorus my sophomore year but my mom made me quit because it was taking too much time away from cheerleading. But I loved it. You'd love it! Dr. Keigwin is the best teacher this school has. If you want, I'll take you to meet him tomorrow during his morning break. I swear, you're gonna love him."

My electives weren't that exciting to begin with. My photography teacher drank whiskey for breakfast, my drama teacher was obviously a frustrated playwright, and my Home Economics teacher was an old lady who still thought learning to make pancakes was the most important thing in the world.

"Okay, Cheryl. I'd love to give it a shot. Will you really come with me?"

"Of course, Bibi. I know Doc's gonna love you. And he's the nicest, sweetest man I've ever met. You'll see."

Cheryl's beauty and popularity amazed me because it gave her power. Not only did she skip her class, but she got me out of mine by inventing a ridiculous excuse about needing to talk to me about the next fundraiser. Teachers loved her, the principal fantasized about her, everyone wanted to be around her. She was nice to everyone from what I could see and willing to help me out. She must have really liked Erasmo.

We walked into Doc's classroom the next morning, classroom 56C. It seems the only things I can remember about high school are room numbers and class temperatures. My history class was 23A and freezing cold. Chemistry was 62C and a simulation of the North Pole. AP English, however, room 14A, was a spa. The first thing I noticed about Doc's class was that it had the right temperature, a strong sign.

Doc was sitting at the piano practicing a piece of music when we walked in. It was my favorite Beethoven Sonata, another sign. After a brief introduction, Cheryl left me with Doc, a short bearded man with tiny round spectacles and a sincere smile. He asked me a few questions and I immediately told him I could play the piano, as though that would grant me an immediate spot in the choir. Next thing I knew I was giving him a mini-concert on the old upright piano in the just-the-right-temperature classroom. I felt at home as I placed my fingers on the keys. When I stopped playing, he smiled and asked me if I was willing to stay after school to practice for competitions and whether or not it would interfere with my other extracurricular activities.

"Well, uhm, I'm a cheerleader now, but I'm going to quit."

"I see. Why is that?"

"I don't like it. It's kind of boring and our football team stinks anyway. Cheerleading's never going to save it."

Doc laughed. "I think you're right. So, would you like to be part of the choir?"

"I'd love to, but, uh, you haven't even heard me sing. I might be terrible, you know."

"Okay. How about we try out your ear first?"

"Try out my ear?"

"Yes, Bibiana, oops, Bibi. That's your nickname, right?"

"How'd you know that?"

"Cheryl already told me about you. She's really fond of you."

"I have no idea why, Dr. Keigwin."

"Call me Doc, dear."

"Okay. So, how are you going to try out my ear?"

"Go stand on the other side of the piano."

I walked around the piano and took a few steps back.

"Okay."

"Now, when I play a note, I want you to tell me what it is."

"What? That's crazy. I can't do that, Doc."

"How do you know?"

"I don't."

"Why don't we just try, then?"

"Whatever you say...but, uh, what does this have to do with my voice?"

"Everything, dear, everything."

"Okay. It's your class."

He played a note and smiled at me.

"Well?"

"What?"

"What's the note?"

"Uhm, G sharp."

"That's right!!! Did you guess?"

"Sort of."

"Okay, let's try another one."

He played another note and looked at me with so much expectation it made me nervous.

"D?"

"Oh my goodness, you're right again! One more just to make sure you're not the best guesser in the world." He struck another note and I hesitated.

"That's an A."

"Oh my goodness, Bibi, you have perfect pitch."

"What's that?"

"You can identify notes just by hearing them." He sat down on a chair and invited me to sit down next to him. "Tell me something, where did you learn to play the piano?"

"Here, in Miami."

"With a teacher?"

"Of course, Doc. I'm not that gifted."

"Ha ha, a sense of humor to boot. What was your teacher's name?"

"Zaida Moreno. I studied with her for about eight years. I tested with a lady named Olga something or other."

"Olga Martinez from the University of Miami?"

"Yep, that's the one. She was really nice."

"And did you graduate? Was this part of a Fine Arts Conservatory?"

"Yeah, but all my lessons were in Zaida's tiny apartment on Calle Ocho."

"I see. Why did you stop studying?"

"Well, I finished my studies last year and didn't really want to stick with it. I wanted to branch out and try other things."

"Like cheerleading, right?"

"Ugh, don't remind me."

"It's okay, Bibi, it's always good to branch out. Do you think you'd like being my accompanist when I need you?"

"Of course I would. Beats jumping up in the air and cheering for a terrible football team."

"Honey, just about anything does, but don't tell Cheryl I said that."

"You got my word."

"In the meantime, I'm going to put you in the alto section. Cheryl says you have a strong voice."

"Cheryl seems to think a lot of things about me that I don't agree with."

"Well, I do, and I'm glad she brought you to me. Don't worry, dear, you'll have nothing but fun in my class."

The bell rang and I gathered up my things. As I walked out the door, Doc told me he'd take care of changing my schedule for me. I was so relieved I nearly hugged him.

That night, I dropped the news to my parents. I wasn't worried they wouldn't accept my decision, but being the good kid in the family, I always told them everything.

"Joo quit the sheerleaders?" My mom asked.

All four of us were having dinner. My dad looked confused. Erasmo guffawed.

"Awww, not cool enough to be a cheerleader? What's the matter? Can't keep up with the cool crowd?"

"Shut up, you jerk. I just didn't like it. It was boring."

"Boring? What, not as exciting as all your little books and homework?"

My dad leaned over the table and grabbed Erasmo by the ear.

"Erasmo, I'm warning joo, be nice." He turned to me. "*¿Qué pasó?* I thought es what joo wanted."

"No, Papi, it wasn't. So I joined the choir."

"*¿Qué?*" My mom asked. "What is that?"

"Chorus, Mami. Singing. Piano. Music."

My dad was relieved. He took a sip of his whiskey. "Good for joo. Es much better. Joo has more talent with music."

"Maybe. Anyway, the teacher's really cool."

"Oh jes? Is he nice teecher?"

"Yeah, he's really nice. He changed my schedule for me and everything."

"Okay, *mi'ja*," my mom said, "whatever make joo happy. No more sheerleading for joo. *Toma*, have more enchiladas."

My brother looked at me and shrugged his shoulders, not sure why his sister was so weird. I sat there and wolfed down my second helping of enchiladas, glad that I wouldn't have to wear a cheerleading uniform anymore. I couldn't wait to get back to reading.

Doc was the first and not the last person who said I would make a great teacher someday. I don't know why he got that impression, but I rode along with it. I was fifteen years old and not even sure I'd be able to go to college. The thought that I could be a teacher someday seemed miles away. But he insisted. He would place a piece of sheet music in front of me on the piano and leave me to direct the choir while he took care of getting us signed up for this or that competition. To my surprise, the students, even the older ones, never complained or questioned my authority.

One day Doc walked back from the main office and stood in the doorway of the classroom. I knew he was there, knew he was watching, but I was so engrossed in the music that his presence failed to distract me. After class ended, he pulled me into his office and promised to give me a late pass.

"Yes, Doc, what is it? Was I doing something wrong?"

"Oh, no, my dear. Quite the opposite."

He looked at me through his little round glasses, a slight grin on his face and that ever present twinkle in his eye. Doc reminded me of Jiminy Cricket, top hat and all.

"Oh, that's good. I think the class likes the song."

"I think the class likes you directing them in the song."

"Huh?"

"Bibi, listen to me. You're different and they know it. You're a born leader, don't you know that?"

"Hell no."

"Yes, I think you do."

"I do?"

He took off his glasses and rubbed his eyes.

"Bibi, what do you want to do when you finish high school?"

"Uh, I don't know really know yet, Doc. I think my parents would be relieved if someone in our family actually made it to college. My brother blew it."

"What do you like to do?"

"Do? Well, let's see. I like to read. A lot. I'm a geek, Doc, in case you haven't figured that out."

"I did, actually."

"You did? Wait a minute, I should be offended." I smiled at him.

"No, no, don't misunderstand me. You're a geek in the best possible way. You like school, you like learning, and you like to do a good job. You're not afraid to shine."

"Hmm, yeah. I see what you're saying. What does this have to do with what I want to be when I grow up?"

"Bibi, you have so many talents. You can sing okay, you can play the piano, and there's no denying you're very smart. Other teachers think you're a model student. What I'm saying is, among those talents, I think there's one you've never thought about."

"Let me guess. Is it my ability to stick ten sunflower seeds in my mouth at one time and eat them one by one?' I loved Doc because he let me be a smart ass.

"No, no, Bibi. Come on, now, let's be serious."

"Okay, Doc. Talk to me."

"You're a great teacher. You *will* be a very good teacher someday."

"What?!" Of all the things I thought I might like to be, teacher was definitely not on the list.

"Yes, my dear Bibi. You are very good at it, and someday, when you're older and have forgotten about me, you will remember my words. Trust me."

"Yeah, okay, Doc. I'll think about that, and don't worry, I'll never forget you. The day I get my first teaching job, I'll give you a call."

"Okay. Now, let me write you a pass to your next class before your teacher sends out a search warrant for her geekiest student."

"Ha ha, very funny."

Doc could've written a book on how to teach. He never treated us like kids. He referred to us as his singing pals. Though most of class time was spent rehearsing for a show or a competition, a lot of times we would end up having conversations about life after high school. Dreams, passions, wishes. Doc never discouraged anyone from pursuing their dream, not even when Carl Switt blurted out in class that his dream was to be a mortician. Doc looked at him and said, "That's fantastic. You'll never have a lack for clients." When Naomi Teele said she wanted to be country singer, Doc stayed after school with her for weeks to help her train her voice. My dreams confused him. The only thing I dreamt about was making enough money to set my parents up for life. Doc would remind me that teaching was my destiny, my true calling. "Forget about money," he would say. "Do what you love and the money will follow."

On the last day of my senior year, I cried as he hugged me. Doc made me feel truly unique and I was going to miss that feeling.

He held me close and whispered into my hear. "No matter what you choose to do in life, Bibi, make sure it's something you wouldn't mind doing for free."

Doc passed away the day I sat in Dr. Lawrence's office and accepted a teaching position. I guess he'd been waiting for me to finally come to my senses and that's why I just couldn't quit. Besides, my salary was so depressing that it seemed I was doing just that, doing what I loved for free.

# Chapter 8

"Miss C, what we gonna do today, yo? You gonna read that book about that Pony kid?"

Chancy was always the first one to speak up. I don't know what kind of power he had in the hood, but whatever it was, it worked. Nobody ever contradicted him. None of the students ever talked back to him or called him names. He kept to himself for the most part, but he was still bad at following rules. He'd get up and go the bathroom without asking, as though I simply did not exist. He would speak out without raising his hand no matter how many times I'd berate him. And he never had his shoelaces tied. It wasn't a rule but I'd made it sound like one. His only saving grace was that he was smarter than I thought. He could read better than most of the kids and always asked pertinent questions about the book.

But like the rest of the class, he spoke a different version of English and I had a hell of a time getting used to it.

"Miss C, I'm figgin' to go to the bathroom," Chancy would say.

"What?"

"I'm figgin' to go to—"

"Figgin' to go?"

"Yeah, Miss C, like, I'm gonna go."

"Oh."

Or Ebony would say, "Miss C, Donte, he trippin'. Tell him to leave me alone."

"Trippin'?"

"Yeah, Miss C. *Trippin'*. You know, like, he tryin' me."

"Oh, yeah, got it. I definitely know what tryin' is. Donte, quit trippin'."

Jazelin would open his mouth and I would find it hard to keep a straight face. He couldn't get through one sentence without saying, "You know what I'm sayin'?" at least three times.

"Jazelin, did you do your homework?"

"Uh, Miss C, I, you know what I'm sayin'? I had to, like, you know, go to, you know what I'm sayin'? I had to go to the store 'cause my momma, you know what I'm sayin'? She had needed some stuff and I ain't had no, you know what I'm sayin'? I ain't had no time, you know what I'm sayin'?"

Their version of English reminded me of Spanglish, a mixture of Spanish and English. Spanglish annoyed the hell out of every Hispanic parent with first generation American kids. Kids like us. For the most part, Erasmo and I could speak Spanish very well. After all, it was our first language. But some words were too hard for us to translate. So we improvised. We said things like "typear," "vacuumcleanear" and "printear." To this day I still don't know the Spanish equivalent for vacuum cleaning.

Spanglish goes even further than that. Words such as "but," "because," "and," "that" and others are replaced by their Spanish equivalents in sentences. My little cousin Barbie is a perfect example of a Spanglish pro. I'd call her from Orlando once in a while to make sure she wasn't having sex or experimenting with drugs. I was annoying like that. Barbie was fourteen when I moved away and *very* hormonal. She always had drama, and she always told me about it in Spanglish.

"Hey, crazy girl. How are you?"

"Oh my God, I have sooo much to tell you, *pero* I don't have that much time *porque* I have soooo much homework *y tengo que limpiar* my room. *Pero* whatever, I'm gonna tell you *un poquito porque* it's juicy gossip. The other day, Carlos called me remember the guy *que* I told you about? *Bueno,* he told me *que* he wanted to take me out *pero* I know my mom isn't gonna let me *porque* she thinks Carlos is a *delincuente,* you know?"

Funny that I would slip right into it. "Yeah, I know, *pero* you have to understand *que* your mom's scared *que* he might make you do something *que* you shouldn't, you know? So be careful *porque* I'll kill you if I find out *que* you're doing drugs. *Pero* if you have questions, *tú sabes que* you can call me, okay?"

I couldn't tell my students to put away their slang words for good. It wasn't fair. So I told them they could speak however they wanted around their friends, or rather, "peeps," but they had to speak correctly inside my classroom. Problem was I had to teach them how to say things correctly in the first place, but what with their At Risk behavior, it was impossible.

They were belligerent, they were insubordinate, they were little monsters, but they were definitely not dumb. And that annoyed me. I wondered if the label was the problem. I mean, someone had stamped "Weird" on my forehead when I was born and I'd done a great job of living up to it. *Maybe that's what they're trying to do,* I thought. I remembered what Namisha had said to me. "Kids will rise to your level of expectation."

I decided to find out why some of them were in the At Risk program in the first place. I could've done the research way before school started, something a real teacher would've done, but I'd been too busy trying to get used to having a real job. Better late than never.

Dr. Lawrence told me my students were falling behind because of their behavior. It's great if a school cares about students who have trouble keeping up, but when I was a kid, having a slow learner or a hellion in a classroom meant a little more attention, a little more planning, and a lot more patience on the teacher's part. It never meant giving up and handing him over to someone else to deal with.

I looked through Chancy's file first. He'd been an above average student until the fifth grade. That summer, his dad got arrested (didn't say for what) and his mom abandoned him. His grandmother got custody. Everything went downhill in the sixth grade. Fights, detentions, suspensions, etc. His grades plummeted. He was labeled a "troubled child." *Well, no shit,* I thought. Losing a mom and dad at the same time will trouble anyone. In the first semester of the sixth grade, Chancy was pulled out of mainstream classes and put into the At Risk program. According to his records, his performance only worsened.

Marcdala was a straight A student until middle school. She got into a fight in the seventh grade. Her record stated that it had been over "race." An African American girl had picked on Marcdala because she was Haitian. I'd honestly never realized there were racial tensions among black people. It's not something they teach you in college. Marcdala's grades started slipping and she was thrown into the At Risk circus. Her grades never recovered either. Her behavior only got worse.

I looked through a few more files and realized most of the kids had been through the same thing. They'd all been good students until something terrible had happened to them. One boy was abandoned by both his parents, one girl was physically abused by her father's girlfriend, another boy was beat up by a group of white kids, etc. They acted out, and how could they not? They got into fights, they disobeyed rules, they disrespected adults. And they'd all been put in one classroom. No surprise, the At Risk program had had twelve teachers in the last three years.

*Twelve teachers in the last three years,* I thought. *Twelve teachers quit.* I sighed. *Boy have things changed.*

Jimmy was this kid in my fourth grade class. He never said much. He would sit at his desk and do his work quietly. He never gave the teacher any problems and pretty much went with the flow. One day, in the middle of a handwriting lesson, he threw his pencil straight across the room. Smack! He laughed as it hit the chalkboard. Mrs. Pratt, a woman who took strict to another level, was momentarily shocked by the interruption. She turned around and faced the class with a half crazy look in her eye.

"Who threw this?" she asked as she bent to pick it up.

"I did." Jimmy was sitting there grinning.

"Why, Jimmy?" She was confused.

"I felt like it."

"Excuse me, young man?" Confusion quickly turned into rage.

"You heard me. I felt like it."

We all looked at each other and the tension in the room intensified. This wasn't the Jimmy we knew.

"You felt like it? What if I feel like marching you down to the principal's office so that we can call your parents?"

"They won't care. They're stupid anyway."

The class let out a collective gasp. Calling your parents stupid was considered a crime. Something about the way he said it triggered something in Mrs. Pratt.

"Jimmy, come with me, please. Miss Bibi, please stand at the chalkboard while I'm gone and write down the names of everyone who misbehaves."

"Yes, Mrs. Pratt." I got out of my seat and quickly made my way to the chalkboard. It didn't take me long because my desk was in the front row. What a surprise. I stood at the chalkboard like a mini-Hitler and made sure everyone stayed in their seats (go ahead and hate me) while everyone whispered to each other.

"Do you think his mom will get him?"

"I heard his parents split up."

"They were always fighting."

"My parents have joint custody."

"I only see my dad in the summer. He moved to Canada."

A lot of the kids in my class had already been through the same thing. Lucky for me, I never had to spend every other weekend with my dad or a whole summer with my mom because in my family, divorce was considered a cuss word. My parents argued once in a blue moon, like when my dad would bring home the wrong toilet paper or forget to take out the garbage, but that was it. Leaving your family was just not an option. Even if you were miserable and secretly wishing your spouse would suddenly develop a permanent case of amnesia, you stayed and worked things out. Without therapy and without lawyers.

Jimmy came back to class the next day, even more withdrawn. I felt sorry for him because the other kids seemed to think it was normal for him to go from a two parent home to a one-parent-struggling-with-bills situation. But there's one thing I remember most; Mrs. Pratt staying after class every day with Jimmy, working with him, helping him with his homework. Mrs. Pratt telling the other kids to "stop picking on Jimmy." Mrs. Pratt sitting with Jimmy's mom once a week to go over his progress. That's what I remember about my fourth grade teacher. Jimmy wasn't sent to a class for kids with special needs. He ended up graduating with me in Honors. One teacher took the time to address his emotional hell and kept him on track. She didn't throw in the towel. She didn't paste a label on him. She did her job.

But someone had thrown in the towel when it came to my students. Not just one towel either. Twelve.

After reading through their files, I was hoping I'd have a better understanding of what living in the hood was like. But to be perfectly honest, I still had no clue. One peek into their pasts was not enough to make me an expert. I didn't know what their homes were like, I didn't know what they did after school, I didn't know anything. For crying out loud, I'd never even driven through the hood. I only knew that it was on the "wrong side" of the I-4.

Ebony gave me my first lesson about the hood. Imagine that. My students were teaching me.

I was trying to keep the class quiet long enough for me to call roll. Ebony was getting in the way of my mission. She couldn't keep her mouth closed for more than two seconds. As I called roll, she made comments under her breath while I tried to get her to stop.

"Ha ha, look at Marcdala's skirt. Girl, you need to get some new rags."

"Ebony, be quiet."

"Okay, Miss C…Jazelin, your 'fro getting long. It look stupid."

"Ebony, I said be quiet."

"Oh, sorry, Miss C…Tevaris, what's wrong with you, boy? You waitin' for a flood?"

"Ebony, I said *be quiet*. Now."

"Okay, Miss C, sorry, hm hmm…ha ha, DiAngelo, I heard your auntie got evicted and—"

After telling her to be quiet for the millionth time, I slammed the attendance book on my desk and looked at her. I was tired, frustrated, and hadn't been able to stop at Dunkin' Donuts that morning for coffee. To make matters worse, Matt hadn't asked me out again. I was bitter.

"Ebony, I've asked you to be quiet too many times."

"Hm hmm." She rolled her eyes at me.

"Ebony, if you don't behave, I'm gonna have to call your mom."

She started laughing.

I could feel my blood rising. "What's so funny?"

"Miss C, you can't call my momma!" She laughed even harder.

"Oh, yeah? Why not?'

"'Cause we ain't got no phone!!!"

This is when a normal person would've given up. This is when a normal person would've picked up their stuff and left. But I wasn't normal. I had a sense of humor and I loved kids. So, naturally, I started laughing. I couldn't help it. I knew my fellow teachers probably would've been shocked by my reaction, would've demanded some kind of reprimand, but I didn't care. Her comment struck me as funny.

My laughter was contagious. It was like a disease that circulated faster than a bad check. Next thing I knew, all of us, Marcdala, Jazelin and DiAngelo included, were overwhelmed with the giggles. I would stop and gather my composure but one look at Ebony and her innocent smiling face and I'd lose it all over again. This carried on for about twenty minutes. Finally, I realized I only had fifteen minutes left to teach the lesson. I wiped my eyes for the last time and faced the class. The look on my face conveyed a serious attempt at being a real teacher, so one by one, they picked up their pencils and sat up straight.

My goal for the day had been to stress the importance of speaking English properly. No ain'ts, no y'all's, no street talk. I started the lesson by asking how many of them wanted to go to college. After a few snickers, more than half the class raised their hands. Pleased that they were behaving, I launched into my grammar lesson. Their good behavior was short lived. I had their attention for three minutes tops before they became engrossed in one another's clothes, mommas, boyfriends, etc.

I looked around the room as they altogether forgot me. *What should I do? Throw erasers? Scream? Get down on the floor like a child and pound my fists? Where is my groove?* My mom came to mind. My mom could get anyone's attention with six words. I'd tried just about everything else so I decided to give the six magic words a chance to save me.

"Guys, listen up." No reaction. "Hey, come on, now. Settle down. That's enough." Nothing. *Here goes,* I thought. "Let me tell you a story."

Instant silence. Everyone stopped what they were doing and looked at me like deer caught in the headlights of a tractor trailer. An invisible director had screamed "Freeze!" on my movie set. I was shocked. I couldn't believe it had been that easy. But I actually had to tell them a story, and I had to give it my all; act out the scenes, get into the characters, etc. *What the hell? It's just a story.*

"All right, I'm going to tell you a story about my mom and what happened to her because she couldn't speak English, okay?"

They all answered at once. "Okay, Miss C."

My mom got into a car accident when I was five years old. It wasn't her fault and nobody got hurt. A man ran a stop sign and crashed into her station wagon as she was heading to pick us up from school. The cop calmed her down while he tried to explain the procedures. Lucky for her, he spoke Spanish, but her luck ended there. An insurance company representative came to see her the next day. The only thing she understood was that she would be getting a check in the mail for damages. My mom, impressed at how quickly things got done in the United States, expected the check to arrive the next day. *Literally.* She would stand by the window every day and hold her breath as the mailman walked to the front door. She would open the door as he tried to insert letters through the slot.

"Es de money?"

"No, lady. No money. Just your regular mail."

He would roll his eyes at the crazy Mexican lady, give her the mail and tip his hat as he turned around. My mom would open every letter, convinced that twenty-five hundred dollars would fall into her lap. Seeing nothing but junk mail she couldn't read, she would sigh and get back to freezing Hawaiian Punch. She did the same thing day in and day out for about six weeks. Every day she would tell my dad the same thing at dinner.

"Fico, no money. Es craysee, no? Maybe they no remember?"

"No, Isabela, joo has to be *paciente.* Es going to take some time, okay?"

"*Sí, está bien.* Okay, more time."

My mom was in the shower when the doorbell rang. It was Saturday and I was sitting in the living room watching *Villallegre,* a Spanish version of Sesame Street. Erasmo was somewhere outside trying to build a ramp for his bike or figuring out a way to blow up the school. I walked to the door and opened it to find Mr. Mailman standing there rolling his eyes.

"Hello, young lady. Is your mom home? I can't *believe* she didn't open the door."

Even at that age I could detect sarcasm.

"What do you want, mister?"

"Just tell her I need to give her something."

I knew she was waiting for "de money," so I ran to the bathroom and told my mom the mailman needed to see her. She practically ran out to greet him in the nude she was so excited, but she managed to throw on a house robe and wrap a towel around her head in less than ten seconds. Seeing your mom in the nude when you're five is not pleasant, especially when you don't know the concept of pubic hair and sagging boobs. Still in shock by the sight of so much flesh, I followed her as she ran to the door holding her boobs in her hands. Mr. Mailman gave my mom a painful smile.

"Jes, meester, I can help joo?"

He was pointing at an envelope in his hand.

"Lady, *money.*"

"Oh! Thanks to God! Oh, jes, de money!" She tried to grab the envelope from his hand, but he pulled back and gave her another evil smile.

"No, no, lady," he said, once again pointing to the envelope, "*money.*"

My mom looked confused.

"Jes, I know es de money! Es for my accident. The inchoorans company say to me they send me de money. I take from joo now."

Once again she made a grab for the envelope and once again he pulled back, frustration in his beady little eyes.

"Lady, for Christ's sake, *money!*" He was pointing at the envelope like Moses pointing at the Ten Commandments.

"*Ay Dios mio*, why joo no give me de money? Joo know, I was having accident, ehm, and the car, joo know, it crash to me. *Ay Dios mio*, my back, my neck, everysing hurt, joo know? I need de money. Plees, give to me." For the last time she made a lunge for it. Mr. Mailman had had enough.

"Oh, Jesus, lady. Can't you speak English? You know? *Habla ingles?*"

My mom looked completely crushed. I contemplated grabbing one of his legs and biting it. Before I could do anything, our next door neighbor Flora ran to my mom's rescue. She'd been watching the commotion from across the street. She smiled at Mr. Mailman and asked my mom what was going on. My mom left nothing out. She waved her hands in the air and told Florita about the accident, her bad neck, the slow inchoorans company and even threw in the fact that she had just made enchiladas and did she want to stay for dinner? Florita was lucky enough to speak both languages, so she relayed the entire drama to Mr. Mailman. Mr. Mailman sighed, took off his hat and gave my mom a long look.

"Would you please tell this crazy Mexican lady the reason I've been standing here arguing with her for the last twenty minutes is because she mailed this letter without a stamp and it needs *money*!" Once again, he pointed at the letter, every vein in his forehead ready to explode. Florita relayed the bad news to my mom and tried really hard not to laugh. *I'm going to bite her too*, I thought. My mom was mortified.

"¡*Ay Dios mio*! I so sorry, Meester mailman! I sink so that joo has de money, and I no put the stamp! *Valgame Dios, ¡qué pena*! Okay, es no problem. I give stamp to joo, meester. Right now." Mr. Mailman had calmed down and was now laughing at my mom.

"It's okay, Miss Casta...Miss Casa...Miss..."

"Mrs. Castellanos, meester. Plees, come in. I give joo some Hawaiian Froot Punch for to drink, okay?"

"Okay, lady."

My mom signed up for English classes the next day, and two days later, Mr. Mailman delivered her check from the inchoorans company. She was so happy.

The kids couldn't take their eyes off me as I told the story. I got really into it. I'd been telling stories about my mom just about my whole life, so it was easy. They started giggling when I imitated my mom's accent, and by the end of the story, they were falling out of their chairs. They asked me to tell them another story.

"I will if you behave for the rest of the day."

Halfway through the lesson, Tevaris, who was sitting behind Ebony, turned to his right and started saying something to DiAngelo. I was just about to reprimand him when Ebony interrupted me. She turned around in her seat and yelled, "Quit playin', T. Miss C ain't gonna tell us a story about her momma if you don't keep your mouth shut!"

The rest of the class spoke up on Ebony's behalf.

"Yeah, T, we wanna hear another story, man. Shut up."

"Come on, yo, be quiet. Miss C gonna tell us somethin' else about her crazy momma if we good."

Finally, finally, there was something I could use to keep their attention. Thank you, Matt. I'd found my groove.

# Chapter 9

My mom has a great laugh. She opens her mouth and nothing comes out of it for a few seconds, after which a dry raspy sound fills up the room and compels everyone to laugh. Just listening to her laugh makes me howl, even if I don't know what on earth she's so amused by. She also has her very own sense of fashion. When I say *very own* I mean nobody else can manage to concoct the outfits she puts together. She'll wear purple pants, a green shirt and brown shoes and think she walked out of Vogue. Her sunglasses are always way too big for her small face, which makes her look like a poorly dressed mosquito, but you can't tell her to take them off because she swears they protect her eyes from the sun. *Yeah, your eyes and just about your whole body too.*

She has a fascination with shoes. Payless Shoe Store was the best thing ever created, in her opinion. Boxes and boxes fill up her closet; red shoes, zebra striped shoes, leopard print shoes, all of which she wears with gold shirts and huge earrings. Sometimes I'd try to enlighten her, but seeing her face go from ecstatic to deflated would kill me and I'd concede that, yes, the red striped sandals go great with the silver purse and the yellow dress two sizes too big for her.

The one thing I love about her most is the way she can tell a story. We'll get to a party and within minutes she will be the life of it. She's not an attention hog; on the contrary, she tries remain quiet and unnoticed even though her clothes scream, *"Look at me!"* Part of the reason she gets away with funny clothes is because she's so damn beautiful. She keeps her hair short, but it's a beautiful, golden brown color and naturally wavy. She always runs her fingers through it as she entertains everyone with stories about either herself or her family. And everyone always eggs her on.

I guess I got my ability to tell a story from her. Thank God for that gene.

And boy can she dance. An eternal bubble of energy and spunk. No matter the music, she can move to it. Swing, rock and roll, salsa, merengue, cumbia.

She's even brave enough to dance to hip hop, a truly laughing matter. She's gotten older, but it's made no difference to her energy level. Mind you, this is always a product of a few tequila shots. She never drinks unless there's music and dancing involved and to get her to have that first shot is always a mission. But one shot is all it takes to get her going. My Uncle Lingero will run after her with a bottle of tequila and a shot in hand.

"*Vamos*, Isabela, *un tequila*."

"*No, no, y no*. No, please, no drinking for me, okay? I no like."

"*Dale, chica*, only one."

After a few prompts, my mom will give in and do the shot. Fifteen minutes later, she'll be running around the party with the bottle, inviting everyone to join her on the highway to Drunken State. By the end of the night, long after everyone has either left or passed out, she will still be going a hundred miles an hour, dancing by herself or trying to get everyone else to join her. And in the morning, she always says the same thing.

"Es the last time I drink tequila. *Ay Dios mio*," she says as she holds her head, "es terrible. I no like to drink no more."

She loves her music, too. When she cleans the house, she throws in a tape of Vicente Fernandez, a Mexican version of Elvis Presley. She sings to herself as she cleans the bathroom, mops the floor, does the laundry, all the things she's done her whole life. And she doesn't complain as long as Vicente's with her for the ride.

When it comes to food, any restaurant will do because it means she doesn't have to cook anything. Her favorites are Chinese and McDonald's, in that order. I used to try to take her to fancier restaurants, but I could always tell she felt uncomfortable and out of place, a feeling I knew all too well. So we'd settle for a couple of Big Macs or chow mein and be done with it. When we were kids, sometimes we'd drive all the way down to Homestead where the Mexican migrant workers live. Best Mexican food outside of Mexico, in my opinion. We couldn't take her to El Torito or Taco Bell because she'd scoff and say it wasn't "real" Mexican food. So we'd drive the hour down to Homestead and let her feel at home once in a while. I know it's hard for her to be surrounded by so many Hispanic cultures other than her own. And yet, she never complains. One Sunday a month is all she needs to get in touch with her roots. That and a few shots of tequila at Christmas.

I love my mom more than anything in this world. There's nothing I won't do for her. Whenever I see women my mom's age sitting at a bus top, I'm almost compelled to stop my car and give them a ride. I always think, *Gosh, that's someone's mom, and she looks so tired.* I hate imagining my mom at a bus stop by herself. Something about the vision makes me terribly sad. She's too sweet and caring and generous and understanding to be sitting at a bus stop.

But damn, she can be an airhead.

She comes home and puts her purse in the fridge, her keys in the freezer and the mail in the utensil drawer. One time, she came home, grabbed the milk carton on the kitchen counter and put it on top of the fridge. She managed to remember to close the refrigerator door. She's not dumb or slow, just focused on something else. On what, we don't know. How she manages to make it home without pulling into someone else's driveway remains a mystery. She lives in another world, one she miraculously comes out of when she has to cook dinner or do the ironing.

Every time I called her from Orlando was an event in and of itself, because she would never remember where I was or what I was doing.

"Hi, Mami."

"*Aló, mi'ja,* how are joo?"

"I'm good, Mami, I just got home from work."

"Oh, jes, bery good. *Pero,* where joo working now?"

I'd sigh. "I'm a teacher, Mami, remember?"

"Oh, jes, of course, baby. *Pero,* joo no work as bartender no more?"

"No, Mami, I quit that job six months ago, remember?"

"Aha. So, no more cruise chips?"

"*Ay Dios mio,* no, Mami. That was two years ago."

"Aha, jes. How joo like Tampa?"

"Mami, I live in Orlando, not Tampa."

She would laugh whole heartedly. "Oh, jes, *mi'ja,* I so sorry, I no remember."

She can be ditzy, but she has amazing talent for bingo and poker and she loves to gamble. She can play just about anything. Dominoes, bridge, poker, gin rummy, even war. The only time her mind is completely in tune with the world is when there are cards and money involved.

She was playing poker one night when her water broke. She was nine months pregnant with yours truly. She refused to leave the table because she had a good hand. My father had to drag her from the poker table and take her to the hospital. She still holds this against him. My dad made the mistake of taking her to Vegas right after they got married. It was like taking a bulimic to a lavish buffet. He had to drag her out of there, too. I once brought up the idea of taking them on a cruise, but when I told my dad there were casinos and bingo onboard, he shook his head. He slipped me a twenty and told me not to mention the idea to my mom.

When I worked at Fridays, some of the guys used to get together on Monday nights for poker night. They never invited me because it was apparently a guy thing. I didn't care too much because I could never get into it. I didn't inherit the obsessive-gambler gene. But I suggested they let my mom play with them.

"Are you crazy?" Alex said.

"Come on, why not?"

"Bibi, we can't take your mom's money."

"Ha, that's what you think. My mom can really play poker."

He raised his eyebrows. "Really? All right, then. Set it up. But it has to be at your place because we can't bring your mom to one of our bachelor pads."

"All right, I'll ask her."

The words were barely out of my mouth before my mom agreed. She looked like a kid on her way to a candy store. My dad, although somewhat annoyed, played the good sport and didn't say a word.

Monday rolled around. My mom made refried beans, fresh salsa and homemade guacamole. If she didn't win, at least they'd remember her when they woke up the next morning with perpetual diarrhea. She ran around the kitchen getting everything ready, stopping to apply orange lipstick just as the doorbell rang. I answered the door. The guys streamed in, all of them looking embarrassed and ashamed of themselves, as though they'd just shown up at my house to rob us rather than to have an innocent game of poker.

They let my mom spoil them. She doted on them like long lost sons as they wolfed down chips and salsa, chips and guacamole, chips and beans. I opened the fridge to make sure we had an emergency back-up of Pepto Bismol. My mom quickly set up the table for the game. I sat off to one side with my dad, who looked amused. We both knew what was going to happen.

Three hours later, the guys walked out of the house, no longer embarrassed or ashamed. They walked out with their tails between their legs because they'd just been given the ass whooping of their lives.

They never asked my mom to play poker with them again. Big shocker.

Technological advances confuse her. When we installed a three way line on the phone, we tried to explain it to her, but she couldn't understand how she could speak to two people at the same time. Such a thing was impossible. The first time she heard the call waiting signal, she got scared and simply hung up the phone. When it rang, she screamed. I don't know what she was thinking. *Did she think the phone was trying to kill her?* Trying to explain email and the world wide web was out of the question. Never mind the world of cell phones, fax machines, palm pilots and DVD players.

Both my mom and dad can understand enough English to have a conversation, but whenever they'd get anything in the mail that looked official, they'd have me look it over. I'd make phone calls for them, fill out paperwork, tear up offers for credit cards. I'd think, *How did you survive when we were kids?*

Logically, I became their personal travel agent. I'd tell them they could call the airline and ask for someone who speaks Spanish, but they'd shake their heads.

"No, no, *mi'ja*, joo do it," my mom would say.

"But why, Mami? It's so easy. You can do it."

"No, I get nerbus. Please, joo call for me and make de reserbaychun."

The first time I booked their tickets online all hell broke loose.

"*¿Qué?* Joo did it on de computer?"

I was sitting at my computer in my apartment, looking over the details.

"Yeah, Mami, don't worry, it's fine."

"*Pero*, how I going to get the ticket?"

"Mami, relax. They're going to send me the flight information via email."

"Email? What is, *mi'ja*?"

"It's hard to explain, Mami, but trust me, they're going to send it to me on my computer."

"*Pero*, how joo get the tickets to me?"

"They're electronic, Mami."

"What?"

"Look, just trust me. I will mail the information to you, okay?"

"*Bueno*, if joo say so, *pero* I no think es okay."

Three flights later they were convinced I knew that I was doing.

She loves to go shopping. Doesn't matter for what, either. I'll casually say, "Hey, Mami, I need a new beach towel." My mom will grab her gigantic sunglasses, pull her purse out of the fridge and say, "Okay, less go chopeeng." Like my dad, she struggles with the pronunciation of certain letters. "Ch" replaces "sh," the letter "j" replaces "y," so on and so forth. At least she tries.

When we were kids, she would lose her temper sometimes, but aside from that, she was a pretty good sport. She'd play Barbies with me and pretend she was having the time of her life. She probably was because she never had a

Barbie as a child. She also loves board games. Trouble, Monopoly, Chutes and Ladders, Candy Land, Hi-Ho Cherry O, Life.

And oh, yeah, Scrabble.

I had a minimal social life in college. I went out once in a while after work so long as I didn't have class the next morning, but that was about it. Most nights, when I wasn't working, I'd come home from school, do a little bit of studying and then set up the Scrabble board. My playing partner was Jacqueline, a cousin who lived two doors down. At the time she was only thirteen, but to us the age difference didn't exist. I would talk to her about school, bartending, boys, everything. She would sit and listen to me and offer me feedback.

"Yeah, I agree," she would say, "you should stick to International Relations." Or she'd say, "Well, from what you told me, John seems like a nice guy, but maybe you should give it some time." And all this while she tried to get a Double Word or a Triple Letter.

My mom would sit off to the side with her Word Search puzzles, stopping only to glance at us once in a while. Before we'd start a new game, I'd offer her a chance to play because I knew she secretly wanted to.

"Mami, you wanna play?"

She would look up from her Word Search, push her gigantic reading glasses up to the top of her nose and shake her head. "No, *mi'ja*, I no sink so. I no bery good."

"All right, Mami, but you can change your mind."

"Jes, *mi'ja*, I know."

One day, I had a brainstorm.

"Hey, Mami, why don't we make it bilingual Scrabble? You can do words in Spanish!"

For the first time, she looked hopeful. "Jes?"

"Yeah, Mami, it'll be fun. You put down words in Spanish and Jacqueline and I will do English, okay?"

"Come on, Isabela," Jacqueline said. "I know you wanna play, *chica*."

She gave in.

It took me two seconds to explain the rules because Super Focused Mom had been watching the whole time.

"Jes, jes, I got it, okay, baby?"

I didn't know what to expect. My heart broke when she put down her first word. Cat. I reminded her she could do words in her own language.

"No, es okay. I want to try de English, too."

"All right, Mami, whatever you say."

We were creaming her but she didn't care. She kept putting down words like mop and top and sit. I was proud of her for trying to keep up.

It was my turn. The letters in front of me were failing to come together. I considered putting down "car" because I was getting too frustrated. Before I had a chance to do anything, my mom, who'd been staring at her letters as though trying to solve the mystery of the Holy Grail, jumped up and nearly hit the ceiling. Jacqueline and I jumped two seconds after.

"¡*Ay Dios mio*! I have de best word!"

"Okay, Mami, hold on. Let me do my word first."

But it was impossible to concentrate after her explosion. I ended up putting "car" on the board because I was dying to know what she'd come up with.

"Okay, Mami, your turn."

She bit her lip and looked at me. She took her sweet time in placing the letters on the board, right on a double word tile. One by one she laid them down as though she couldn't believe she'd been so clever.

"B-E-R-D-A-, and Y!" She clapped her hands and lit up a cigarette.

Jacqueline and I looked at each other, looked at the word, then looked at my mom. She had a silly grin on her face. The mosquito looked so happy. I cleared my throat.

"Mami, what is that?" I could already feel the laughter building up. I tried not to look at Jacqueline because I could tell she was ready to lose it.

"What joo mean, *mi'ja*? Berday."

"Ber-day?"

"*Sí, mi'ja*, like, joo know, *Happy Berday to Joo, Happy Berday to joo, Happy Berday to Bibita, Happy Berday to joo!*"

It was too much. One look at Jacqueline and we were on the floor. My mom, who should've been offended, started laughing. Her mouth opened and her face turned red and I swear I could practically see the laughter on its way out. It burst into the kitchen and destroyed us for ten minutes. When I couldn't take it anymore, when my stomach felt as though I'd just done three hundred sit-ups, I calculated her score. No way in hell was I going to take "berday" away from her. She had just created a new version of Scrabble. Jacqueline and I dubbed it "Ghetto Spanish Scrabble."

She played with us every night after that. She used words like "choogar" for "sugar," "jes" for "yes," "choos" for "shoes." To this day, I can't play a game of Scrabble or listen to the birthday song without thinking of her.

I have no single complaint about her, bad clothes and all. Not only was she my only friend as a child, she was my personal chauffeur.

"Mami, can you take me to the library?"

"*Claro*. Let's go."

"Mami, can we go to the movies on Saturday? I want to see *Karate Kid*."

"*Sí, mi'ja*, we will go."

"Mami, can you make enchiladas today?"

"Jes, my choogar, whateber joo want."

"Mami, can we go to the movies? I want to see *Karate Kid* again."

"Oh, jes, me too. Okay."

She denied me very little.

The day we were moving into the huge home near Westwood Lake, my dad announced the previous owners had left their sixty-five-year-old upright piano behind. Well, they didn't actually leave it. My dad bought it for about a hundred bucks, a lot of money back then. For me, it was love at first sight. The upright Kimball called to me the minute we walked in the door. Ten seconds later, I was signed up for piano lessons.

Piano made sense to me like open heart surgery makes sense to a doctor. Sheet music was like a code I found easy to break. It was another challenge, another game, another marvelous way of annoying Erasmo. Nothing could've made my parents more proud, not straight A's, not a trophy in bowling, not an award for spelling. The ability to play the piano went above and beyond what they'd expected of me, and they bragged about me to everyone.

My mom would drive me once a week to Zaida Moreno's house in Little Havana. Every Wednesday at three, I would sit with Zaida in her tiny apartment while she told me to *sit up straight keep your hands flat keep up to the tempo don't slouch don't slouch coño I said don't slouch*. Zaida thought I was the bee's knees. I never gave much thought as to whether or not I was good. I just loved sitting at the piano and letting my hands roam all over the keys, in awe of the way notes came together and created such beautiful sounds. But she'd always fawn over me and fill my already-huge head with praises. She made me believe I was truly talented. Different. Not just a fat kid.

My whole family believed my talent for music was in the genes. My dad claimed I got it from my grandfather Paco. My mom swore it had to be from my Uncle Antonio. Uncle Antonio used to get drunk at parties and pull out his guitar. He'd always play the same song, "Hotel California." But he couldn't really play and he couldn't really sing so my dad would argue back and say

I definitely got it from Grandpa Paco, who'd never picked up an instrument in his whole life.

Cuba versus Mexico versus Cuba versus Mexico.

My mom would always buy me something after my piano lesson. She wouldn't take me to the mall and spend five hundred dollars on me. The reward always revolved around food, no surprise. She would take me to McDonald's or Burger King or Pizza Hut or Dairy Queen. I would eat my treat on the way home. We'd drive back to Southwest Miami via Bird Road, right through the heart of Coral Gables. I loved that drive home. Coral Gables was full of beautiful Spanish style homes and streets shaded by overgrown Fica trees. I'd look out the window as I wolfed down my Big Mac and wonder what kind of people lived in those homes, and I'd wonder why we didn't have one. I'd let myself pretend I lived in one of those homes with a mom who didn't have to wear a uniform and a dad who didn't come home from work looking like he'd just been run over by a truck. Those massive homes and perfectly manicured lawns gave birth to my dreams. *Someday*, I would say, *I'm going to make enough money to buy my parents one of those homes.*

No matter their financial situation, my mom would always find a way to reward me for a straight A report card. She would put aside a little bit of money from every single one of her low paychecks. I would get a new lip gloss, a new pair of shoes, a new Barbie. It was her way of letting me know how proud she was. I didn't need gifts to get good grades, being that I was Super Geek, but it was still cool.

She'd also make an extra effort to get us name brand clothes, even though she'd tell us it was materialistic and ridiculous. We knew she was right, but we still wanted jeans made by Sergio Valente or Sassoon or Gloria Vanderbilt. We couldn't afford the real kind and this is where you appreciate a place like Miami, because no matter what it is you want, you better believe there's someone out there ready to sell you a great imitation. We wore imitation designer clothes and nobody ever knew the difference. Even my dad busted out and got himself a pair of fake designer jeans. He looked like a Cuban cowboy. However, the Sandal Queen stuck to her leopard print pants.

The year I was turning thirteen, gold nameplates were the thing to have, as though teenagers needed a reminder of who they were. God forbid you wore a nameplate around your neck that wasn't in either cursive or mock Chinese letters. I wanted a nameplate so bad it hurt, but I couldn't bring myself to ask for one. I knew my parents' financial limits and had gotten used to getting my clothes from Kmart. I figured a gold nameplate was really expensive, so I kept my wish to myself.

A few days before my birthday, my mom came into my room as I was getting ready for school. She was practically jumping up and down. She looked like a giant sized Mexican jumping bean.

"Oh, choogar, joo are going to love the present I get for joo!"

"Really?" I looked at her suspiciously. "Why?"

"Oh, joo will see!" She clapped her hands. "Es beautiful! Joo are going to love it!"

"Okay, Mami, but you didn't have to get me anything big."

"Oh, no, choogar, es no big, *pero* es bery nice." She jumped her way out of my room and left me with my enemy, the mirror.

The day rolled around. My birthday fell on a Sunday that year and we were going to celebrate at the beach with the rest of my Cuban family. As I slipped into my bathing suit, I could already hear Tia Josefina and Abuela Guillermina.

"Joo are getting more fat."

"Don't eat too much, eh? *Estás muy gorda.*"

I put them to the back of my mind and reminded myself I could go to jail for drowning someone. My mom came into my room with my birthday present and gave me a big hug. It was only six thirty in the morning but she was already borderline spastic.

"Come on, *mi'ja*, open it!"

"Okay, Mami, okay. Hold on, let me get my shorts on."

"No, no, no. Open now, please. Joo are going to love it!"

I gave in. I stood in front of my mom in my one piece whale suit and carefully tore off the wrapper. It was a jewelry box! *It can't be,* I thought. I held my breath as I opened it.

It was exactly what I had wished for. A gold nameplate in cursive letters. It was shiny and beautiful and cool and...*oh, shit,* I thought. I took a closer look at it and came to the startling realization that my sweet mom had spelled my name wrong. Instead of Bibiana, it said Viviana.

"Joo like it, *mi'ja*?" She smiled at me hopefully.

No way could I tell her she'd gotten my name wrong. I wasn't hurt, so why spoil her happiness? I could tell this present probably meant more to her than me. She was proud of herself.

"Mami, I love it!" I hugged her and quickly put it on. "I love it, Mami, and I can't wait to show everyone at school." As though I had five hundred friends or something.

Everything would've been fine had Tia Josefina not shown up at the beach. My brother and my dad had been warned not to say anything about the nameplate. Everyone decided to play along with it. Except my aunt. She loved pointing out mistakes, and my mom was always making them.

The minute she saw my gift, she announced loudly that my name was spelled wrong. My mom was over by the barbecue getting herself a piece of chicken. She turned when she heard Josefina.

"*Tia*, be quiet. It's fine. It's not wrong."

"*¿Qué?* No, no, no. That's no the way joo spell Bibiana."

My mom came over.

"*¿Qué pasa?*" She took a bite of her drumstick.

"Isabela, *¿qué te pasa, eh? No le pusiste el nombre bien, chica.*"

My mom looked at me for confirmation and I nodded.

"Why joo no tell me?" She didn't look hurt but I still felt like crying.

"Because I don't care, Mami. It doesn't matter how it's spelled. It's still my name, you know." I bit my lip and glared at my aunt. She smiled wickedly and walked away.

I looked back at my mom, who by now had devoured the entire drumstick, cartilage and all. I had to give her credit. No matter how hard Josefina tried, she could never get under my mom's skin. It's like everything she ever said to her would simply pass her by. She started laughing, amused at her ability to forget such a simple thing as how to spell my name. Soon, we were both laughing. I was relieved that she wasn't hurt, glad that I didn't ruin her one proud moment. She took the necklace back and had it changed anyway. Believe it or not, I still have it.

My mom rules.

# Chapter 10

A few days before I graduated from high school, my dad and I went for a walk after dinner. It was a ritual. We first started walking when I was thirteen, when I was convinced being skinny would solve all my social problems. Personality and charm meant nothing to me at that age, only a flat stomach and a body that didn't make me look like a potential linebacker for the football team.

My dad was more than happy to walk with me because it meant one thing: the freedom to fart in public. It was so embarrassing. We'd be walking along, saying hello to the neighbors, stopping to remark on this or that new plant. My dad would let it rip. No shame at all. It would've been okay if his farts were the silent but deadly kind, but they were unbelievably loud and more potent than any nuclear weapon. So help me God, sometimes I'd look at the flowers and see them wilting. Dogs would cross their eyes and lay down, neighbors would look at us and giggle. I tried many times to make him stop.

"Papi, please. Don't do that. It's so embarrassing!"

"No, no, everysing that comes from de body es natural."

There was absolutely nothing natural about him embarrassing the hell out of me. I was already an outcast, and the Fart Champion wasn't helping.

That day, he asked me what I wanted as a graduation present. I considered asking him to stop farting for the rest of his entire life but knew it was pointless. You can never defeat bowel movements.

"A gift? What do you mean? For what, Papi?"

"Joo know, for de graduation. I no can buy joo a car, but maybe I sink so I can give you somesing." My dad could not pronounce "th" to save his life. It was always replaced by an "s."

"Oh, I hadn't thought about that." In truth, I'd done nothing but think about it. I knew a lot of kids at my school would probably get a new car or a trip to Europe, but I also knew asking my parents for any such thing would make them feel bad.

"We could go see *abuela* in Mexico."

"Ah, okay."

"We could drive there, you know? A road trip." It was just an idea, but I was hoping he'd buy it.

"Drive to Mejico?"

"Yeah, Papi. Just imagine it. We could sell one of the cars and you could buy a van, an old one like Tio Santiago used to have in California. Drive from Miami to Guadalajara."

Silence. We kept walking along, swatting at mosquitos and wiping the sweat off our foreheads.

"Okay. We do that. We drive to Mejico and stay for two weeks, and then we sell de van and fly to Miami. Es a good idea."

"Really, Papi? Can we do that?"

"Jes, *mi'ja*, es no problem. I like de road trip, like you say. *Pero* plees, no take the keys from de hotel, okay?"

I was stunned. I'd never thought my dad would agree to the crazy plan, but he did and even looked happy about it.

"Okay, Papi. I'll help you look for a van."

We continued our walk and a few moments later he let out the loudest, smelliest fart of all. *Mexico, here we come.*

Two weeks later, after we'd bought the van, we set out on our road trip. My brother decided to stay back and keep the house safe (which meant more parties than you can imagine) while my mom, my dad and I drove through Florida, Alabama, Mississipi, Louisiana and finally Texas. By the time we got to the border of Mexico at Laredo, Texas, I was sure I would die from my dad's farts before I got to see my grandmother again. Two of my uncles, Ramon and Miguel, were waiting for us on the Mexican side. We picked them up just across the border and they helped my dad navigate the van all the way to Guadalajara.

The roads were relatively safe in Mexico, but some parts were kind of scary. We drove through areas where there were no streetlights and no yellow lights on the road to guide us at night. There were, however, a multitude of crucifixes placed alongside the highway, as though to guide us straight to heaven. I immediately thought people had placed them there at random, as though they'd been on a walk and said, "This looks like a good place for Jesus." I thought this out loud and Tio Miguel started laughing. He explained their real significance (death at that particular point) and I looked around the van for a hole to crawl into. I felt so stupid. When it came to books and school,

I excelled in every subject, but like my brother would say, "Common sense is the least common of your senses, dumb ass."

It took us three days to get to Guadalajara, long enough for me to consider getting an oxygen mask for the next time. If there ever was a next time. When we parked the van in front of my grandmother's house in downtown Guadalajara, a group of anxious relatives awaited us. Okay, it wasn't just a group. To be honest, it looked like the population of a small country. My mom has sixteen brothers and sisters, all of whom took "be faithful and procreate" to a higher level. I had cousins in Los Angeles but they paled in comparison to the amount of cousins I had in Mexico, some of whom lived with my grandmother. Sandra, Maria, Lourdes, Ximena, Guadalupe, Mario, Kenya, and Carla all lived with my grandmother. Their own mother, my Aunt Bianca, had passed away at the age of thirty-three. She had gone in for a routine tube-tying operation and ended up getting too much anesthesia. "God was sending us a message," my cousin Lourdes said to me. "Birth control is the work of the devil." I could see where my mom got her "sign" theory from.

After two weeks of eating tacos from a street vendor and sitting on the doorstep talking to my cousins about America, my dad came to me one morning, cigarette and lighter in hand, and told me it was time to go. The van was sold, the mission accomplished. My dad had to get back to work. My mom had loved spending time with her family, but she, too, had to get back to work. Summer school was right around the corner and the school cafeteria awaited her.

"Bibi, ees time to go," my dad said to me that morning.

"Uh, okay, but can I stay?"

"Stay? *Pero*, for what?"

"I'm not ready to go back. I want to stay here for a while."

"Oh. How long joo want to stay?"

"I don't know. Until I run out of money?" I'd worked a part time job at Pizza Hut throughout high school and had about five hundred dollars saved up, which to me meant I could stay there forever.

"Oh. Joo no want to go to college?"

"No. Not yet. I don't know what I want to study anyway. I just want to have fun for a while, you know, Dad? Live a little." I thought my dad would be crushed by the news. I had three full scholarships to study music thanks to the help of Doc. Turning them down was probably the dumbest thing I could've done, but back then it didn't matter. I was determined to do something different for a change. Something unexpected of me. He sighed as he put the cigarette in his mouth and lit it up. As he took his first drag, he squinted his eyes and looked at me. He exhaled the smoke and shrugged his shoulders. I thought for sure he'd say no. But my dad's never been like that, never one to say no unless it's something he knows will be bad for me. "Okay, joo want to stay, joo stay. *Pero* when de money is over, joo come home. Be nice to your *abuela*, okay?"

"Okay, Papi, I will."

"Okay, I tell your mami. She's going to be bery upset."

"Thanks, Papi." I got up and hugged him.

He held me tight and kissed me on the cheek. "*Ten cuidado, mi'ja.*"

"Don't worry, Papi, I'll be very careful. Promise."

And with that, I buried the nerd for good. The nerd never would've done such a thing. The nerd would have gone back to Miami, gone to college, continued being the good kid, the overachiever, the perfectionist. There was no room for the nerd in Mexico. Only the new thin me with the wild streak.

My mom cried uncontrollably when we said goodbye. I put on a brave face and told her not to worry. It was the first time in seventeen years that we would be apart for more than a few hours. She gave me her blessing with tears in her eyes and told me she was going to miss me. I hugged her little body tightly and promised I wouldn't do anything stupid.

Never make promises you know you won't keep.

After the first few weeks, I started to think five hundred dollars was going to last me more than a year. Everything was so cheap. I spent money on bus rides to small villages outside the city (my grandmother loved to send me on errands) or on six-packs of beer for my uncles. I treated my cousins to *paletas*, *taquitos, aguas frescas* and *fresas con crema,* a day at the ice skating rink inside the Hyatt hotel, a day at the zoo. I never counted my stash but it never felt like I was spending a fortune. And my cousins thought I was rich. To them, relatives from *el otro lado* who were able to afford a flight down south were more than well off.

If they only knew.

My grandmother, seven female cousins, two aunts, one old dog and a paranoid schizophrenic uncle lived on the second floor of a building in Sector Reforma, a short walk from El Centro. The house had five small bedrooms, a very sorry-looking bathroom and an ancient kitchen. There was a water tank on the rooftop, and whenever you wanted to take a hot shower, you had to throw combustibles into the heater in the bathroom and wait a few minutes for the water to heat up. That's if there was water in the tank to begin with. With so many people living under one roof, getting your turn in the bathroom required a lot of patience. Usually I went last, because I didn't have a job or anything to do except help my grandmother find her pocketbook among the scattered clothes and endless amount of dirty dishes.

My grandmother is a remarkable woman. She had her first kid at the age of thirteen and didn't stop popping them out until she was forty-seven. Shocking, I know, but this was Mexico, where having a kid never meant sitting down and looking at a bank account statement to determine if you were financially ready. Never mind the Catholic factor. No birth control for my grandmother. I never met my grandfather because he died before I was born. I once asked my grandmother why she stopped at seventeen children, and to my surprise, she said, "Your grandfather died, *mi'ja.*" She looked at me seriously for a moment and then started laughing, as though she realized she probably would have ended up having two dozen kids. I though it would've been a funny thing to say to someone. "I have two dozen kids" as opposed to "I have two brats."

My grandfather died of alcoholism after spending a lifetime trying to make a living for his large family. "Well, he didn't really try too hard," my grandmother would say. "He was much better at spending money on booze and sleeping with other women." She didn't look tired or bitter when she said this, simply resigned to her lot in life. As though this was to be expected of all women.

No matter how tough her life had been, she had an incredible amount of energy. She seemed to outlast everyone. She would wake up before anyone else and start making *frijoles fritos* and fresh tortillas for breakfast. Before I'd even have the chance to wash my face or brush my teeth, she'd drag me to the local *mercado* to buy whatever she needed for the day. Fresh fruit, chicken, meat, milk, eggs.

Whereas my mom is shy and timid, my grandmother is her polar opposite. She is afraid of nothing and nobody. Everyone in the Mercado knew her as Lupe, short for Guadalupe, and as we'd walk through the market, everyone from the fruit vendor to the local *borrachos* would say hello to her. The queen of her own barrio. She never questioned my decision to stay with her. In fact, she'd say how much she admired my courage. She would tell me we have the same wandering soul, the same desire to see the world. Of course, she had never had the chance. They were, to put it mildly, piss poor. No trips to Europe for Lupe.

Her face is lined with wrinkles, lines on her face and hands that represent all she has lived, all she has endured and suffered, including the loss of one of her daughters, my Aunt Bianca. Most days, after everyone had left for work and we'd finally found her dentures somewhere in the chaos, we would sit at the kitchen table and talk. I would ask her questions about my family and she'd answer them as though she'd waited all her life to be on my private talk show. Even though she could never remember where she'd set things down, her memory for all other things is sharp and intact. We would sit in the tiny kitchen drinking instant coffee while she took me back into her life, her history, her face animated and alive as she told me stories about her children and what Mexico was like when she was a child. Mostly I loved hearing about my mom. I asked a lot of questions about her because I wanted to know what she'd been like before she'd experimented with orange lipstick and perfected sandal throwing.

To my surprise, my mom had a similar childhood to mine. She was never picked on for being fat, but because she was shy and gullible and ready to believe people were inherently good, other kids took advantage of her. She was clumsy and forever tripping over something. Her clothes were hand me downs and her shoes were always falling apart. She was picked on a lot and pushed around by other girls, but instead of fighting back, she would say nothing and simply come home to Lupe and cry. She had no friends and spent most of her time looking after her younger brothers and sisters, making sure they'd had something to eat. She was very close to my grandmother growing up, so close that when my grandmother told her she had to move to Los Angeles to be with her older sister Esmeralda, the separation nearly destroyed her. As much as she fought the idea of living on "the other side," my mom reluctantly got on a train and head north. She never returned to Mexico to live. She met my dad, fell in love and stayed in America to pursue a better life. To chase the American dream.

Those sad stories about my mom would make me want to get on a plane and fly home. They would make me miss her terribly and ache for her warmth. I'd always thought my mom had been born with rollers in her hair and a funny accent, never once imagining that she had often gone hungry and tired from so much responsibility. To me, my mom was that crazy lady who'd mispronounce things and then laugh at herself. The woman who would drop everything and cheer me up if I was upset about something. The woman who never complained about not having a moment to herself. The thought that my mom had once been sad or hungry made my stomach turn.

My grandmother showed me pictures of her when she was a child, old black and white snapshots worn away at the edges. She was a very pretty little girl in spite of the rags she was wearing. She was always smiling in these pictures, a skinny little girl with straight brown hair and dimples. I saw no traces of worry in her sweet face; only innocence and unadulterated happiness, as though having to care for her brothers and sisters was perfectly normal. The nerd inside me would kick me and curse me for staying in Mexico, but I'd quickly bury her even further. I was on a mission.

Although Lupe has more energy than a classroom full of kindergarten kids, she would take a break in the afternoon and have her siesta. After too many cups of instant coffee, the last thing I'd want to do was sleep. I'd leave her to her nap and walk around the city with my little notebook, prepared to write every thought that came into my head. I never wrote a damn thing, though. I would get too caught up in watching people to sit down and write everything bouncing around in my head. Whenever I did stop to write, every thought I'd had for the past two hours would vanish from my mind and I would sit there staring at my journal willing it to give me some kind of inspiration. It never did. I doodled and scribbled a whole mess of nonsense. It was clear to me that I wasn't cut out to be a writer. Not yet, anyway. The revelation that I would want to sit down one day and write would come to me years later. For the time being though, I was a wanderer with an empty journal and a heart full of dreams.

I'd walk the streets of Guadalajara on most days in a stupor, amazed that I was doing such an unexpected thing in my thus far nerdy life. I'd look at people and wonder what their lives were like, what their families were like, where they lived, who they loved. I'd stop and stare at old buildings and imagine what they must have looked like hundreds of years ago. *Probably the same*, I would think. Dark skinned men and women with adorable kids would stare at me curiously. I was half Mexican but I looked every bit American. My clothes seemed to scream "tourist" and the fact that I was a seventeen-year-old girl walking around alone was enough for people to want to stare. Their stares only reinforced my desire to do something different. I liked standing out for once.

I would walk through Mercado San Juan de Dios, a giant market that catered to both locals and tourists, a place where you could buy anything from a fake "Hard Rock" t-shirt to a steaming bowl of *menudo*. Vendors would see me as I came close to their stalls and go into a frenzy. It seemed like a competition to see who could yell the loudest at the American tourist. They made your average salesman look like a rookie. At first, I would smile and say, "No, thank you," but after a few weeks they started grinding on my nerves. They would try to say something in English until I'd turn to them and say something in Spanish so they'd stop harassing me.

"*Oh, ¿eres Mejicana?*" They would say.

"*Claro que sí.*"

"*Andale pues, guerita.*"

From there I would walk through Plaza Tapatia, an enormous plaza full of people walking to and from work and groups of American tourists in Hawaiian shirts and way too large cameras. Sometimes, because I ached to speak English, I would stop and talk to them. Timid I was not, I was starting to discover.

One day I walked up to man in a Hard Rock New York t-shirt. He was standing with a group of tourists whose cameras looked like weapons they were so huge. "Hello, there. Where are you from?"

"Oh, you an American?" He looked pleased to see another Yankee.

"Yes, but I'm staying here with my grandmother. My mom's Mexican."

The group came and stood around me. I felt like a movie star.

Hard Rock Man smiled sincerely. "Wow, that's great. We're all from Wyoming."

"Wyoming? Cool. How do you like Mexico?"

"It's beautiful. The people are so friendly here. What a nice experience for you, huh? Where's home?"

"Miami."

"Miami, huh? Great. Well, are you homesick yet?"

This question always made me stop and think. *Am I? Not really. Not yet.*

"Nah. Sometimes I miss a few things, but I like it here for now."

"Oh. Are you in college?" A painful reminder.

"Nuh-uh. Don't know what I wanna do." I'd smile and try to look wise and deep, like a world traveler with intense observations. I must have looked like a moron.

"Well, you've got the rest of your life to figure that out, don't ya?"

*Yes I do*, I remember thinking. "Yep, you're right! I'll figure it out eventually."

"Good for you, dear. I'm sure you'll have a great time. But hey, don't drink the water!"

"Ha, I'll keep that in mind. Have a great trip!"

I walked away and thought, *Silly man, everyone knows Montezuma's revenge only attacks white people.*

As much as I liked talking to my grandmother and helping her find things she'd misplaced (her pocketbook, her glasses, her bra, her teeth), I was growing restless. I wanted to see more of the country. I wanted to continue burying the fat nerd. The more outlandish the adventure, the further away I'd get from her. I would think about this at night as I sat on the rooftop of the house and stared at the lights of the city. I'd look far into the distance and see the mountains and wonder what lay beyond them, what new parts of me awaited my discovery. As the days went on, I fell more in love with my new life. *I'm going to start all over again*, I'd think. *Reinvent myself into something out of this world.*

But in order to do that, I had to keep moving. Keep venturing, keep exploring this new me. I'd already been to most of the surrounding villages riding on very old school buses that posed as proper transportation. The bus drivers would steer these old buses as though they once dreamed of being race car drivers. The fact that I could have died in a terrible accident never phased me. When you're young, you tend to think you're invincible and incapable of dying. Ah, ignorance is bliss.

I would sit surrounded by shy women who didn't know what to make of the young girl with headphones in her ear, surrounded by chickens and more chickens and older men who would sneak looks at the "gringa" from the "other side." More than once, I'd catch someone looking at me, checking out my clothes, clothes that were probably made in a factory somewhere in their own country. I'd smile at them and say, *"Buenos dias."* They'd timidly smile back and utter good morning, their eyes looking everywhere else but directly at me.

My grandmother and I were sitting in the kitchen one morning when I told her I wanted to go to the west coast. I was fascinated with the Pacific Ocean because it was the first ocean I'd seen as a child. Something called me to it, an old memory. When I was five, we all piled into my Tio Santiago's van and drove down to Guadalajara. All of us (cousins, aunts, uncles, the dog) hopped on an old Greyhound bus (we were too many for the van) with enough food to feed a small army. We headed for a small fishing village on the west coast of Mexico. We camped on the beach in tents and spent four days in Melaque, swimming in the freezing cold water and eating fresh fish.

We ate *paletas* while my brother and I taught our Mexican cousins how to build a sand castle, the ice cream dripping down on our chins and onto the sand as we frantically tried to keep the water from washing away our creation. I don't remember any American tourists, any McDonald's, any Hyatts.

Melaque was a vacation spot for families from the city who wanted to bask in the sun and jump into the small waves crashing along the shoreline. It was a memory I had always held onto and I wanted to go back and see it all over again, remember a time when my Aunt Bianca was still alive, a time when life was simple and innocent.

My grandmother didn't say anything as I told her my plan. I told her I would go to Melaque for a few days and have a look around. From there I would get on another bus and head north to another beach town. "And from there, who knows?" I said. I promised to be careful, swore to call her any chance I got and practically got down on my knees and begged. No need for me to beg, though, because she smiled and put her hands in the air. "Sí, mi'ja, está bien." She let me go, only if I promised never to mention anything to my mom, who would've fainted at the thought of her daughter traveling anywhere by herself, even if it was her own country.

The next morning, my Uncle Miguel took me to the bus station and helped me buy my ticket. He asked me over and over again if I was sure I wanted to go. Eventually he gave up when he realized I was on some weird mission. He must have thought all Americans are crazy. He blessed me before I got on the bus and shook his head as I hugged him. I took my place on the bus and immediately put my headphones on. I waved to him as the bus pulled out of the station. I had a huge smile on my face.

The bus ride was about five hours long and took us through some of the most amazing scenery I'd ever seen. It was lush and tropical, mountains and mountains of green. A jungle that held promise of adventure. It was so different to Miami, where every mountain was made of concrete. The old bus sputtered as it went up and up until I thought for sure we were never going to come down. The narrow road was steep, the curves dangerously sharp, and still I was not afraid. I felt like a world traveler embarking on an important mission, a writer with a story to find, a teenage kid with no direction but a whole lot of guts.

When I arrived in Melaque, I didn't really know what to do so I did the first thing that came to mind: *find something to eat.* The village was just as I remembered it. The houses were more like shacks put together at the last minute, the streets looked as though they'd been dug up only the day before and as in most Mexican villages, a plaza with a gazebo took center stage. I found the local *mercado* and walked around taking it all in. The sun, the sound of waves crashing, children laughing and following me around.

The world traveler in me loved it but I started to panic when I realized there was no place for me to sleep except under the stars with an old blanket my grandmother had shoved into my bag when I wasn't looking. She had also packed a few sandwiches and fresh fruit. I got a lump in my throat when I thought of her. Before panic got the best of me, I stopped at a stall where a plump older lady was selling chopped coconut in little plastic bags. *Yum.* I bought one from her and smiled. I got up the nerve to ask her where I could find a place to stay. She looked me up and down, confused by the question.

"Where to stay?" she said in Spanish.

"Yes, is there a hotel here maybe?" I was hoping that in the more than ten years since we'd been there, somebody had thought to build one. I was wrong.

"No, *mi'ja*, there's no hotel here. This is not a tourist beach." She looked worried. "Are you here alone, *guerita*?" *Guerita* means "blondie" in Spanish.

"Yes. I came from Guadalajara." She could see that I looked positively terrified. *So much for being a world traveler*, I thought.

"*Ay Dios mio, hija*, you shouldn't be traveling alone, a young girl like you. Come back here at five when I'm finished with my day and I'll take you to my house. It's very small and I have six children, but you'll be safe and warm, eh?"

I thought it over for half a second. *What are my options?*

"Okay, *gracias. Muchas gracias, señora.*"

"*Sí, mi'ja, andale pues.*"

I couldn't believe she was going to let a total stranger like me stay with her. When I was a kid, my mom refused to let me go to any slumber parties and if she'd known what I was up to back then she probably would've had a heart attack. It was only two o'clock and I had three hours to kill, so I went and sat on the beach. Little kids came up to me every five minutes trying to sell me something. Mango on a stick, an umbrella, hollowed out conch shells, whatever they could to make some money. They were so sweet looking, those kids, and although I wanted to buy something from all of them, I didn't have as much money as I'd thought. I would never survive for long if I started buying souvenirs I'd probably lose anyway.

Besides, mango gave me diarrhea.

I sat there and watched everyone around me, who in turn watched me. I tried hard not to stare, tried to keep me eyes focused on the horizon, tried to think about something other than the fact that all eyes were basically on me. I didn't like being a movie star *that* much. But I noticed how happy everyone looked in spite of their humble surroundings. They looked like they were enjoying every second of their break from whatever struggle they were going through. *These people are living*, I thought, *really sucking it up*. I thought about what my cousin Lourdes had said to me when I asked her why everything shut down for two hours in the afternoon.

"They don't do that in America?" she asked.

"No way. Nothing ever seems to close, not even on Sundays."

"*Hijole*, not even on Sundays?! You mean people work on that day? What about the holidays? Easter? Christmas?"

"Lourdes, everyone works all the time in America. That's just how it is. You know, they're all chasing the American Dream." I said it as though it was a crime.

"The American Dream? What's that?"

"Well, it's something like this. You try to do really good in school so you can get into college. You go to college and study really hard so you can graduate and get a piece of paper that will help you get a steady job with benefits."

"What do you mean 'benefits'?"

"Benefits. You know, health insurance and stuff like that, so you don't have to pay for anything when you see a doctor."

"You have to pay to see a doctor if you don't have insurance? Why?"

"I don't know. That's just the way it is."

"We get free health care here. We never have to pay for anything like that. So what happens if you get sick and you don't have insurance?"

"You get to sit in an emergency room in a hospital for a long time before anyone sees you, and then they hand you a bill. It's usually a lot of money."

Lourdes looked baffled. "Okay, so, what happens after you get the job with benefits? Is that the American Dream?"

"Oh, no, not quite. You get a nice job with some company and then work really hard so they'll promote you. When you get promoted, you get your own office and secretary and by then you're married to someone with a nice job, too. You buy a big house together in a safe neighborhood, have a few kids, a cute dog, two nice cars and vacation twice a year somewhere."

"And then what?"

"And then what? Well, you keep working until you're old enough to retire, keep trying to get a better promotion or a better job somewhere else, keep trying to make more money so you can buy more things."

"Things like what?" She loved to ask questions.

"Oh, you know, a boat, a second home, an island, whatever. Somewhere along the way, you've made enough money to put your kids through college, and then they start it all over again. By the time you retire, you have enough money in the bank to live on, and then you get to live your life however you want. Voila!" The idea that I might end up doing that very same thing sent shivers down my spine. *No, no, no*, I said to myself, *I want to be different. I want my life to be spectacular.*

"Oh, that's kind of sad."

"Well, that's the American Dream, and that's why many places stay open on Sundays. You understand?"

"Yes, I understand. In America, people live to work. Here in Mexico, people work to live. To eat. To stay alive and keep your family together, but work is not the most important thing to us. We always make time to enjoy life with whatever little money we have. So what happens to all that money you save when you die? You can't take it with you, you know."

"I know, Lourdes, and that's why I'm here in Mexico with you and not at some college doing what everyone thinks I should be doing."

"I knew I liked you."

"Yeah, I like you, too, Lourdes."

I was starting to feel more than slightly sunburned. I got up from my little spot on the beach and once again headed for the village. My throat was dry and I was aching for a cold drink so I wandered into a little shop not far from the lady selling coconut. The shop was old and dark inside and all the products on the shelves looked like they'd been sitting there for a century waiting for someone to save them. The man working behind the counter was chewing on a piece of sugar cane when I walked in, and he looked me up and down, trying to make up his mind which language he should throw at me. I said hello to him in Spanish and asked him where the Coke was. He pointed to a cooler in the corner and I smiled at him. He smiled back and checked out my ass as I walked away from him.

I was feeling around inside the cooler trying to find the coldest can of Coke when I heard something that made my heart stop. The voice of a woman speaking English. *Can it be that I'm not the only traveler?* I thought. I began to get excited because I realized how much I was aching for conversation in English.

Talking to myself just wasn't enough for me.

I peeked through the shelves and looked at her. She had long silvery hair held together by a clip and she was wearing a long white cotton dress with a funky pattern on it. It reminded me of the clothes I'd seen hippies wearing in old pictures of *Time*. She wasn't a young woman, but it was hard to tell how old she was. Long earrings dangled from her ears and her wrists were an interesting display of bracelets, as though she'd just kept adding them to her arm in an attempt to break a world record. She spoke to the man with the funny mustache behind the counter, and from the way she was speaking, I could tell she had been to the shop more than once. She stood there and chatted with the man for a few minutes, throwing in Spanish words here and there. The man seemed to understand her just fine, which threw me off. *Why didn't he speak English to me?* I thought.

I was rooted to my spot and realized that sooner or later he was going to start wondering if the cooler had swallowed me, so I came from around the shelves and walked back to the counter. She turned to look at me and did a double take. I was pleased she had noticed me. Well, how could she not? It wasn't every day that a seventeen year old girl with very American clothes wandered around a village with less than five hundred residents.

She looked at me from head to toe not once, but twice, and then smiled warmly.

"Hello there, young lady."

"Hello."

"What in the name of God are you doing here in Melaque?"

*So much for small talk.*

"I'm staying with my grandma in Guadalajara. We came here when I was a kid and I guess I just missed it. So here I am." I shrugged and felt like kicking myself for not having something more mature to say.

She raised one of her hands to her face. The bracelets made a jingling sound as they slid down her arm. "Dear Lord, did you come here by yourself?"

"Uh-huh." I took a sip of my Coke.

"On a bus?"

"Yep."

"Alone?"

"Uh-huh." I burped and giggled. "Sorry. It's the Coke."

"That's okay, young lady. What's your name?"

"Bibiana." I didn't want her to keep asking me questions without asking her some myself. It would have been rude. "What's your name? Do you live here? Where are you from?" I could no longer contain my excitement on being able to speak English. I loved the feel of the words as they rolled off my tongue.

"Good God, you are a curious one. Well, let's see, my name is Eva, I live here in Melaque, but I'm originally from Wisconsin."

"Wisconsin, really? How on earth did you end up here?"

"Jesus, my dear, that's a very long story and right now I'm in the middle of making dinner for my family, so I must head back home. Would you like to come over for dinner? Do you have a place to stay?"

*Her family?* I thought. My curiosity was reaching an all time high. *Maybe she's harboring more people I can speak English with.*

"I kind of have a place to stay, I think. The lady selling coconut in the market offered to let me stay in her house tonight with her six kids."

"Oh, that's Juanita. She's a very sweet woman, but her kids will drive you crazy, and her husband likes to drink a little too much. God only knows what he'll try to do to you when you're sleeping. Come along now, we'll go over and see Juanita on the way to the house and I'll let her know you're staying with me."

I couldn't decline her offer. The thought of some drunk old man trying to fondle me gave me the creeps.

After thanking Juanita for her generous offer, we made our way through the market. What a sight we must have been. Me with my backpack and Coke in hand, Eva in the long white dress and silver mane. Everybody knew her. She said hello to everyone we passed and even stopped a couple of times to inquire about this or that sick relative, always grabbing their hands and muttering comforting words in her broken Spanish. She kept introducing me to everyone as though I was a long lost grandchild. I didn't say much because I was still marveling at the miraculous change of events. Being a traveler was turning out to be more fun than I had anticipated.

We left the market and started climbing a rocky path up the side of a mountain. I couldn't see any more houses, or rather, shacks, and I briefly wondered if Eva was just some crazy old lady who was going to slaughter me the minute we left the last remnants of civilization. As the path got steeper, I started to breathe a little heavier. Eva had no problem at all climbing the steep path. For a second I thought she was going to break into a run, she was so quick and agile.

When I thought for sure my legs were going to give out and my lungs were going to explode, we took a turn around a bend and there stood the most amazing house I'd ever seen. It looked as though it had been planted into the side of the mountain and grown into itself just like the many trees surrounding it. It was a split-level structure with huge windows and a porch that protruded along the side of it as if in defiance of gravity.

We were greeted at the door by Mick, a young man who could've come straight out of a surfer magazine, Sharon, an older woman who had a cigarette in her mouth and a paint brush in her hand, and Kyle. Kyle looked at me with a half crazy look in his eye, and then quickly looked behind me as though to make sure no one had followed us. *What have I gotten myself into?* Mick, Sharon and Kyle gave me a once over and immediately launched into question mode.

"Where are you from?"

"Are you Mexican?"

"Is that your real hair?"

"Do you have issues?"

"Are you here to stay?"

"Do you work for the government?"

Eva told them to leave me alone and get back to whatever they were doing. They shrugged and wandered off in separate directions as Eva led me into the kitchen. We hadn't said much on the walk. In fact, we'd said nothing at all because I couldn't keep up with her. Eva put my backpack in one of the rooms and poured me a glass of wine. She calmly went about preparing dinner. I'd never really had wine before, but because I was so nervous and jittery, I decided not to question my drink options. I was lucky enough to have a place to sleep and it was too late to run back into town in search of Juanita.

Eva's "family" seemed a bit weird to me but she made me feel comfortable. I took a sip of my red wine and asked her if I could help her with anything. The warm red liquid tasted funny but I kind of liked it. Holding a glass of red wine made me feel more grown up, in spite of the fact that I had less than three hundred dollars to my name and still no clear direction.

"Jesus, no, honey. You relax. You must have had quite a day." I noticed every one of her sentences seemed to be sprinkled with Jesus or God or Lord.

"I guess so. The bus ride wasn't too bad."

Eva started peeling an onion.

"Don't let them scare you, dear. They're nice folks. Just a little lost, God help them."

"Who?"

"Mick, Sharon and Kyle. My family."

"Are they your kids?"

"Kids? Not really, but I think of them as family. They've lived with me for a really long time." She stopped peeling the onion for a second and racked her brain for a memory. "Mick's from Australia. He came here about seven years ago in search of the perfect wave, God bless him. Well, it didn't take long for him to realize Melaque doesn't really have much to offer except a breathtaking sunset and nice people. When I met him, he'd run out of money and was sleeping on the beach trying to steal money from the local kids. I convinced him to stay with me for a couple of days and he never left."

"You let him stay? Just like that?" I took another sip of wine.

"Yes, dear, just like that. I realized, and so did Mick, that he was really searching for something inside himself. Well, he found it and decided it was a life here with me, in my funny house in the mountains."

"Wow. Cool. What about Sharon? Is she an artist?"

Eva sighed as she set the onion aside and began chopping up a green pepper.

"Sharon wants to be an artist. She's originally from New York City. I met her flying back here from Wisconsin one year. She was on her way to Mexico City for a brief vacation, but I got the feeling she was running from something. We had a nice chat on the plane, and as we picked up our luggage at the baggage claim in Mexico City, I gave her my address and told her she could come visit whenever she wanted. She showed up on my doorstep a week later, piss broke and crying. Turns out she was running from a very wealthy family and a high society fiancé. I took her in and she's still here, too."

"Amazing. And what about Kyle? Is he okay?"

"What do you mean, 'okay'?"

"Well, he looked sort of, you know, paranoid. Like I was the FBI or something."

"Good girl. You're intuitive. I like that. Kyle's not crazy, even though he looks it. Kyle joined the army when he was eighteen and went AWOL only a few months later, God help him. He hitched a ride into Mexico and somehow ended up in Melaque. What is it about this place?"

I smiled and shrugged. I waited for her to keep telling me about Kyle because he was the most intriguing of the three. She stopped chopping the green pepper and refilled my wine glass. I was drinking it too fast, but I didn't care because I was starting to feel like I could listen to Eva talk forever. Her movements in the kitchen were calm and focused, and she exuded something I couldn't put my finger on, something I definitely wanted. She looked at ease and happy with her life.

"Okay, so how did Kyle end up here? With you and your funny house?"

"Oh Lord, he drank too much one night and got into a fight with one of the locals. They asked me to come down to the jail and interpret for him. They agreed to let him go because I promised to bring him here and talk some sense into him. I did, eventually, and he stayed. But he's always been afraid some men in uniform will come and get him and drag him back to some barracks in Colorado. That's why he's so paranoid, Jesus help him. "

"Oh."

I desperately wanted to ask her about her history. I wanted to know how she'd ended up living in a house in the mountains with three potential lunatics. I wanted to ask Mick if he would teach me to surf and pick apart Kyle's brain. I even wanted a drag off one of Sharon's cigarettes. But the wine was making me sleepy, so sleepy in fact that when Eva led me to the rocking chair on the porch to watch the sunset, my eyes closed immediately and darkness swallowed me whole. My last thought as I slipped into a deep sleep was that I really should've called my grandmother and told her I was okay. But I'm half Mexican, and to us, there's always *mañana*.

The next morning, I woke up to the sound of crashing waves. The view from the porch was truly spectacular. Giant cliffs surrounded the beach on both sides, as though trying to protect the little village from unwanted visitors. I guess it worked because aside from Eva, The Lost Trio and myself, there was nothing but locals.

I'd been moved from the rocking chair to the hammock and a thin blanket had been put over me. Someone had taken off my shoes and placed them next to the rocking chair. I sighed and inhaled the fresh air. The waves crashed into the shoreline as the sun slowly made its way into the sky. The air was cooler up at the house and I hugged the blanket tighter to my body, wondering if I was the only one awake. I pictured Kyle standing behind the sliding glass doors peering through a pair of binoculars and the thought made me giggle. I was dying of thirst and hated the way red wine tasted in my mouth one day later but I didn't want to make any noise.

Panic hit me when I realized I hadn't called my grandmother. I practically flew out of the hammock and off the porch at the thought that my grandmother might be worried sick about me. I made such a commotion outside putting on my shoes that I was sure I'd woken up the whole nuthouse. I opened the sliding glass doors and walked through the living room on the way to the kitchen, hoping there was a phone I could use.

Sharon, Kyle, Mick and Eva were sitting at a round wooden table in the kitchen eating what looked like a breakfast buffet for marathon runners. *Chilaquiles, quesadillas,* refried beans, scrambled eggs, toast, bacon, *birote, conchas*…it was Denny's meets Taco Bell and my mouth watered at the sight of it. I'd fallen asleep the night before and missed any kind of dinner, and aside from a can of Coke and some chopped coconut, I hadn't had anything of substance to eat in far too long. They all looked at me as I stood there like a deaf mute drooling at their breakfast. I was ready to dive in but my bladder begged for relief.

"Good morning, Bibiana. How did you sleep?" Eva had the soft voice of someone who's dealt with armed robbers and potential rapists, like someone who has never lost their patience and yelled at the top of their lungs.

"I slept okay. I was really tired. I'm sorry I missed dinner."

"Oh, it's okay. Would you like some breakfast?"

"Yes, I would love to eat something, but right now my bladder's about to burst. Where's the bathroom?"

Eva gave me directions and I practically ran.

Eva's bathroom was a museum in and of itself. Every single spot on the walls was covered with something. Pictures, trinkets, bumper stickers like "Question Authority" and "Free Tibet." There were more pictures in her bathroom than we had in our entire house in Miami. I sat on the toilet and peed like a racehorse while I took in the exhibition. I washed my hands, smoothed out my hair and checked my breath. No surprise, it was disgusting. I put a little bit of toothpaste in my mouth and scrubbed it on my teeth with a finger. After I rinsed and checked it again to make sure the smell of my breath wouldn't kill the Lost Trio, I made my way back to the kitchen, back to the greasy bacon and *tostadas*.

Sharon looked up from her plate when I walked back in and smiled through a mouthful of beans and eggs. She moved over and patted the chair next to her.

"Actually, Eva, I have to make a phone call. I promised my grandmother I would call." I felt childish saying it. The night before I had felt like a middle aged woman enjoying a glass of red wine and suddenly I was a teenager again.

"Don't worry, dear, she's not worried. I already spoke to her."

"YOU WHAT?!"

"Calm down, Bibiana. Jesus, you truly are an excitable young lady."

"Sorry. I'm finding this whole scenario a little out of the ordinary for me. How did you get in touch with my grandmother?" I sat down next to Sharon and put enough food on my plate to feed every one of my relatives for six weeks, including the dog.

"I figured you would have a contact number written down somewhere so

I looked through your backpack and found it in your journal. I hope you're not offended."

"You don't have to worry about nothing," Kyle said as he looked at a point behind me. "Eva wouldn't never do nothing bad. She didn't want your grandma to be all up in a tizzy cause she ain't heard from you in forever."

I tried to decode what Kyle had just said to me. I knew it had something to do with Eva not trying to steal any of my stuff. What could she steal anyway? My money was in my pocket and all I had in my backpack was an old sandwich, a dead apple and my walkman. I was so hungry I didn't care that she had looked at my journal. Most of what I'd written was nonsense anyway. "What did she say?"

All of a sudden I had a vision of Eva on one end of the phone trying to explain to my grandmother that her granddaughter was staying with three strangers and that she was okay, and then I pictured my grandmother on the other end, her teeth somewhere else but in her mouth and farts coming out of her ass every ten seconds. It was too much for me. I laughed out loud.

"What? What's so funny?" Mick said.

I was laughing so hard that it was making him laugh, too. Before I knew it, all of us were sitting there laughing at the top of our lungs. I suddenly felt at home. Laughter is an extraordinary bond. After I calmed down and told them I was laughing at a really old memory that had nothing to do with them, I dove into my breakfast.

"Anyway, what did she say?" I stifled a giggle.

"Your grandmother is very sweet, Bibiana. Does she have dentures?"

Oh dear God. I was ready to lose it again but there was food in my mouth and it would've landed all over the Lost Trio.

"Yeah, she does. She always takes them out and puts them down somewhere and then makes me look for hours until I find them. She probably didn't have them in when you called."

Sharon took a sip of orange juice and looked at me not unkindly. "Are you close to her?"

"Oh, yeah, without a doubt. We're all pretty close, to be honest."

She looked towards the ocean, sadness dripping from her face. "Must be nice to have a family like that."

"Yeah, it is." I hate seeing people sad so I immediately started rambling to fill up the silence. I just started talking off the top of my head like someone who's just snorted a line of cocaine. "My dad farts all the time in public which is really embarrassing and my mom wears orange lipstick and rollers but that's not too bad because my brother can be really mean so mean that he sometimes catches lizards and wears them as earrings just to scare me and I have a paranoid schizophrenic Uncle Javier who's always lighting matches in his bed under a blanket which makes my grandmother really mad so mad that she yells at him and eventually her teeth fall out of her mouth from so much effort and they fall somewhere and get lost and the reason I was laughing before was because I was thinking about my grandmother trying to talk to Eva without her teeth and the fact that she farts like a champion."

Mick, Kyle, Sharon and Eva stared at me openmouthed, like I was a wild animal on tour with a traveling circus that had ended up in their kitchen. Mick coughed and covered his mouth, Sharon put out her cigarette and tried to suppress a smile but then she looked at Kyle, who for once was staring directly at me and not at the imaginary soldier in the background. He quickly glanced at Eva as though waiting for her approval to go ahead and laugh. She looked around the table and then at me sitting there stuffing my face with more beans just to stop myself from rambling and started laughing.

Mick, Kyle and Sharon quickly joined in and once again we sat there clutching our stomachs at the thought of Lupe farting and spitting through her gums.

Eva wiped her eyes and took a sip of her tea. "Don't worry, Bibiana. Your grandmother knows you're okay. I told her I'd let you stay here for the night and she thanked me profusely. If you like, you can call her again, but I don't think it's necessary."

"I don't think so either. Besides, she's probably running around the house as we speak trying to find her bra."

After breakfast, Eva's "kids" went off to do whatever it was they enjoyed doing (surfing, painting, looking out for spies) and Eva led me to the porch. She sat on the rocking chair and I dove back into the hammock. She hadn't asked me to leave nor offered me advice as to where to go next. I was relieved. I wasn't thrilled at the prospect of getting on another chicken-laden bus, and I also didn't think I'd be lucky enough to find such interesting hosts in the next beach town. I wanted to talk to Eva and find out how she had ended up so far away from Wisconsin.

"Eva, why are you here?"

She sighed and took a sip of her tea as she looked at the vast expanse of the Pacific Ocean. "Lord, honey, it's always a man."

"A man? What do you mean?"

"I came to Guadalajara in college on a student exchange program. I was tired of doing the same old thing and although my parents wanted to send me to Europe, I convinced them to let me come to Mexico. I'd seen pictures of it in travel brochures and something about this country called to me. While I was here, I met another student, the son of a rich Mexican politician, and we fell in love. His name was Francisco Miguel Flores." She sighed and looked back at the ocean. "Francisco and I had a love affair that summer. Neither of our parents approved of our commitment to each other, so we ran off after the summer and eloped." She looked lost in a memory. Really far gone. So I did what I always do. I pulled her right back.

"What happened?"

"We came here to Melaque for our honeymoon. We rented a little shack close to the beach from one of the locals and spent two weeks soaking up the sun and meeting everyone. Francisco said it was the first time he'd ever really felt like he was part of his country. I made him promise we would come back here and live here for good one day. Unfortunately, our marriage pretty much ended at the end of our honeymoon. His parents disowned him and we moved back to Wisconsin after I begged my parents to give him a chance. They did, but it wasn't long before Francisco realized Wisconsin wasn't where he wanted to live and I wasn't the woman he was destined for. He said I was too American, too typical, too mainstream." She sighed heavily. "If he'd only known."

"What were you really like?"

"Me? I was different, but he couldn't see it. I tried getting him interested in art and museums and books, in living a life without greed, without being a slave to money, but he was still hellbent on making more of a life than his dad had. But I loved him so much I followed him to New York City, where he made his fortune as a Wall Street broker."

"Did you have kids?"

"No. Doctors told me I couldn't have any and it put more strain on our relationship. We stayed together for nineteen years, him with his mistresses and me with my social work. I spent my time working in shelters for abused wives." She put her hands in the air and shook her head. "One day I woke up and realized I was still wishing for another life, so I asked him for a divorce and took a small portion of his fortune. God bless him. I didn't mean to take it, but I think he felt too guilty. He gave me enough money to live the rest of my life in peace. I hopped on a plane and came here, and the rest is history, as they say."

"You've lived here since then? In Melaque?"

"Yeah. It was the only place that had ever made me feel at peace with myself. I sit here every night and think about things. Life, choices, family. Mostly I think about Francisco and wonder where it went wrong, but I don't regret anything. I've lived here for over twenty years and have had the happiest times of my life."

"Don't you get lonely? Don't you miss America?"

"Sometimes I get lonely, but it only lasts for a day or two. My three kids keep me company and make me laugh. As for America, it's always a plane ride away. You see, dear, the only thing I wanted was to be free, to live my life however I saw fit, even though it meant giving up fast food and mass transit. And Lord knows I have enough money to get by until my dying days. I think I'm doing something meaningful. I've helped three people find themselves, as people say, and that's more than enough for me. And then, of course, I get lucky enough to run into someone like you, God bless you, and it reminds me that life is full of chance encounters."

I mulled over her words and wondered what she meant. I looked far from someone who could leave her with any kind of worldly wisdom. I looked more like someone who needed a huge helping of wisdom. To go, please.

"Bibiana, what the hell are you doing here?"

I was taken aback by her words, mostly because she'd used the word "hell."

"I don't really know."

"What do you want to do with your life?"

I swayed gently in the hammock and gave it some thought. "Uhm, nothing concrete. It's hard to explain. Right now I like meeting new people and getting to know where they come from, what they're doing, where they're going. I feel like I'm learning something, not just about them, but about me. All my life I've been a good kid, you know? I've always been a good student, a good daughter, a good everything. I had three scholarships to study music but I decided to pass them up and well, live a little. Do something different for a change. I know I'll end up going to college someday, but for now, I like being free like this. You know what I mean?"

"Lord, honey, more than you know. And forgive me for saying this, but don't put off college for too long. Education is very important, honey. You'll learn a lot of things you might need someday. And believe it or not, it opens your mind."

"I know, I know. I'd like to go to college someday, but not until I know what I really want to be. Why waste my time?"

147

She nodded and then looked at me with concern. "Lord, honey, what are you going to do in the meantime?"

"I was hoping to see more of Mexico, maybe head north towards the bigger beach towns where I won't have to rely on a chance encounter to find a place to stay. I only have about three hundred dollars and I'm not sure how long that's gonna last, so I guess I'm just going to play it by ear."

"Dear God, I do admire your sense of adventure, but you can stay here as long as you like. It's nice having someone new to talk to, and you're different because you didn't come with any baggage, if you know what I mean."

"Don't tell me I'm normal, Eva!" I giggled. Nobody had ever said I was normal.

"No, dear, you're not normal. Just sane."

She got up from the rocking chair and patted me on the head before turning around and going back inside the house. *Sane*, I thought. I wondered how long that would last. I was secretly afraid too much time around my crazy Uncle Javier would somehow affect me, as though schizophrenia was something I could catch if I wasn't careful. I got that sleepy feeling I sometimes get after eating too much. I felt myself falling backwards into a serene darkness as the crashing waves sang to me their sweet lullaby.

# Chapter 11

I stayed with Eva and her loony tunes for a week before hopping onto a bus again. I'd had enough of Kyle's questions about whether or not I *really* knew who my dad worked for, Mick's mood swings and Sharon's sad droopy face that I just couldn't fix. I loved talking to Eva, and had it not been for her patience and good cooking, I probably would have tied up the Lost Trio and forced them get over their drama or else. I hated the thought that someone was suffering and that I was basically too young and too inexperienced to help them.

When I wasn't looking, Eva slipped two hundred dollars in my backpack. It had to have been her because everyone else was broke. I found the money when I got on the bus to Barra de Navidad and rummaged around my backpack for my walkman and my journal. She had put the money between two pages of my journal and on one of them she had written me a note.

*Bibiana—*
*You are a good soul, remember that. You will do good things, large and small. Find your place in this world and stay there. Above all else, be happy and remember you have a home here.*
*Peace and God Bless,*
*Eva and the Gang*

I felt a pang of sadness as the bus pulled away from Melaque. I had grown to like Eva and the Lost Trio because they were slightly off center. Different. Unique. Like me. They made me laugh. I watched little kids running alongside the bus, waving their hands in the air and not minding that fact that they were inhaling poisonous gases and eating a whole lot of dust. I looked for Eva's house up in the mountain but it was too far up. Already the week was starting to seem like a dream, so I took out my pen and wrote everything down in my journal, Kyle's paranoia included. I finally realized what a journal was for. I wrote and wrote as the bus traveled through the mountains and didn't stop until my fingers started to ache and my pen ran out of ink.

I never made it too far. After Barra De Navidad, I went to Puerto Vallarta for a few weeks and then all the way to Mazatlan, where I stayed for two months. I say "all the way" because it makes me feel like I might have traversed an entire continent when in reality I only traveled a few hundred miles. I found cheap places to stay and basically wandered through all three places writing down my thoughts and lying on the beach.

Sometimes I'd wonder if I should have stayed with Eva for longer, but then I would meet another traveler and realize I needed to have my own chance encounters, needed to get out there and meet people, learn something from them. As much as I sometimes wanted to meet another Eva with an amusing family, it never happened. Instead I met young travelers from all over the world: Australia, New Zealand, England, Ireland, China, Japan, Ohio. I did end up learning a lot from them, like essential swear words and how to make a spear out of a Bic pen, a rubber band and a needle. It was all fun and games and one really bad hangover until all I had left was enough money for a bus ride back to Guadalajara, a journal with no more empty pages to write in and enough memories to last me a lifetime.

As close as I was to my mom growing up, my desire to do something different and off the wall seemed to shut out any thoughts of calling her just to let her know I was okay and still alive. I left that up to my grandmother, who somehow convinced my mom I was always "out" whenever she called. I thought about her from time to time, especially when I'd meet someone who reminded me of her, but homesickness didn't hit me until I got on the bus back to Guadalajara. Guilt overwhelmed me as I thought about how lonely she must have been without me for so long. I thought about her sitting all alone in the living room after my dad had gone to sleep with no one to talk to. Who was she going to the movies with? Who was picking up the disasters she created in the supermarket? Who was helping her put rollers in her hair and look all over the house for her car keys?

I got a huge lump in my throat at the thought of my mom being sad and lonely and realized my journey had to come to an end. I could only be selfish to a point; I was young, I was a wanna be gypsy, I was many things other than a bookworm and a good daughter, but at heart, I was my mom's best friend, and you don't do that to friends.

I returned to Guadalajara and spent a few more weeks with my grandmother. I wrote down my thoughts into a new journal. The house was still chaotic and Uncle Javier had gone from trying to set himself on fire to trying to blow up the dog. I settled back into the circus like someone who has never known another life. I was starting to like the noise and fights and potential fires because it gave me a lot to write about.

My cousins fought a lot, mostly because they were all trying to put food on the table and still hurting from the loss of my Aunt Bianca. I stayed out of their arguments because it wasn't my place to interfere anyway. I was just a visitor who had no idea what it was like to be hungry, to be bone tired, to wish things were different, to pray for a financial miracle. I was eighteen years old and ready to start my own struggle. Doing what, I didn't know, but after Eva and the Lost Trio, Uncle Javier's lunacy and my grandmother's missing teeth, I was ready for anything.

I called my dad and he put me on a plane two days later. He sounded relieved when I told him I needed to come home. I could hear him light up a cigarette. Somewhere in the background I heard my mom yelling at my brother for using the car without her permission because she missed her favorite bingo night. I couldn't wait to get back. I said a thousand tearful goodbyes at the airport (everyone insisted on seeing me off) and headed back to Miami, convinced that living with Lupe and seven female cousins on different PMS cycles was not a solution to my restlessness. I desperately missed my mom and the way she always smelled of Oil of Olay.

I returned to Miami thinking about what Eva said about college. I wanted to go, but my scholarships were gone and I knew I'd probably have to enroll at Miami-Dade Community College (we called it Grade 13) and eventually FIU. My parents weren't poor, but they couldn't afford any kind of tuition, so the day after I got back from Mexico, I applied for a job at TGI Friday's as a waitress. I had to pay for college and Friday's looked like a fun place to work.

I don't know what possessed me to think they would hire an eighteen year old with Pizza Hut experience as a waitress. The time I spent slicing pan pizzas and refilling the salad bar meant nothing to the manager who interviewed me. However, he did think I had a nice personality (and probably nice tits) and decided to give me a job as a hostess. My tasks included seating guests in the right stations so as not to bombard a waiter or waitress all at once and confuse the kitchen, blowing up balloons for all the little monsters who came with their parents, wiping down the menus that looked like textbooks and answering the phone.

You would think these tasks would be enough to keep someone entertained and busy for hours, but by the end of the first week, I was pulling my hair out. I was so bored. For Christ's sake, I'd just spent a year in a foreign country, how could anything top that?

I liked greeting guests at the door and walking them to their table with the checked tablecloth. I did not like leaving them in the care of a waiter wearing red and white stripes and zero personality. I wanted to be a waitress because it looked like so much fun. I thought it was almost glamorous. Why, I don't know, but I'll blame it on television. It can make anything look fabulous.

Waiters and waitresses were always standing by the service bar laughing and playing practical jokes on each other. I was always standing at the front being polite and courteous. They were making over a hundred dollars a shift and I was making about a third of that. Even though I lived with my parents, I knew I'd never be able to pay for college on what I was making. After two weeks of twiddling my thumbs, I decided to approach the general manager, Teddy Cross.

If Teddy Cross were an animal, I'd have to say he was a bear. Not the cute cuddly kind you see on the shelf at Toys 'R' Us, but the kind that wouldn't hesitate in ripping your head off. Every single part of his body had too much flesh. His arms were the size of my legs, his legs looked like two tree stumps and his voice was loud enough to knock you down. He never spoke in a calm manner, rarely said hello to anyone and mostly stood around the kitchen yelling at the Haitian cooks who, thankfully, couldn't understand him.

When I approached him, Teddy was sitting at a small two-top in the far corner of the restaurant going over paperwork. It was a Saturday afternoon, right about shift change. The day shift waiters were running around like maniacs trying to get their salt and pepper shakers refilled. The night shift waiters were inspecting ketchup bottles, making sure they were properly refilled. Everyone knew better than to bother Teddy unless he was barking out orders for a refill on his coffee or a clean ashtray.

I'd met him briefly on my first day. I say briefly because he shook my hand and looked me up and down before storming off to yell at some unfortunate cook. I knew approaching him without ear plugs or a concealed weapon was bold, but then again, I'd just spent about a year in a Third World country. I wasn't about to let Teddy intimidate me. I sat down at the table with him and he looked at me as though I'd just interrupted the birth of his first child.

"Hi, Teddy."

"What do you want?"

"Sorry. I didn't mean to interrupt you, but—"

"What do you want?"

"I wanna be a waitress."

"Who the hell are you?"

"Bibiana. Bibi. I'm a new hostess. I just started two weeks ago."

"Hm hmm." He went back to scanning his paperwork.

"I know you're busy, but I wanted to—"

"Forget it. You're not getting a raise."

"I don't want a raise."

He looked up at me. "So what's your problem? I'm busy. Get to the point."

"I just told you what my point is. I wanna be a waitress."

"Why?"

"Why? Because being a hostess *sucks*."

He put down his pen and chuckled. "It sucks?"

"Yeah, it sucks. It's about as interesting as watching the grass grow. I hate standing around and I've inhaled enough helium to last me a year. I want you to give me a chance as a waitress. I swear I'll be good at it."

"Do you have any experience?"

"No. I mean, I worked at Pizza Hut in high school, but that's about it."

"And you think, based on your experience at Pizza Hut, that you can be a waitress?"

"I don't base it on that. No, sir."

"Then why the hell do you think I should make you a waitress?"

"Because I have a personality. Because I actually like people. Because my parents can't afford to pay for college and I have to foot the bill and making six dollars an hour for blowing up balloons and cleaning menus will do nothing but land me in an insane asylum and besides I just spent a year in Mexico doing literally nothing and now I have to make something of my life but blowing up balloons and cleaning menus isn't enough for me no way I have too much ambition and I like school and please give me one chance if I screw it up you can always fire me or send me back to being a hostess." I was out of breath.

Teddy put the end of the pen in his mouth and started chewing it. He stared at me for a few minutes while I waited for him to reach across the table and strangle me. "Okay."

"Okay what?

"You can be a waitress."

"I can?"

"I hope so. I've never done this before, you know, promoted a hostess so quickly, but you have something I like."

153

"What's that?"

"Guts. You're a brave kid."

"I didn't plan on being one, honestly. I just turned out this way."

"Whatever. Work your shift tonight and you'll start training tomorrow morning. Don't be late."

"Okay, Teddy, thanks."

I got up quickly before he changed his mind.

"One question, Bibi."

"Sure."

"What the hell were you doing in Mexico?"

"Uhm, trying to find myself."

"Ha. Did you?"

"Nope. I found three lunatics, though."

"Well, if you're ever wondering who you are, there's always the mirror in the ladies' room."

"I know, Teddy. I wipe it down about three times a night."

"Get out of here, you smart ass. Make me proud."

"I will."

After that, my life flew by me at an alarming rate. I never got the chance to think about where on earth I was going because any thoughts of the future would be rudely interrupted by a fat middle aged man asking me for a refill on his Coke or a frustrated mom asking me for more salad dressing. It was that or I was engrossed in writing a paper or studying for an exam. I somehow made it through community college and into a FIU by surviving on loads of coffee and having patient restaurant managers.

My parents never bugged me about what I was going to "be" or what I was studying. They were happy enough that I was actually in college. Me, the daughter of illiterate immigrants. The only thing they hoped was that I wouldn't want to "be" a prostitute or professional drug addict. My parents were simple people who just wanted to see me happy.

I once asked my dad if he wished we were rich.

"Rich? I am bery rich."

"No, you're not, Papi. We have used cars and hardly ever go on vacation. Mami never buys new clothes and we don't get an allowance. You're not rich."

"No, mi'ja, I am. I wake up every morning time and breathe in and out, joo know? I has a bery good wife, nice cheeldren and a roof on my head. We no has problems and we has de food to eat. Es enough for me. I am rich. Joo

154

remember what is importan', and joo always be happy, okay?"

"Sure, Papi." But I wasn't so sure.

Since I was the one footing the bill, I decided to study something I liked. The greatest thing about putting yourself through school is that you basically get to decide what you want to study. For all my parents knew, I could've been majoring in Parks and Recreation learning how to teach a mean game of kick ball and they wouldn't have cared one bit. I decided to major in International Relations simply because it had the word "international" in it. I took classes like Population and Geography of Africa, Latin American Studies, US Foreign Policy after the Cold War. With each new class, I learned more and more about the world and it gave me a sense of adventure; I soaked in new cultures, new ideas, new theories and spent days dreaming of the day I would trek off to India or Russia or South America.

College did nothing but fuel my imagination and I was grateful for it. *There's so much out there*, I would think, *and I desperately want to be a part of it*. I imagined myself going to live in a Third World country on a humanitarian effort. I pictured myself helping people rebuild their communities. I let my imagination run wild; I would do something meaningful and passionate, something that would go down in history. It was in college that I began to embrace the idea of making a difference. Not a small one either. Oh no. It had to be on a grand scale. And I truly felt that with every A I got, I was closer to an "international" job somewhere.

*Give me the world*, I would think. I wanted to see it all and I wanted to make a difference. I couldn't decide how, but it sounded damn good whenever I'd talk about it to whoever wanted to listen. That person was usually Linda, a woman ten years older than me and a full time waitress. She was like the sister I never had, the girlfriend I longed for when I was a kid, the mom who could understand plain English. I spent a lot of time at her house drinking pots of coffee, talking about my classes, my dreams, my goals, my everything. She would listen patiently and tell me to never stop dreaming. "It will keep you young," she would say. Naturally, she became my closest friend aside from my mom. And she loved to have me around because I'd imitate my mom for her whenever she wanted. She loved her, and well, who couldn't love a woman wearing orange lipstick?

Linda would call my house sometimes just for the hell of it, knowing very well I wasn't home. She got a kick out of my mom's accent.

"*¿Aló?*"

"Hello, Mrs. Castellanos, is Bibiana home?"

"Oh, Linda, how are joo?"

"I'm good, Mrs. C. How are you?"

"Oh, Linda, I'm bery good. Joo know, working and cooking. I'm so bery tired sometimes."

"I know, I know. Where's Bibiana?"

"Bibi? No, Linda, she es at joonybersity. She estudying bery hard, joo know? She bery smart."

Linda would giggle. "Oh, okay."

"Jes, someday she going to be having a bery good job. Joo want to leave message?"

"No, Mrs. C. I'll call her later, okay?"

"Okay, my choogar, I tell her when she get home. Okay, bye bye."

I used to hang around this guy in high school, one of the kids in my chorus class who seemed to be obsessed with me for reasons I will never know. His name was David Goldberg, and yep, you guessed it, he was Jewish. Like Linda, he loved to tease my mom. He'd come over to my house sometimes after school because I was always too nice to say no. My mom would greet us with a tray of frozen Tang (she got tired of Hawaiian Punch).

"Hi, Mrs. C, how are you today?"

"Oh, Danny, how are joo?"

"Mrs. C, you making fun of me?"

"What joo mean? Why joo say that?"

"Are you calling me a Jew?"

"What? What are joo talking about, Danny?"

"See, you said it again, Mrs. C. You're calling me a Jew." He would wink at me and I'd grimace.

Embarrassed, my mom would attempt to clear up the misunderstanding. Danny would stand there trying not to laugh.

"No, no, Danny, joo are bery wrong. I say 'joo' as in 'joo and me,' okay? No 'joo' as in 'Joowish,' okay, baby? Joo want some frozen Tang?"

"Okay, Mrs. C, I'm just teasing you."

"Oh, joo are so craysee, baby." And she would laugh and slap his hand.

Lucky for me, Linda trained me to be a waitress. I practically ran behind her as she instructed me to *pick up that plate, refill that Coke, get that little kid some more crackers.* Her energy and her spunk won me over from the very beginning, and she took a liking to me because I never questioned anything she made me do. I learned how to balance three plates on one arm, take two drink orders without running back to the bar and balance two glasses in one hand. I dropped a lot of stuff in the beginning but she never yelled at me. She would laugh and tell me not to worry, eventually I'd get the hang of it.

But I still did a lot of stupid things.

A waiter ran up to me in the middle of my first training shift and asked me to get a container of steam out of the storage room for the espresso machine. I was halfway there when Linda stopped me and made me think about what he'd asked me to do. "Bibi, a container of steam?" She patted me on the shoulder and told me not to be so gullible, which was like telling me not to breathe.

I started going to her house a few times a week when I didn't have class or a paper to write. She had three young boys, Jordan, Keith and Christopher. Her husband was appropriately named Monty. Every word out of his mouth was a quote straight out of Monty Python. He made me laugh and never made me feel uncomfortable. Both Linda and Monty are two of the nicest people I will ever know. They welcomed me into their family as one of their own, and it was only a matter of time before I got to know her parents, his parents, her friends, his friends, their entire nucleus of warmth. They were struggling to make ends meet; Linda waiting tables and Monty working as a carpenter/handy man. They worked long hours but always maintained a positive outlook on life. No matter the disaster, Linda would always say the same thing. "Oh, honey, it could always be worse." And this after a broken leg, a car accident, a fire. They were such a close family that at times it was hard to figure out where one ended and the other began. I was thrown into the mix as a spicy afterthought, the extra pepper in the salad.

I spent more time with Linda and her tribe than I spent trying to establish a relationship with a guy. I'd never had a good friend like Linda, and it was nice to know that after so many years of mistrusting women, I'd finally found someone who liked me for me, the girl who imitated her mom to a tee, played hide and go seek with the boys and dreamt of changing the world one order of mozzarella sticks at a time.

Linda is just the kind of friend everyone needs. As I got older, we stopped talking as much. I'd send her postcards from wherever I was when I was on cruise ships, call her whenever I was back in town. When I moved to Orlando, was talked even less. It wasn't that we weren't as close, but distance can do that to a friendship. Still, no matter where I was, no matter how long it had been since I called her, I knew that I could always pick up the phone and pick up right where we left off. No recriminations, no "Why haven't you called me you ungrateful bitch?" None of that nonsense.

Usually when we called each other, we'd always start off with, "Are you sitting down?" followed by:

"Oh, Bibi, Eric broke his arm."

"Linda, my period is three days late!!!"

"The doctor says I need a hysterectomy."

"I've gained three pounds, Linda."

"Monty wants to quit his job."

"I got a job as a teacher!"

"Jordan broke his leg skateboarding. But oh, well, I suppose it could be worse, right?"

Both Linda and I are convinced she must have done some terrible things in her past life. Tragedy is constantly lurking around the corner. Broken limbs, car accidents, dead pets. And as much as she is optimistic and all smiles, sometimes she'd hit a really rough patch and call me out of the blue.

"Oh, Bibi, I'm having a bad day. Can you imitate your mom for me? Come on, I need a pick me up."

And I would. I'd tell her the latest Isabela Castellanos adventure and make her laugh.

By my senior year in college, I had gone from being a spastic waitress to a full time sarcastic as hell bartender. The nerd was still in there somewhere, dying to get out, but I hid her well. I hid her in a thin body, I hid her behind my sarcasm and my tough shell. I tucked her away in a far corner of my mind and made sure she never got a chance to speak up. It was easy to keep her out of my new life because there was no room for a nerdy fat girl in a spectacular life. No room for her at all.

Working in a restaurant allowed me to further tap into a new side of myself, a side I had only glimpsed in Mexico. A side that was curious, adventurous, imaginative and more than ready to drink tequila. A side that was prepared to put a few drops of Visine in someone's drink if necessary. I discovered the world of alcohol. The only time I'd ever really gotten drunk was in Mexico, when a couple from Russia took me under their wing for a night and introduced me to vodka. Bad, bad hangover, but it had been a fun night. So I started going out after work as long as I didn't have school the next day. Most of the other bartenders were guys, and they treated me like a little sister. They'd take me out to a bar, buy me shots and then make sure nobody hit on me. I was a commuter student in college, and although I never had the "go away to college" experience, I still learned to party and have fun like the rest of them. I learned the value of Tylenol after a night of drinking. I quickly learned that there was nothing like cold apple juice in the morning to quell the nausea. I also learned that guys always seemed more attractive and interesting after a few drinks. Hmm.

What seemed most hilarious to me, however, was the fact that even though my parents couldn't afford to pay for college and I had to work full time, it never seemed to bother me. I thought it set me apart. Frat boys would come in hordes on some nights and tip me nearly enough money to pay for an entire semester. I would smile at them and flirt as they'd hand me outrageous tips and think, *Ha, your parents are putting me through college, you moron, and I'll probably get much, much further than you ever will.*

The bar was my stage. I entertained regulars with stories about my family while I'd briefly wonder what I was going to do after graduation. Sometimes when I'd get off work at three in the morning and drive home knowing I had to study for an exam or finish a paper, I'd pray for my college life to end. Then there were days when a customer would hand me a fifty dollar tip and I would think bartending was the only thing I wanted to do. Or could do.

One day after college graduation, I was sitting in my bedroom thinking about what I was going to do next. It was a lot of pressure. I flirted with the idea of going back to Mexico just to see if Eva and the Lost Trio were still alive, but I knew it would do nothing for me except prolong the real world. I considered going to graduate school, even law school, but I was so tired and worn out from working and studying full time that three more years of school seemed like a death penalty. And besides, a whole other world was waiting for me. There was a difference to be made, but I just had to figure out which one I wanted to dive into.

I got several job offers to go into sales from some of the regulars, but that meant working in Corporate America. There was no way in hell I was going to go that route. Most of the salesmen who came into the bar were terribly unhappy, grossly unhealthy and horrifying at telling jokes, especially after three shots.

What I was going to do with the rest of my life seemed like the question of the century for every bar regular at Fridays.

"So, Bibi, what the hell is your major again?" Sal would ask. Sal was the most obnoxious, the most annoying, and the most regular of all the drunks. The only thing that seemed to redeem him was the fact that he was the best tipper.

I'd sigh and brace myself for another attack. "International Relations, Sal. I've only told you that about, oh, let's see, five thousand times?"

"Yeah, yeah, that's right. So what are you gonna do with that? Huh? Go to law school?"

"I don't know. I think I've told you that about, oh, let's see, five thousand times?"

"You don't know? What the hell's wrong with you, kid? Why go to college?"

"Shit, Sal, I don't know, maybe to learn something? Broaden my horizons?"

"Ha! Well, aren't you special?" Sal would look at the other regulars and snicker. "Ha! We got ourselves a scholar!"

"Yes, Sal, a scholar, but that's much better than being a drunk whose life revolves around Stoli and tonic, you asshole."

The other regulars would laugh and slap the bar as though they'd heard the funniest joke, and what would Sal do? What he always did. Order another drink and hand me a ridiculously high tip as though to thank me for reminding him what an idiot he was.

I got little help from my family.

Erasmo: "At least you graduated from college, dork. Can I borrow five hundred bucks?"

Mom: "*Mi'ja*, es okay, somesing will happen to joo and joo will know what joo want. Be *paciente* and wait for de sign."

Dad: "Get a job with de goberment. Es good benefits, good health inchoorans."

I was so stressed out about what I was going to do that I snapped at everyone. I yelled at my mom because she ruined one of my shirts when *she* did the laundry. I nearly beat the shit out of my brother when I caught him trying to give away one of my stuffed animals to his girlfriend. I snapped at my dad when he asked me to play the piano for him. I was a miserable bitch. If I didn't find a real job soon, I'd probably end up smashing a bottle of vodka over Sal's head.

That day after graduation, I sat on my bed and looked out the window, praying for it to give me a sign. *Something has to happen soon*, I thought. *I'm going to go crazy if I don't figure out what to do next.* The phone rang and I stared at it like someone who's seeing the devil for the first time. I knew it was Fridays. I knew they were calling me to come in on my day off, my first day off from school and work. I let it ring about five times until the little Catholic girl on my shoulder poked me and reminded me that I was, after all, a good person.

"Hey, Bibi." It was Mike, one of the restaurant managers.

"Hey, Mike. Let's cut to the chase. What do you want from me?"

"I need you to work tonight." *Shit, shit, shit!*

"No, I have to study for a final, Mike."

"You're full of shit, Bibi. You graduated yesterday, remember? So, here's the deal: Alex's mom got into a car accident and he's a mess. He can't make it and nobody else will answer my calls. Come on, it's Wednesday night. It'll be slow, a no-brainer."

Dealing with drunks and happy frat boys was anything but a no-brainer. It was more like an iron man competition for my patience.

I sucked at saying no twice and I really cared about Alex. He'd bailed me out more than a couple of times. I looked at myself in the mirror as I held the phone to my ear and nearly vomited at the sight. I had bags under my eyes because my parents had taken me out to dinner the night before to celebrate and I had gotten very drunk. My parents took it as a sign that I was celebrating, whereas in reality I was miserable and confused. I didn't want to end up as a bartender for the rest of my life.

Locking myself in my bedroom contemplating my future probably would've driven me out of my mind, so I decided to go in to work. If anything, it would keep my mind off of everything. It also gave me a sick sense of satisfaction to be able to squeeze a little more money out of the frat boys and their parents.

"Oh, all right. I'll come in, but I swear, Mike, I'm not going to be social, okay? I'm in a bad mood, you got that? *A very bad mood.* I'll play the barback roll, okay?"

"Whatever you say, kid. I'll see you at five. Oh, and hey? Congrats on graduating. What are you gonna do now?"

"Mike, I've decided to come in for you. Don't ask me to make any more decisions right now."

I hung up the phone and jumped in the shower, my first that day.

One decision is all it takes to change your whole life.

When I walked up to the bar, I said hello to the other bartender, Patty, and calmly told her I was in a very bad mood and probably shouldn't deal with any customers directly. Patty wasn't used to me not smiling and laughing, but she took the news like a trouper and said I could just hang out and restock the beer, the ice, take out the garbage, wipe down all the bottles and just basically try to be invisible. This suited me just fine, but by the end of the night, I was honestly starting to ache for conversation with someone. I can only stay quiet for so long.

I was walking around the bar checking for dirty ashtrays when I passed two men in expensive suits. They were older men and definitely not regulars. They were far too refined and sober. As I stood by them pretending to clean down the bottles, I heard one of them talking. He had a slight accent I couldn't put my finger on. I loved accents because it usually meant that person would be able to enlighten me on whatever country they came from. I'd had enough of being quiet so I asked him where he was from.

"Where I am from?"

"Yeah. Forgive me for eavesdropping, but being that I'm a woman and naturally nosy, I couldn't help but hear your accent. Sorry."

"Oh, no, don't be. I'm originally from Austria." He paused as I stared at him waiting for him to elaborate. "Uh, actually, I was born there, but I just moved here from Hawaii, and before that I was in Paris, before that London, and before that I was in Greece."

"Wow!" Now here was someone I could talk to. He had salt and pepper hair and looked old enough to be my dad. He had a kind face and a non-threatening look in his eye. In other words, he didn't look like a nasty pervert.

"What about you?" he said. "Where are you from?"

"Uh, I was born in East Los Angeles, but we moved here when I was seven. My dad thought there was too much crime in LA so we moved here. What a genius, huh?"

Both men started to laugh and all of a sudden I felt like I was being interviewed for the CIA. What was I studying? When was I graduating? How do I feel about public speaking? Do I want to travel? We talked for about an hour, mostly me answering their questions about who I was and what I was doing with my life, or rather, what I wanted to do. I told them I wanted to do something different, something out of this world. They'd nod their heads at each one of my answers as though an invisible questionnaire existed in their heads. Likes people, check. Has a personality, check. Can speak Spanish, check. Willing to travel, check.

I excused myself for a moment because I had to change a keg. When I walked away, I saw the older man lean over to the younger one. I knew they were talking about me. I smelled a job offer of some sort, but I hoped it didn't involve nudity or dancing. I came back to the bar and started wiping down another bottle when the older man called me over.

"Bibiana, I want to ask you something."

"Sure." I came over and stood in front of them, ready for the blue ribbon.

"My name is Helmut, and this here is Edward." I shook both their hands.

THE WHOLE WIDE WORLD

"We work in the travel industry and we both think you would be an asset to our company."

"Oh, what kind of company?"

"We'll get to that. To put it bluntly, we like you. We like your personality and sense of humor. You obviously like people."

I shrugged and raised my hands in the air. "What can I say? My mom and dad raised me right."

"We can see that. So, would you be interested in a career that involves a lot of traveling?"

"Yes, of course."

"Okay, I'm going to give you my business card with my direct line. When you see my card, you'll know who I am and what we do, so just take the card and think about it. If you decide this is something you want to do, give me a call. I'll make sure you get taken care of." He reached into his jacket pocket and pulled out a card. "I hope you make the right decision. Oh, and can we have the check?"

"Sure, I'll get it for you." I raced around to the computer and printed out their check. "Here it is."

I was trying hard to keep cool, but I really wanted to snatch the card out of his hand and run to the bathroom so I could read it in private. He took the check and handed me his card. I didn't look at it right away because I didn't want to seem too desperate. They paid their bill, left an outrageous tip and walked out. I promised to think "it" over.

The minute they were gone, I pulled the card out of my pocket and stared at it. I was shocked. Stunned. Surprised. Ecstatic! The card read, "Helmut Meyer, Vice President of Norwegian Cruise Lines." *Oh my God*, I thought. Cruise ships. Travel. Islands. Fun. Fun. Fun! I could not contain my happiness that night. Somehow I knew my life as a bartender was over. I knew I would leave and never look back. I knew my life was starting at last. I hugged Patty, hugged the manager, got home and woke up my parents and hugged them, too. My mom was too tired to ask me anything and my dad didn't have his dentures in, so any kind of explaining would have to wait. Besides, I couldn't hold a serious conversation with my dad when his teeth were in a glass on the bedside table.

I was on my way to a spectacular life. And much too quickly, I forgot about making a difference.

# Chapter 12

I called Helmut first thing the next morning to confirm it wasn't a scam. After a brief introduction and trivial chit chat, his personal assistant set up an appointment for me with the Human Resources person. I had to go down to the Port of Miami and see Nancy Tyler that very same day. *Wow*, I thought, *I made a really good impression on those men.* I typed up my résumé, picked out my best outfit and even polished my nails. I didn't want to tell my parents anything until I'd gotten the job, so I ran out the door with résumé in hand as my mom handed me a cup of coffee in a Styrofoam cup.

"Where are joo going, *mi'ja?*"

"I'm going to change my life, mom."

"Changee your life? Your life no good now?"

"Yes, Mom, it's great, but this will make it better. I'll tell you what it is when I get home, okay?"

"Jes, *mi'ja, andale. Dios to bendiga.*"

I hugged her tightly. "Thanks for the coffee, Mami. You're the best."

I made it to the port in record time and found the office building where my future awaited me. I was nervous and wondering if I'd remembered to put on deodorant. A very kind old woman led me to Nancy Tyler's office. She looked at me as she held open the door as if to say, *Honey, you have no idea what you're about to endure.* I walked in and saw an anorexic looking woman with short hair and glasses seated at a large desk. She looked me up and down as I walked in and didn't even bother to smile. She pointed at the empty chair in front of her desk impatiently and straightened out her size zero suit jacket.

"Okay, Bibiana," she said as I sat down across from her. "Did you bring your résumé?" She was eyeing me with contempt and suspicion. I wondered what Helmut and Edward had told her about me. I handed her my résumé and cleared my throat as I waited for her questions.

She looked over it for what seemed like an eternity and then finally set it down. She crossed her hands on her desk. She looked like a five year old trying to play grown up and I nearly giggled. I begged my imagination to leave me alone.

"So, you have no experience working on cruise ships, do you?"

"Uh, no. Actually, working on ships had never even crossed my mind until I met Helmut and Edward."

"You mean *Mr. Meyer* and *Mr. Nowak.*"

"Yes, of course. They told me I could call them by their first names," I said innocently.

"Hm hmm, well, isn't that wonderful for you." *What a bitch,* I thought. "How exactly did you meet them?"

"Didn't they tell you?"

"No, not really. It's not my place to ask where they get their girls from." *Oh, shit, she must think they met me in a strip club.*

"Uhm, I was working one night at Fridays, you know, *bartending...* with my shirt on, of course."

"Fridays?" she asked me suspiciously.

"Yes, Fridays. Red and white stripes, potato skins, mocha mud pie. That place. I thought I put that on my résumé?"

She looked at it again and then set it down after a second. "Uh-huh, very well, you're right, I must have overlooked that."

*How could you overlook that?* I wanted to ask. *For God's sake, you're the Human Resources person.* I started to tell her how we met when she cut me off in mid-sentence.

"Do you know what working on a cruise ship is like?" *Jesus, she is dumber than I thought.*

"No, of course not, being that I've never been on one, Ms. Tyler. But I'm really excited about this opportunity and I think I'll like it."

"You think so, do you? Well, let me give you a brief description of life on a cruise ship. You'll work every single day for at least ten hours for six months at a time. You will get very little time off in port and if you do, I doubt you'll be able to enjoy it because you'll be exhausted from working so many hours. You will live in a cabin with someone else, and believe me, it's the size of your closet at home. You'll have to deal with passengers who are mad because they didn't get the cabin their travel agent promised, they didn't get the dinner time their travel agent promised, and they didn't get to book the right tour on time because their travel agent didn't tell them about it. On top of that, you'll have to deal with people from all over the world; different cultures, different languages, different values and ideals. You will always have to be nice because if we get one bad comment about you, you're off the ship. Now, how does that sound to you?"

To be honest, it sounded horrifying, but I knew she was only trying to scare me. I wasn't about to give her any kind of satisfaction.

"That sounds all right to me. I lived with my grandmother and ten relatives in Mexico in a home that looked pretty much like a cave and I loved it. Sometimes I'd have to wait for hours to get my turn in the shower and I've never seen so many roaches in my whole life. I've been working ten hour shifts for the last four years on top of going to college, so I don't think the work load's going to be too much for me. As for dealing with angry passengers, I'm not worried at all. You wouldn't believe the kind of people I had to deal with at Fridays."

She gave me a sinister smile and cleared her throat.

"Bibiana, we get thousands of applications every day from people all over the world dying to get a job on cruise ships. Sometimes they have to wait six months to a year for a chance. Most of the people you'll be working with won't appreciate the fact that you waltzed right into this job without having to wait. I recommend you keep your chance encounter with Mr. Meyer and Mr. Nowak to yourself. You won't want them to get the wrong idea. Do you understand me?"

*So, there it was,* I thought. *The moron thinks I slept my way into the job.*

"Of course I understand, but once I tell them I'm *gay*, there will be no way for them to get the *wrong* idea. But don't worry, I'll keep it to myself. Thank you so much for the advice." My fake smile hurt my face but I held onto it until I left her office. The fact that I was getting on a ship in three days was enough for me to forget how horrible she was.

When I got to my car, I jumped up and down at my twist of fate. I sat in my car and looked at the brochures she'd given me, glossy pictures of the *MS Seaward*, the *Winward*, the *Norway*, the whole wonderful fleet just waiting for me to explore them. I drove home with the radio blaring "I'm Free" by Kenny Loggins and it made me want to stop my car on the highway and dance like a crazy person. *There is a God,* I remember thinking, *and boy does He like me.*

The night before I was supposed to sign on the *MS Seaward* and sail out of Miami, some of the bartenders took me out for a few drinks. Okay, it was more than a few. We consumed about half a liquor store. I got home at two in the morning with enough tequila in my system to make my Mexican uncles damn proud. I managed to make it to my bedroom without falling over. As soon as I turned on the light and saw my waterbed, my old desk and the curtains my mom had made for me, the reality that I would be away from home for months and months hit me hard. Too hard. Alcohol can do that to you. It can take the slightest of feelings and magnify it by three hundred percent, be it sadness or happiness.

I looked around my room and felt like crying. *How can I leave my mom again? How can I be so selfish? What is she going to do without me? Jesus, what am I going to do without her?*

I crept into my parents' bedroom and woke my mom up. She got up as though she hadn't even been sleeping. I realized she'd been waiting up for me, something she always did no matter how old I was. She could never go to sleep knowing one of us was "out there" somewhere.

Without saying a word, she led me back to my bedroom. I sat down on my waterbed and three shots of tequila nearly toppled me over.

"*Mi'ja*, joo has been drinking. *Ay Dios mio*, joo are going to be like your *tios*."

"No, Mom, it's okay. I'm okay, really. I'm not drunk."

She sat down next to me and smoothed my hair, which smelled like a whole pack of cigarettes. "What's wrong, *mi'ja*, eh? Why joo wake me up?"

I couldn't hold back the tears anymore, not when Jose Cuervo was basically egging them on.

"Oh, Mami, I'm so scared. I, I…I'm scared to leave home, to leave my bed and my room and this house and you and Papi and the way you always iron my clothes and make me breakfast and take care of me when I'm sick and…and…" I was crying so hard I couldn't talk.

"Es okay, *mi'ja*, es okay. Don't cry, baby."

"No, Mami, I, I, I went to Mexico and left you here by yourself with Papi and I know you were so lonely without me and now I'm going to do it to you again and and and that's so mean. I'm sorry, Mami, maybe I shouldn't go."

She looked at me so tenderly that it made me cry even harder.

"Ay, *mi'ja*, don't be craysee. Es what joo wanted, no? Joo want to see de world, no? I no want joo to estay here and be sad. Joo go and has some fun and joo call me, okay? I know joo will love it, *mi'ja*, so no cry, okay? And remember, *mi'ja*, if joo no like it, Mami and Papi will be here for joo, foreber and eber. Joo can come home when joo want, okay, *mi'ja*?"

In my heart, I knew she would be devastated once I left. I knew she would sit in her rocking chair in the living room after my dad had gone to bed and miss someone to watch scary movies with. I knew she would go to the mall and wonder why I wasn't behind her picking up the messes she always made. I knew she would probably cry as she looked at my empty bedroom with the curtains she had put so much love into. I knew she would look at pictures of me when I was fat little kid in elementary school and wonder if I was happy. I knew she would go to bed every night and say a prayer for me. I knew how much she loved me, but I also knew that more than anything, she wanted me to be happy, and that meant letting me go.

As I walked up the gangway to my new life, I silently thanked God for giving me such wonderful and understanding parents, even though my dad's bowel movements were embarrassing and my mom's lipstick never matched what she was wearing. They were my family and I loved them.

I spent the next year and a half working on cruise ships as a purser. I was the information girl. The go to person. The one you came to when you needed sea sick pills or lost your cabin key. It was an absolute blast at first, like everything is when it's new. I thought they would put me on the ship as a bartender, but to my surprise, they made me a keeper of all vital information. It really didn't bother me that on most days I worked ten hours straight without a day off. It didn't annoy me that my cabin was the size of a shoebox and that I had to share it with Paula, a Canadian girl who thought nothing of bringing crew members back to the cabin to have sex while I tried to get some sleep on the top bunk. I thought working on a cruise ship was glamorous and exciting.

Passengers came to me with every one of their troubles and I always tried to help them as best I could. It was so nice to deal with sober people for a change. I laughed at some of the questions I got my first couple of weeks, but eventually, complete and utter stupidity started to wear me down. *People can't be this dumb*, I would tell myself. When I wasn't lying on crew deck working on my tan or trying to hold a serious conversation with a Norwegian officer in the crew bar, I answered really dumb questions while I tried in vain to keep a smile on my face. I couldn't help but think about what I'd really like to give them as answers. I knew I couldn't say what I really wanted because Nancy Tyler had made it very clear to me that I would be kicked off as soon as someone wrote a bad comment about me, but that didn't stop my mind from wondering.

"What time is the midnight buffet?" someone would ask. *Are you serious?* I would wonder.

"Do you work here?" *No, I like wearing epaulettes and a white uniform. It's quite the rage!*

"Do you live on the ship?" *Uh-uh. We get flown home every day in a really fast helicopter.*

"Do those stairs go up?" I'd be too speechless to think of a witty reply.

"Where is the elevator that goes around the ship?" *Sir, this is not the Willy Wonka Chocolate Factory.*

"Do I need my passport in Key West?" *No, but you should take some kind of weapon. The Oompa Loompas are really restless.*

After a few months of ridiculous questions, I was seriously starting to doubt the education system in America. But then I'd walk up on deck as the sun was setting and see the ocean spread before me like an endless dream and embrace my new life. I probably could have gone to graduate school after college. I could've gotten a job with a company and climbed the corporate ladder. I could've done a whole lot of things, but working on cruise ships was perfect for me. It was spectacular.

Cruise ship life was like a fraternity party magnified by three hundred percent. The crew on the *MS Seaward* had more energy than all of New York City on a Saturday night. We were like a drunk representation of the United Nations; all the delegates were about my age and convinced being slightly inebriated was the only way to deal with annoying passengers. I met people from all over and then some. Croatia, Turkey, India, Russia, England, Ireland, Canada, Norway. All of us stuck on a giant party boat, all of us forgetting about life on land, the real world. Everyone with the exception of the captain and the officers worked seven days a week and partied every single night. We would all get together in the crew bar and drink ourselves into a merry state.

One night, I was in the crew bar with my nymphomaniac cabin mate, Paula. We were bonding over shots as usual, even though most of us had to get up in a couple of hours and face passengers without any trace of tequila on our breath. Somebody made the sad mistake of asking me about my family.

"So, Bibiana, where do you come from?" Istvan asked me. Istvan was a dancer from Hungary and so beautiful it made my eyes hurt.

"I'm from California, but I grew up in Miami." I sipped on my beer, my second that night. Istvan got even more beautiful.

"But you are not an American, this is right?"

"Yeah, I'm American, but my parents are Hispanic."

"Hispanic? From Spain?"

"No. My mom's Mexican and my dad's Cuban. I'm a cross between black beans and tortillas."

Istvan laughed and toasted me with his drink. "Tell me about your family."

170

"My family? Like, my parents?"

"Yes, your mom and dad. They are nice?"

"Yes, they are nice, but my mom is crazy and my dad thinks farting should be made an Olympic sport."

The other crew members at the table giggled.

"What do you mean your mum's crazy? Is she really nuts?" Sophia asked me. Sophia was a dealer in the casino. I had never seen her without a drink in her hand and a cigarette in her mouth. She was from London and really loud. All the guys said they loved her legs, and not because they were actually nice, but because she spread them for just about everyone except the captain. I liked her in spite of the fact that everyone thought she was a tramp. She was always nice to me.

"She's not nuts, but she's definitely close. She's just quirky."

"What do you mean?" Istvan asked. "What is this 'quirky'?"

"Quirky, Istvan, means that sometimes she comes home and puts her purse inside the freezer and her keys in the oven. She talks to herself on most days and usually manages to knock over everything in the supermarket. She also speaks English with a really funny accent."

Paula jumped into the conversation and asked me to imitate my mom. "Bibiana, tell them that story about when your mom knocked over the mannequin in the department store! I love that story!"

"You mean when she beat the shit out of a doll?"

"Yes!" She looked at the other crew members and gave the thumbs up sign, as though I was a movie they should really see.

"Okay, if you insist." I didn't need much prompting. I loved telling stories about my mom. "But first I need another shot."

Paula ran to the bar immediately and came back with another shot of tequila. Down it went.

My mom could've won an award for being the biggest klutz. There was nothing she touched that didn't cause an avalanche. In grocery stores, she was that woman who would grab an orange from the pile and cause all of them to come crashing down. In department stores, she would knock over one rack of clothing, therefore causing it to smash into another one until the entire junior miss department looked like a gigantic domino display. My brother and I would always be right behind her picking up the chaos while she wrung her hands and said *Ay ¡Dios Mio!* We were so used to the commotion my mom would cause that after a while we began to enjoy it. We'd actually bet on how much time it would take for my mom to create a mess.

It was a day before Halloween. Erasmo, my mom and I went to the mall because Burdines, a department store, had the best Halloween shop in town. Masks, costumes, fake guns, face paint. My mom wanted the best costume because there was a contest at the Bingo Hall and if she won, she would win a free month of bingo. Both of us were still teenagers, a time when most kids would be mortified to be caught in the mall with their moms, but being around her never phased us. Being around her was free entertainment.

Burdines was swarming that day with kids, parents, frustrated employees, drug dealers and hired hit men. There were so many people that it was hard to figure out where the mannequins began and real people ended. Enter victim. It was a mannequin of a little girl with its back to us, and it was wearing something cool like Ralph Lauren or Guess, clothes we couldn't afford, hell no. It did look like a real little girl at first, so I'll give my mom some credit. As we walked passed it, my mom, who was closest to it, bumped into it and then stopped dead in her tracks. The mannequin started to sway on its fake shoes and looked ready to fall over.

"*Ay, ¡Dios mio!*" my mom said way too loudly. So loud in fact that everyone in the area stopped what they were doing and paused to look at my mom. I looked at my brother, he looked at me, and then we looked at my mom, who looked absolutely mortified.

"I no mean to bump into joo, *mi'ja.* I'm so bery sorry." There she was, innocently carrying on a conversation with the doll, completely unaware that it was stiffer than a rock and not responding to her.

"Maaami," I said.

The people around us started laughing, and if that wasn't enough, my mom grabbed the mannequin by the arm and continued her apology.

"Joo know, I no pay attention. Okay? I'm so bery sorry. Where is your mami, *mi'ja?*"

Everyone was laughing their heads off, as though my mom had been hired by Burdines to make an ass out of herself. I grabbed my mom and tried to move her on, but as she took a step, she ripped the doll's arm off. She took one look at it and turned into a complete bonafide maniac.

"*Ay, ¡Dios mio!* I broke de arm! I reep it! Please, someone call dee 911! I reep de arm!"

There was nothing we could do. My mom was truly convinced she had single-handedly torn off a little girl's arm and we were all laughing too hard to tell her otherwise. My brother put his big arms around my mom and hugged her.

"Mami, it's a doll! Calm down! You didn't rip her arm off. She's not real!"

She looked at the arm, at the lifeless doll and then at everyone laughing at her. She continued to make a spectacle of herself.

"Oh, okay. I put dee arm back for de little girl. Okay? Es no problem." She tried to get the arm back into the socket, her face twisting in concentration as she struggled to make everything right. The crowd seemed to have doubled in those few seconds. Tiny beads of sweat popped up on her forehead as she tried desperately to put the arm back in.

A manager came over to my mom after a few minutes and grabbed the arm out of her hand. "Uhm, really, it's okay, lady. I'll fix it for you."

"Oh, meester, so sorry. I no can fix for joo. I break de arm, joo know? *Pero*, es okay, no? She no living, joo see? She is no for real, so es okay."

"Yeah, lady, it's okay. Move on, now."

We convinced my mom to buy a clown costume. After all, she was good at making people laugh, orange lipstick and all.

After that night in the crew bar, everyone started saying *Ay Dios mio* whenever something went wrong. *Ay Dios mio, I dropped a drink. Ay Dios mio, I missed boat drill. Ay Dios mio, I slept with a casino dealer and it was awful.* I became the crew bar stand up comedian. It wasn't like someone would hand me a microphone and order me to tell jokes. They would hand me a shot and ask me to imitate my mom.

It was after one night of imitating my mom that Andy, one of the ship's photographers, came over and sat next to me at the bar. He was English, handsome in a very posh way and had one of those accents going for him.

"You're very funny, you know."

"No, I'm not. I just imitate my mom really well."

"Yeah, but it's still funny. You have so many stories to tell. Are they all true? Is your mum really like that?" God, I loved that accent.

"In a million years I couldn't make those stories up. She's really that way."

"Brilliant. You should write them down someday."

"Write them down? I've never thought about that."

"You should. I'd read them." Andy was flirting with me, which wasn't a good thing. He was known to be a playboy and I'd already been warned to stay away from him.

"Look, you don't have to feed me compliments, okay?"

"Settle down. I was being honest."

I looked at him and tried to figure out if he was just making small talk to get into my pants. Two shots of tequila and I was hoping he would be.

"Where are you from, Andy?"

"England, and you?"

"Originally Los Angeles, but I grew up in Miami."

"Brilliant."

"Is everything brilliant to you?"

"Yeah, mostly. Even though we invented the English language, we can't seem to utter any other words except brilliant and lovely. Sorry." He shrugged and took a sip of his beer.

"Hey, I was only teasing you. I really like your accent, by the way."

"I love your mum's. You really make me laugh."

"I do my best. Ready for a shot?"

"Absolutely."

Even though I drank enough on most nights to kill a small elephant, during the day I answered silly questions with a smile on my face and continued to love being on a cruise ship. I got a wicked tan, made friends with people from all over the world, traveled throughout the Caribbean, Alaska and Europe and even managed to acquire a nice English boyfriend. Nerdy Fat Girl was definitely gone. Andy was one of the photographers on the ship, someone who annoyed the passengers as they boarded the ship, ate dinner, got off the ship in every port, dressed up for formal night. It seems Andy was never without his camera. We managed to form a relationship if anything because we were both on the same ship and clueless.

At the end of my first contract, Andy asked me if I'd like to go to England on vacation to meet his family. No, it wasn't what you might think. We were both young and crazy and half drunk all the time, so naturally, we thought it was something serious and probably going somewhere. I agreed to go to England with him, and why the hell not? I'd never been there and was really curious if they drank warm beer or not.

# Chapter 13

I was more than a teacher, really. I saw myself as an entertainer of sorts. Stand up comedy at its rawest. I had finally figured out that the only way to get the kids to behave and sit still was to throw in stories about my mom while teaching them a lesson. For them everything had to be broken down to a story because it was the only way they would learn, or rather, would like to learn. So far, they'd heard about Mexico, my bartending experience, college life, cruise ships and growing up as a fat kid, but nothing, absolutely nothing made them laugh as hard as when I imitated my mom. Not even stories about my dad's farting-in-public fiasco.

I was right about *The Outsiders*, though. Ponyboy became a hero to them, as did Dally and Johnny. The students loved to make comments about each character. To them, they were real people that needed to be called out.

"Miss C, I don't like that Dally guy. He's mean," Ebony would say.

After every chapter, Jazelin would put his two cents in. "Yo, Miss C, I think Dally the coolest, you know what I'm sayin'? 'cause he's like, you know what I'm sayin'? He tough and he remind me of my momma, you know what I'm sayin'?"

Chancy was the hardest one to please. "Miss C, I can say something? Uh, I think, uh, like, Johnny? I think he crazy. He shouldn't have stabbed that boy. And Sodapop even though he got a funny name, I think he okay but he don't take care of his little brother, you feel me? And like, that girl Cherry? Why she gonna like Dally? 'cause he cool, Miss C? I don't think he cool. I think he dumb. But I like Ponyboy 'cause he likes to read. Miss C, we can read that book they reading?"

"Which one, Chancy?"

"That wind book. It sound cool."

"Oh, *Gone With The Wind*?"

"Yeah, that's it. We can read that next?"

"Yes, we might be able to read that next."

Chancy was much smarter than I thought.

At first I read to them as they followed along, sometimes three kids sharing one torn up paperback (the trials of teaching in a poorly funded program). It was hard to get them to sit still and be quiet at first, but there was something about the book that instantly sucked them in. After a few tries, I started picking different students to read, and it was always chaotic. Everyone wanted a chance to read. I would think to myself, *Well, this isn't so bad after all. I've made them want to read. I'm doing something right.*

Chancy finished the chapter for the day, and of course, asked me if I would tell them a story about my mom. They had been good, they reminded me, so I dug into my brain frantically searching for a story. I mean, my mom had done some pretty outrageous things in her life, but I was getting to the point where I would have to start making stuff up. Either that or hope and pray she would do something funny and call me to tell me about it. As I stood there racking my memory, Marcdala raised her hand.

"Yeah, Marcdala, what's up?"

"Miss C, what happened to your boyfriend from…what was that place you said? England?"

"Uhm, well, it didn't work out. We broke up because he wanted to stay on cruise ships and I wanted to come home."

I didn't want to tell them what really happened. Truth was I got tired of cruise ships after two eight month contracts and decided to do something else. When I got back home, Andy didn't look quite so attractive anymore. Being on land changes everything because you see people differently. The Andy I saw horrified me. He drank too much, had zero ambition and didn't have any kind of religion. I ended things and got a job at the Hard Rock Café in Miami. Andy stayed on cruise ships. And that was the end of that.

"Okay, but what happened when you went to see his family? Did you call your momma? Did she miss you?"

"Yeah, I called her, and yes, I missed her, and oh my God I just remembered the funniest story about her. You guys wanna hear it?"

"Yes!"

They were all looking at me expectantly, each one sitting perfectly still at the edge of their seats. I looked at the clock and saw that I had ten more minutes till the bell rang. They'd been pretty good so I decided to reward them. Besides, they were about to get to that part in *The Outsiders* where Johnny dies and I didn't want to end class on a sad note.

My parents liked Andy the moment they met him. Finally they had met someone with a different accent, which to them was a bonding factor. We stayed with my parents for one night (Andy slept on the sofa, of course), and the next day they drove us to the airport. As we stood at the gate saying goodbye, my mom reached out and grabbed Andy's arm and pulled him close.

"Plees, when joo get to de England, joo tell Bibita to call me. Collect, okay? Es okay, I has the money to pay. Okay, baby?" She pulled out her wallet from her oversized bag and opened it to reveal a few dollar bills. I groaned. "Joo see? I has de money. We bery good family, and Bibita es a bery nice girl, okay? So, joo tell her to call me so I no worry."

Andy smiled and said nothing. I don't think he understood her.

"Mami, I'll call you, I promise. But listen, when I call you, it's going to be nine a.m. your time, okay?"

"*Sí, sí.*"

"So, when the phone rings at nine, you answer it, and no matter what the lady says, you say 'yes.' That's it, just say 'yes.' You got it, Mami?"

"Oh, of course, my choogar. Jes! I say jes! Okay, es no problem. Joo has a bery good time and joo call me, okay?"

I leaned over and hugged my dad, who was desperate for a cigarette. Airports make him uncomfortable. I bent down and hugged my mom. Her lipstick was bright pink that day and she'd decided to take the rollers out of her hair. Thankfully, she didn't look sad. She was getting used to the fact that I liked to keep moving. Andy hugged both my parents, which was unlike him, being that he was, in fact, English, and we walked towards the terminal.

At the last minute, I turned around to look at them one last time. The odd couple. My dad had his arm around my mom and she waved at me. I was kind of sad to leave them, but hell, I was headed to England. My life was getting more spectacular by the minute.

After a seven hour flight over the Atlantic and an hour train ride, we finally arrived at his home. Home is not the correct word, actually. Mansion would be more exact. Andy had never told me much about his family, mostly because we were always too caught up in making last call at the crew bar to think about anything else. I was greeted by his mom, his two sisters and his uncle Pat. In Hispanic families, if you don't see each other for just one day, you usually greet each other with a strong hug and millions of kisses. Not so with his family. They greeted one another as polite strangers and didn't even make any comments about one another's appearance. *What a weird family,* I thought. My family would've said I looked too fat, too skinny, too old, too young, too tired, too tan, too whatever. I welcomed their silence.

The time came for me to make my collect call. Andy's mom insisted I make it direct but I knew my mom would've been mortified. I got a hold of the operator with the lovely British accent and told her it was a reverse charges call. I was praying my mom would remember what I told her. When she answered the phone on the first ring, I let out a long sigh.

"*¿Aló?*"

"Yes. I've got a collect call from Bibiana in the United Kingdom. Do you accept the charges?"

"Bibi? No, she no here."

A brief pause.

"No, no, madame, Bibiana is *calling you*. Do you accept the charges?"

"No, lady, Bibita is on vacachun. She es in England with her boyfren. Joo want to leave message, lady?"

Time for me to cut in. "Can I say something to her?"

"Oh, please. She's mad, luv!"

"Mami, Mami, it's me! Bibiana! Say yes, okay?"

"*Ay Dios mio*! Oh…jes, lady! I pay! I pay for de collect call, okay, lady?"

The operator was laughing. "Oh, bloody hell! Is that your mum?"

"Uhm, yeah."

"She's crazy, luv! She reminds me of my mum. Go on, then. You can speak now."

"Thanks."

The class laughed wholeheartedly during the story. The bell rang and they gathered their belongings while I reminded them to do their homework. Chancy took his time getting his things together, which was odd. Usually he ran out the door before anyone else. After everyone had gone, I sat down at my desk and started going over my lesson plans for the next day. He still didn't leave, though. Instead he made a huge production of putting his stuff away in his beat up backpack. I stared at him until he looked at me.

"What's up, Chancy?"

"Yo, Miss C, you can give me a ride home?"

"Say that again."

"Uh, will you please give me a ride home?"

I didn't know what the rules were as far as driving kids home, but honestly, I didn't care. For the most part, I'd been left alone. Once in a while, Dr. Lawrence would stop me in the hall and ask me how it was going, but since I'd managed to keep all of them out of in-school suspension and jail, he and everyone else assumed I was doing a great job. For all they knew I could've been teaching them every cuss word in the English language and they wouldn't have been the wiser.

"Sure, Chancy, I'll give you a ride home."

He gave me a funny look, as though his question had been strictly hypothetical. "Miss C, you can't give me no ride home. You know where I live?"

"Yeah, Chancy, you live in the hood. West Parramore. Big deal." I stood up and gathered my things together.

"Yo, Miss C, you crazy. You can really give me a ride in your nice car?"

"Yeah, I can, and by the way, my car is not that nice. In fact, it's about to die."

"But Miss C, I live in the hood, yo. It's kind of scary."

"Oh, come on, are they gonna do something to me in the hood because I'm white?"

Chancy jumped back in shock. "Shoot, Miss C, you ain't white."

"I'm not?"

"No, Miss C, you're Hispanic. You're one of us."

There you go. I was no longer the white kid trying to do good for the poor black kids. To them, I was an equal. I was, as I had always wanted to be, accepted. I agreed to give him a ride home and his whole face lit up like a light bulb. It was reason enough for me. Seeing Chancy smile was like running into Jesus Christ on the street. A miracle.

Chancy followed me out to the school parking lot. We got into my little red Honda monster and Chancy immediately changed the radio station and found something he liked. He turned up the volume, laid back in the seat and smiled. As the bass boomed out of my speakers, I pulled out of the lot and onto Robinson Street. Most everyone was gone for the day, which was a good thing because I really didn't want anyone to see me with a student in my car, a student who thought my car was clearly designed to be a moving night club.

I drove past the now empty school, past Lake Eola and its beautiful fountains, past tall buildings, yuppy-filled cafes and happy hour bars. Chancy kept the smile on his face, kept grinning from ear to ear even as we crossed under the I-4 and drove right into the hood. I kept driving, waiting for Chancy to tell me where to turn.

When he realized I had no idea where I was going, he sat up a little bit and told me to *make the left after the second light, then a right, and then another left, go down a little, Miss C, okay...hey, there go my cousin Tonilda, no don't*

179

*stop Miss C she crazy keep going make a left at the stop sign and then a right ha ha ha there go Shaquila she's a who'e okay Miss C it's the third house on the right uh-huh pull in Miss C uh-oh there's my grandmamma and Uncle Morris.*

I pulled in and turned the music down. Chancy put his hand on the door handle and looked at me. "Come on, Miss C. Turn the car off. Don't be scared." I looked at his grandmother and uncle, who were sitting on the porch with an angry dog, all three of them looking back at me like I was the anti-Christ. I turned off the ignition and got out. There was no way I could've driven away without explaining who I was and why I'd decided to give Chancy a ride home. Chancy got out of the car, walked ahead of me up the battered steps and onto the porch where the suspicious three sat. Uncle Morris, who was puffing on a pipe, looked me up and down and then back at the dog. The dog wagged its tail and waited for me to do something. I bent down to pet it and it growled so I quickly jumped back and cleared my throat.

"Hello, I'm Miss Castellanos, one of Chancy's teachers."

His grandmother stood up from her chair and gave me a long look. She was a heavyset woman with tired eyes that stared at me with contempt and suspicion. She gave a Chancy a sideways glance and then looked at me again.

"Hm hmm, must be bad if you drove out here yourself."

"Excuse me?"

"I know why you're here. What'd he do now?"

"Oh, uh, nothing. He asked me for a ride home, that's all."

"That's it?" She looked at Chancy, who was picking at his 'fro. He shrugged and pulled his pants up to his waist. *There's a first*, I thought.

"Grandma, I'm thirsty. I'm gonna have me some soda. Miss C, you want some?"

"No, it's okay."

His grandmother grabbed him by the ear as he tried to make an escape.

"You pour Miss C a glass of lemonade and bring it out here, you hear? And you better put it in a nice glass, young man. Go on, now."

Chancy went inside the house and left me on the porch with his grandmother and Uncle Morris. She sat back down on her chair and patted the empty one next to her. There was really nothing for me to do but sit down and pretend I didn't feel grossly uncomfortable. I tried to pet the dog again but he growled as soon as my hand got near him.

"Stop that, Boy. You behave." His grandmother looked at me and smiled earnestly. "He's a mean old dog, that one. By the way, my name is Ruthie and that's Morris, my brother."

At the sound of his name, Morris turned and looked at me as though seeing me for the first time.

"Morris, say hello. This is Miss Castu...Miss Ca...Miss..."

"Miss C. The kids call me Miss C."

"You hear that, Morris?" She was practically shouting now. "You say hello, Morris!"

He coughed a little and put his finger on his hearing aid. "Hello there, Miss C. Welcome to our palace and gardens." He winked.

I suppressed a giggle. Ruthie leaned over and pinched his arm. Morris flinched and slapped Ruthie's hand away.

"Crazy old man," she said. "He thinks we live in a palace with a great big ol' garden! Shoot, if I didn't love him so much I'd put him in a home for crazy people."

"I heard that, Ruthie. Hm hmm. Always calling me crazy. Ain't nobody understand me like Boy does, ain't that right?" The dog wagged his tail and leaned into Morris's leg.

"Is that his name? Boy?" I said.

"Hm hmm. Easiest name in the world to remember. I hate those names people give to dogs, stupid ass names like Duke and Spot."

Ruthie pinched him again. "Don't you go swearin' around Miss C. We have to show her we're a nice family, ain't that right, Miss C?"

"Well, to be honest, I do quite a bit of swearing myself sometimes, not in front of the class, of course. But once in a while it's good to curse out your anger when nobody's listening."

"Amen, honey. Now, tell us a little about yourself. We ain't never had no teacher come around to see us. Where you from?"

"We're originally from California but my family moved to Miami when I was seven."

Chancy came out the front door with a cold glass of lemonade. I don't really like lemonade because it always leaves a lump in my throat, but it was unbearably humid and my tongue was dry.

"Thanks, Chancy." I took it from him and gulped half of it down I was so thirsty.

"Lord have mercy, you sure was thirsty, Miss C."

"Hm hmm, I sure was."

Chancy started running down the front steps but didn't get too far before Ruthie's strong arm grabbed him and pulled him right back.

"And where do you think you're going?"

"Come on, Grandmamma, I'll be right back. I'm goin' round the block to see Maxwell."

"The hell you is! I told you I don't like that boy. He ain't good people. I heard he's in a gang. West Parramore Boys or somethin'. Uh-uh, you stay here."

"Grandmamma, please, I won't be but ten minutes."

She let him go and raised her finger at him. "Ten minutes, young man, and when you get back you're going to help me 'round the house, you hear? Huh?"

"Yeah, Grandmamma. Peace, Miss C!"

"See you tomorrow, Chancy."

Chancy ran across the yard holding his pants up and quickly disappeared. Ruthie took a sip of her lemonade and looked at me again.

"So, you was saying? You from Miami?"

"Hm hmm. I grew up there."

"You white, Miss C?"

"I beg your pardon?" I looked at her and wondered if it would always be a standard question for me. I mean, it was pretty obvious to me that my skin, in fact, was white. Okay, so maybe a little tan, but white in general.

"You don't look white. I don't know, you look mixed."

I coughed on my sip of lemonade. "Mixed? Hmm, haven't heard that one yet. But yeah, I guess you can say I'm mixed." *Mixed up.*

"Mixed how, though? Your parents, where they from?"

Morris took a puff on his pipe and joined in on the conversation. "If you ask me, she look like a Indian."

"Indian?" Ruthie and I said in unison.

"Hm hmm. The feather kind."

"Oh Lordy, Morris, you sure is crazier than I thought." Ruthie shook her head back and forth and fanned herself with an old magazine.

"It's really okay, Ruthie. My grandmother's part Aztec Indian. I've never seen her wearing any feathers, though."

Uncle Morris looked at me and winked again. "Hm hmm, I told you, Ruthie. She a Indian."

I laughed and took another sip of my lemonade.

Ruthie stopped fanning herself. "Aztec Indian, Miss C? Like, from Mexico?"

"Uh-huh. My mom's Mexican. You know, the refried beans and tortilla kind."

Ruthie licked her lips and shook her head. "Oooh, girl, I love Mexican food. And your daddy? Where he come from?"

"My dad's from Cuba. The real I-hate-Castro-and-I-have-a-solution-to-Cuba's-problems kind."

Ruthie laughed out loud.

"Girl, you're funny. No wonder Chancy likes you."

"He does?"

"Oooh, girl, he's always going on about you and that crazy momma of yours. Tell me somethin', did your momma really get into it with the mailman?"

"Say what?"

"Yeah, Chancy had told me that story about the stamp and the accident and the fruit punch. Lord, I don't know if he told it right, but it sure sounded like your momma's a funny lady."

"Hm hmm, she sure is. Crazy as hell, too."

"Honey, we're all a little crazy. Lord knows we need to be nowadays." She paused for a moment and stared out onto the street. "Tell me, now, Miss C, you plannin' on sticking around?"

"Well, to be honest, I've got some tests to grade and I should probably go to the gym, plus I promised my mom I'd call her tonight."

"No, no, Miss C. I mean, are you gonna stick to these kids for the whole school year?"

"Oh. Yeah, of course, unless I get fired for giving Chancy a ride home."

"Hm hmm, you won't."

"Nah, I probably won't. Anyway, why does everyone keep asking me that question? I feel like everyone's expecting me to have a nervous breakdown. It's like some people want me to fail."

"Jesus, girl, those kids ain't easy. Sometimes I can barely handle Chancy, let alone Ebony and Marcdala and that crazy boy Jazelin."

"Yeah, they're pretty tough sometimes, but they're all right. I think they've gotten used to me and my erratic mood swings."

"Hmph. All's I know is Chancy talks about you all the time. He don't complain about going to school anymore. The other day he asked me to take him to the library."

"He did?!"

"Uh-huh. Said he wanted to read *Gone With The Wind*. Lord have mercy, child, I nearly fainted." She scratched her head and looked at me curiously. "I don't know what it is you're doing, baby, but it's working. Chancy's never wanted to read. I never thought that boy would ever be the same after his daddy got arrested and his momma left."

I bit my lip. *Don't say something stupid.* "Yeah, I know about that. I'm sorry."

"You don't need to be. It was bound to happen sooner or later. His daddy was no good and his momma was heading towards nothing but trouble with him."

"Does Chancy ever hear from them?"

"No. Once in a while his daddy calls from prison, and his momma, well, we ain't heard from her since the day she left." She sighed heavily. "Never could help my daughter. She ain't never listened to me when I told her not to get mixed up with that boy. I'm just grateful she had the common sense to leave Chancy to me and Morris. I'm making sure he don't make the same mistakes, but Lord, he's had some awful teachers. It's like they all give up before they've even given these kids a chance."

"Yeah, I know, but I'm not going anywhere, Ruthie. That's a promise."

"You sure, Miss C? You know, it's easier said than done."

"I'm sure." I paused for a moment and thought about what I was saying. "Well, unless I win the lottery."

Ruthie laughed and grabbed my hand. "No, I still think you'd stick around."

"I'd love to have that option right now, Ruthie. Teacher's get paid shit."

As soon as the word was out of my mouth I wanted to kick myself, but she laughed even harder.

"It's okay, honey, like you said, it's good to curse that anger out."

"Yep, it is. Anyway, I have to get going. Thanks for the lemonade, and please remind Chancy to do his homework." I got up and turned to Morris. "It was nice to meet you, Morris." Morris didn't look at me. "Hey, Morris," I said a little louder, "nice to meet you!"

Morris looked up at me and took a puff on his pipe. "Okay, Pocahontas, you take care, you hear?"

I laughed and turned to Ruthie, who had gotten out of her chair and was holding her arms out to me. Before I had a chance to hold out my hand, Ruthie grabbed me with her huge arms and bear hugged me so hard I thought I was going to puke all over her.

"You take care, Miss C, and thanks for stopping by. Honey, you're welcome anytime, you hear?"

"You got it. Next time I make enchiladas I'll bring you some, okay?"

"Girl, don't you make me no promises!"

"Too late."

I leaned down to pet Boy and he didn't growl. I walked down the steps and got into my car while Ruthie stood on the porch yelling at Morris for calling me Pocahontas. I waved and drove away. When I turned the radio back up, it was on the station Chancy had picked. I left it right there and drove home to Puff Daddy.

# Chapter 14

After our incredible make out session and heart to heart chat, I thought Matt would call me, seek me out in between classes or ask me to have lunch with him. I thought for sure he'd ask me out again or at the very least, make up excuses as to why he was not getting down on his knees and proposing. Unfortunately, Matt did none of those things. Whenever I'd see him in the hallway, he'd wave at me and smile but he'd never stop and talk to me. He would dart out of his classroom quickly after school as though fleeing the Nazi regime. As though I was Hitler.

I didn't know how to deal with the situation. A part of me wanted to storm into his classroom and demand an explanation and another part of me wanted to beg him to *please, please like me*. I wanted to be alone with him again. I wanted those eyes to look at me again, eyes that had seemed to see right through me. I ached to have another conversation with the guy I was sure was my soul mate. He had been ignoring me for about three weeks and I was one miserable bitch. I was bitter.

When it came to relationships, I was a complete disaster. Andy had been the only guy I'd dated for more than three months and I'm pretty sure that was only because a) he had a cool accent, b) we were nearly always drinking and c) when you're stuck on a cruise ship, you end up dating guys you would never in a million years date on land. I didn't know the rules of dating. I didn't have five different girlfriends I could call up and beg for help. I had Linda, though. "Should I call him? Should I say something? Should I ask him out instead of waiting?" I asked. Linda told me to be bold and make the next move. "What's the worst that can happen, right?" Ever so optimistic. My mom told me to be patient and, of course, wait for a sign. My brother told me not to waste my time with him because he was probably way out of my league. He offered to set me up with one of his redneck friends before I hung up on him. My dad said nothing. He liked to stay out of my love life.

Matt hadn't said two words to me since our night at the Ale House and it was really starting to depress me. My depression carried over into everything. My runs got shorter, my naps got longer, I stopped eating altogether and started losing what little ass I had to begin with. Ben and Jerry silently cursed me from the freezer for ignoring them and I stopped dreaming up ways of embarrassing Mrs. Coleman. Even stories about my mom were starting to suffer, which wasn't good because after all, it was my groove.

Kids can sense anything. It's like they're built with a special radar designed to pick up distress signals. If you're happy, they love you. If you're mad, they do things to make you explode. If you have PMS, they know better than to do anything wrong and if you're sad, like I was, they turn into caring little angels. I just couldn't hide it from them. I was good at masking my emotions around adults, but when it came to kids, it seemed unnatural to feign happiness.

Chancy started to show up for class on time and Marcdala finally gave in and started showing me how smart she really was. Jazelin stopped picking on Tevaris and Ebony quit making fun of everyone's clothes. It was a few weeks before the Christmas break and I had zero energy. I should have been happy my students were really good for once and ready to learn something, but I was upset about the whole Matt-is-ignoring-me situation. The last thing I wanted to talk about was the discovery of America or grammar.

"Yo, Miss C."

I was sitting at my desk calling roll. "Yeah, Chancy."

"Why you so sad all the time?"

"What?" I looked up.

"Man, what's wrong with you? You look like you wanna cry all the time, you know what I'm sayin'?

"Chancy, I'm just tired, okay? I'm not sad. I promise. Get your homework out and let me finish calling roll."

Ebony raised her hand.

"Go ahead, Ebony."

"Miss C, how come you isn't married?"

"Come on, now, rephrase that sentence and ask me the question like I've been teaching you to."

Ebony sighed and twirled her pencil in her left hand. "Okay. Miss C, *why aren't you married?*"

"Good, Ebony, it's good to know you've learned something."

She stared at me and waited for an answer to her correctly put question. The rest of the class looked at me as though my answer would solve every puzzle in the world.

"I don't know why I'm not married, Ebony. Some people meet their soul mate and some people just don't. I guess I'm not lucky. I thought I found mine, but apparently I was wrong." I put down my pencil, put my face in my hands and stared at my students, students who were staring back at me wondering what was wrong with Miss C. Marcdala raised her hand.

"Yes, Marcdala," I sighed.

"Miss C, are your parents still married?"

"My parents?"

"Yeah. Are they still together?"

"Yes. Of course they are. They've been married for over twenty-five years."

"Wow. That's a long time."

"It sure is."

Jazelin sat up in his seat. "Miss C, how your parents got together? 'cause you had said that, you know what I'm sayin'? You had said your momma's from Mexeeco and your daddy's from Cuba. How they met, you know what I'm sayin'?"

I was too tired to correct his grammar. "That's a long story." I sighed again and picked up my pencil.

"Come on, Miss C, tell us how they got together. You haven't told us a story in a long time."

Jazelin was right. I'd been in a funk. *Enough is enough.* "You know what? I'm going to tell you a story about how my parents hooked up."

Marcdala started giggling. Everyone else followed her example.

"What's so funny?"

"Miss C, you said hooked up."

"Yeah, so?"

"I didn't know teachers said that."

"Well, Marcdala, I'm not most teachers. You wanna hear the story or not?" I smiled for the first time in weeks.

"Yeah, Miss C!" the class yelled.

My mom got across the border illegally. She didn't swim across the Rio Grande or pay a coyote thousands of dollars to cram her into an eighteen wheeler with thirty other hopefuls. She simply got across the border by turning herself into something she definitely was not: a hippie.

It was the sixties. While my mom hand washed piles and piles of clothes and helped my grandmother raise sixteen kids, America was fast becoming an organized festival of sex, drugs and Janis Joplin. As thousands gathered in Washington DC to protest the Vietnam War, my mom stood in the tiny living room and protested my grandmother's decision to send her to America. She was sending her to live with her older sister Esmeralda. She was terrified to leave her mom, afraid to go somewhere she'd only heard about from other people. "Why do I have to go?" she kept asking. "Because life will be better for you," my grandmother said over and over again. The real reason Lupe wanted to send my mom to Los Angeles was because my mom was dating a class A drunk. She didn't want to see her end up marrying a loser with no job.

After months of begging and crying, my mom finally gave up arguing with Lupe. Lupe was a force to be reckoned with. The letters from Esmeralda started to arrive. Along with the letters, Esmeralda sent pictures of flower children and detailed instructions on how to pronounce "American citizen." Eventually, Esmeralda sent a box with bell-bottomed pants and a flowery shirt. My mom tried on the clothes and posed for Lupe, and when Lupe thought my mom was pronouncing "American citizen" well enough, she wrote to Esmeralda and set a date for my mom's arrival in Tijuana. The plan was Esmeralda and her husband Santiago would cross the border, pick her up in Tijuana and bring her back through like any other ordinary young woman smoking loads of marijuana and listening to *Free Bird*.

My mom really looked like a hippie, too. She had long, light brown hair (our ancestors were originally from Spain), and a fair complexion. She was thin and had straight white teeth even though they sometimes couldn't afford toothpaste. Good genes go a long way.

My mom got across the border and made it into the United States without any problems. When the US Immigration Officer asked my mom where she was from, she said "American citizen" like someone who's grown up eating fried chicken and apple pie. The Immigration Officer smiled and winked at my mom as Santiago drove the van towards her new home.

She settled in with her sister and husband and soon got a very illegal job at a clothing factory in downtown Los Angeles. She took the bus to work, slaved away for hours with no breaks and said very little to the other Mexican women. For the first few weeks, she was lonely and homesick and missing the smell of *tierra mojada*, the wet soil of her homeland. She wrote to Lupe once a week and begged to come home, but Lupe would always write back and tell her she had to stay at least one year. If after that year she still wanted to come back to Mexico and marry the drunk, she would honor her wishes. My mom, always the good daughter, obeyed her.

In another part of the world, my dad Federico was fleeing the Castro regime in Cuba. After months of planning and clandestine reunions, my father and ten other men stole a Cuban military boat and sailed into the Caribbean. Their captain was inexperienced but determined to get them out of Cuba safely. They brought very little with them; bread, water, bananas, a dog. As the boat sailed away from the island, Federico looked at his *patria* getting further and further way, wondering for the first time in his life if he would ever see his family again. Like the others on the ship, he was leaving everything behind with nothing but his memories in one pocket and his dreams in another, sailing away to a foreign country offering freedom and opportunity.

Too bad the captain of the ship had no idea what he was doing. They quickly ran out of water, food and gas. The boat began to drift in who knows what direction and the dog rapidly became the next potential meal.

They got lucky on their seventh day when a Coast Guard boat from Honduras spotted the drifting vessel and picked them up. From there, they were sent to Mexico City. America was offering political asylum to Cuban refugees, so they were transported to Los Angeles. Even the dog managed to make it. As much as Federico was sad to leave his family behind, he was more than ready to dive into the many opportunities America had to offer.

He couldn't speak a word of English or drive a car, but Federico and his best friend Canino got a job working construction, a job that paid more than he'd ever earned in his whole life. While Fico (short for Federico) learned how to weld, lay tile and put up drywall, Isabela silently cursed everything around her and counted the days when she would be able to return to her country. To the nice young man who promised to give her the world even though he always smelled like a bottle of Jose Cuervo.

There was a diner at the bottom of the factory where Isabela worked. Every morning before hitting the sewing machines, Isabela would sit at a table by herself and have coffee and a donut. It was the only thing she ate because it was the only thing she had learned to pronounce in English. The other ladies in the factory either flat out ignored the light-skinned *Mejicana* or teased her until she could do nothing but walk away from them. She was used to being picked on.

Federico had breakfast at the same diner every morning with his best friend Canino, someone he had grown up with in a little town on the outskirts of Havana. Canino was in love with Isabela and eternally obsessed over her hair, her skin, her body, the very ground she walked on. Federico never said much whenever Canino talked about her, and each day when Isabela would get up from her table in the corner and make her way up into the building, Canino would tell Federico he was someday going to work up enough nerve to ask her out. Federico would nod his head and keep his thoughts to himself.

That Isabela noticed Canino first was no surprise. Canino was loud, funny, boisterous, oftentimes obnoxious. He was handsome in a rebellious sort of way, a Cuban James Dean. His black hair was always perfectly slicked back as though he was waiting for his big break in Hollywood. The other ladies were always talking about him, wishing he would ask one of them out. None of them ever said much about Federico, and why would they? Whereas Canino was explosive and animated, Federico was quiet and reserved, a cigarette always in his hand and an expression of serenity on his face.

Isabela would often think about Canino throughout the day, but she would quickly forget him the minute she remembered her favorite drunk in Mexico. *One year*, she would think as she sewed buttons and zippers onto shirts and pants. *One year and I will leave this country full of crazy people and big cars behind me.*

Every morning Federico would swing by Canino's tiny apartment and together they would take the bus to the diner. From there, a *gringo* in a big truck would scoop them up, a truck with ten Cuban men already crammed in the back of it, all of them intent on making it in America. They were usually silent in the morning, each one lost in their own thoughts about the families they'd left behind in Cuba, the women who'd sworn they would wait for them to return, each young man drowning in the memory of waves crashing on Varadero beach, nights filled with rhumbas and zarzuelas, Cuban cigars and *mojitos*. Federico would look at the city around him and wonder what dreams he may have had when, as a kid, he lay in his bed free of any kind of responsibilities. Whatever they were, Federico rarely had more than a few moments to think about them. The *gringo* would watch them work and yell when necessary, which wasn't often. These young men from Cuba were hard workers and respectful of the man with the dollars. The *gringo*, in return, would sometimes reward them on Fridays by bringing them a case of Coors.

After a long day under the hot California sun, the truck would drop them off at the diner and each would find his way home. Federico always walked Canino to his apartment from the bus stop, mostly because he liked his company and enjoyed walking, enjoyed it even though his body ached and his mind craved for something other than learning how to put up dry wall. One day, after weeks of rambling about his obsession for Isabela, Canino told him he was going to approach her the next day.

"You are?" Federico looked at him from the corner of his eye, trying to feign indifference.

"Yes, Fico. It's time. If I don't ask her out soon, someone else will. She's very beautiful. That hair, those lips, those eyes, those..."

"Yes, yes, I know. What if she says no to you?"

Canino smiled confidently. "She won't, Fico. You see, she will be mine."

"Ah, okay, whatever you say, Canino."

"*Bueno, chico*, I see you tomorrow."

"*Sí*, okay. See you tomorrow."

Tomorrow was a bad day for Canino. Federico never turned up at Canino's apartment to wait for him. He went straight to the diner and calmly approached my mom and spoke to her softly. He looked her in the eyes, asked her if she'd like to go out with him some time, and just like that, Federico stole Isabela from Canino. Isabela never found out about Canino's obsession, and although Canino stopped talking to him for a few weeks, eventually he got over it and was Federico's best man at their wedding only six months later.

What was it that made Isabela forget her boyfriend in Mexico? What changed her mind so quickly about returning to her homeland? It was nothing too complicated, you see. Federico was handsome in a dignified way. He had soft hands and gentle eyes that could see through anything. He was unafraid in a country that intimidated most immigrants. He was a hard worker, a go-getter; sensitive and intelligent and more than willing to give Isabela a good life in the United States. She forgot the drunk and gave her heart willingly to the man with ambition and passion.

"And the rest, as they say, is history." I looked at the class expecting some kind of reaction, but they were oddly quiet.

"Miss C, that wasn't funny at all. How come you didn't imitate your momma?"

"Jazelin, it wasn't supposed to be a funny story. You asked me to tell you how they got together and I did." I was disappointed.

"Yeah, but, you ain't got something funny to say?"

"Say that again, Ebony."

"Oops. Don't you have a funny story about them you could tell us? Please?"

I was tired at that point. Not only tired, but even more depressed because it just reminded me that Matt and I might never have a story.

"Miss C, do they ever fight?" Marcdala asked.

"My parents? No, not really."

"Never?"

"Uhm, no. I mean, they bicker once in a while, but they love each other. My mom must really love my dad, though, because he has dentures and farts all the time." The class giggled. Suddenly, the light bulb in my brain went off like a siren at a nuclear power plant. "You know what? I do have a funny story, but maybe we should wait until tomorrow. I should really give you a lesson on the discovery of America. I've been spoiling you with too many stories, and the only thing you'll have learned by the end of the year is my family's history."

The whole class gave me a collective "Awwwwwww" followed by "Come on, Miss C!" "Please?" "We'll be good for the whole week!?" and "I'll stop picking on Tevaris."

They were bribing me and I was miserable enough to let them get away with it. I gave in too easily. Depression can do that to you.

"Oh, all right, but you better come through with your promises, because if you don't I'll never tell you another story, got it?"

"Yes, Miss C!"

# Chapter 15

Whereas I was a late bloomer when it came to dating, Erasmo, being the cool jock that he was, got an early start. He was born with the ability and good luck to attract women of all ages. My mom scolded him and his teachers pulled his ears when he was bad, but he'd always find ways of charming them. In high school, he went from one girlfriend to the next like someone who thought women were recyclable products. I would just start getting used to one of them when he'd quickly change his mind and move on to another victim.

After he graduated from high school, he blew off college and got a job as a stock boy at Publix Supermarket. My parents weren't surprised or angry because it was obvious Erasmo never enjoyed school. He liked parties, playing baseball and dating the entire girls' soccer team, but when it came to academics, he lacked the focus. I was book smart and he was street smart. Kind of sad, really, because Erasmo was intelligent when he put his mind to it. Too many years of "You should be more like your sister" probably got to him.

He worked full time and tried to give my parents money for bills at home. They always refused to take anything from him. We're talking about a Hispanic family here. It's perfectly acceptable for children to live with their parents as long as they wish, so long as they respect the rules of the house. My mom would do his laundry, clean the mess in his bedroom, cook for him, clean for him, breathe for him. In her eyes, Erasmo could do no wrong, not even when he borrowed her car without telling her.

Marie was a check-out girl at Publix and a senior at a private Christian Academy. Erasmo fell in love with her at first sight because she represented everything he wasn't; she was smart, ambitious and driven. She also had zero tolerance for my brother's nonsense. She ignored him whenever he tried to talk to her and refused to go out with him. She knew he had a reputation. Eventually, after weeks of leaving flowers on her car and incessant badgering, Marie agreed to go out with him.

One date was all it took for them to fall in love and become permanently joined at the lips. We really liked Marie and prayed he wouldn't dump her for someone else. She never laughed at my mom's lipstick, always asked me questions about school and never flinched whenever my dad would fart. Lucky for us, Erasmo was completely smitten with her and stuck to her like glue. They dated for five years, the time it took for him to get his act together and become a corrections officer and for her to finish college. They got engaged soon after she graduated, and boy were we relieved.

Even though it was completely acceptable in the twentieth century, they decided not to move in together. Her parents wouldn't allow it and God only knows Marie probably would've changed her mind once she realized what a complete slob she was about to marry.

A few weeks before the wedding, Linda was over at my house for a change drinking Cuban coffee, a legal version of liquid cocaine. One shot is all it takes to get your heart beating a mile a minute. No wonder Cubans spoke so loudly; it had to be the coffee.

As my mom moved around the kitchen preparing dinner, Linda asked her how she felt about my brother getting married.

"Oh, Linda, joo know, es bery nice. I like Marie bery much. She's nice girl, joo know?"

"Yes, she is." Linda took a sip of her coffee and lit up a cigarette.

"But...joo know, I sink so they chould have move in together for some times."

"What?!?" I was shocked. I couldn't believe my mom was cool with *living in sin*. "What do you mean, Mami?"

"Oh, joo know, joo sink so that joo know someone, *pero*, let me tell you somesing, joo no know someone until joo live together. Oh jes."

Linda giggled and looked at me, pleading with me to beg my mom to explain.

"Mami, why do you say that? What happened to you and Papi when you moved in with him?"

"*Ay Dios mio*, so bery much." She grabbed Linda's pack of cigarettes and lit one up, loving her one moment of attention. "When I met your papi, oh, joo know, he was so nice to me. He hold my hand, we go to de movies, we eat de ice cream, *pero*, let me tell you somesing, we always kiss kiss but no touch! I was good girl."

"Uh-huh, so?"

"When we gotten married, I was veerjin, joo know? I no sleep with no one because my mama always say to me, 'Why he buy the cow when he get de milk for free?' Joo know, Linda?"

My mom loved Linda because she was the only friend who'd ever stuck with me. Linda nodded as she took a drag on her cigarette.

"So then what happened, Mami?"

"*Bueno*, the night of our wedding, I was so bery happy. I love him, he love me, and your grandma was bery happy I was gotten married. Our first night together, your papi was bery good to me. He was gentle and he kiss me soft and—"

"Mami, please, I don't need to hear the details." Hearing my mom talk about sex with my dad was as bad as walking in on them, if not worse.

"Ah, sorry. We go to esleep that night, and the next morning I get up and go to de bathroom. *Ay Dios mio.*" She put her right hand on her chest and looked up at the ceiling. "Joo know what I find?"

"What, Mami?"

"Your papi's teeth in a glass! *¡Valgame Dios!*"

Linda and I nearly fell out of our chairs. My mom started laughing, too, which wasn't good, because it only made us laugh harder. We laughed for what seemed like forever until we finally got a hold of ourselves.

"So, then what happened?" I said as I wiped my eyes.

"Oh, choogar, I was so deesellusion, *pero* I loving him, joo know? So I grab de teeth and wash them in de sink, *pero* when I try to put back in glass, I don't know, my hand do somesing funny and they fall in toilet. *¡Ay Dios mio!* I pick them up, put them back in glass, and I no tell your papi. No tell him, okay?"

Linda was clutching her stomach and choking. I couldn't breathe.

"I won't tell him, Mami, I swear."

"Bery good. So, es why I sink so Erasmo and Marie chould have lived together for little bit, okay? Es good esperience."

The bell rang just as I delivered the last line of the story. As they gathered their things, they put in their two cents about my mom.

"Yo, Miss C, your momma's crazy!"

"Miss C, we can meet your momma?"

"Miss C, can you call your momma and put her on speaker phone?"

I promised to call my mom and put her on speaker phone at the end of the year as long as they continued to behave and do their work. They promised and walked out while I got my things together. As soon as the class was empty, I sat down at my desk and felt oddly at peace. My students were sometimes bad enough to make me want to throw chairs, but the knowledge that I could get them to be good for the rest of the year was enough to brighten my mood. I even forgot about Matt as I put my attendance book away and straightened out the desks.

I took my time driving home because I knew the only thing waiting for me was a quiet apartment, a bottle of red wine and *Jeopardy!* When I pulled into my parking space, I saw Matt sitting on my front door step with flowers in his hand. I wanted to run into his arms and kiss his whole face, but I controlled myself. I had been depressed for a full three weeks and I was determined to make him pay for it.

He stood up as I walked towards the door. "Hey."

"Hey."

"How are you?"

"Great, Matt. How are you? How's your dad?"

"My dad?" He looked confused for a minute. "Oh, yeah. He's good. Back to work."

"Good, glad to hear it."

His enormous presence was blocking the entry into my apartment. I stood there waiting for him to say something.

"Uh, I got these for you." He handed me the flowers, a dozen beautiful tulips. My heart skipped a beat because I'd told him tulips were my favorite flower. I couldn't believe he'd remembered.

"Wow. They're beautiful." I took them from him and dangled my keys. "Uh, this is where you move to the side and let me open my door. You're way too big for me to tackle." He nervously moved to the side. "You can come in, if you like."

"Yeah, I'd love to."

Matt looked absolutely terrified. I wondered if he thought I was going to attack him the minute we got inside. I opened the door and held it open for him as he crouched and walked in. He gasped as he looked around my apartment. I went to the kitchen with the flowers and wondered what the hell I was going to put them in. I didn't have any vases because no one ever sent me flowers. I grabbed the empty coffee pot, filled it up with water and made it a home for the tulips. Matt laughed at my inventiveness.

"I'll get you a vase next time." *Next time?* "I like your apartment. I like the way you've done it up."

"Yeah, well…"

I looked at my apartment for the first time as though seeing it through a stranger's eyes. I had pictures on the walls from my cruise ship adventures. Pictures of Jamaica, Cozumel, Croatia, Norway, Greece, Spain. From my year in Mexico; a picture of Eva and the Lost Trio, a picture of my grandmother and my two million relatives, a picture of me and three other travelers on the beach in Mazatlan.

I looked at my other belongings and cringed. My furniture was an uneven combination of Pier 1 meets Target, Target being the winner, of course. A teacher's salary was simply not enough for a fabulous sofa from Pottery Barn. I also had enough books piled up against the wall to make any librarian respect me. I was glad that at least it was clean and for once the plants looked like they were finally coming out of their coma.

"Wow, looks like you've been to a lot of places, and you weren't kidding when you said you liked to read."

"I wasn't kidding about anything that night, Matt." He looked at me and sighed, fully understanding what I was referring to. "What are you doing here, Matt?"

He sat down on my futon. "I'm here to tell you that I'm sorry."

"Sorry? For what? Wait a minute, were you the one who hid all my chalk yesterday?"

He laughed and shook his head. "You're amazing, you know that?"

"I've been called off-center and quirky and weird and oh, yeah, different. This is the first time for me with amazing."

"No, I mean, you're amazing because you always find something funny to say."

"Bartending did it. You have to be a smart ass all the time otherwise you get labeled as boring and bitter. Hey, do you want something to drink?" I opened the fridge and called out his options. "Let's see, I have water, water, water...oh, I have a bottle of red wine."

"It's four o'clock in the afternoon."

"So?"

"You're nuts. Just give me some water, please."

I poured him a glass of water by grace of God. My hand was trembling so bad I thought for sure he'd hear my one ring rattle against the cup. I thought about my options. I could break down and tell him I was miserable he hadn't talked to me, or I could play the cool nothing-phases-me card, which I was definitely good at. I didn't have time to decide because when I turned around to bring him the glass of water, I ran right into him. I stopped it from spilling all over him and stared at the buttons on his shirt. He was standing so close to me I could see tiny pieces of lint clinging to his shirt. *I want to be a piece of lint right this minute*, I thought.

"Sorry," he said, as he towered over me.

"Oh, uhm, here." I took a step back and handed him the glass of water. He grabbed the glass and set it down on the counter. He took my hand and tried to pull me close but I resisted. I was crazy about him but I still had self respect.

"Look, Matt, you can't—"

"Bibi, let me talk first. I came here because I wanted to talk to you. There's something you need to know."

"Are you gay?"

"What?! Oh, for Christ's sake, no!"

"Sorry. I just had to make sure."

"After the way we kissed, do you really think that?"

"No. It's just my defense mechanism kicking in. I have a feeling I'm not going to like what you're going to say, so I thought I'd build myself up for the worst."

"Bibi, I'm not gay. I'm just, I'm, I have, I think—"

"Come on, Matt, I'm a grown up. Spill it."

"Let's sit down, okay? Please?" He was looking at me intently, almost desperately.

"Come on." I took his soft hand and led him back to my battered futon. We plonked down on it and I turned to face him.

"Okay, whatever it is, it can't be that bad. Let's hear it."

He looked at me long and hard, not sure how I would handle his next words.

"I kind of have a girlfriend." He let out a long sigh.

His words knocked the wind out of me. *My soul mate is seeing someone else? How is that possible?* "Kind of? What does that mean? What kind of 'kind of' are you talking about?"

"Well, remember when I told you I went up to New York to see my dad?"

"Uh-huh?"

"That wasn't the only reason I went up there."

"Okay, so—"

"We kind of split up before I left, but in the past couple of years we've been on and off. We've been together since high school." He swallowed and looked at me, waiting for a reaction. I didn't know what to say. I mean, what could I say? I sat there and waited for him to keep explaining.

"We grew up together, you know, in the same neighborhood. She was like an annoying little sister, but I don't know, from one day to the next she went from chasing me around and bugging me to demanding that we get married. Her parents and my parents are good friends, her sister married my brother, her brother married my sister... everyone thought it was logical that we get married, too. But..."

God I loved hearing that "but." It gave me hope. "So what happened?"

"I guess I started wondering if maybe there was someone else out there for me. I loved her, I still love her in a way but it's just not right. I know it sounds cheesy but she's not 'the one.' I moved down here to get a new start, you know, give us time apart. I thought maybe I'd realize we were meant to be together. But it hasn't happened. She's more like a good friend I don't want to hurt, you know?"

"Not really, but I'm listening. So, why is she still "kind of" your girlfriend?"

"Sometimes I get lonely down here, without my buddies and stuff, and she's almost like family. You don't just forget about someone you've been with for such a long time. So I'd fly up there, she'd fly down here, we'd get back together and then fight and break up. I haven't found the right time to permanently end things, and I really want to because she deserves someone else, someone who'll give her what she wants. A home, a family, a life, all that stuff you girls love to dream about."

"You don't want that?" *Uh-oh, I thought, what if he wants to be a playboy for the rest of his life?*

"Of course I want that, just not with her. I know I have to end things and when I went up to see my pop I was fully prepared to tell her to move on. But I couldn't. The look in her eyes killed me."

Fair enough. He was a nice guy. I couldn't be a bitch and tell him to dump her ass and marry me, so I went from being a jealous wanna-be wife to a friend.

"Matt, you have to do what makes you happy, you know. If you keep stringing her along, she's going to keep thinking you'll end up married. That's not fair to her. I would hate you if you did that to me. You're going to hurt her, trust me, but in the long run you'll be doing her a favor. Unless you're still wondering if she's the one for you? Are you?" I really wanted to know. I certainly didn't want to be second choice.

He looked at me for a few seconds and then grabbed a piece of my hair. His finger quickly got tangled in the curls, so for the next few minutes we giggled as he tried to escape the monster on my head.

"Maybe you're confused," I said.

"No, not anymore."

"Why not?"

"Remember when we met in the library before school started? When you nearly killed yourself tripping over that chair?"

I cringed. "How could I forget?"

"You were so funny and cute. There was something about you I couldn't put my finger on, something I wanted to investigate."

"Sure, that's understandable. You wanted to get to know the faculty lunatic."

He laughed and grabbed my hand. "I couldn't stop thinking about you that day. Every time I thought of something else, your face would pop into my head and it drove me crazy. I flew up to New York knowing I had to break up with her because if I didn't, I'd always wonder what it would be like getting to know you."

"But you didn't break up with her."

"Nope." He let go of my hand and looked around my apartment. "I guess I took one look at her face and lost my will. I chickened out."

"Oh."

"Yeah."

He got up from the futon and started looking at all the pictures, pictures of me trying to find my place in the world. He stopped at a picture of me and the Lost Trio.

"You're a free spirit, aren't you?"

"Hmm, I guess so. Why do you say that?"

"It's obvious. I mean, look at all these pictures." He swooped his arm around the apartment. "All these books and stuff. You've done more in your life than I ever have. You've done things I wish I'd had the guts to do."

"Oh please, Matt, you still can. How old are you, anyway?"

"Thirty-three."

"That's my favorite number."

"Hey, me too."

"Why?"

"Don't know." He paused for a moment. "Reminds me of someone."

"Jesus?"

"Hey! How did you know that?"

"Same reason. And I've always thought something extraordinary is going to happen to me when I turn thirty-three."

He shook his head and stared at me. "You scare me."

"I scare you? Why?"

"You just do. We have too many things in common. I'm not talking about liking the same kind of ice cream and stuff. I mean bigger things."

"Hm hmm, yeah. I'll agree with you on that one." It *was* kind of freakish. The whole number thing spooked me. "Well, it's nice to know we share the same faith. I would have a hard time telling my parents you're an atheist. That shit would never fly with my mom."

"It wouldn't sit well with my Irish Catholic parents either."

"Are you going to sit down again? My neck's starting to hurt."

"Yeah, sorry." He sat down next to me and every single hair on my body came to attention. "That night scared the shit out of me, you know."

"It did?"

"Yeah, it scared the holy hell out of me. I'd never met anyone like you, so free-spirited, so funny, so, so—"

"So crazy?"

"No. So different." Once again, he got up from the futon and went to the kitchen. He grabbed the glass of water, and downed it. He walked back to the futon and sat next to me again, but this time he grabbed my hand. More things in my body came to attention.

"So my hair didn't scare you?"

"Stop that. I love your hair." He grabbed a tiny piece of it again and thankfully it didn't strangle his finger. "That night freaked me out because I felt something I'd never felt before. I don't know, it just felt so good to talk to you, like I'd known you forever."

"You know what? Me too."

"Really?"

Matt was being so open and honest and so unlike any guy I'd ever dated that I knew trying to play the tough girl would be pointless.

"Yeah, really. I've never been good with relationships. This is going to sound bad, but I'd always get bored around the three month mark. I'd realize it was never going to go anywhere, so I'd end it. I mean, why waste their time? But believe it or not, we'd keep in touch. They liked having a girl around who could shoot pool and throw a football." Matt crossed his eyebrows as though I was speaking to him in Chinese. "I like playing football, I like fishing, I like mountain biking, I like all those things most girls don't. So the guys would call me, tell me all about their girl problems. Sooner or later they'd hook up with someone who felt threatened by me and voila, that would be the end of that." He gave me a sad look. "Hey, it's not like that. I have a best friend in Miami and her name's Linda. She's like an older sister to me. And it's okay, I don't mind being alone."

"You don't?"

"Well, I didn't until I met you. You took me out and took advantage of me, you swine, and now I'm crazy about you and I don't know what to do." I punched him lightly on the stomach.

"Really?"

"No lie."

"Hey, I really wanna hear you say you're crazy about me again, but let me ask you something. Why do you like doing all those boy things? Were you a tomboy? You didn't really tell me that part the other night."

"Nu-uh, not really. I was a chubby wanna-be-cool little sister. I like football and fishing because I wanted my brother to like me so bad I learned to do things just to make him happy."

"Did they?"

"That's a whole other talk show."

"Okay, but mountain biking?"

"Yeah, I like mountain biking. I used to be a little chubby when I was a kid and it's the only thing aside from running that helps me stay in shape." *You are a big fat liar.* "I don't know, it's just fun to me. I'd rather be outside getting all sweaty and nasty than walking through a mall looking for the latest sale. Besides, being outdoors helps me think."

"Yeah, like you *really* need help with that."

"Now who's being sarcastic?" I poked his stomach and he grabbed my hand.

"I'm just kidding. Do you hate me?"

"For—?"

"Come on, the girlfriend thing."

"Should I?"

"Bibi, I barely said two words to you in the last few weeks. I haven't called you, asked you out, nothing. I've ignored the shit out of you. Aren't you mad?"

"Uh, right now I'm in shock that you, a man, fully admitted everything you did wrong. I thought I was going to have to torture you a little bit. Damn, Matt, you ruined my game."

"Bibi, are you mad? Come on, stop avoiding the subject."

I wasn't sure what I felt. I still thought he was the only man for me but I didn't know how to handle the girlfriend. "Okay, I'm not really mad. If I was, you wouldn't be sitting here right now without any broken limbs." I cocked my head to one side and looked at him, the man with diamond eyes and adorable crooked teeth. "One thing, though. Why didn't you tell me about her on the first day? What did you say her name was?"

"Her name's Ingrid." He continued playing with my hair. "To be honest, I wasn't prepared that night. I mean, I knew I liked you, but I didn't know I would like you *that* much. You showed up and pulled the rug out from under my feet before I'd even had the chance to stand on it. It didn't seem like the right time to tell you, and anyway, I hadn't planned on kissing you or anything like that."

"And why the hell not?"

"Calm down, you nut. I didn't think you liked me, didn't think you'd even let me kiss you."

"Really? That surprises me."

"Why?"

"I thought 'I WANT YOU' was written all over my face."

He burst out laughing and grabbed my face with his hands. "God, you kill me." He kissed me softly and pulled back, not sure if he'd done the right thing. I was ready to take his clothes off but resisted. That "kind of" girlfriend was still lingering. "I thought you were way out of my league, Bibi, especially after you told me about all the things you've done and all the places you've been. I couldn't imagine what the hell you would want with a guy like me."

A family, a life, a future. A story. Dare I say it? Something normal.

"I'm not out of your league, Matt. Hell, I think we're playing on the same team."

"You're not kidding. So, what now?"

"What do you mean?"

"What do you wanna do?"

"About us? About this? About the world?"

"About us."

"What can I do? You're the one who still has a girlfriend. As much as I want to hold your hand and tell you I think you're the best thing that's ever happened to me, I can't be number two, second choice, an experiment."

"What are you saying?"

"Matt, you've got unfinished business, and if there's anything I've ever learned from my dad it's that you can't walk out the door when you've still got one foot walking in."

"Your dad told you that?"

"Yep."

"Smart guy."

"That he is."

"So, basically, what you're saying is you want nothing to do with me until I'm truly a free man?"

"I knew you were smart."

"Okay. I can respect that." He got up all too quickly and pulled the keys out of his pants pocket.

"Are you leaving?"

"Yeah."

"Are you mad?"

"No."

"Then why are you leaving?"

"Because it's nearly five and I've got some *unfinished business* to attend to. I need to book a flight to New York."

"What?!? Now? Right this minute? Wait a second…" I got up and tried to grab the keys out of his hand. Call me crazy, but the fact that he was getting ready to break someone's heart bothered me because I knew it was my fault.

"Bibi, don't be ridiculous. I'm not about to screw this up a second time, okay? I can't stop thinking about you even when I'm sleeping and the thought of not being around you depresses me. I need to break it off with Ingrid for good."

"Just like that? Are you sure?"

He sighed and put his hands on my shoulders. "What's you're favorite number?"

"Thirty-three."

"What was your favorite toy?"

"Sit 'N Spin."

"Who's your favorite funny guy?"

"John Cusack."

"Favorite movie with him in it?"

"*Better Off Dead.*"

"You see? We're made for each other."

He pulled me into his arms and I didn't resist. He kissed me hard and strong as though he was leaving for war.

"See you later. I'll call you."

"Okay."

I watched his tall figure walk towards the door, watched the man with the sensitive heart and caring eyes stop and look around my apartment before looking at me one more time.

"Hey, Bibi?"

"Yeah?"

"You'll need to teach me some Spanish."

"No problem. Here's your first lesson. You ready?"

"Yeah."

*"No me olvides."*

"No me olveedes? What does that mean?"

"Don't forget me."

He smiled and shook his head. "Not on your life."

Matt walked out the door and I stood there for five minutes, rooted to the spot in my living room where he'd kissed me, already wishing he was back. Then I ran to my bedroom and jumped up and down on the bed like a little kid before I heard something snap. *Shit*, I thought, *I'm going to have to buy a new bed and I'm flat broke.*

After Matt left, I got in my car and went for a drive. I had no idea where I was going but it didn't matter. The world looked beautiful to me, like a place I was truly happy to be in. A place that no longer confused me, a place that didn't make me feel like an outsider, a place I deserved to be. The sun seemed brighter, the air felt cooler and I felt like a million bucks and then some. Three weeks of agony and depression faded in my mind as I slipped in a Van Morisson CD and played my favorite song, "Into The Mystic." As Van filled my car with his soulful lyrics, I held my hand out the window and let the wind have its way with it. I didn't even notice that I was sweating and probably running every red light. I was so happy I wanted to yell.

Somehow, I ended up in the hood, right in front of Chancy's home. It was the kind of thing only someone like me would do. I could've driven to Lake Eola and walked around, I could've gone to the book store, the mall, the moon, but no, I drove to the hood without even thinking about it. I pulled into Chancy's driveway and turned off my car, wondering if anyone was home. Boy barked as I got out of my car, but as soon as I got close enough, he stopped barking at me and starting wagging his tail. I bent down and pet him for a few minutes and wondered what in the hell had possessed me to go there.

Before I got a chance to knock, Grandma Ruth opened the door and walked out onto the porch. She had a spatula in her hand and was chewing on something. I realized I'd shown up while she was cooking dinner. Whatever she was making smelled damn good and I smiled as she looked at me up and down.

"Lord have mercy, look what the cat dragged in."

"Hi, Ruthie."

"Is Chancy in trouble?"

"No, no, not at all. I was in the neighborhood and thought I'd drop in."

"You was in the neighborhood? Girl, what's wrong with you?"

"What do you mean? You said I was welcome any time."

"Come on, now, don't you play games. You must be here for a reason."

"Okay, Ruthie, you got me. Chancy told me you were making something good for dinner and I invited myself over."

"Girl, get your ass inside. You look like you need something to drink."

"You ain't kidding."

She looked at me hard for a few seconds because I couldn't stop smiling.

"Why you smiling, Miss C?"

"Really? Was I smiling?"

"Girl, you're whole face is shinin'. Seen that look before a million times. Hm hmm. You're in love."

I wanted so bad to tell her what happened with Matt, but if I told her, Chancy would find out I was in love with Mr. Connelly and tell the whole class. I loved my students, but there were some things that needed to be kept private.

"Maybe. You got something cold to drink, Ruthie?"

"Do I ever. Let's go inside so you can tell me all about Mr. Connelly before Chancy gets back from football practice."

"What? How did you, when, why—"

"Honey, there's something you need to learn about kids. You can't hide anything from them. They all know you got it bad for Mr. C, so there ain't no use in you tryin' to hide it from them, okay?"

"Damn, they're smart."

"Smarter than most people give them credit for. Come on, now, follow me."

Morris was sitting on the couch and slowly stood up when he saw me.

"Well, well, if it ain't our own Miss C."

I went over to him and kissed him on the cheek and hugged him.

"Girl, what you doin' here? Chancy in trouble?"

"No! Come on, now, Morris, Chancy's not that bad."

"He's not? Just the other day he hid my dentures. Spent a whole damn day looking for them things."

"Believe it or not, Morris, my brother and I used to do the same thing to my dad. We thought it was hilarious."

Morris scratched his head and sat back down. "Ain't nothing funny about an old man running around flappin' his gums. Shoot, I ain't find them till night time." He shook his head and went back to watching television.

I followed Ruthie to the kitchen. She stood in front of the stove, her forehead wrinkled in concentration as she tasted something from a large pot. Satisfied with the taste, she poured me a glass of fresh lemonade. I took it from her and sat down at the kitchen counter. I glanced at the fridge and noticed she had more pictures on it than I had in my entire apartment. Chancy in his football uniform, Chancy wearing a Santa hat, one of Morris and Boy on the porch taken just at sunset.

As I stood there momentarily entranced by the intimacy of looking into someone's childhood, I felt the side of my lips curling up into a smile. Sometimes my students drove me so crazy that it was easy to forget that they, just like myself, had once been children with nothing but innocence and dreams in their eyes. She stopped what she was doing and looked at me out of the corner of her eye. I smiled at her because I couldn't stop. Love was spilling out of me onto her counter and probably into the food. I wanted to hug her, hug Morris, hug the whole world. Never underestimate the power of true love. I was so happy I even forgot about my broken bed.

"Come on, now, don't keep me in suspense, girl. What happened?"

"I think I'm in love, Ruthie."

"Shoot, you ain't gotta tell me that. It's written all over that pretty face of yours. Is it Mr. Connelly?"

"It sure is." I sighed and put my face in my hands.

"Hm hmm. So? Did he ask you out?"

"Well, sort of. We went on a date about three weeks ago and had an absolute blast."

"A blast? Is that what you call it?"

"Uhm, yeah. I mean, we had a really good time. We just talked and talked and then eventually attacked each other in the parking lot."

"Say what?" Her eyes opened so much I thought they were going to pop out of her head.

"It's a harsher way of saying we got it on."

"Oh, okay. Gotcha. So you kissed him? On the first date?"

"Yeah, why not?"

"Honey, you come from a different generation. Never mind that, though. So then what you did?"

"Nothing. I drove home, he drove home, and then he didn't talk to me for three weeks."

"See? That's why you don't 'attack' each other on the first date. Hm hmm."

"No, it's not like that. He had a girlfriend. I mean, has. I mean, well, he's going to break up with her."

Ruthie shook her head and took a sip of her lemonade. "Honey, they all say that." She sighed heavily.

"No, Ruthie, let me explain. I swear, it's not what you think."

I told her about the tulips, the girlfriend, the number thirty-three incident. I even told her about breaking my bed and how I just didn't care. She moved around the kitchen as I plead my case, silently wishing she would agree that we were made for each other.

"Well, honey, you sure is convinced he's the man for you. But be careful. Things ain't always what they seem."

"What do you mean? Do you think he lied to me?"

"No, no, baby, I'm sure he meant it, but you ain't known him that long, you know what I'm saying? Don't give your heart to him so quickly, okay? That's all. I don't wanna see you get your heart broken. You seem like a nice girl."

She was right, of course. For all I knew, Matt was feeding me a load of lies just to get into my pants. Still, I was glad she thought I was a nice girl.

"Okay, I'll be careful. Anyway, I better get going. I just wanted to stop by and say hello."

"So soon? Baby, you just got here." She looked hurt that I was leaving so quickly. "You don't wanna stay for supper?"

"I'd love to, but I have that bed situation to take care of. Hopefully I can buy another one without having to file for bankruptcy. It's part of that whole 'teachers get paid shit' theory."

She laughed and took my empty glass of lemonade. I patted Morris on the shoulder and waved goodbye but he was too engrossed in a program about crocodiles to notice me. Ruthie walked me out the door and stood on the front porch with her hands on her wide hips as I got in my car.

I pulled onto the street and noticed she was trying to tell me something. I rolled down my window.

"I'm waitin' on them enchiladas!"

"You got it. I'll bring some over as soon as I can! Thanks for the lemonade!"

I watched her walk back inside the house and headed home. I decided the bed could wait. I would just have to sleep on the futon until I figured out how to ask my dad for some money.

I eventually got tired of driving around aimlessly and went home. I'd played every single Van Morrison CD I owned. I pulled into my apartment just as the sun was setting. The first thing I saw when I walked in the door were the tulips. I sighed and lay down on the futon. I knew I'd have to get used to backaches for the time being. Happiness settled over me like a warm blanket on a cold night and I hugged myself. *For once*, I thought, *my life makes sense*. I'd found someone who seemed to think I was normal, I was no longer terrified to walk into my classroom, and I even considered being nice to Mrs. Coleman. Even though it was still early in the day, I felt my eyes closing from the sheer exhaustion of not having too much to worry about.

I should have known it would never last.

# Chapter 16

I woke up the next morning totally confused. I was still wearing the clothes I'd worn the day before because my little nap on the futon turned into a whole night's sleep. I looked at the time, jumped in the shower and got dressed in record time. The animal on my head clung to me as I ran to my car, notes falling out of my bag and my zipper still undone. If there was one thing I hated more than anything it was being late. I sped all the way to the school on I-4 and for once didn't worry that I might be pulled over. I wove in and out of traffic like a maniac and basically ignored all road rules. I even used my horn a few times.

Like I said, I hated being late.

I walked in the door of my classroom just as the bell rang, completely out of breath. For once, I was the last person to walk in the door. Even Chancy had beaten me, and from the look on his face, I could tell Ruthie had told him about Matt. They were bound to find out sooner or later. I gave Chancy a look as though to say, *Open your mouth and I will never give you a ride home again.* Chancy looked back at me as though he was saying, *Okay, Miss C, I got you.* I winked at him and grabbed my attendance book, totally and completely unsure what I had planned to teach that day. Just as I finished calling roll, Dr. Lawrence walked into my classroom unannounced. The whole class fell silent as his large presence filled the doorway, every one of my students wondering who was in trouble this time.

"Hello, boys and girls. How is everyone today?"

Everyone started speaking at once. I sighed and wondered if they'd learned anything from me at all.

"Yo, man, I'm tired."

"Dr. Lawrence, you play football?"

"Hey, Dr. Lawrence, Miss C's cool! Her momma's crazy."

"Dr. Lawrence, my auntie say hello!"

I told them to *please be quiet sit still show some respect we have a visitor.*

Miraculously, they obeyed and calmed down. Dr. Lawrence looked at me and raised his eyebrows as though he couldn't believe they'd actually listened to me. I smiled back at him sheepishly and then noticed Matt standing in the doorway behind him. My heart stopped as he met my eyes and for a moment I forgot where I was. The only thing I could see was his crooked smile and the twinkle in his eyes. He winked and I nearly fainted. All this within a few seconds. Dr. Lawrence cleared his throat and broke the spell.

"Miss Castellanos, Mr. Connelly is going to watch your class while you and I go for a walk. There's something I want to talk to you about."

My heart dropped and I suddenly felt like I was going to puke. Every single negative thought possible ran through my mind. *Oh, shit, he found out I gave Chancy a ride home. Uh-oh, he knows about Matt. Oh my God, Ms. Davis and Mrs. Coleman complained about me. Ah crap, my stories are inappropriate.* Whatever it was, it had to be bad news. Dr. Lawrence hadn't said very much to me so far and asking me to go for a walk was surely a sign that I had royally screwed up.

I swallowed and looked at him in fear as we walked out the front doors of the school. We crossed Robinson Street and walked onto the empty field in front of the school where the soccer team practiced.

"Is everything okay?"

"Yes, yes, no need to worry, but there's something I need to talk to you about."

"Look, if this is about me giving Chancy a ride home, I swear I can explain."

He stopped dead in his tracks and looked at me. "You gave Chancy a ride home?"

"Uh-huh."

"When?"

"A few days ago. Last week or something." Beads of sweat popped out on my forehead and I felt my armpits turn into Niagara Falls. *Great,* I thought, *not only am I going to get in trouble for God knows what, now I'm totally busted for giving Chancy a ride home. Moron. Moron. Mo-ron.*

"Hmm. Why did you give him a ride home, Miss C?"

"Well, to be honest, he asked me to. I'm sorry, Dr. Lawrence, but I didn't know the rules and I know ignorance is no excuse but when I said yes he smiled and he was so happy and I've never seen him look so—"

"Calm down, Miss Castellanos. You're not in trouble." He laughed and shook his head. "I'm simply surprised."

"Why?"

"Miss C," he said as we resumed our walk, "most teachers think the 'hood' is a war zone. They think they're going to get shot, jumped, raped, you name it. Not you, obviously."

"Well, to be honest with you, I was pretty scared of the kids and the whole idea of the hood when I first started. I didn't know what to expect. You told me they were bad kids, you told me they were At Risk, you told me most of them had been in trouble with the law. I thought I was going to have a classroom full of hardened teenage criminals, but wow, I was so wrong."

He smiled and looked at me. "What do you think now?"

"They're just kids, Dr. Lawrence. Kids. We've all been kids, haven't we? Yeah, they like to try me sometimes, but they're not that bad. In fact, they've grown on me."

It was so true. I looked forward to looking over Marcdala's homework. I enjoyed hearing Ebony hum to herself. I loved watching Chancy as he read *The Outsiders*. I loved them because I knew they liked me, liked me even though I wasn't their color or came from a completely different background.

I felt accepted.

"Well, I know you've been doing a great job. Chancy's grandmother called me and thanked me for hiring you. You see? I knew you were different, and that's why this walk is so difficult for me." He sighed heavily.

"Oh my God, am I getting fired?"

"Fired? Miss C, do you have any common sense?"

"Actually, no. My brother's always said it's the least common of my senses."

"He's right. Of course you're not getting fired. I asked you to take a walk with me because something's come up."

"Something's come up?" I was totally confused. If he wasn't firing me, what could it possibly be?

"Yes. I got a call today from West Orange High School."

"The school way on the other side of town where the rich kids live?"

"Yep, that's the one." He paused and stroked his chin with his massive hand. "They're looking for a Spanish teacher."

"A Spanish teacher?"

"They called me because they can't seem to find anyone and I always seem to help them out, so I recommended you."

"Me? Me? You recommended me?" I couldn't believe it. Spanish was the last thing I'd ever thought I'd teach, let alone in a high school.

"Yes, you. You're Hispanic, aren't you? You speak Spanish, don't you?"

"Yeah, I can speak it okay, but that doesn't mean I can teach it."

"Well, let me ask you this, did you think you could teach the At Risk students?"

"Hell, no."

"What do you think now?"

"Okay, you got me. But it would mean leaving Howard, my students, Chancy, Marcdala, Jazelin."

"Hm hmm."

"Wow."

"I knew you'd be surprised, but you have to remember something, Miss C. The decision is all yours. I only promised to mention it to you. That doesn't necessarily mean you have to go. This isn't the military. You don't have to make a decision right now, but they'd like you to start in February. That should give you enough time to think it over."

We kept walking along in silence because I was too stunned to speak. Being offered another position in a school full of rich white kids was the last thing I'd ever expected. After a few minutes, Dr. Lawrence cleared his throat.

"Miss C, can I be honest with you?"

"No, go ahead and lie to me."

"Very funny, young lady."

"I'm kidding." I patted him on the shoulder.

He grabbed my hand and squeezed it and then let it drop.

"Miss C, I've been a principal for, oh, about twenty years. I've seen new teachers come and go, some good and some bad. I've never seen a teacher stick to the At Risk students for more than three months, and you've done more than that. Not only have you stuck to them, you actually like them. You must've been a bad kid when you were in school." He chuckled.

"Me? A bad kid? Oh, no, that's where you're dead wrong. I was a really good student. I loved school, loved homework, loved reading, loved everything a nerd would love. I was Super Geek."

"Really?" He looked surprised.

"Why is that so hard to believe? I don't look like a reformed delinquent, do I?"

"No, of course not, but I never would've taken you for a nerd. I've always thought you were a bit of a rebellious young lady."

"Well, you're right about that, too, actually. Right after high school, after being told I was different and weird and odd and strange and too many things

216

to even remember, I kind of buried the nerd. Don't get me wrong, I still like to read and watch documentaries, but I stopped letting people run all over me. I guess I found another voice."

"Maybe that's your key to success with the students. You don't let them run all over you."

We'd already walked around the track twice. I wondered what was going on in my classroom and whether or not Chancy had blurted out to Matt that he knew about us.

"I don't know about that, Dr. Lawrence. Those first few weeks were rough. It wasn't until I started telling them stories about myself and my crazy mom that they calmed down and starting behaving. I swear to God, it worked like magic."

"Don't swear to God, please."

"Oops, sorry."

"It's okay. Stories about your momma? What kind of stories?"

"Oh, well, stories about her misadventures in the real world. Like when she beat up a mannequin in a department store, like when she dropped my dad's dentures in the toilet and didn't tell him, like when she got into a huge fight with the mailman. You know, normal stuff."

Dr. Lawrence laughed loudly and put his hand on his stomach. "Your momma did all that?"

"You have no idea how much she's done. I'm hoping I'll have enough stories to get me through the school year, but if I run out, I can always pick on my dad's family."

"Well, I have to say it's the most creative method I've ever heard of. But if it works for you, it's fine with me."

We walked back to the entrance of the school, the entrance I'd grown to love with its massive white columns and red brick walls. Before he opened the door, he looked at me sadly.

"Miss C, going to work at West Orange would be a great opportunity for you, so think it over."

"Yeah, I will."

"But there's no reason I can't be honest with you, right?"

"Yeah, we covered that."

"I'd miss having you here. I know the kids would be devastated and I don't know how I'd ever be able to replace you."

"You'd have to find someone who has a neurotic crazy mom just like mine, someone who can tell stories."

"I don't think that would be easy."

"No, you're probably right."

I was trying to keep the moment light because I didn't want to imagine the torture I was going to put myself through over the holiday break. *Just my luck,* I thought. I was happy and for once I wasn't thinking about what I'd rather be doing with my life. *Why does this always happen to me?* I thought.

"Do whatever will make you happy, Miss C. Just remember that, okay?"

"Okay, Dr. Lawrence, I will. And thanks for the walk," I said as I walked towards my classroom.

I went up the stairs, down the corridor full of beat up lockers, made a left at the end of the hallway, walked past three classrooms and finally came to mine. I stood outside the door and tried to hear what was going on, but I couldn't hear anything. They were completely quiet. Matt was a much better teacher than I'd thought.

I opened the door and found them all writing furiously on a sheet of paper. Matt was sitting at my desk looking like my soul mate, of course, and he smiled shyly as I walked towards him. The students pretended to keep working on their assignment, but I knew they were watching us, knew we had to be very, very careful.

"Thanks, Mr. Connelly. What did you make them do?" I was trying to be as professional as humanly possible but my lips kept tugging up at the corners in a desperate attempt to smile. I must have looked constipated.

"I told them to write an essay on how they like living in America."

"Hmm, that's interesting. I can't wait to read them."

"So how was your walk?" From the way he was looking at me, I could tell he had no idea what it was about.

"Uh, it's not something I want to tell you right now, okay? I'll tell you about it later," I whispered.

"Gotcha. Okay, listen," he said loudly as he wrote something on my notepad, "here are the names of the students who misbehaved while you were out."

The class stopped what they were doing and Chancy snickered loudly.

"Man, what you talking about? We was good."

"Yeah, Miss C," Ebony protested, "don't believe him. He's lying. We *were* good." She gave Chancy a know-it-all look and for one brief moment I saw a black version of me. Chancy shrugged his shoulders.

"Whatever."

I turned to Matt as he got up from my desk.

"Thanks for looking after them," I leaned in and whispered again, "Were they really that bad?"

"Nah, I needed an excuse to write something down. I'll catch you later— God you smell good."

I turned and faced the blackboard for a moment so the students couldn't see the stupid grin on my face. When I sat down at my desk, I saw the note Matt had written for me. Before I read it, I looked up at the students to make sure they weren't staring at me. To my surprise, they were back at their assignment.

The note said:

*Christmas around the corner. Want to be with you. Call you later.*

My heart nearly burst with happiness. Matt wanted to spend the holidays with crazy me even though we'd only had one real date. I remembered what Ruthie told me and decided to slow the train down. *Priorities, priorities,* I said to myself. My priority over the Christmas break was going to be deciding whether or not to transfer to West Orange. I was going to need peace and quiet, long runs, endless glasses of wine.

But the thought of waking up next to Matt on Christmas morning was too tempting, enough to make me forget West Orange and teaching Spanish to a new set of students. Already I was visualizing Matt and me exchanging Christmas presents, watching *It's a Wonderful Life,* having dinner in his apartment (I hadn't seen it yet but it looked cozy and warm in my dream), discussing our future, what we would name our kids.

And then I realized something that sent chills down my spine.

There would be no Christmas for me in Orlando.

There would be no quiet nights with Matt in his cozy apartment.

There would be no regular turkey dinner on Christmas Day.

There would be no discussions about my job offer.

There would certainly not be any peace and quiet.

Lucky for me, I was going home for the holidays.

Back to Miami. Northern Cuba. The capital of Latin America. It was an unspoken rule with my family. You can go ahead and live your own life, go ahead and make friends and experience whatever you want, but your ass better be home for Christmas. And see, it posed a dilemma. If Matt wanted to be with me over the holidays, he'd have to spend them with me and my family, the Cuban side of my family.

My mom's Mexican family was interesting if not a little on the drunk side, but they were miles away. Not one of them had been brave enough to follow their sister to Miami. My dad's family, however, was an entirely different story. They made my mom's family look normal.

*Poor, poor Matt*, I thought.

# Chapter 17

My dad was the first one in his family to leave Cuba. The only one who realized Castro was a maniac who was going to destroy their lives and take away their freedom. When he said goodbye to his three brothers and two sisters, his mom and dad, they told him Castro wouldn't be around for much longer and why didn't he just wait? My dad adamantly refused. He told them to stop praying for miracles and get out while they could. None of them listened at first and stayed behind waiting for the day when Castro would be disposed of.

Boy did they wait a long time. One of them, my Uncle Rodolfo, is still waiting.

My Aunt Josefina was the next genius to leave. How she got out, I don't know. There are some things my dad refuses to talk about (most Cuban men tend to be stubborn). She joined my dad in Los Angeles with her four kids, Carlos, Ophelia, Anabel and Jose. Our cousins. Oddly enough, we never saw much of them growing up in LA. I think they were terrified of my uncles.

When we left LA and moved to Miami in 1978, Josefina followed soon after. Minus the husband, who found the women in Los Angeles far too beautiful to leave behind. She landed in Miami with not a leg to stand on and stayed with us for a few weeks, no surprise in a Cuban family. You always help a family member out, even if you get on each other's nerves and drive each other crazy. That's just the way it is.

A Cuban is a Cuban is a Cuban, and you're forever bound by loyalty and ties that run too deep to question.

Then came the Mariel Boat Lift in the early eighties. The only thing I remember seeing was boatloads and boatloads of refugees on television and camps that had been set up under Interstate 95 near downtown Miami. Thousands and thousands of people running away from a Communist regime. Moms and dads and children and ex-convicts convinced America would give them what they'd lost. Their freedom. Little did they know America would also offer them the opportunity to get hugely into debt and crap insurance options. Little did they know they would come to Miami and never learn how to speak English because the majority of the population already spoke Spanish.

The thought that I had a Cuban grandmother and grandfather had never crossed my mind. Abuela Guadalupe was the only one I'd met and besides, my dad never talked about his family or his past. Boy did things change. The Mariel Boat lift transformed both the city of Miami and my dad. For the first time in our lives, he seemed to come to life. His parents, Guillermina and Paco, and his mentally handicapped brother, Luis, were coming on one of those boats crammed with hopefuls. Every day he would wake up at the crack of dawn and drive down to Tamiami Park to look for the names of his parents and brother on the lists of new arrivals. Every day he would come home and pour himself a whiskey after work, light up a cigarette and say, "Es okay, maybe tomorrow, eh?"

Erasmo and I were so excited to have another set of grandparents that we stopped fighting and helped my mom prepare the extra bedroom. We went to Kmart just about every day and bought clothes, towels, soap, Doritos. As though we were preparing for the end of the world. We were, in a sense. We were preparing for the end of our world, a world that was quiet and safe and free of drug lords and thieves. A world free from a constant attack on my weight problem, my brother's bad grades, my mom's cooking, anything subject to an opinion.

Cubans are very opinionated people. Just ask my relatives.

One Sunday morning, I woke up before anyone else and walked into the living room, excited beyond belief to have the TV to myself, only to find my dad sitting on the couch smoking a cigarette. He looked sad, a look I wasn't used to. My dad never said much, but when he did, he was always optimistic.

My brother came home one day with a broken arm after a skateboarding accident.

My dad: Es okay, es just a little swollen. Joo need some ice.

My brother: Papi, I think it's broken.

My dad: No, no, es okay. No *problema*. Joo be okay tomorrow.

My brother: Papi, I think it's broken.

My brother went to bed that night with a broken arm that swelled to gargantuan proportions by morning. The next day, my dad took one look at his arm and grimaced.

My dad: *Mi'jo*, I sink so es broken.

My brother: Yeah, Papi, I told you that.

My dad: Okay, les go to de hospital. They fix it.

Out came the cigarette. My dad was calm, cool and collected. Erasmo and my dad left for the hospital while my mom went from zero to hysteria. No matter the injury, my mom could graduate it from "nothing to worry about" to a near death experience. All she had to do was look at a little blood and scream at the top of her lungs and it instantly hurt much more than you imagined.

Thank God for my dad and his cigarettes.

When I walked into the living room that morning, ready to make the television my personal entertainment slave, my dad looked trapped in another world far away from our home in Miami, a world I'd only come to know through my daily adventures on Calle Ocho when we first moved to Miami. To me, Cuba was just like Little Havana: noise, loud music, strong Cuban coffee, an annoying cigar, shouting and more shouting. I never asked my dad questions about what Cuba was really like as I felt absolutely no need.

"Hi, Papi."

He smiled when he saw me and held his arms out. *"Ven acá, mi niña."*

He was always quiet but always affectionate. Cubans are touchy-feely kind of people, the kind of people who never turn down an opportunity to kiss and hug. I walked towards him and let his arms envelop me. I inhaled Old Spice and cigarettes.

"What are joo doing up so early, *mi'ja*? Es only seven."

"I couldn't sleep. I had a dream that I'd failed my math test. It was horrible, Papi."

He laughed and hugged me closer and invited me to sit on the couch next to him. I climbed up onto the ancient green couch and snuggled into his large belly. He put his calloused hand on my head and smoothed my hair tenderly.

"Es okay, Bibita, joo no fail math test. Joo bery smart, joo make me so proud."

"Papi, why do you look so sad? Are you sad?"

"No, *mi'ja*, I not sad. I'm bery happy now, joo know? I no seeing my mami and papi for a bery long time."

"How long, Papi?"

"Ha! For bery long time." He sighed heavily. Twenny years."

"Twenty years? That's forever, Papi!"

"Jes, long time, *pero* now they coming here to Miami."

"I know. I can't wait. What are they like, Papi?"

"What are they like? Oh, *mi'ja*, they are bery good people. Bery nice. Joo are going to love them."

"Are they going to live here with us?"

"Jes, *pero* only for a little bit, no too long. I soon find them *un apartamento*."

"Do you think they'll like it here?"

"I don't know, I sink so. Es gonna be bery differen', joo know?"

"What's so different about Miami?"

"Oh, *mi'ja*, America is so differen', *pero* es good. Es better living here now. *Pero* Cuba, Cuba was so—" He stared into the distance, lost in memories.

I yanked him right back to my talk show. "Cuba was so what, Papi?"

"It was so nice. So beautiful. Before Castro, many Americans come to Cuba. For vacachun, for business, for de music and de people. The most beautiful place in de world."

"So why did you leave? And why are your parents coming? Why are so many people leaving now, Papi? If it's such a great place, then why didn't you stay there?"

He sighed and picked up a cigarette. "*Mi'ja*, some sings too complicated for joo now, *pero* one day when joo are older, I going to tell joo everysing, okay? Joo wanna watch TV?"

Boy did I wanna. Erasmo usually had control over the television, which meant I was forced to watch one of two things; either a football game or a very boring fishing program. I preferred watching *H&R Puff N' Stuff* or *Land of the Lost*, so you can only imagine how much time we spent fighting over the remote control. But no matter what I did or said, no matter how many times I'd go running to my mom, Erasmo would always win and I would end up learning yet one more thing about bass fishing.

Lucky for me, as we got older we stopped arguing so much. He stopped picking on me, stopped annoying me, stopped calling me names and pulling my pigtails. In fact, he stopped noticing me altogether. I'm convinced my brother knows nothing about what my life was like between the ages of eighteen and twenty-four. That's okay, though. He knows enough about me now to make up for it.

But damn, we sure had a funny relationship growing up.

It didn't stop with the remote control. No, that would've been ideal. We argued over everything. I mean, *everything*. I would do everything I could to get him to like me, to think I was cool. Little did I know I was really annoying the hell out of him.

For example.

"The Dallas Cowboys are the best football team ever."

"I think so, too," I would say.

"Why are you such a copycat? Why do you always have to copy me?"

"I am not."

"Are too. You're such a dork."

Or better yet.

"The Dallas Cowboys are my favorite football team," he would say loud enough for me to hear.

"Not me. I like the Dolphins."

"The Dolphins are crap! How can you even say that?! Didn't I tell you to like the Cowboys? Didn't I? You're such a dork!"

Back and forth. If I agreed with him, he'd get mad. If I opposed him, he'd get mad. I could never win, but I soldiered on for years, convinced he would like me sooner or later. Unfortunately, it was much, much later.

Lucky for us, we got away with using a few words because my parents couldn't figure out if they were cuss words or not. We got to say things like *crap* and *sucks* and *damn*. My poor mom went around using these words because she eventually picked them up from us. She would say, "Crap, I burn de rice," or, "Damn, joo are driving me craysee!" We would stand there and giggle because nothing is funnier when you're a kid than hearing your mom use a bad word.

God forbid we ever said *coño* or *carajo*, though. If we ever did, she would go from being the sweet mom who held me close to a complete maniac. It was her anger, followed by her sandal, followed by a solid hour of yelling, followed by a lecture on how they'd worked hard their whole lives to give us this, that and the other. And we'd feel so bad we'd promise to stick to crap and sucks and damn.

We also drove our dad out of his mind. He was a very patient man, but sometimes we asked for it. We violently protested their smoking habit once we found out cigarettes could kill them. When we realized our pleas weren't working, we decided to hide their carton of cancer sticks. The mother of all mistakes. Off came the belt and we ran. Ten seconds later, we gave them back.

We no longer had Donna's Slip N' Slide, so we improvised. On weekends, my dad took a second job painting houses. Logically, we took his plastic sheets and poured dish soap all over them and took turns slipping and sliding in the back yard. Problem was, such things as sharp rocks existed. We tore sheet after sheet. After the umpteenth time, my dad sat us down and talked to us, which was more torturous than anything else. The way he spoke to us and that disappointing look in his eye was enough to make us sob hysterically.

Sometimes, when we'd done something horrible, we'd ask him to hit us instead. It was so much easier to forget. But no, we'd get a lecture on how hard he'd worked, how much he wanted us to have a better life, how much he loved us and so on and so forth and sob, sob, sob.

We also did things to him out of sheer amusement. His hair was literally a silver afro. He had a full head of hair and tried to keep it as short as possible. One time, he let it get pretty long. It didn't grow down, though, it grew out and up. One Saturday afternoon, he fell asleep on the old green couch. His head was resting back, his mouth open in sweet abandon, a man lost in his dreams.

Both of us noticed the shoebox of rollers sitting on the kitchen table. Mom was nowhere in sight. We came up with an idea. It seems Erasmo and I only got along when we were both doing something naughty.

Twenty minutes later, our dad was lying on the green couch with a full head of rollers. We even considered putting lipstick on him but fell short of courage. Ten minutes later, my dad woke up and went to the bathroom. Five seconds later he was running all over the house, half yelling and half laughing.

"*Coño*, these cheeldren are driving me craysee!"

We couldn't have the television or the radio on during dinner, so we had to satisfy ourselves with each other's company. Which meant Erasmo and I would sit there and argue about everything. Most days, my dad would calmly ask us to settle down and be quiet. Most days, we would listen to him. Most days, my mom would take off her sandal. But the best days were when my dad lost his patience. He would say the funniest things, and even though we'd be scared into silence, we'd still laugh about it later.

When he'd had enough, my dad would put down his fork, take a deep breath, look at us and say, "*Me están encendiendo el higado,*" which literally means, "You are setting my liver on fire." Or he would say, "*Me están revolviendo la comida,*" which means, "You are mixing up my food."

So whenever we'd start fighting at the dinner table, Erasmo would lean over to me and whisper, "We should stop fighting, Bibi, because we're gonna set Papi's liver on fire." Or I'd say, "Stop pinching me, Erasmo, Papi's gonna get mad and we're gonna mix up his food."

We'd giggle and get along for about ten seconds.

My dad has some pretty outrageous concepts about the world, so naturally, we laughed at him.

"No, Papi," Erasmo would say, "there are no such things as UFO's."

"Huh, that is what joo think, *pero* I saw one. Joo no remember? When we driving through New Mexico?"

Erasmo and I would look at each other and laugh. *Our dad's crazy*, we would think.

My dad truly believes in the existence of UFO's. The only reason we don't know more is because the government is withholding the evidence. Along with that, my dad believes strongly in the following:

There is a cure for cancer and it will never be revealed because too much money will be lost.

"Yeah, okay," we'd say, "That one sounds believable."

AIDS was introduced as a method of population control.

"What do you think?" Erasmo would say.

"Uh, let's give him that one. I can buy that."

The education system in America is going down the drain for one simple reason. They want to keep everyone stupid.

Erasmo would look at him and say, "Don't think so, Papi. Look at Bibi. She's a dork."

The only reason Castro is still in power is because the US Government wants him there, for reasons that remain a mystery.

I'd poke my brother in the ribs. "Don't even touch this one. You know how he gets. His liver will be set on fire."

"And I don't know enough about Cuba anyway, so let's keep quiet on this one."

But back to my brother.

He knew I looked up to him. He was very aware that I would do anything he told me to do simply because he was my second Jesus Christ, the other person in my life whom I worshiped and adored. Unfortunately, he rarely made me do things that weren't hazardous to my health. He convinced me to eat the green part of the watermelon by telling me it would make me strong and cool just like him. I did, and forty-five minutes later, I was praying to the ceramic God, the toilet. My mom took off her sandal when I told her the truth and chased Erasmo around the house until she pegged him, which took the Sandal Queen all of five seconds.

On my fifth birthday, my dad gave me two choices: anything I wanted from Toys R' Us or a day at Disney Land. I knew Erasmo wanted to go to

Disney Land, but I defied him. I chose Toys 'R Us because I wanted a new bike. As we walked around the store, nothing seemed to capture my attention until I stumbled upon the most beautiful bike I'd ever seen. It was pink and had a banana seat, along with streamers on the handlebars and an adorable white basket with a flower on the front. Love at first sight.

My brother pulled me aside and gave me a talking to.

"Bibi, you can't get this bike. It's a girl bike."

"But I'm a girl, Raz."

"Yeah, but if you get this bike, you'll never be able to hang out with me and my friends. We won't be able to take you to Dead Man's Alley with that thing."

Dead Man's Alley was an abandoned lot where Erasmo and his friends had built their own ramps and potential death traps. I'd wanted to go there since the day I'd heard about it, even though it scared the holy hell out of me.

Like I said, I worshiped him.

He convinced me I really wanted a Mongoose dirt bike. My dad bought me the boy bike, confused at my sudden change of heart. We drove home that day, me totally excited at the prospect of going to Dead Man's Alley even though I'd really wanted the Pink Dreamsicle.

I rarely got to ride that damn bike at first. I quickly figured out he'd told me to get it because he wanted it for himself, the jerk. I would stand on the front porch yelling my lungs out, trying to get my mom to come outside and throw her sandal at Erasmo.

"Mami, tell Erasmito to give me back my *bicicleta*! Mami, pleeeaaaasssse!"

But Mom was always too busy freezing Tang or fruit punch. My brother would taunt me from the street, laughing at my crying and whining. I got fed up really quick.

"All right, fine, if you don't wanna give me my bike, I'm going to ride your Huffy!"

"Go ahead, I don't care."

He and his friends laughed as I huffed and puffed my way towards the back yard. With more confidence than I really had, I stormed into the back yard and rescued his old Huffy with the huge banana seat from cobwebs. It was way too big for me but I didn't care, I had a mission to accomplish. I struggled just getting up on the seat and reaching the pedals, but after a few attempts, I rode out onto the sidewalk desperately trying to stay on and waited for Erasmo to get mad and yank me off.

But he didn't. Instead, he watched me as I rode down the sidewalk. I say "down" because our house in East LA was at the top of a small hill. Halfway down towards Delmar Avenue, a very busy street, he stopped riding my bike and screamed at the top of his lungs.

"It doesn't have brakes, Bibi! It doesn't have brakes!"

Uh-oh. All hell broke loose as Erasmo and his friends tried to catch up to me and stop me before I got run over by a low-rider. As I got closer, adrenaline and a basic desire to remain alive kicked in. There was a tree at the bottom of the hill, a very large tree that looked liked my savior. It seemed to hold its arms out to me as I turned the bike and dove right into its solid foundation. Crack, smash, ouch, ayyyyyyy! The bike crumpled and I hit the grass like someone sliding into second base. Nothing in my body broke except my self esteem. I started crying immediately, not because I was in pain but because I knew I had to make my brother sorry. And I did. He never got on my Mongoose bike again.

Lying in bed that night, I felt triumphant.

It was when I moved to Orlando that our relationship changed. He was married by then and father of a beautiful little girl named Savannah. Being a father completely changed him. Turned him into someone else, someone I couldn't get used to. He'd never taken any kind of interest in my life, never knew where I was or what I was doing. For a few years, we were as close as the sun is to the moon. But when I moved away, I started getting weird phone calls from him, calls I never knew how to handle.

"Hey, Bibi, what's up?"

"Nothing. What's up with you? How's Savannah?"

"She's good. Other than that, it's the same old crap. What've you been doing? How's Orlando?"

"It's okay."

Silence.

"That's it? It's okay?"

"Yeah, I mean, what else can I say?"

"How's your love life?"

Silence.

"Bibi?"

"Yeah?"

"How's your love life?"

"Do you really want to know?"

"Yeah, man, come on. I'm your older brother, remember?"

I'd always want to point out that aside from being my older brother, he'd always been my torturer, my master, my very own Hitler. But I never could. I was Catholic, which meant I was supposed to be *all about forgiveness.*

"Uhm, it's okay. No, actually, it sucks."

"Hang in there. You know, I can always set you up with Donald. He always asks about you."

Whatever. Donald always had grease under his fingernails and reminded me of Pig Pen from the Peanuts gang. He was also missing a few teeth, which meant he had the potential of getting dentures someday, just like my dad. No thank you.

"Thanks, Raz, but I think I can manage."

"All right, sis. So, when you coming home?"

"Uh, don't know. Soon. Really soon."

The phone calls confused me, but little by little we made our way back to each other. I'd call him once a week and fill him in on my latest teaching story, tell him Chancy's momma jokes, complain about being homesick. We'd talk about our childhood, always playing the remember-this-remember-that game. He never said he was sorry, never brought up the torture or the teasing. Neither did I. Until I went home one weekend.

We went out on his boat, a brother and a sister out for a day of fishing. We spent most of the morning slicing squid for bait and trying to find the right spot on the big blue. We took a break in the afternoon and popped open two beers. We sat on the bow of the open fisherman and let our legs dangle. We didn't say much at first, just sat there enjoying the sun and the breeze. After the third beer, we were laughing our asses off. We brought up all the crazy things we'd done as kids, my mom's adventures, my dad's funny afro. He suddenly got quiet. When I looked over at him, he had tears in his eyes and was looking off into the distance.

"Hey, Raz, what's the matter? You okay?"

"Yeah, man, I'm cool. It's nothing."

It killed me to see a man cry, killed me even more because it was my brother.

"Are you sure? You having problems with Marie?"

"Nah, it's not that." He wiped away a tear on his shirt sleeve.

"Come on, dude, talk to me. I'm a good listener."

He looked at me, tears sliding down his beautiful face. "I was just sitting here thinking about how mean I was to you, you know?"

"Come on, Raz, forget about that. We were just—"

"No, dude, seriously, I was an asshole. And you know what kills me? I don't know who the hell my sister is. I don't know what you've been through, I don't know what you've done in the past few years." Another tear slowly made its way down his face. He didn't bother wiping it. "I wasn't there for you like I should've been, man. I never wanted you to be around me, and you know why? Because I was always so jealous of you. You were always the smart one, the talented one; Bibi can do this and Bibi can do that and Bibi is so wonderful and why can't you be more like Bibi? But you know what?"

"Raz, stop it. I mean it, okay?" Now I was crying.

"No, let me tell you something, dork." He put his arm around me. "You are so fuckin' cool, man. I am so proud of you. I brag about you to all my friends."

"You do?"

"Yeah, man, can you blame me? You've always done whatever the hell you wanted. And you know what? I wish I *had* been more like you." He grabbed my head and put me in a headlock. "You are one crazy chick, dude."

"You don't need to remind me. I think I inherited craziness from Mami."

He started laughing and let me go. "I believe it. Hey, do you forgive me?"

I looked at him sincerely. "Raz, I forgave you a long time ago. I mean it."

He grabbed me again and hugged me. "Cool. You ready for more fishing?"

"Let's do it."

By the time I met Matt, I'd already been living in Orlando for a little over a year. During the first three months of my "solo" flight, I went home only once, and that was just to pick up the rest of my stuff. During the next three months, I went home about six times, each time using the excuse that I needed to get "one more thing." During the next three months, I went home nearly every weekend.

You see, no matter where you go, there you are.

I started missing my family in more ways than one. I missed helping my mom get ready for bingo, talking to my dad about that crazy man Fidel, sitting at Linda's house drinking gallons of strong coffee, taking the air out of my brother's tires when he wasn't around. Things like that. But admitting my loneliness would've been a big, big mistake. Dad would've rented a U-Haul and come up to Orlando to move me back home. He would've looked at me and said, "I told joo." I hated that.

So, I'd talk to them and laugh and tell them stories just to make them think I was still doing fine on my own. I always left out the fact that on most nights, my only companions were a bottle of red wine and a calzone from Pisa Pizza, or that the only people who seemed to know me better than anyone else were the night staff at Blockbuster. My ability to lie developed into a monster I couldn't control. I made up friends, events, more friends, more events, bullshit, bullshit, bullshit. And they always bought it. They thought I was living a jet-set kind of life on a poverty-line kind of salary. They believed I knew exactly what I was doing and where I was going.

Finally.

Don't get me wrong. I wasn't suicidal or so depressed that I couldn't get out of bed. Just plain old homesick. Not having a solid group of friends only made it harder. When Matt walked into my life, he didn't change it so much as turn it on its head. It was weird to come home and have messages on my answering machine, even weirder to find little notes on my car or a rose on my desk.

I thought I was the only one marveling at the miracle of Matt's presence in my life, but I was very mistaken. My family was more than surprised and excited about Matt. Judging by their reactions when I told them I was a) coming home for Christmas *and* New Year, b) bringing somebody with me and c) bringing someone who wasn't a woman, I'm convinced Erasmo, the Sandal Queen and the Fart Champion thought I was gay.

"You're what? Did I hear you correctly?" my brother said in hushed tones.

"Yep. You heard me. I'm bringing a guy home."

"A guy? You mean, like, a *guy* guy?"

"What do you mean a '*guy* guy'? Of course he's a guy!" I sighed into the phone and lay back on my still screwed up bed.

"What's his name? Where's he from? What does he do?"

"Slow down, Raz. Jeez, I got a headache and you're not helping."

"Oh, that's right, I forgot it's Saturday, which means you probably went out last night and got smashed."

"Nooooo, I'm not a drunk, you know. I just had one too many glasses of red wine." My head hurt just thinking about it. "I gotta go."

"No, you didn't answer my questions about the guy guy."

I yawned and scratched my stomach. "All right. His name is Matt Connelly. He's Irish Catholic, which should make Mami very happy. He's not a communist, which means Papi will let him into the house. He's from New York, he's a teacher just like me. Oh, and he hates the Cowboys."

"He what?! And you're still bringing him to meet me?"

"Yep. Deal with it. We can't all be Cowboy fans. Besides, he's about ten feet taller than you and probably not the best person to get into an argument with."

"I was only kidding, you moron. I can't wait to meet him. You haven't brought a guy home since that English dude. Have you told him about us?"

"What do you mean?"

"You know, about our *familia*. I think you should warn him, you know."

"You ain't kidding. But I'm afraid to tell him because he might back out on me."

"Nah, he won't. You're the coolest chick, man. He's probably crazy about you."

I laughed to myself. "Erasmo, that's only the second time in my whole life that you've ever called me anything besides moron or dork or dumb ass."

"Don't get used to it."

"I'm going to hang up now. My head is going to explode."

"All right. See you soon."

The truth is I was terrified of telling Matt about my family. I wasn't ashamed of them, not in a million years. But taking him to meet my tribe was like taking a lamb into the slaughterhouse. Like I said, Cubans are very opinionated people. I could already imagine their reactions.

"*Dios mio, que grande.*"

"*Ay Dios mio, un gringo.*"

"Joo Catolic?"

"Joo do drugs?"

"Joo have nice family?"

And all this before, "Nice to meet you" or "Welcome to our home" or "Would you like something to drink?"

Erasmo wasn't the only one who tortured me when I was kid. My Abuela Guillermina and my Tia Josefina made him look like the sweetest brother on earth. The first words out of their mouths would always be a comment about my appearance, and if that wasn't enough, they'd usually add something to remind me of my bleak future as a fat, ugly, mop-haired young woman.

"Joo are too fat. Es no good. No boys will like joo."

"Your hair. Es ugly. Joo should brush it, Bibita. Es why joo no has no boyfriend."

"Joo need to lose weight. Joo will neber get married."

"Why joo no has no friends? Es because joo are fat, *seguro*."

"Why joo always reading? Joo need exercise or joo will die bery fat."

And I would stand there and smile and try to be polite even though each comment would hit me like a slap in the face. After ten minutes of heavy criticizing and raised eyebrows, they'd kiss me and hug me and move on to the next victim. My fat legs would walk me back to my room and I'd take one look in the mirror and consider shaving my head. Instead, I'd pick up my latest novel about teenage angst and go back to my fantasy world where nobody stood in front of me and attacked everything from head to toe.

That's what my family is like, though, and like it or not, I couldn't trade them in for nicer relatives with manners. I also couldn't tell them to stop being so mean, because they'd argue with me and tell me they were saying it *for my own good.* Yeah, telling someone they're fat and ugly is the best way to boost self-esteem. Whatever.

And now I was taking Matt to meet the Critical Crew.

We decided to take his car because it didn't look like it was about to die a miserable death. He showed up on my doorstep early Saturday morning with fresh bagels and coffee. Another dream come true. A man with food in his hand. *I am so blessed,* I thought. He grabbed my suitcase out of my hand and put it in the trunk of his car and off we went. Down south to a foreign land. I almost felt like I should ask him if he'd packed his passport.

Miami is like a foreign country and I'm not kidding about that.

For the first few miles, we were both quiet. Matt sensed there was something on my mind and respected my silence, but eventually he cleared his throat and interrupted my thoughts.

"Hey."

"Yeah?"

"What's up?"

"What do you mean?"

"You haven't said much." He looked at me with a worried expression. Instinctively, I leaned over and kissed him. He smiled. "You okay?"

"Yeah, think so."

"You wanna talk about it?"

"Hmm, don't know."

"Come on. What's going on? Are you regretting taking me to meet your family? Am I rushing things?"

"Oh my God, no way. I'm actually flattered. I can't believe it."

"Then what is it? Is it the job offer at West Orange?"

"Not really, to be honest. It's, it's—"

He sighed and grabbed my hand with his free one. "Hey, tough girl, don't you trust me? Usually you can't keep your mouth shut."

I gave him a sideways glance.

"I don't mean it in a bad way, Bibi. I love listening to you, really, but I can tell something's bothering you. Come on, give it up."

I sighed and looked out the window at the flat landscape. "You're right. The thing is, I'm scared shitless."

"Scared? About what?"

"You meeting my family. Matt, they're nuts."

"Nah, they can't be that bad. Come on, my family's pretty crazy, too."

"No, no, no, you don't understand. I'm pretty damn sure you've never met people like them, and I'm very sure you've *never* been to a place like Miami."

"I can handle it, okay? I'm a tough guy from New York, remember?"

"Yeah, but your accent's not going to save you this time. Trust me. You're going to be bombarded by a lot of things."

"Okay, okay. So, why don't you tell me about them first? Tell me now because this landscape is boring and if you entertain me it will make it more interesting. Huh? What do you say?"

"You really want to hear about them now? If you do, you might turn this car around and drive right back to Orlando."

"I doubt that." He leaned over and kissed me. My knees turned into silly putty.

"Well—"

"Come on!"

"Okay. Let's see, where do I start?"

I thought about lying to make my family look less neurotic and more normal, but that would've been pointless. In three hours he was going-to witness the entire circus.

"Okay, well, my Tia Josefina is pretty critical no they're all critical they will criticize everything about you in less than ten seconds and my Tia Raquel always wears this apron around her neck that has a fake penis underneath it and she'll lift it up and show you and laugh because she thinks it's hilarious her husband my Uncle Lingero is always wearing a wife beater t-shirt and whereas I have a wild animal on my head he has a wild animal on his back it's that hairy and wait till you meet my grandmother oh boy you better prepare yourself she doesn't speak English and she'll be annoyed that you're not Cuban but that's okay because my dad will like you just because you're not a communist he hates Castro FYI and yes he will probably fart in front of you so please don't be surprised when the fumes hit your nose and you feel like passing out—" I paused.

Matt was laughing. "Go on."

"You want more? Okay my brother is the biggest Cowboy fan in the whole wide world but I told him you like the Jets and he's okay with it I think my mom well you've heard about my mom her clothes never match and she'll fawn all over you because she'll be so excited that I brought a guy home oh and the food oh my God the food don't be surprised if you see a dead pig roasting in our back yard in a Chinese box I'll explain that later but yeah the food is grossly fattening but delicious I hope you got some solid workouts before this trip and Matt honey be prepared to drink endless shots of tequila because for some reason they like to pretend they're Mexican once in a while especially when the mariachi band shows up don't look at me like that trust me they've probably hired one for Noche Buena and—"

"Nochay booena? What's that?"

"Oh, that's right, that's another thing I have to explain. We don't celebrate Christmas Day like most of the American world. We throw a huge party on Christmas Eve."

"Really? What's that like?"

"What's it like? Well, let's see." I knew I should shut my mouth, but being that I'd spilled the beans about everyone, why stop? "Everyone comes over our house or my Uncle Lingero's house doesn't really matter because they live right next to each other. My grandmother and my Aunt Josefina live about two blocks away, and my other relatives live within a mile."

"Why do they live so close to each other?"

I sighed. "Oh, Matt, do you really know nothing about Cubans? Remember this, they stick together. Living in the same city isn't enough for my family. They have to live close enough so they can come over every chance they get and voice their opinions on everything without having to drive anywhere."

"Interesting."

"Interesting? No, I wouldn't call it that. I'd call it mortifying because you never get one moment of peace."

"But you don't sound like it bothers you too much, though."

"To be honest, it doesn't. I love my family, even though they always criticize me and make me feel like a piece of bad artwork they can always judge."

"You're not a piece of bad artwork."

"Ha! That's what you think. Wait till you talk to my Tia Josefina."

"What else? This is hilarious. Tell me more."

"You actually want to hear more?"

"Bring it on, Bibi."

Three and a half hours flew by as I talked nonstop about growing up in Miami surrounded by my dad's family. He laughed when I told him the story about Erasmo making me memorize the names of every football team and didn't even flinch when I told him he'd probably have to dance salsa and merengue with one of my aunts. The more I talked, the more he seemed to look forward to the experience. It wasn't until I looked out the window and saw the familiar landscape of Miami (signs in Spanish, bad drivers) that it hit me.

No matter what the occasion or impending disaster, it was always good to go home.

# Chapter 18

I decided to let the students have a mini-Christmas party on the last day of the term. It was only fair, as every one of them had been more than good and had actually made an effort to learn. If there was anything I remembered about school and holidays, it was the excitement of waking up and looking forward to a Valentine's celebration or an Easter party. I was lucky enough to have teachers who used any excuse to have moms take over for a day. We'd stuff ourselves with cupcakes, candy, pizza, Doritos, ice cream, soda, you name it. All the things we weren't allowed to eat on a daily basis.

Well, to be honest, my house was a little different when it came to food.

Because my parents were so poor growing up and had suffered through real hunger pains, there was little they denied us when it came to food. Most kids would come home and have a healthy snack, like an apple or jell-O. Not us. We'd come home from school and eat TV dinners or chicken pot pies. Sometimes I still get a craving for the fried chicken TV dinner with the brownie and corn. We'd eat homemade pizza (a piece of toast with Ragu sauce and a slice of American cheese), Entenmann's donuts, Little Debbie snack cakes that my mom brought home from work. Never mind the fact that we'd have dinner in less than three hours.

Sometimes, when my mom would tuck me into bed, I'd look at her sadly and tell her I *needed* some ice cream.

"Ice cream, *mi'ja*? *Pero*, es bery late."

"I know, Mami, but I really *really need* some. I have a hard test tomorrow."

She'd sigh and smooth my hair. "Okay, I bring joo some. Joo want some milk, too?"

"Hm hmm. Yes, Mami."

And still I'd wonder why I was big enough to wear my mom's clothes.

I had such fond memories of junk food and parties that I knew my teaching experience wouldn't be complete without a good high-calorie festival.

Apparently, it was a first for them.

"Miss C, what should we bring?" Marcdala asked.

"Bring whatever you can. I don't care, as long as it's not flammable or sharp."

Jazelin bolted out of his chair. "Yo, Miss C, I can bring a boom box?"

"What was that?"

"Yo, sorry, Miss C. *May I* bring a boom box?" He looked at me hopefully, as though he'd just asked me if I would let him into heaven.

"Well—"

The class pleaded along with him until I gave in. After all, what was a party without a little bit of music?

"Okay, bring the boom box, but hey, you can't bring any music that has cuss words, you got it?"

"A'ight, Miss C." Jazelin walked over to Chancy and they did some funky thing with their hands that I couldn't duplicate, not in a million years.

"Miss C, Miss C!"

"Yes, Ebony?"

"Miss C, uhm—" She looked around the room and hesitated for a moment.

"What is it, Ebony? What's up?"

"Uhm, Miss C, can I sing a song?"

All the kids started snickering and "awwwwwing" and basically let her know they weren't down with it.

"Of course you can." The class started to complain again but I stopped them before Ebony's self-esteem vanished into thin air. "Come on, you guys, let's be nice, okay? Show some respect."

"But, Miss C," DiAngelo pleaded, "she ain't no singer."

"She's what?"

"I mean, she can't sing."

"How do you know?"

"Uhm, well, I don't know, yo. She don't look like no singer."

Ebony had obviously had enough. She stood up and put her skinny arms on her waist. "I can sing, okay? *I can sing.*"

"Ebony, calm down. I'm going to let you sing, okay? Now, sit down."

But Ebony wasn't having it. She seemed to go somewhere else for a few minutes and I stood there, my hands on my desk, transfixed by her conviction.

"Miss C, I can sing I don't care what they say I can sing. I sing all the time when noone's around I sing at the top of my lungs in the shower and it sounds good Miss C and I'm gonna be a singer someday I'm gonna be a singer because that's what I really wanna do Miss C so please let me sing because it's my dream y'all heard? I can sing."

She spoke so passionately and vehemently about her belief that everyone, even Jazelin, got quiet. She gave DiAngelo a look so full of hate it should've killed him instantly and sat down.

I cleared my throat. "Okay, honey, no problem. If you really want to—"

She opened her mouth and started singing, of all things, "Amazing Grace." And for a moment I forgot where I was. Ebony's voice boomed into the classroom, an angelic voice that took my breath away. We all sat in silence as she sang the whole song. My God, her voice was beautiful. It nearly brought tears to my eyes it was so sweet and perfect. When she was done, I looked at DiAngelo. He looked like he didn't know where to put himself.

"Miss C, I think we should let Ebony sing." He looked at Ebony. "Damn girl, I ain't know you can sing like that."

Ebony smiled triumphantly and sat down. I cleared my throat and composed myself. Her voice reminded me of Doc for some reason and it made me want to cry.

"Well, like I said, we're going to have a party on the last day before the Christmas break and yes, Ebony's going to sing. Jazelin's going to bring a boom box and we're all going to stuff ourselves with enough junk food to give us a heart attack. A'ight?" I smiled and clapped my hands. The entire classroom hooted their appreciation.

Chancy looked at me out of the corner of his eye and smiled. "Yo, Miss C."

"What's up, Chancy?"

"You said, 'a'ight'."

"Yeah, so?"

"Why you saying that, yo? You always be telling us to talk right and say this right and raise your hands and show respect. Now you talkin' like us? What's up with that?"

I laughed and walked over to his desk. "Does it bother you, yo?"

He laughed and picked at his 'fro. "Nah, Miss C, it's cool. It's a'ight, yo. You can chill, Miss C. You cool."

"Good. Now get your notebooks out. We'll talk about the party at the end of class."

The *transfer to West Orange* dilemma weighed heavily on my mind as I gave the students a lesson on how to write a letter. Freudian slips left, right and center.

"Now, kids, you always need to write the address on the letter. For example," I walked to the chalkboard, "you would write, 'West Orange High School,' uh, I mean, uh—" My mind drew a blank.

"Why would we even write to that school?" Marcdala blurted out. "That's way on the other side of town, Miss C. We're not going to that school."

"Yeah, that's where all them rich white kids go." Jazelin rolled his eyes.

"Uh, well, it was just an example. Let's move on."

More gibberish on letter writing. *You need an address, a name, the date, all that good stuff that makes a good impression.*

"Make it short and sweet. Don't tell them you won't accept the job offer unless you're, uh, I mean, try to get your point across and, and—"

The class gave me a funny look, like they'd all seen my mind walk out the door.

"Sorry, guys, it's the holidays. I'm a little distracted." I gave them what I hoped was a convincing smile.

"Miss C, what you gonna do for Christmas? You goin' home, Miss C?"

"Yeah, Chancy, I'm going home." I was relieved they hadn't looked into my mind and seen the tempest of confusion and turmoil. "But listen, we need to get through this lesson, otherwise we won't be able to talk about the party."

They must have felt something in the air, the quiet before the storm. They sat quietly as I droned on and on about how to write a proper letter to Biggie Smalls. Lessons meant more to them when I included someone they knew, and that someone was usually a rapper or a movie star or a relative. We got through the lesson with no interruptions, and once I was done, I had them write a sample letter to whoever they wished.

As they wrote, I sat at my desk and looked around the room. *We've come so far*, I thought. In less than a month they had gone from unruly, totally out of control teenagers to attentive young children, and all thanks to my mother. I made a mental note to give her more money for bingo. I even thought about buying her new lipstick.

My thoughts went from West Orange to Matt in about two seconds. Two seconds after that I fell into what-will-sex-with-Matt-be-like thoughts.

My mother raised me to believe I couldn't have sex until marriage. This was a standard rule for me; there was no deviating from the norm, no justification for having sex before a ring on the finger, no way out of it, no way, no sir. I accepted it because nobody had ever wanted to sleep with me in the first place. No serious boyfriends, just a little bit of deep kissing and petting here and there, nothing to write home about.

Until I went to Mexico. Until I opened my eyes and saw a whole other world waiting for me. Until I realized there was no room in my *soon to be spectacular* life for a virgin. Until I realized the last thing I wanted to do was get married. My parents had a seemingly good marriage but I regarded the institution as something that would hold me back from chasing every silly dream running through my head. *If I got married, how will I travel to Africa?* I would think. *Or backpack through India? Ride the Trans Siberian Railway?* Mexico had helped me grasp that wondrous sense of freedom you can only get when you're sitting on an old bus with nothing to your name and a journal full of dreams and thoughts. I realized that if I waited until I got married to have sex, I would probably wait a long time. A very long time. I wasn't happy about that.

Enter John.

John was a bartender at Friday's. He was considerably older (a whole five years); a quiet, mysterious young man with dark, brooding eyes and incredible sex appeal. I loved him the moment I laid my eyes on him. That first look, that first smile took my breath away and rendered me helpless. He had an air of danger and intrigue rolled into one and it was powerful. It drew me to him like a magnet.

I would love to say we had a steamy, torrid affair. I would love to say we ended up seeing each other for years. I would love to say so many things about the first guy who stole my heart and then tried to give it back. But I can't. Because nothing really happened except that we went out for a few drinks one night after work, had a little too much and ended up in his apartment. That was the end of my virginity and my life as a sweet, obedient Catholic girl. John and I saw each other a few more times, but it went absolutely nowhere. He kept telling me I was too young. "You're just gonna hurt me, Bibi. Sorry, but it's bad timing."

Basically, he dumped me. I suffered for about, oh, let's see, three hours. Which doesn't say much for my feelings. I mistook sexual desire for love, and once I realized the difference, life when it came to the opposite sex became much easier for me. Problem was, I was no longer a virgin and was living with the guilt. I'd wanted to have sex; it was my decision, my choice, but still the guilt and shame failed to leave me. I carried it around like a backpack full of Bibles.

I knew I had to tell my mom, as it would be the only thing that would make me feel better, even if she took off her shoe and smacked me a few times. I told my mom everything and keeping such a serious thing from her was torture. If

I thought for one second that she would fly off the handle and call me *a-slut-a whore-a disgrace*, I never would've told her. I came to her with the news simply because my gut told me she would accept it as though I'd just told her I'd made a hundred dollars that night in tips. Still, I was a little afraid.

"Mami?"

She was ironing my dad's shirts. *Not good*, I thought. *Hot appliance in her hand.*

"Uh-huh?"

"Mami, I have to tell you something." My heart was pounding and I could barely get the words out.

"Uh-huh, okay, what is it, *mi'ja?*"

"What would you do if I told you I wasn't a virgin anymore?" It took me forever to get the words out.

She turned the iron off (good sign) and looked at me. Not sadly, not angrily, not anything. Just looked at me as though she was trying to make up her mind how she felt about it. I held my breath.

"What joo want me to do, eh? Joo want me to sew joo back up?" And she laughed as she said this. Relief washed over me. "*Ay, mi'ja*, your mami no es old fachun like joo say." She laughed again while I tried to figure out what this strange woman in front of me had done with my mother. "*Ay, mi amor*, let me ask you somesing, okay?"

"Sure, Mami."

"Why joo wait so long?"

Dear, dear. You think you know your parents until the day they come out with something remarkably contradictory to everything you were brought up to believe. My confession brought me even closer to my mom, but don't misunderstand me. She accepted the fact that I had sex, but that didn't mean I could have it under their own roof or anywhere near them. It was something they preferred not to think about, some peculiarity about my behavior they found slightly disturbing. Oh, well. You can only ask for so much when it comes to Hispanic parents. Lucky for me, mine were more liberal than I'd thought.

Matt and I hadn't made love—as opposed to having sex, of course—because something was telling me to wait. Besides, just the idea of it was enough to make me crazy. I looked around the classroom at my students and instantly felt my face get hot. *How can I sit here and think about sex right in front of them? How dare I?* I looked out the window instead. Gone was the shame once I pictured Matt taking off his shirt, kissing me softly on the neck as I took off my shoes and unbuttoned my pants. The passion, the intensity, the build up. Just as my shirt was coming off, DiAngelo yanked me right back from my own porn movie.

"Miss C?" DiAngelo was standing at my desk staring at me with a funny look on his face.

"Oh, sorry. Yes, honey?"

"Miss C, I finished. What you want me to do?"

"Just leave it on my desk. The rest of you do the same as you finish, and before we dive into party mode, I'll have you some of you read them out loud to the class."

Big mistake.

"No, Miss C, mine's stupid!"

"Miss C, I ain't do it right, yo!"

"Miss C, you straight trippin', I ain't gonna read my letter to the class."

"Uh-uh, no way, yo. I ain't gonna make a fool of myself."

I stood up and put my hands on the desk.

"Hey, hey, hey, slow down. First of all, you all sound like you haven't learned a thing from me. Why the *ain't's*? Come on now, behave. If you don't know what you're doing wrong, you won't know how to do it right, okay?"

Silence.

"And I swear, if anybody laughs, you're out of the party. I'll send you over to Mr. Connelly's classroom during the party and you'll have to lick the chalkboard."

The class went into a frenzy.

"No, Miss C!"

"Okay, Miss C, we *will* be good!"

"Miss C, *I'm not* going to laugh!"

I laughed in spite of myself. I'd never used the chalkboard threat and I could see why it worked for Matt. "All right, then. Finish up."

They finished their letters and placed them in a neat stack on my desk. The last one to finish was Chancy, no surprise. He was always the last one, but the one who always seemed to put the most thought into an assignment. Man, I loved that kid.

The class sat quietly while I looked through the letters. They were all equally afraid to have to read them aloud, but I figured public speaking was just as important as how to string a sentence together. The class sat quietly as I read one after the other to myself, secretly pleased at their improvements. They weren't one hundred percent perfect, but good enough to make me feel

I was actually doing an okay job. I decided to pick Jazelin's letter because it was addressed to his mother. I was curious as to what he needed to let his momma know.

"Jazelin?"

Jazelin covered his face in his hands and shook his head. "No, Miss C, come on, now. Don't make me read it."

"Get up here right now. Come on." The tone in my voice meant I was serious.

"A'ight, Miss C, a'ight." He came to the front of the classroom and grabbed the paper I was holding out to him.

"Shoot, Miss C, I don't wanna do this, yo."

"Come on, Jaz, just read it. I'm sure it's fine, and don't worry, if anyone laughs, it's straight to the chalkboard." I smiled and winked at him. Jazelin turned around slowly and cleared his throat.

"I wrote a letter to my momma 'cuz there some things she need to know, you know what I'm sayin'?"

He turned his head and looked at me. I nodded my head in encouragement. "Go ahead."

"Dear Momma, uh, I am writing you this here letter 'cuz Miss C made me and you need to know a few things about me 'cuz you don't never aks me. I am doing good in school and I don't cut up so much 'cuz Miss C she gets mad and starts trippin'. I don't like when you holler at me 'bout nothin' just 'cuz you is tired from workin' all the time. It ain't, I mean, it's not my fault that my daddy don't love you like he should and you gotta be workin' all the time. I am trying to be a good son 'cuz I know you think I will end up like my Uncle Big D the one locked up. I am not like him, Momma, so stop hollerin' at me to get my shit, oops, sorry Miss C, my stuff together. Miss C is a good teacher and she want me to learn and get a education 'cuz she say it will open doors for me. I am sorry you have to work so much and that we don't got, I mean, don't have a nice crib, but some day I am gonna get a good job and you won't have to work in no factory no more. And I won't get into no more trouble like fights and stuff 'cuz Miss C say we gotta be nice to people and not hit them when we mad. I love you, Momma. The End."

The class said not a word, not even a snicker or a giggle. Jazelin had a "bad boy" image and his letter shocked everyone, including myself.

"Jazelin, look at me."

"Yeah?" The scowl was gone from his face. He even looked a little sad. Defeated.

"Jazelin, that was absolutely fantastic! I am so proud of you!"

I got up from my desk and came around to hug him, but he stepped back as though I had bubonic plague.

"Hey, come on. I was just going to hug you."

Big, big no-no in the school system. I could've been accused of child molesting.

"Nah, Miss C, don't hug me, yo. That's embarassin'."

"Okay, how about a handshake?"

"A'ight, Miss C. Let me teach you how we do it."

The class laughed as I tried to mirror his complicated movements. First a punch, then a shake, then a grab, followed by elbows touching and finishing off with a fist on the chest. Sign language straight from the hood. When I finally got it right, the students started clapping and cheering. I felt like an idiot but I laughed anyway.

Jazelin broke the ice and made everyone want to read their letters to the class.

"I can go, Miss C?"

"Miss C, my letter is better!"

"Miss C, pick me, pick me!"

The bell rang as we got through the last letter. They packed up their things while I gave them their homework assignment. I promised we'd talk about the party the next day. Once they were gone, I sat at my desk, no energy in me whatsoever. I liked teaching, but it was more exhausting than anything I'd ever done. It was like being on stage at all times. West Orange High School popped into my head again. I sighed.

Like I said, one decision is all it takes to change your whole life.

# Chapter 19

South Beach, Coconut Grove, Downtown, Key Biscayne, Coral Gables, the Design District. Exciting, happening, beautiful, rich in color and rich in gorgeous people. Billion dollar homes and massive yachts. A second home for movie stars, famous musicians, wealthy drug lords. A truly amazing place full of palm trees and endless warmth.

But that's just a tiny part of it, and it's the only part you normally see on television. There's so much more to Miami than breathtaking models and awe inspiring homes. There are seriously bad drivers, poor neighborhoods, miles and miles of traffic no matter which way you're heading and oh, yeah, a whole lot of Hispanics.

When we first moved to Miami, there was a considerable amount of Cubans. Cubans who'd come over in the early sixties fleeing from Castro and his message of "equality." Lawyers, doctors, businessmen and artists fled to Miami and made their mark. They quickly became the movers and shakers in politics and business, people with no money but an incredible amount of passion. Miami thrived. Neighborhoods went from all-Anglo to all-Cuban in a blink of an eye. Our neighborhood near Westwood Lake was one such example.

But it was cool. We never faced any kind of discrimination, never got any complaints about the fact that we roasted pigs in our back yards. The Cuban population grew and grew because Miami welcomed it. The Mariel Boat Lift in the early eighties turned Miami into a set out of *Scarface*. I'm not kidding. When Castro told the people they were free to go, he also opened up his prisons and said, "You're free to go, too." So we got it all. Innocent people desperate to get to America to live a better life and criminals dying to get to Miami to, well, commit more crimes.

Surrounded by so many people from my dad's country, it was hard for us to think of ourselves as American. We spoke Spanish freely, talked loudly in public places and played our music whenever and wherever, with not a care in the world. We celebrated the Fourth of July, but we put more energy into celebrating Carlito's birthday or Ophelia's baptism or Luisito's First Communion. We saw Cuban flags way more often than we saw American flags. Cuba seemed to be everywhere you went.

In my mind, there are two types of Cubans, in the same way that there are many types of Americans (Texans, Rednecks, New Yorkers, etc.). I've broken Cubans down into two groups, White Cubans and Ghetto Cubans. Let me make something clear, though. This is how *I* see it, this is how *I* have separated them in my mind. Neither group is superior to the other; they are simply different. Way, way different.

That said, here's my breakdown.

White Cubans are successful businessmen, doctors, lawyers, professors, artists. Ghetto Cubans are construction workers, factory workers, guys who help you move for fifty bucks, ladies who do manicures and pedicures out of their own apartments in Hialeah, the ultimate Ghetto Cuban suburb. White Cubans take vacations in Europe, Ghetto Cubans take vacation on Sundays and they spend it at the beach or at someone's house. It depends on whose turn it is to cook. White Cubans send their children to expensive Catholic schools and universities. Ghetto Cubans send their children to public schools and tell them over and over again to get good grades so they can get scholarships so they can get a good job so they can make money so they can support their parents when they're older.

White Cubans never kill pigs and roast them in their back yards, absolutely no way in hell. Too savage, too uncivilized, too raw. Ghetto Cubans not only kill pigs, they invite everyone and their brother to come over and taste it, as though having the best tasting pig is a contest. White Cubans have great insurance plans and go to the best doctors in town. Ghetto Cubans know someone who knows someone who has a brother would can pull your tooth or get you antibiotics for fifty bucks. White Cubans drive nice new cars and live in beautiful homes. Ghetto Cubans drive cars that were bought for a hundred bucks from the brother of the friend of the guy who pulled your tooth, cars that break down often and have to be taken to that other guy who has a friend who knows some cool guy who can fix it for seventy-five bucks. And they live in an apartment they rented from the uncle of the friend of the guy who fixed their car. It's one long chain of I-know-somebody-who-knows-somebody-who-knows-this-guy-that-can-hook-you-up-for-nothing. White Cubans use their fingers to point things out. Ghetto Cubans use their mouths to point out the *mamacita* walking across the street or as a way to ask you to get them something. White Cubans hire landscape companies to make their front yard look like something out of a magazine. Ghetto Cubans mow the lawns themselves, but they'll pay Little Juanito from around the corner two bucks to put the mowed grass into trash bags. And Little Juanito, who's always out to make a fast buck, will do it gladly.

But there's one thing both groups have in common; there are Cubans, and then there's everyone else. Cubans, for the most part, believe they are the superior race. The best doctors come from Cuba, the best baseball players come from Cuba, the best food comes from Cuba, the best music comes from Cuba. The absolute best comes from Cuba. Cuba is number one. And if you don't believe me, just ask a Cuban and they'll set you straight.

My family is one hundred percent Ghetto Cuban, and I'm proud of them, but I can't deny I once wished for a White Cuban family. I can't say I didn't want to live in a big home in Coral Gables and go to an expensive Catholic school. I'd be lying if I said I never imagined my parents driving nicer cars and wearing expensive clothes. I wished for these things not because I was ashamed, but simply because I wanted something better for them. Something better for all of us. Little did I know I was the only one with these wishes. We could've won the lottery and I swear my parents wouldn't have moved out of Miami to save their lives.

*I am rich*, my dad once said.

Sadly, my grandfather died two years after he got to Miami. High cholesterol, diabetes, heart failure. I don't remember too much about him, just the fact the he would wolf down steak and white rice even though everyone told him he shouldn't. He was very stubborn. Sometimes I would sit on his lap and play with the hair growing out of his ears, something I found fascinating. He never looked happy, though. Grandpa Paco was sad to die in a foreign country, and it was only when he took his final breath that I got a sense of what it's like to lose a mom or dad.

A couple of days after the funeral, Erasmo and I ran into the master bedroom with a dilemma. He was trying to get me in trouble for breaking a glass in the kitchen, I was trying to get him in trouble for burning one of my stuffed animals. My mom was standing outside the bathroom door with her face in her hands. Erasmo and I looked at each other and quickly forgot the war.

"What's wrong, Mami?" I asked.

She looked at us, eyes brimming with tears. She put a finger to her lips, the universal sign for *shut your mouth*. We walked over and stood by her near the bathroom door, unaware of what awaited us.

From inside the bathroom, we heard the shower running and the sound of a man heaving and crying. It was awful. I felt like we were violating some kind of law, like we shouldn't be listening in on my dad's grief. Our dad was a rock. A pillar. A monument of strength and patience. A man with calloused hands and a hard body. Hearing him sob was too much for me so I ran out of the room and locked myself in my bedroom. Unable to face a sad situation, I picked up a book and started reading. Clue number three: *Bibiana is unable to face reality.*

We never mentioned what we'd heard or questioned his inability to open up to us. The next day, my dad was back to normal, and his strength made me proud. I decided I'd be like him. Strong, cool, patient, private. Selfish, really.

My parents sold our four bedroom home near Westwood Lake the year I was in Mexico and it broke my heart. I had so many memories of my bedroom overlooking the front yard. It wasn't very big, but it had been a safe haven for me. It was where I'd stood in front of my mirror a million times and cursed my appearance, the very same place I'd tried on my first cheerleading uniform and felt good about myself. My private library, exercise room, fast food restaurant.

They bought a three bedroom townhouse in the heart of Westchester, a little community a few blocks away from Westwood Lake. Westchester was a good place to live because it was close to everything. Everything was twenty minutes away. Well, back then it was. When the population swelled to an alarming number, everything became an hour away and a mission.

The good thing about Westchester is that no matter what you want, you can find it. Strip malls with sub shops, pharmacies, hair salons, bowling alleys. Places where you can send money to Cuba, a telegram to Cuba, your soul to Cuba. Traditional barber shops where serious political discussions are held and always, always a tiny Cuban bakery right next door. A place where you can find pastries filled with guava and cheese (root canal potential), fresh Cuban bread and cakes for birthday parties.

Sedanos Supermarket is a block from their townhouse. To this day, my dad walks there every evening after dinner and gets together with his pals, Cuban men his age who think they most definitely have an answer to the problems in Cuba. They stand around in front of the grimy supermarket (it's pretty nasty) and offer their solutions heatedly and with passion. You would think they'd tire of this subject, think they'd move on and talk about something else like baseball or the latest movie, but we're talking about old boys from Cuba. Nothing is more important than the fate of their homeland.

So here's the layout. My parents live in townhouse number eight. Next to them is my cousin, Jacqueline, and her husband Jose aka Cuba (imagine that). Next to them is Caridad, an old lady with more opinions than Joan Rivers, and in townhouse number five we find my Uncle Lingero, his crazy wife Raquel and his teenage daughter, Barbie. My grandmother and my Aunt Josefina, along with my mentally handicapped Uncle Luis, live only two blocks away. My other Aunt Consuelo and her son Israel live in an efficiency around the corner from them. Aside from them, I have a dozen so-called aunts and uncles and cousins and second cousins who don't share my blood. Just the fact that they all come from the same place in Cuba, a little town outside of Havana called Guira De Melena, makes them family.

And it was Matt's turn to meet the whole cast.

We took the Florida Turnpike down to Miami, truly the most boring piece of highway you'll ever encounter. Nothing but flat landscapes and rest stops brimming with people heading the other direction to Disney World. As soon as we entered Dade County, Matt felt a change in the atmosphere, and not in a good way.

"Did you see that guy? He just cut me off!"

"Yep."

"Jesus Christ Almighty, doesn't anyone use their turn signal down here?"

"Nope, and don't take the Lord's name in vain."

"Sorry." Seconds passed. "Damn, did you see that guy? He just flew by me. He must've been going about a hundred!"

"Yep," I nodded.

Seeing the person you love suffering from road rage can be a turn off. A big one. I tried to get his mind off the other drivers by holding his hand. Didn't work.

"Damn it to hell, no wonder you left!"

I caressed his hand and kissed it, and eventually he calmed down. Never underestimate the power of affection.

"Bibi?"

"Yeah?"

"Do you think your family's gonna like me?" He looked a little scared.

"Of course. They're gonna love you, I promise."

"Even though I'm not Cuban?"

"Yes, even though you're not Cuban."

"Are you sure?"

"Look, Matt, Cubans can be judgmental and harsh and critical, but if you're honest and a good person, they'll know right away and take you in. Be prepared, though. None of them speak English."

"None of them speak English?"

"Uh, well, my mom and dad do, albeit somewhat badly, but they can get their point across. They'll make an effort, so don't worry."

"Okay, but what about the rest of your family?"

"My cousins are just like me. They've got the English language down pat. My uncles and aunts and my grandmother, no. Don't know a damn word." I shook my head.

"How long have they been in the States?"

"Most of them have been here over twenty years, I think."

"What? Twenty years? And they still don't speak English?"

"Nope. Trust me, it annoys me. When my dad came to this country, he knew he didn't have a choice but to learn English. Same with my mom. But remember, they arrived in Los Angeles a long time ago. It was unforgiving. Miami's not like that. There are so many Hispanics here that learning to speak English isn't really necessary. They don't assimilate into American ways unless they move to some place like Minnesota or Ohio."

"Really?"

"Hm hmm."

"Elaborate."

"I'm telling you, just about everyone speaks Spanish. You'll see. Sure, there are still a lot of white people in Miami, but they're dwarfed by the amount of Hispanics, and not only Cubans anymore. Miami's become the capital of South and Central America. Added to that are all the people from the islands in the Caribbean. They've pushed the white folks north, like to Ft. Lauderdale."

"No, shit? Jesus, I mean, wow, I never knew that."

"Not many people do. Ask someone from Nebraska what they think Miami's all about and they'll bring up South Beach. Oh, get off on this exit."

"The Bird Road exit?"

"Yeah." My heart started beating faster just at the thought that home was only a few miles away. "Anyway, as I was saying, there are a lot of subcommunities within Miami."

"Like what? Is it like New York and the five boroughs?"

"I can't say. I've never been to New York, but I think you have more people from around the world. New York is a true melting pot. Miami's a melting pot of South America and the Caribbean." I paused and thought about it. "For example, Kendall used to be an all-white suburb, but it's recently become Little Bogota. Then there's Doral, what we call Doralzuela because it's been flooded with Venezuelans. There's Little Buenos Aires, Little Haiti, Little Jamaica, Little Nicaragua; just about everyone in the southern hemisphere has made a place for themselves."

"What about Mexicans? You didn't mention them."

"Oh, yeah, how could I forget? Most of them live in Homestead because they come over to pick tomatoes and strawberries and oranges and everything else that's pickable. Not many Mexicans in Miami proper, though."

"Hmph. So your mom has no family here?"

*What a perceptive man*, I thought. *No wonder I love him.*

"No."

I looked out the window. This was home. No matter how much I'd cursed Miami, no matter how many times I had gotten to work or school pissed off because three thousand people had cut me off or failed to let me get into the next lane, it was still home. And I missed it terribly.

"Bibi?" Matt sounded alarmed.

"Yeah? What's wrong?"

"Uh, you weren't kidding. Look!" He was pointing at all the strip malls. "So many signs are in Spanish."

I looked out the window and saw what he saw. Envios a Cuba, Carniceria Argentina, Farmacia Garcia, it went on and on. "I told you."

"Wow, this is pretty unbelievable."

"Yep." I was proud. "Hey, you need to make a left on 99th Avenue."

"Okay."

He made a left and we drove past Sedanos. It was only eleven in the morning so I didn't bother looking for my dad.

"Okay, make a right at the second entrance of the townhouse complex."

He made a right into The Courts of Birdwood.

"The Courts of Birdwood?" he asked. "Sounds like something out of Robin Hood."

"Funny you say that. I used to think the same damn thing."

As we pulled into the parking space in front of number eight, he grabbed my hand. "Told you we were made for each other."

My parents' townhouse is conveniently located right next to a dumpster. One morning, my dad walked out to take out the garbage and found the body of a dead man. Shot in the head. My dad became a local celebrity. People would come around and knock on the door to get the juicy details. Each time he told the story, the details got more and more exaggerated. Cubans are born with the ability to take a fender-bender and turn it into a ten car pile up with multiple deaths.

I took one last look at Matt before we got out of the car. I was afraid his first encounter was going to ruin everything and I wanted to remember the fact the he liked me pre-Castellanos madness.

"You ready?" I said.

"You better believe it."

I inserted my key into the lock and didn't even get a chance to turn it because my mom opened the door. She looked out of breath. She'd been peeking through the shades.

"Oh, my Bibita!" She grabbed me and hugged me hard and I hugged her back just as tightly. She smelled of Oil of Olay.

"Hi, Mami. I missed you."

"Oh, me, too, baby." She looked up at Matt, way, way up. "Hello." She looked at him shyly.

"Hi, Mrs. Castellanos. My name is Matt."

Just the fact that he'd pronounced my name right confirmed that he was my soul mate. He leaned down and she kissed him on the cheek.

"Hello, Matt. Please, please come in. Joo tired? Joo want some coffee? Orange joos? Somesing?"

Matt chuckled and looked at me. "I'd love some coffee."

"Come, come, follow me."

We walked to the back of the townhouse into the kitchen. Their place was small, but it was cozy. Like me, my mother felt every inch of wall space deserved a picture or painting or crucifix. Matt tried to look at all the pictures, but I stopped him before he caught sight of my First Communion picture. I hated it because it was B.D.—Before Dieting.

My dad was sitting at the kitchen counter smoking a cigarette. He got up as Matt's presence seemed to fill up the entire back half of the townhouse. He came over to Matt and held out his hand.

"Hello, nice to meet joo."

"Hi, Mr. Castellanos. Thanks for letting me spend Christmas with you and your daughter."

"No, no," he laughed, "please no call me Mr. Castellanos. Joo can call me Fico."

"Feeco?" Matt looked at me.

"Yeah, it's short for Federico." I winked at him.

"Okay, Feeco."

My mom quickly produced four tiny cups of liquid cocaine. As we sipped the espresso, my mom stole glances at Matt and kept looking at me with a secret smile on her face. I wondered what she was thinking, wondered if she thought I'd paid him to pretend to be my boyfriend.

Matt hit it off with my father right away. How he managed to win him over so quickly I will never know. Within minutes they were engrossed in a political discussion about Cuba, my dad's favorite topic. I sat there quietly, feeling like a judge on a panel. This was the deciding factor. I could never be with someone who didn't get along with my parents. A lot of people don't let their families decide their life partner, but to me, Matt's approval of my family and vice versa was crucial.

My mom told me to follow her upstairs because she needed to show me something, which meant the minute we got to her bedroom, she was going to ask me for bingo money. I squeezed Matt's arm and asked him if he was okay, but before he had a chance to answer, my dad nodded and told us to leave them alone. Matt smiled reassuringly and I followed my mom upstairs.

"He is so bery nice," she said as she closed her bedroom door.

"You think so, Mami? You just met him."

"No, Bibita, I know. The way he look at joo, I don't know, es so bery nice. I sink so that he love joo."

I started laughing and suddenly felt embarrassed. "Come on, Mami, I just met him, you know."

"It don't matter, *mi'ja*. He is the one joo are going to marry."

"Mami!" My face got even hotter.

"Believe me, *mi'ja*, I has a feeling. He is the one for joo."

"Okay, Mami, whatever you say."

"Hm hmm." She paused and then looked at me with that special grin. "Ehm, *mi'ja*, can joo give me some money for de bingo?"

My mom was so predictable. I pulled out the twenty I'd put in my pocket when I was getting dressed that morning and gave it to her. *At least she's not running out to buy crack*, I told myself.

The rest of the morning was a blur. My mom made a supersonic-high-cholesterol-breakfast-of-champions, a staple in most Cuban homes. Fried eggs cooked not in olive oil, but in lard. *Manteca*. I berated her for continuing to use lard because it was so bad for them. My mom laughed and said they were both healthy and did Matt want another fried egg? Matt looked like someone who'd just walked into a Denny's after spending six months in a desert. He consumed everything my mom put on his plate. My mom took this as a positive sign. During breakfast, they asked Matt about his family. My mom slyly threw in the important question.

"So, ehm, do joo believe Jesus Christ?"

I cringed. "Mami!"

Matt said, "Don't worry, Bibi." He looked back at my mom and smiled. "Yes, Mrs. C, I believe Jesus Christ."

"Ah, okay, es bery good."

After breakfast, I decided to take Matt for a drive and let him digest the mountain of food before the evening festivities. Lucky for us, we'd arrived on Noche Buena (which means Good Night). We snuck out the door and into his car before the circus had a chance to attack him.

It was time to take Matt on my very own trip down memory lane.

# Chapter 20

I love Miami, love it because it's where I grew up, love it because it's my hometown, my roots, my hood. But talk to someone who has "escaped" from Miami and moved north and this is what you'll hear:

"People are so rude."

"I hate Miami. The traffic sucks."

"Nobody speaks English."

"Everyone expects *you* to speak Spanish."

"People are so rude."

"The humidity is disgusting."

"People don't know how to drive."

"Everyone's always on their fuckin' cell phone."

"There is no culture, nothing to do."

"People are so rude."

I don't hold these comments against them. At one point, I despised the whole city of Miami too. I used to say the same thing. *Everything sucks. There is nothing to do here. Not a beautiful thing to be found anywhere in this entire fuckin' city.* But then again, there wasn't a pretty thing to be found inside of me either, so what the hell did I expect? You could've plucked me out of Miami and dropped me into Eden and I still would've found reasons to complain.

But I love Miami now. I love the craziness, the bad drivers, the obnoxious humidity, the models, the wanna-be's, every last Haitian who has managed to make it over. I love the fact that you can go from one extreme to the next within minutes. Drive through Overtown and you're right smack in the middle of the projects. Head south a couple of blocks and bam, you're on swanky Brickell Avenue where only the very wealthy can afford to live. Very, very wealthy.

I love it because it's sunny and warm and hectic and one big adventure if you let it be. It is so many things at once and yet so simple; it is *alive*. It has indescribable energy, energy that is like a magnet forever pulling me back. Culture? I'll show you culture. Drive through Little Havana and *don't stop*. Park your car and get out. Sit down in a little café and order a *café con leche* or a *guarapo*. Listen. Watch. Soak it in with an open mind. Drive down to Old Cutler Raw Bar on US-1. Sit down at the bar, order a drink and I guarantee you're going to see every single part of Miami represented. Plain old white folks, Mexicans, Rednecks, Cubans (White *and* Ghetto), African Americans, Jamaicans, White Trash; lawyers, doctors, landscapers, strippers. Take a look around and you'll see all these people sharing one space and getting along.

Spend a Sunday at Crandon Park Beach on Key Biscayne. But you better get there early. Like seven in the morning kind of early. Get there after eleven and forget about getting a barbecue pit. Cubans don't play when it comes to getting the best table. My dad used to wake us up at five thirty in the morning on beach days. We'd get there as the sun was rising and stay until the sun went down. The whole family, too. Aunts, uncles, cousins, friends of the family. Walk around Crandon Park and you'll find that just about every single table has at least one of the following: a domino game, a radio blaring salsa music, loaves and loaves of Cuban bread, Chek soda (Strawberry, Grape, Cherry, Pineapple), a box of *pastelitos* and *croquetas*, coolers full of Bo-weiser (Spanglish for Budweiser).

Walk down to the water and prepare yourself for one of the prettiest beaches in South Florida. The water may not be very deep, the waves may not be huge, but wade in the water on a good day and you can look down and see your feet. In the summer, the water gets so warm you feel as though you're in a bathtub.

Culture is everywhere. You don't have to go to an art exhibition or a play to find it. You can find it in a park, in a supermarket, in a nightclub, in barbershops, in Hialeah. You can find it if you keep an open mind and forget the language barriers.

Miami will always be the place I call home. It was the city that gave birth to my dreams, the city that let my imagination roam freely, the place I ran away from time and time again only to find myself yearning for it, aching for the music and the noise. For my family. For my childhood. I love Miami because it is *different,* and I can identify with different.

I took Matt to all my favorite places. All the places I remembered fondly. Matt kept looking out the window, trying to take in everything I was pointing out, but it was hard for him because he was too focused on bad drivers. He kept shaking his head and raising his hands in the air in complete confusion.

"Look, Matt, that's where I used to bowl."

"That guy's gonna kill someone."

"Look, that used to be a roller skating rink."

"Uh-huh, cool. Damn, this guy's tailgating me."

I carried on anyway, "This is Tropical Park."

"Really? It's pretty big damn it why won't this asshole let me get in the next lane?"

My love meter was quickly going down. Road rage is a big turn off. Ignoring me when I'm trying to share a part of myself and my childhood is asking for it.

"Matt, listen to me. I mean it."

He looked at me worriedly. "What's the matter?"

"You need to understand something, okay? Bad drivers are everywhere and there's nothing you can do about it. Nobody's gonna use their turn signal, nobody's gonna let you in the next lane even if you have your indicator on. In fact, they're gonna speed up just to piss you off. People are gonna jaywalk like you wouldn't believe. When the green arrow turns red, you better believe up to four cars are gonna run it. And yes, people are gonna speed past you. Oh, and let me not forget the MOC's."

"The what?"

"The MOC's. Morons On Cell phones. When the car in front of you is going ten miles an hour in a thirty mile an hour zone, I can guarantee you it's some moron on their cell phone."

"Isn't there a law against that?"

"No. But I'm pretty sure some big lawmaker's daughter is going to get killed someday because of a MOC and he'll push for a law. But for now, there's nothing you can do about bad drivers. Cussing and swearing and getting pissed off and not paying attention to me is not going to stop that asshole from driving two inches behind you, okay? So, do me a favor and focus on your on own driving and forget about everyone else except me, deal?"

He leaned over and kissed me on the nose. "Okay, Sledge, I'm sorry. I didn't realize what I was doing."

"It's okay. Now drive. I want to take you to this great park on the water."

I guided him through Coral Gables with the Fica tree tunnels down to Old Cutler Road, a road that cut through a neighborhood that made Coral Gables look like the projects.

"This is really something else, Bibi. Wow, look at these homes."

"Yeah," I said dreamily. I was remembering too much. "I used to drive down here with my mountain bike and park at that roundabout we just passed. You see that trail?" I was pointing at the wide sidewalk. "That trail goes all the way down to the park I'm taking you. I'd ride my bike all the way down to Matheson Hammock, sit on the grass and read my book or study."

"By yourself?"

"Yeah, by myself. Why?"

"Didn't you have any friends?"

"I thought we covered this, Matt."

"Well, you said you didn't, but I don't know, I thought you'd been exaggerating."

"No, I wasn't. I told you about my friend Linda, but she's married and has kids and well, she doesn't have much time for that kind of stuff."

"Oh. That's so sad. I don't like to think of you doing all these great things by yourself."

He said it with so much sincerity it made my heart hurt. "Matt, you're so cute. Don't worry, funny guy, I liked being by myself, okay? Really."

And I did. I'd gotten used to having me as my only companion. Me and my imagination and my dreams.

We pulled into Matheson Hammock Park and Marina. The road into the park took us through about a mile of mangroves. We reached the end of the road, which brought us to Biscayne Bay. There was a manmade atoll, a giant saltwater swimming pool that was surrounded by a wide path and huge rocks. You could either sit on the rocks and fish, go swimming in the atoll, or, if you were me, ride your bike on the path and come to rest on the little patch of grass just next to the atoll. That tiny little part of the world was my slice of heaven.

Matt and I walked around the atoll slowly. He didn't say very much. I could tell he was taken aback by the beauty of the place, much as I had been. He held my hand and asked me more questions about my no-friends childhood. Finally, we plonked down on the grass.

"This place is amazing. It's so relaxing." I sat Indian style and he lay down and put his head on my lap. I looked at him. His eyes were closed and he had a tiny smile on his face. *I'm dreaming*, I thought. *I can't believe I found this guy.* He fell asleep on my lap and I stared out into the ocean. For once, I thought of nothing. Within minutes, my eyes were closing so I lay down as well. I drifted off to sleep and dreamt of a giant pig chasing Matt and me around my parents' house. The Pig was wearing an apron with a fake penis

262

and orange lipstick. Matt shook me awake just as the Pig farted and laughed.

"What! What!" I looked around. I had that feeling you get when you spend the night at someone's house and can't remember where you are the next day.

"Bibi, it's getting kind of late. Don't you think we should head back?"

I looked at my watch. It was four. Just thinking about my family attacking me and my appearance and Matt was enough to make me want to keep driving all the way down to Key West. It was painful.

"Hey, you okay?" Matt said as we walked back to his car.

"Sort of. Seeing my family can be pretty stressful."

"But you don't mind it too much, do you?"

"Well, yes and no. Like I said, I love them. But the attack on my appearance always propels me right back to childhood. Back to when I was fat and fat and fat and nerdy and ugly and bucktoothed and frizzy haired."

"You were?" We got into his car and started driving back to Westchester.

"Yeah."

"You only told me you were a little chubby, kiddo."

"I was too embarrassed. But there's nothing I can do now to stop my mom from pulling out the photo albums."

He grabbed my hand and punched me lightly on the chin. "Come on, Sledge, I don't care what you looked like before." He made his tough guy accent even stronger just to make me laugh. "All right, tuff guy, let me tell ya somethin'. Kid, you got what I like, so don't worry about it, eh?"

I laughed and pinched his nose.

As we drove back to my house, a strong smell permeated the entire city of Miami. I knew that smell better than I knew anything. It was the smell of pigs roasting in back yards all over the southern half of Florida. The smell of pork seasoned with a mixture of orange juice, lemon juice, salt, pepper and garlic. It made me hungry.

When we got back to the townhouse complex, there were no more empty parking spaces so we parked on the street. I could hear the music and the shouting already, even from around the corner. We walked into the house, which was empty, and straight into the back yard, which was crowded. I swear my family performed just as I'd rehearsed it in my head a million times. Too fast, the drama unfolded.

On cue, Aunt Raquel came over to Matt and shook his hand. She said hello and lifted up the apron and showed Matt the fake penis. I could tell she'd already had more than a few shots of tequila. She leaned over to Matt and very slowly said, "I like *joo*. Joo like *me*?" Matt laughed and looked at me for help.

I kissed my aunt and told her she was crazy and took Matt to meet my Uncle Lingero and the wild animal on his back. Lingero was wearing a wife beater t-shirt, shorts, black socks and sandals. A fresh-off-the-boat outfit. Lingero grabbed Matt by the arm and said, "Joo see pig?" Matt shook his head. Lingero dragged him over to the pig like a caveman proud of his kill, while I went around and kissed everyone on the cheek.

"*Hola, Tia.*" Kiss, kiss.

"*Hola, Israel.*" Kiss, kiss.

"Hey, Jackie." Kiss, hug, kiss.

Matt came back to me as I was saying hello to my Aunt Josefina. First words out of her mouth were, "*Vaya, estás muy flaca. Tienes que comer.*" Now I was too skinny. Now I needed to eat more. *Damn it, some people are never satisfied.* As expected, she made comments to me in Spanish about Matt's size, Matt's Americanness and Matt's inability to speak Spanish. As though I hadn't already noticed these things myself. A part of me wanted to strangle her but one look at Matt and I felt better. He didn't look the least bit uncomfortable.

We found my brother, who was holding Savannah. Savannah jumped out of Erasmo's arms when she saw me and ran up to me screaming, "Habibi! Habibi!" She'd added "Ha" to Bibi and had no idea that her nickname for me was the word for love in Arabic. I picked her up and hugged her. She looked at Matt and leaned over so he could take her in his arms, which he did. I salivated at the thought that someday Matt would be holding our child like this. *Snap back to reality, you moron,* I thought. *You haven't even slept with him yet.* Matt and my brother shook hands and instantly hit it off. They talked about football and cars and other manly stuff while I looked around for my mother. I zeroed in on my target and laughed out loud.

My mom was wearing black pants for a change. And she was wearing black shoes. She'd even thrown on a one-colored shirt, and it was red. Her hair was out of rollers and looked beautiful. But her lipstick was orange, her shirt was on inside out, and yes, her shoes were black but they were two different types of shoes. She was holding a bottle of tequila and was trying to get my grandmother to do a shot.

As I looked around, I suddenly felt a sense of relief. I looked at Matt laughing at something my brother said as he handed him a beer. I looked at my dad yelling at my uncle, yelling even though he was right next to him. I saw my aunt pull the penis trick on one of the neighbors and then fall down. She was pretty wasted. I saw the whole circus for what it really is. Music.

Dancing. Laughter. Love.

Family.

At the end of the night, after everyone had gone home with enough pork in their system to keep their stored fat supply stocked for a lifetime, Matt and I went to bed. Well, I went to my bed and my mom pulled out the sofa bed for Matt, of course.

Some things will never change.

# Chapter 21

The rest of the vacation flew by. By the end of the two weeks, I felt I'd known Matt my whole life. Problem is, we never discussed West Orange. Every time he'd ask me about it, I'd tell him I didn't want to think about it just yet. *Bibiana is unable to face reality.* The words bounced around in my mind and gave me a headache.

We left on a Sunday morning. We weren't leaving empty-handed, though. We were leaving with three rolls of paper towels, two packs of toilet paper, five gallons of purified water, three huge Tupperware containers full of leftovers, new towels, a rice cooker and a bag of fresh fruit. I could never leave the house without something. It made my mom feel better to know that, should I break down on the highway, I would at least have something to wipe with and enough food to last me three days.

We said our goodbyes to everyone. As usual, I promised to call my mom the minute I walked in the door of my apartment. I knew she would be agonizing for three and a half hours until I let her know I'd made it back to Orlando safely.

Matt pulled up to my apartment and turned the car off. Suddenly, neither one of us could think of what to say. We'd talked nonstop for three and a half hours and yet now that my bedroom was ten feet away, we couldn't bring ourselves to look at each other. I cleared my throat.

"Uh, so."

"So."

"Do you want some water before you—"

"Yes."

He grabbed my suitcase out of the trunk and we walked into my apartment. All the plants were still alive. I took it as a good sign. Being alone after two weeks of being surrounded by maniacs was too much, though. Far too tempting. We took one look at each other and knew what was going to happen. Clothes disappeared in two seconds, inhibitions followed right after.

The little Catholic girl on my shoulder was nowhere to be found. And sex with Matt was just what I'd expected. Forget about making love; we had sex like two people stranded on an island who have just found each other. We fit together like two pieces of a puzzle. I finally understood why my mom had asked me why I'd waited so long in the first place.

Miraculously, after what seemed like hours (it always seems that way at first), we got out of bed and ordered something to eat. We fed each other and caressed each other and held hands and oh Lord anybody looking at us would've puked.

Even though I couldn't imagine not being with him for a second, I asked him to go home.

"Why?" He looked sad.

I sighed heavily. "Matt, we have to go back to work tomorrow, and I need to think about what I'm going to do."

"You wanna talk about it?"

"No."

"Why not?" Now he looked annoyed. "Come on, Bibi, you've talked to me about everything else. Why not this?"

"Matt, I can't explain it. I'm just like this. Whenever I have a problem, I deal with it myself. Once I've worked it out, I'll talk to you. Please understand."

"Bibi, this won't work out between us if you do this all the time. Come on, you're supposed to trust me." He was right, but I'm stubborn.

"I know, I know, but you gotta understand me. I've always handled the big things by myself. It's not easy for me to bring in a third party, even when it's someone I love." *Uh-oh. I said the L word.*

"Someone you love?" He no longer looked annoyed. Now he looked alarmed. *Oh, shit*, I thought. *Way to go, idiot. You just ruined everything.*

"Well, I didn't mean to say, I, uh, I meant to say that I am, uh," I shrugged.

"Do you love me, Bibi?" His eyes got even wider, as though he couldn't believe it. "Really?"

I stared at him and was just about to lie and say no when he leaned over and got two inches from my face. I could smell pepperoni pizza on his breath.

"Well guess what, tuff girl?"

"What?"

"I love you too."

I just about fainted. The fat girl had finally done good. Before we fell into bed again, I pushed him out the door. The word *Love* was getting in the way of the words *West Orange* and *transfer* and *Grandma Ruthie* and *Uncle Morris* and *Chancy* and *Ebony* and *Marcdala* and *Jazelin* and *Doc Keigwin* and *expectations*, words that were crowding my mind and confusing me more and more by the second.

Matt left and I fell back into bed. No surprise, I fell right asleep and gave no thought to West Orange.

I walked into class the next day with a spring in my step. I missed my students and couldn't wait to hear about their holidays. What I didn't know was that when students are away from you for more than a few days, they tend to forget the rules you've established. So Chancy walked in ten minutes late, Ebony ragged on everyone's clothes, Jazelin nearly punched Tevaris because he accidentally bumped into him, DiAngelo refused to sit down even though I threatened to call his auntie. Chaos. I felt like I was back at day one. Marcdala was surprisingly absent. *Where is my smartest student when I need her?*

"Hey, settle down, you guys."

They quieted down for two seconds and started all over again.

"Come on, now. What is this? What happened to all of you over the break?"

They all responded at once.

"Miss C, how your Christmas was?"

"Miss C, you seen your momma?"

"Yo, Miss C, check out my new sneakers!"

It was the last thing I needed on my first day back. I hadn't given much thought to taking the job at West Orange, but suddenly it seemed like the best option. The easy way out. I didn't want to use a story to calm them down, either. First of all because I didn't have one and secondly because I wanted them to start behaving on their own. Because they liked me. Because they respected me. Because I could chill, you feel me?

The first half of the day was a disaster. It was like a movie set with a bad director. Lines were forgotten, actors spoke out of turn, nobody was where they were supposed to be: in their seats. I gave out three detentions, raised my voice a dozen times and rubbed my temples constantly. It was an *I need to get some Xanax* kind of morning. During my planning session, I went to see Dr. Lawrence. I was hoping he'd tell me the position had been filled and that I no longer had to torture myself, that I was going to have to stick to the kids who were driving me crazy.

Dr. Lawrence was in his office. He looked up as I walked in the door.

"Well, well, how are you? How was your vacation, Miss Castellanos?"

"It was great. How was yours?"

"Too short, much too short." He shook his head. "What's going on? You look like you need to talk."

"It's about West Orange.

"Okay. Shoot. Have you made a decision?"

"No, not even close. I just want to ask you a few questions." I sighed and looked out the window. "Dr. Lawrence, what will happen to these kids if I leave?"

"What do you mean? Like, who's going to take over?"

"Uh-huh. Are you going to hire someone else?"

He took off his glasses and rubbed his eyes. "To be honest, I'm not sure. I've been toying with the idea of mainstreaming them back into regular classes. I've been thinking about eliminating the At-Risk program."

"Oh, wow, that's pretty major. But why?"

"You've brought them a long way, you know. I've seen what you've been doing. I know they're not dumb, Miss C. They just needed someone to set them on the right track, and I think you did."

I thought about that morning and shook my head. "Nah, they're back to being uncontrollable."

"It's the first day back after the break. All the kids are rowdy, so don't worry. They just have to get used to you again."

"Whew, that's a relief. West Orange was starting to look tempting."

He chuckled. "Well, what are you going to do? You know they need an answer soon."

"I don't know, Dr. Lawrence. I think mainstreaming the students would be a great idea, so that's a point for the Transfer-to-West-Orange team. I can definitely see Marcdala in the gifted program even though I think Mrs. Coleman is ignorant and conceited." Dr. Lawrence laughed out loud, very un-PC-like behavior. "But then I think about the rest of them, about how they make me laugh, about the fact that they do behave and listen to me, and that's a point for the Stay-at-Howard-and-Go-Nuts team. Here I feel like I'm making a difference. I'm not sure I would be making a difference at West Orange."

"Hm hmm. Sounds like you got one heck of a baseball game in your head." He winked and I laughed. I thought it was more like a game of fierce dodge ball.

"Sorry, I usually break decisions down into teams. It's easier for me." I sighed and played with a paperweight on his desk. "I'm confused."

"Miss Castellanos, I don't know what to tell you except do whatever will make you happy."

I sighed and rolled my eyes. "Dr. Lawrence, that's the problem. It's always been about me, me, me. Sure, it would make me happy to have a classroom full of perfectly behaved kids. It would make me happy to teach something like Spanish because it would be so easy. It would make me happy to work in a nice school with new desks and central air-conditioning and a computer all to myself. But that would make a whole classroom here very *un*happy. And I don't think that's fair. I go back and forth. I think I want to stay one minute, but then I think working at West Orange would be so much better. You know?"

He stared at me for a few seconds and didn't say anything, as though he was trying to find the right words for me. "Miss C, would you like a few days off to think about it? Something tells me this decision is more important to you and has more significance than I thought."

"Are you crazy? And let the kids drive a substitute teacher out of her mind? Come on, Dr. Lawrence, I'm not that selfish. Don't worry, I'll figure it out."

He laughed and got up from his desk, a sign that meant he was sick of hearing me ramble. I got up, shook his hand and walked out the door. Back to the chaos.

When the students came back to class, I was prepared. *No more nonsense,* I told myself as I wrote on the chalkboard. *They will listen to me and like it.* They walked in looking defeated and exhausted, like mummies on Prozac. Still no Marcdala. They sat in their chairs and looked ready to fall asleep. Uh-oh, I thought. Matt must have let them have it.

"Hey, what's wrong with you? You guys look like you've just gone through boot camp."

Ebony raised her hand. "Miss C, I'm sorry about this morning. Sorry I was cuttin' up."

"Miss C," Jazelin piped up, "I'm sorry I pushed Tevaris 'cuz it was wrong and I know you don't like that."

"Yo, Miss C," DiAngelo said, "Mr. Connelly was mean."

I raised my eyebrows. "Is that right?" So that's what it was. They must have had to lick the chalkboard. "What did he say?"

Chancy snickered and sat up straight. I noticed his shoelaces were untied. *Someday he's going to trip and break his arm and remember me.* "Chancy, tie your shoelaces before you open your mouth." He rolled his eyes and tied them slowly. "So, what happened?"

"Mr. Connelly said we better be good in your class 'cuz if not he was gonna take us outside and make us run and I hate runnin', Miss C." All the students spoke out at once, all of them agreeing wholeheartedly with Chancy's comment about running. *Yeah, but you like running your mouth, don't you?*

"All right, well, let's get to work. Our lesson today is on the structure of the US Government."

Not what they wanted to hear. They complained under their breath as they took out their notebooks and pencils. I'd drawn a flow chart on the board, with the White House at the top. Ebony interrupted me before I had a chance to say anything.

"Miss C, why we gotta learn this? It's boring."

I couldn't agree with her more, but I still had to do my job.

"Ebony, believe it or not, you need to know this. You'll end up using this knowledge someday."

"What for? I wanna be a singer, remember?"

"Yeah, well, even singers learn this stuff in school." Kurt Cobain came to mind. Learning the difference between the House of Representatives and the Senate hadn't helped him much. "Trust me," I lied, "this stuff can be pretty interesting."

And before I knew it, I was remembering my mother. I'd said exactly the same thing to her one day. I put down my notes and looked around the class.

"All right, I wasn't going to tell you a story today, but because you came back and apologized for your behavior this morning, I think I should reward you. And besides, this has something to do with what you're going to learn today."

The mummies snapped out of their Matt-induced comas and sat up in their chairs. I cleared my throat and prepared to tell them by far the funniest story about my mother. As they looked at me, their eyes full of expectation, all thoughts of West Orange vanished.

# Chapter 22

My dad came home one day with an American passport, and no, it wasn't stolen. He'd gone down to the Immigration building and filled out the paperwork, studied the questions and passed the exam. And he'd done this without telling anyone. He flashed his passport at me and my mom.

"I am no longer a fucking Cuban. I am now a fucking American!"

I laughed out loud and looked at my mom, who looked terribly annoyed. One eyebrow was raised and she was looking at my dad suspiciously. There was something else on her face too. Raw jealousy.

Two seconds later, my mom was on the phone. She didn't even ask me for help this time. She got the number for INS, requested the paperwork in her funny accent (she refused to ask for an operator in Spanish, as though this alone was enough to get her a passport) and waited patiently for the exam questions to arrive in the mail. After the *inchoorans* incident, she knew better than to harass the mailman the next day.

I came home one day from school to find my mom sitting at the kitchen table with her head in her hands. There were papers spread out all over the table. I thought she was crying and quickly ran over to her.

"Mami, what's wrong?"

She looked up at me. She wasn't crying but looked thoroughly confused.

"Ay, *mi'ja*, I no understand. Everysing is so hard, joo know?"

I grabbed one of the papers in front of her, one page of citizenship questions. They were in English.

"Mami, why did you request to take the exam in English? Nowadays you can take it in Spanish. You made a mistake, Mami."

She sat up straight and shook her head with conviction. "Ah, no, Bibita, I no take de test in Espanish. No, no. If I want to be American, I speak de English only, okay?"

She was doing it to get back at my dad, who'd been smart enough to take the test in Spanish. I put my stuff down and decided to help her. I mean, how

273

hard could the questions be?

"All right, Mami, let's start with an easy question. What are the colors of the American flag?" I looked at her expecting the answer to shoot straight out of her mouth.

"Oh, es easy. Three."

"No, no, Mami, what are the *colors* of the American flag?"

"Ahhhh." She laughed and shook her head. "Sorry. Thirteen."

"No, no, Mami!" I was growing impatient. "Listen carefully. What are the *colors* of the American flag?"

She thought about it for two seconds and raised her finger in the air. "Ah, jes, I know. Fifty!"

She got the number of stripes, the number of stars and the amount of colors on the flag, but not the right answer. I started laughing because I couldn't help myself. My mom started laughing too and we didn't move on to the next question for five minutes.

I wiped my eyes on my shirt. "Come on, Mami, let's get serious."

"Jes, *mi'ja*, okay."

"Okay, Mami. If the President of the United States dies, who becomes President?"

She smiled knowingly at me. "Ay, *mi'ja*, that one is bery easy. His wife!"

Oh Lord have mercy. We laughed even harder. It took us another ten minutes to get serious again. Getting through the questions was going to take us a century.

"Mami, come on, please. Okay, let's see." I tried to find an easier question. "Okay, here's one. What is the capital of the United States?"

"Los Angeles?"

"No."

"Miami?"

"No."

"New Jork?"

"No! Mami, think about it." I was trying my hardest not to laugh and it was making my throat hurt.

"Wacheengton?"

"That's right, Mami! You see? You got one right."

But that was the only one. The harder the questions got, the more absurd her answers. I decided the best way for her to pass the exam was if she actually learned the structure of the government. I didn't want her to memorize answers she could easily mix up. I found time to sit down with her every day for two months. I brought in backup, too. Index cards, an old civics book, pictures of the President and the Vice President I had cut out of magazines. I even drew the White House on a sheet of paper. After two months of too much laughing, she could finally get most of the answers right. Most, but not all. This is my mom we're talking about.

Test day rolled around. She was nervous and jumpy and terrified. We sat in the waiting room at INS with all the other "aliens" and waited for her turn. Just when I'd finally calmed her down and reassured her that everything was going to be fine, a very large old woman walked out into the waiting area with a clipboard in her hand. Everything about her was square. Her face, her hair, her glasses, her body. She was very serious looking, a "Don't mess with me" kind of woman. She called out my mom's name and my mom turned white. Somehow, she stood up and walked over to the Cubed Monster. Her legs were trembling so badly I thought she'd collapse before she made it. It reminded me of the Lion in the Wizard of Oz, that scene where he's walking down the long corridor to meet the Wizard. I chuckled and put my head in my hands. *Please God*, I thought, *please make her remember red, white and blue.*

About twenty minutes later, my mom walked back out into the waiting area with the Cubed Monster in tow. She refused to look at me and instead focused on her shoes, which happened to be red, white and blue. I wondered if she'd worn them on purpose. The Cubed Monster had taken off her glasses and was wiping her eyes with a tissue. *Oh, crap, she screwed up so royally she made the lady cry.*

"Is this your mother?" she said as I walked up to them.

"Yeah, why? How'd she do?" I gave her a hopeful look.

She shook her head and pinched the bridge of her nose. "Honey, let me tell you something," she said in a southern drawl, "I've been doing this job for over twenty years, and in my entire life nobody has ever explained the United States Government to me the way your momma just did."

"Oh God, what did she do?" I looked at my mom but she was still engrossed in her American flag shoes.

"Oh, honey, she was just too much. She tried to draw me a picture of some house, she told me all about her brothers and how she crossed the border illegally." She paused and chuckled. "And for every question I asked, she said either 'Red, white and blue,' 'Thirteen,' or 'Fifty.'" She started laughing openly. "Oh, honey, I haven't laughed like that in a long time. Your momma's something else."

"Great, but did she pass?" I held my breath.

"Anybody who can make me laugh that hard deserves to stay here." She turned to my mom and grabbed her hand. "Miss Castellanos, welcome to the United States!"

My mom shook her hand and looked like she wanted to bear hug the Cubed Monster. She put her hand on her chest and looked at the sky, "*Ay Dios mio*, I so relief, joo know? Sank you so bery much."

"You're welcome, and have a nice day."

Not long after that, my mom came home with an American passport. She flashed it in my dad's face.

"Joo see? I no longer a fucking Mexican. I now a fucking American, and I pass my test with de English only. Ha!"

I replaced *fucking* with *damn* when I told the story, but it made no difference. The students laughed and shook their heads and called my momma crazy. It was easy to start the lesson after that. Easy until Marcdala walked in the door.

"Hello, Marcdala." She stood at the door with her arms crossed. She looked pissed off. "Where have you been?"

"Do you really care, Miss C? Huh? Do you?" She was all attitude.

"Of course I care. Marcdala, what's wrong with you?"

"What's wrong with me, Miss C? I'll tell you what's wrong with me." Everyone stared at her as though she'd completely lost her marbles. "My friend Tashae's in Mrs. Coleman's class and she told me that you were gonna transfer to West Orange to teach them stupid white kids."

Uh-oh. I started to sweat. "Where did Tashae get that from?"

"From Mrs. Coleman. She told her."

"Why did she tell her that?" I could feel my blood starting to boil. The whole situation was *setting my liver on fire*.

"She told her that 'cause Tashae was saying how you're the coolest teacher 'cause I told her all about you and how she wants to be in this class instead of Mrs. Coleman's 'cause Mrs. Coleman is mean and boring. So Mrs. Coleman told her you were gonna transfer to another school and to forget about being in your class."

I was so mad I couldn't see anything but the color red. I rarely get angry, rarely lose my temper, but when I do, it's not pretty. I focused on my breathing as I looked at the students. They were looking at me as though to say, "Is that true?"

Marcdala walked back to her desk slowly and kept her eye on me. She no longer looked mad (it was my turn to assume that emotion). She looked hurt and disillusioned. Chancy gave me a dirty look and slumped down in his chair. Jazelin snickered and said, "I knew it." Ebony put her head down on her desk and started humming. Everyone else glared at me. The fact that I hadn't said anything confirmed what Marcdala said.

"All right, guys, give me a second. I'll be right back."

I walked out and knocked on Matt's door. He took one look at me and his eyes widened. "Hey, what's wrong? You don't look too happy."

"Matt, can you watch my class for a few minutes?"

"Yeah, sure. What's going on?"

"I promise I'll tell you later. Promise. Right now I need to take care of something."

"You look really mad. Don't do anything stupid, okay?"

"Settle down, tuff guy, I'm not armed and I don't have any rat poison on me."

"Good. Go on, then."

I squeezed his hand, turned around and walked down the hallway. I peered into Mrs. Coleman's classroom and found it empty. I checked the teacher's lounge, the cafeteria, even the ladies' room in the front office. Nothing. I finally found her in the library. She was sitting at a round table by herself, grading papers or writing down all the reasons why she loves herself. As usual, she was wearing a perfect little outfit straight out of Ann Taylor Loft, an outfit that probably cost more than one of my car payments. Lucky for her she had a rich husband. The *bitch*.

I walked right up to her and didn't even give her a chance to say anything.

"I need to talk to you right now, and outside."

"Uh, well, I'm kind of busy right now. The students are doing research for a Global Warming project and I need to be here in case they have questions. I don't leave my students alone like some of us do." She smiled and I considered stabbing her with her pencil.

"Okay, well let me outline your options. You can sit here and let the kids watch while I make you look like an idiot, or you can leave them with the librarian and come outside with me because if you don't your kids are going to get a firsthand lesson in how to put somebody in their place." I leaned over and got really close to her face. I smiled. "Well, what do you say?"

She huffed as she got up from the table and followed me out the door. The minute we were outside, I turned on her.

"Who the hell do you think you are?" I tried to remain calm and keep my voice down even though Satan was threatening to take over.

"What is this about, Miss Castellanos? Why did you drag me out here? You know, I have a lot of important things to do and I don't understand why you—"

"Why did you tell Tashae I was transferring to West Orange?"

"Oh, so this is what it's about. It's true, isn't it?"

"It's none of your business. You had no right to tell her anything. You have no right to talk about me to your students."

"Oh, please, stop being so dramatic. What's the big deal, anyway?"

"What's the big deal? I'll tell you what the big deal is. I happen to like my students. I happen to think some of them are smarter and wiser than ten of your gifted-with-no-social-skills students put together. I care about them and don't want to hurt them. And you have no right to tell them something you haven't even confirmed."

"Calm down, Miss Castellanos. I only said it because we all know you're going to take that job." She shrugged and gave me an honest smile. "Come on, think about it."

Her honest smile killed my anger and replaced it with curiosity. "What makes you so sure I'm going to take it?"

"You'd be dumb not to. Besides, it's logical. Nobody ever sticks to those kids." She looked at me and took a step closer. She put her hand on my shoulder. I looked at it, then back at her. She let it drop and sighed. "Listen to me, okay? And please don't take this the wrong way."

I decided to back down. She no longer had that smug look on her face. "I'll try not to."

"You seem like a nice person and those kids love you. They're always talking about you and how much fun you are. Believe me, it annoys me. And yeah, I'm jealous, okay? I said it. I shouldn't be because we're supposed to be playing on the same team, but I can't help it."

I liked the fact that she used the team analogy. One point for her. "I'm really not that fun, trust me. So, what are you trying to say?"

"Transferring to West Orange is a really good opportunity. Just think about it. You'll be teaching Spanish, an elective. The kids will be in your class because they chose it. And it's a much nicer school. Their classrooms are newer, their media center has computers and—"

I cut her off before she could continue throwing points at the Transfer-to-West-Orange team. "I know, I know. Trust me, it's crossed my mind. But I still need to think about this a little more, okay? Can you do me a favor?" Never in a million years did I ever think I'd ask The Cat for a favor.

"Sure."

"Don't mention this to anyone until I've made a decision."

"All right, I won't. But think about it. Shoot, I wouldn't hesitate." We walked back into the school. "Hey, can I ask you something?"

"Sure, Mrs. Coleman."

"You can call me Trisha, by the way."

"You can call me Bibi."

"Bibi?"

"It's my nickname."

"Okay, Bibi." She giggled. "Did your mom really beat up a mannequin?"

I shook my head and chuckled. "She sure did. Who told you that?"

"Tashae. I guess you tell them stories about your mom and then Marcdala tells Tashae."

"Do you have a crazy family?" I asked.

"Believe it or not, I do."

"Well, if you're ever having trouble keeping your kids in line, yank out a story. It works like a charm."

She smiled and headed towards the library. "I'll keep that in mind," she said over her shoulder.

I watched her as she walked back to the library and felt bad. I shouldn't have judged her so quickly. I laughed because it's exactly what I'd told my students. "Give people the benefit of the doubt," I had said.

I got back to my classroom just as the bell rang. The students walked out the door and didn't say a word to me. Most of them didn't even give me a look. Chancy sat in his chair and refused to leave. Once they were gone, we had a staring contest for about twenty seconds. He won.

"Yo, Miss C, tell me the truth. You gonna leave?"

"I don't know, Chancy. Maybe."

"But why, Miss C? You don't like us no more?"

"Chancy, it has nothing to do with that, okay? Believe me."

"Then why you wanna leave? You had a fight with Mr. Connelly?"

"No, Chancy." I really needed to be alone. I hated that look in Chancy's eyes. It said, "But you promised."

"Chancy, listen, I can't talk about this right now. Okay? Why don't you go home?"

"You can give me a ride?"

"Sure," I said. "Come on."

I dropped him off in front of his house and kept driving. Thank God

279

nobody had been sitting on the front porch. I couldn't face Grandma Ruthie or Uncle Morris or Boy. The only person I could face was the asshole living inside of me, the altogether too-selfish-too-self-centered-too-unsatisfied asshole.

I drove home to Van Morrison. Van always makes me feel better.

# Chapter 23

When I got home, I did something I hadn't done in a long time. I sat at my piano, the old upright Kimball who'd never failed me. No matter the problem, I'd always been able to place my hands on the keys and let go. It soothed me in ways only a musician can understand. It helped me look at things in a different light.

I decided to play my dad's favorite song, "Malaguena." A very powerful and moving piece that truly tested the capacity of my fingers. As soon as I started playing, the Nerdy Fat Girl materialized and sat next to me on one side. The Skinny Chic turned up and sat on the other side. *Oh, great, just what I need now.*

"So, what's your problem?" The Nerdy Fat Girl said.

Skinny Chic gave her an evil smile. "What do you think, fatso? I'm confused."

"I guessed that. You're never satisfied, are you?"

"Come on, don't start. And hey, didn't I bury you?"

"You sure did. Well, at least you tried. But guess what? You can't hide me forever."

"Obviously. So what do you want?"

"I want to talk to you. You've been ignoring me for a long time. Way too long."

"Hey, I had a damn good reason to bury you, okay? You made me miserable."

"No, it wasn't me. It was all those other people who made you miserable. And right now I'm the only person who's gonna talk sense into you."

"Talk sense into me? About what?"

"Come on, stop being so stubborn. We both know why you're confused."

"We do? I don't think so. If I knew why I was so mixed up, you wouldn't be sitting here, would you?"

"Whatever. Let's get to the real issue here, okay?"

"The real issue?"

"Yeah, the real issue. What's really confusing you?" She gave Skinny Chic an innocent look.

Skinny Chic bit her lip. "Well, I don't know. No, I do know. The thing is, I thought I was happy, you know? Really happy. I like teaching and my students have grown on me. And I met this guy, you see. And he's crazy about me. I was starting to feel like I'd finally gotten my shit together. But—"

"But what?"

"There's another opportunity for me now. And I kind of feel like it's something better for me."

"Oh, give me a fucking break. You always think there's something better. That's why you went on a diet and destroyed me, right? Because you thought your life would be better as a skinny chic?"

"You're damn right I thought that, you stupid fat bitch. Because of you, I had no friends. Because of you, everyone picked on me and made me feel like an outsider. Because of you, I felt like a disease nobody wanted to catch. You made my life a hell."

"So what happened? You went on a diet, you became a cheerleader and then what?"

"Ugh, you're so annoying. Okay, I hated it. I still felt like I didn't belong. I still felt different."

"Yeah, so much so that you decided to make it your thing. It's like somebody threw you a ball that said, 'You Are Different' and you ran with it. Ran with it all the way to Mexico."

"What does Mexico have to do with it?"

"A lot, you idiot. We both know why you decided to blow off college for a year. We both know why you hopped on those buses and turned yourself into a wanna-be gypsy."

"I did it because I really wanted to."

"Bullshit. You did it because you were convinced you could never be normal and part of something ordinary. You did it because you wanted to remain different. You did it to bury me for good. You did it because you were trying to prove something."

"Okay, so maybe you're right. But I came back and went to college just like everyone else, didn't I?"

"Yeah, and you were skinny just like everyone else too, right? But then what happened? You had all these dreams about making a difference and changing the world and blah blah blah. Where did those dreams go, smart ass?"

"Stop being so mean."

"I'm not being mean. I'm being honest. I'm trying to help you. So, think about it. What happened after college?"

"You know what happened. I got a job on cruise ships."

"Why?"

"What do you mean why? I would've been stupid to turn that opportunity down."

"Why?"

"Because it was different. Spectacular."

"Not because you really liked it, though. You did it because it was something else that set you apart from all the people who'd picked on you. You did it because you secretly couldn't wait to get to your high school reunion and tell everyone what a wonderful life you've had."

"No, that's not true." The Skinny Chic began to squirm.

"Yes, it is, and I'm sorry if this hurts. The truth always hurts. And I have to carry on. You got off cruise ships and then what? What did you do?"

"I went back to bartending."

"Why?"

"Because I couldn't think of anything else. And you have to admit, the Hard Rock was a great place to be a bartender."

"Why? Why didn't you just go back to Friday's? Why didn't you get a job in some dive bar?"

"Because the Hard Rock was exciting, it was cool, it was fun, it was different." She sighed. "Spectacular."

"Here we go again. Look, I have to be really honest with you. You've always done things for the wrong reasons, okay? You've done all these things because you think it makes you more interesting. More unique, more special. More 'spectacular.' You're so lame."

"Can you blame me? All my life I've been told I am different. When it wasn't somebody picking on me because of you, it was somebody telling me I was talented or smart or special. What was I supposed to do?"

"You were supposed to do what your dad's always told you to do. What Doc always told you to do. Do what makes you happy."

"But those things did make me happy." She scratched her head. "Didn't they?"

"Did they really? If they really made you happy, then why did you stop doing them?"

"Because I got bored. Because I started thinking there was something better out there."

"And you thought moving to Orlando would fix everything? You thought moving into an apartment in a suburban community would solve your problems? You thought moving away from the people who really love you, the people who have never put any expectations on you, would kill your restlessness?"

"Stop being so melodramatic."

"Oh, shut up. I know why you left Miami. You left because it had too many memories of me, Nerdy Fat Girl. You left because you were trying to get away from me and everything I made you feel. You ran away."

"Whatever."

"Whatever is right. You should've listened to your dad. No matter where you go, there you are."

"What are you trying to say?"

"You blamed Miami for everything. You blamed it for your misery, your lack of direction, your anger. But let's be honest here, it wasn't the city you didn't like. It was *you* in that city."

Skinny Chic started crying.

"You've never been able to admit the truth to yourself, and that's why you'll never be happy. Bibiana, someday you're going to have to stop and take a good look around you because guess what? *You are not the center of the world*. Nobody's keeping tabs on your life. Nobody really cares whether you travel to India or backpack through Africa. Nobody cares if you've seen the world or worked at the Hard Rock. The people who really love you, the people who really care about you, just want to see you happy. You don't have to prove anything to them. The only person you're trying to prove anything to is your miserable self. To me. Because I've always been here and you know it. Because I live inside of you. Because deep down inside, you hate me and you want to forget I ever existed."

"Why are you doing this to me?"

"Why? I'll tell you why. Because if you don't stop and realize what you're doing, you're going to walk away from something you really wanted. You know what your problem is? Everything has always been easy for you, and now that it's gotten tough, you want to take the easy way out."

"That's not true. I've had to struggle."

"Yeah, right. You don't know what struggle is. You wanted to play the gypsy and your dad let you. You wanted to go to college and you did. Why?

Because your parents love you and they gave you a home and all the support in the world."

"But I still had to pay for it myself."

"Big fucking deal. Welcome to the real world. You're not the only one who's had to pay for school. You wanted to be a waitress, bam! Done. You asked to be a bartender and two seconds later you were pouring vodka tonics. You wanted to travel and live an exciting life, and what happened? It was handed to you on a silver platter. You wanted a job at the Hard Rock and you got it, just like that. You wanted to move to Orlando, and just like that, they welcomed you. Honey, you don't know what struggle is."

"You are so evil."

"Too fucking bad. For the first time in your life, you've decided to do something that isn't so fabulous. Something normal, ordinary. You've decided to be a teacher, but it's just not good enough, is it?"

"That's not fair. I'm confused because there's another teaching job."

"And?"

"I think it might be better for me."

"Damn it, listen to yourself! When will anything ever be enough? Listen, I'll be the first one to say you've lived a full life. There's no denying that. You are one lucky bitch who always seems to be in the right place at the right time, and I'm not saying you shouldn't have done those things, but you need to think about why you did them in the first place."

"I know, I know. I was running. Okay, I'll admit that. Now leave me alone, will you?"

"Are you nuts? I'm not leaving you alone now, not when you seem to be listening for once. Tell me something, what do you think will happen if you take that job at West Orange? And be honest."

She shrugged. "I think I'll like it."

"For how long?"

"For as long as I can. I don't know, I can't predict shit like that."

"You can't predict anything because you don't ever commit to anything. You go into new jobs thinking you can always quit and do something else."

"Damn it, you are so right."

"Of course I'm right, you moron. I'm the Nerdy Fat Girl, remember? The know-it-all, the show-off, the teacher's pet."

"Please don't remind me." Skinny Chic looked over. "Hey, let me ask you something. Why did you turn up now? Why didn't you turn up when I was hopping from one job to the next?"

"How could I? Every spectacular job you took buried me even more. There was no room for me on a cruise ship, no room for me behind a cool bar. So I stayed back, hoping you'd come to a point like this. And here I am." Nerdy Fat Girl was smug and Skinny Chic let her be.

She crossed her arms on her chest. "All right. So what now?"

"Well, think about it. You think West Orange will be better? Okay, fair enough. It's not a bad thing to want more out of life, right? But be honest. You know what's going to happen if you take that job. You'll get there, it'll be new and fun and exciting. You'll have students who are nothing like Marcdala or Chancy, students who sit down when you tell them to and turn in their homework on time."

"Yeah, and then?"

"You'll get bored. Admit it. And you'll want to kick yourself because you were actually making a difference at Howard. Because you were doing what you originally wanted to do back when you were in college. But like magic, something else will come along and you'll go with it and next thing you know, you'll be the only thirty year old with fifteen different jobs on her résumé."

"You think so?"

"Honey, I know so. I've been watching you for a long time, don't forget that. I know how you are. And you know what? It would be a real shame if you left Howard. You know why? Because until that job offer came up, you were happy. You weren't thinking, 'What next?' You weren't wondering if there was something more exciting out there. I think this job offer was a sign."

"Oh, don't start with that sign stuff. Besides, how could it be a sign?"

"It's obvious. It's a sign that you have to stop running. You have to stop worrying what everyone else thinks of you."

Skinny Chic's temper got the best of her. "I do *not* care what people think of me!"

"Oh, puh-lease. You do. You have always cared, like it or not. You care because deep down inside, you still want to belong. You still want to be accepted. And you know when that started? It all started when—"

"Look, I know when it started, okay? It started in the second grade when Mrs. Connor told me I was her favorite student even though all the kids hated me. It started when Rudy punched me in the stomach and called me a whale. It started when I was the last kid picked for kickball. It started when Melissa handed out birthday party invitations to everyone except me. It started when everyone got invited to junior prom and I had to sit home with my mom. It started when that stupid football player told me I was weird. It started when

286

someone pushed me in high school and called me a Chorus Geek. It started when senior prom rolled around and I had to go with one of my cousins. It all started back then. And you know what? It ended when I buried you in Mexico. And now you're back and I hate you."

"That's too bad. But here we are again, and this time you can't bury me."

"Yes, I can."

"No, you can't. You can't because I am who you really are. And you know what? Big deal. You *are* different. There's something about you that sets you apart. You're not better than anyone else, but you're unique. And that's a very cool thing. So stop trying to prove something to the world. Who cares what everyone thinks? Stop trying to prove that you're this larger than life person who can do anything, go anywhere. *Stop running.* And for God's sake, stick to what you love. Admit it, you love what you're doing right now, even though it's not spectacular or exciting. You love it because it's what you've always wanted to do."

Skinny Chic was defeated. "I know. You're right. You've always been right."

"You better believe it."

"I think I know what I need to do. No, I'm sure of it."

"Then do it. And do me a favor, okay?"

"What?"

"Don't try to bury me again. You know you need me."

"Got it. But can you do me favor?"

"Sure."

"Please don't show up on my legs and hips. I'm happy with my body."

"Okay, but don't feed me quite so many Doritos or so much Ben and Jerry's anymore. The temptation is too much."

Skinny Chic laughed. "You got it."

They looked at me and nudged me in the ribs.

"All right, you two, that's enough. Go away."

I got up from the piano and picked up the phone. Matt answered on the second ring.

"Matt?"

"Hey, you okay?"

"Yeah, more than okay. Can you come over?"

"Of course, tuff guy. I'll be right there."

Twenty minutes later, Matt was knocking on my door. He hugged me and pulled me away from him.

"Are you okay?" He looked sincerely concerned.

"Yes, I am. Can we sit down?"

"Yeah, yeah, sure."

We sat down on my futon. My piano was still open and I stared at the bench, shadows of Nerdy Fat Girl and Skinny Chic still lingering.

"Hey, talk to me. You had me worried, you know."

"I know, and I'm sorry I couldn't come to you with this."

"Why couldn't you? You didn't strike me as someone who has a problem talking."

"Yeah, I know. Me, the eternal entertainer. Look, Matt, there are a few things you need to know about me."

"More than I already know?"

"Oh, hell yes. Way more. Thing is, I'm a little more complicated than you think. I feel like I've been lying to you in a way."

"Oh, shit, don't tell me you have a boyfriend tucked away somewhere."

"No, no, not at all. It has nothing to do with that. Besides, I don't do that. It's hard enough for me to share myself with one person, let alone two."

"Okay, so what is it?"

"Look, Matt, I'm not as spectacular and wonderful as you think. Okay? I'm just an ordinary young woman trying to make sense of the world."

"Nothing wrong with that, kiddo. Everyone's trying to do that."

"I know. But I think I misled you. I made you think I know exactly who I am and where I want to go. I told you all about my adventures and cool jobs because I thought you'd like me more. I've always thought people won't like me unless my life has been extraordinary and out of this world."

"But it has been, Bibi. I'm almost jealous of you."

"Oh, God, please don't be. To be honest, I'm tired of running around. I'm tired of trying to impress this imaginary audience in my head. I'm tired of trying to be this remarkable person. Do you understand?"

"No. Explain."

"Matt, when I was a kid, everyone picked on me because I was fat and smart. I know tons of people have been abused for the same reasons, but I let it get to me. Too much. So I did all those things because I wanted to prove that I wasn't just some fat kid. I wanted to prove that I was better than them."

"That's perfectly normal."

"Yeah, I know, but I took it too far. The reason I've never been able to stay in one place is because I kept thinking I had to do more. I've always had to get the cooler job, live in a cooler place, date a cooler guy."

"Does that mean you want to date someone cooler than me? How dare you!" He pulled me close to him. "You're never gonna find someone like me, tuff girl. We were made for each other."

"I know, but I don't want you to have the wrong impression of me."

"Look, you don't have to explain. I know where you're coming from, okay? And besides, I happen to like this weird person you are. I like the fact that you're different. It's not every day I meet a girl who's willing to armwrestle."

"Ha ha. Cute, Matt, cute. But seriously, I'm just trying to let you know that deep down inside, I'm still an insecure fat chic." Nerdy Fat Girl got up from the piano and kicked me. "Well, not so insecure anymore. I'm working on it." Skinny Chic stood up and gave Nerdy Fat Girl a high five.

"Hey, chill, fruit cake. We all got issues. So, what are you gonna do?"

"What am I gonna do? Stay at Howard. Stick to the At Risk program. Try to keep my boyfriend in line."

"Oh, so now I'm your boyfriend?"

"Yep. Deal with it. No backing out now, sir." I leaned over and kissed him.

"Nope, no backing out now."

# Chapter 24

It was the last day of school. We were watching the end of *The Outsiders*. I looked around the classroom as Johnny told Ponyboy to "Stay gold." Not a dry eye to be found. I caught Chancy drying his eyes on his t-shirt. As soon as the movie was over, I turned the television off and switched on the lights. The last thing I wanted was to end the school year on a sad note. I cleared my throat.

"All right, guys. Party time!"

The students quickly forgot Ponyboy and Johnny. They jumped out of their chairs as though I'd just told them we were going to the moon. I sat down at my desk and left them in charge of setting up the Carbohydrate Festival. Within minutes, my huge desk was covered with Cheetos, Doritos, chocolate chip cookies, cupcakes. One look at it and I could feel my ass getting bigger. *Shit, I'm going to have to run an extra two miles today.*

Jazelin brought out the boom box. Marcdala and Ebony pushed some desks back and created a dance floor. They were making too much noise but I didn't care. Nobody seemed to care. Dr. Lawrence was so relieved I'd decided to stay that I could've taken the kids to a nightclub and it wouldn't have phased him. They wolfed down the treats while they danced their little bodies away. It was one huge bump and grind festival. They tried to get me on the dance floor but I adamantly refused. I could only go so far to fit in. Give me salsa or merengue, and I'll dance for hours. Hip hop? I don't think so.

Jazelin grabbed Marcdala and pulled her to the center of the dance circle. They started rubbing up against each other and dancing in a way that made me blush. Matt walked in the door and Ebony immediately grabbed him. If I thought I'd look stupid dancing to hip hop, it was only reinforced by the sight of big Matt trying to keep up with Ebony. Nothing beats watching a white guy trying to get down. He even had the white man overbite. I roared.

As I watched the chaos unravel around me, I hugged myself. I felt good. Relaxed. At peace. Matt and I were going to Mexico to meet my family over the summer. We were going to head out to Melaque to meet Eva and the Lost Trio. Her last letter to me had been the carrot too juicy to pass up.

> *Dear Bibiana,*
>
> *Lord knows it has been a while since I heard from you, but I pray to God you are well. Not much has changed around here. Well, to be honest, we've had a few adventures. Mick went out on his surfboard and got bit by a shark, God bless him. Nothing too serious, my dear. He only ended up losing an arm but it hasn't stopped him. He still runs out every morning trying to catch waves that don't exist. Sharon is having an art exhibition in Guadalajara in July. She is very excited and her family is coming down for the occasion. I don't like them, God forgive me, but she seems to be looking forward to it. As for Kyle, well, what can I say? Kyle has grown ever more paranoid. The other day I caught him looking under my bed with a flashlight. He said he was looking for a pair of his binoculars but I know better. I think he's convinced I am the CIA. Jesus, I can only do so much.*
>
> *Last I heard you were teaching. I cannot tell you how happy this makes me. I have a feeling you have found your place, and it is a good one. I knew you were destined for greatness.*
>
> *I hope you can come back here someday and sit with me on the porch. It would be nice to catch a sunset with you again. And bring someone if you like. Something tells me you are no longer alone, and I hope I am right.*
>
> *God bless you, Bibi. Please come see us soon. We still remember you and that crazy family you told us about.*
>
> *Love to you.*
>
> *Eva and The Gang*

*Destined for greatness*, I had thought. Being a teacher may not seem so spectacular to some, but I thought it was. It was much more than that. It was where I belonged.

Chancy turned off the boom box in the middle of a song. The other kids booed and yelled at him.

"Yo, man, why you trippin'? Turn it back on!"

"Chancy, I was just gettin' down with Princess, yo. Quit playin'!"

Chancy came up to me. "Miss C, Miss C!"

"Chancy, don't yell. I'm right in front of you."

"Miss C!" He pulled his pants to his waist. "Miss C, you gotta call your momma and put her on speaker phone! You promised!"

All hell broke loose.

"Yeah, Miss C, call your momma! You had told us you were gonna call her if we was good!"

"Miss C, I can talk to her?"

"Come on, Miss C, do it!"

The class started chanting, "Call her, call her!"

I looked at Matt for reinforcement and he winked. He mouthed, "Do it."

"All right, all right. But be quiet as I get her on the phone. If there's too much noise, she'll get confused and hang up."

Forty bodies dragged their desks to the phone. You could've heard a pin drop as I dialed the number. *Please be home, please be home.* She answered on the first ring.

"*¿Aló?*"

"Hi, Mami. It's Bibi."

"Oh, my choogar. How are joo?"

A few kids started giggling and I put my finger to my lips.

"I'm good, Mami. How are you? What are you doing?"

"Ay, *mi'ja*, I so tired. I just getting home from de work. What are joo doing?"

"I'm working, Mami."

"Cruise chips, *mi'ja*?"

"No, Mami."

"Oh. Bartending?"

"Nope."

"Ah, I know! Joo are teeching, no?"

"Yep."

Chancy looked ready to explode. *Hold on*, I mouthed.

"Mami, I'm in my classroom, and my students want to say hi. Okay?"

"Your students?"

"Yeah."

"They are there with joo?"

"Yeah, Mami."

"*Pero*, how they going to say hi to me?"

"You're on speaker phone, Mami."

"Ah? Espeaker phone?"

I sighed and looked at Matt. He put his hand over his mouth and stifled a giggle.

"Look, Mami, just say hi, okay? Say hello to my students."

"Ah, okay." There was a brief pause. I could imagine my mom trying to figure out how she could say hi to forty kids at once. Everybody held their breath and waited for her next words. "Hi, cheeldren!"

They all said hello in unison.

"How are joo? Joo like my daughter? She es bery nice, joo know? I loving her, and I sink so she is loving joo, so joo be good, okay?"

Marcdala blurted out. "We love you, Mrs. Castellanos. I wanna go to Mexico someday!"

"*¿Mejico?* Jes, es bery nice place, *mi amor*. Bery nice."

"Mrs. C," Jazelin said, "your daughter cool."

"Cool? Jes, I sink so. She always complain she cold."

We all started laughing.

I sat back and let the kids ask her questions. She was exactly as I'd portrayed her to be. Funny, quirky, alive...different.

I sat back and let her take over. I looked at my students, the forty kids I never thought I'd be able to handle, and smiled. *Damn, it feels good to be part of the whole wide world.*

# Chapter 25

Imagine this. It's the first day of school. A young woman in her early twenties with untamed hair all the way down to her waist is standing in front of a classroom, a classroom full of unruly teenagers from the hood who can't stay in their seats. Her name is written on an old chalkboard, a dilapidated attendance book is on her ancient, beat up desk and the only sound you hear is an air conditioner trying desperately to stay alive. It is not the only sound you hear. The students are picking on each other, calling each other names and basically being monsters. You see a young woman trying to get control of her class. She is not strict. She is trying to remain cool. The kids say "Yo" as she calls their names, and one by one she checks them off in the attendance book that looks ready to fall apart. She asks them to take out a sheet of paper and the students complain. She takes a deep breath and says, "All right, let me tell you a story." All forty kids get quiet and look at her expectantly.

And she smiles.

THE END

Printed in the United States
26728LVS00003B/203